CU00588195

Netta Muskett was born in Seveno
Kent College, Folkstone. She had a
at first teaching mathematics bef

the then owner of the 'News of the World', as well as serving as a
volunteer during both world wars - firstly driving an ambulance
and then teaching handicrafts in British and American hospitals.

It is, however, for the exciting and imaginative nature of her
writing that she is most remembered. She wrote of the times
she experienced, along with the changing attitudes towards sex,
women and romance, and sold millions of copies worldwide.
Her last novel 'Cloudbreak' was first published posthumously
after her death in 1963.

Many of her works were regarded by some librarians at the time
of publication as risqué, but nonetheless proved to be hugely
popular with the public, especially followers of the romance
genre.

Netta co-founded the Romantic Novelists' Association and
served as Vice-President. The 'Netta Muskett' award, now
renamed the 'RNA New Writers Scheme', was created in her
honour to recognise outstanding new writers.

PLASTER CAST

Netta Muskett

HOUSE OF
STRATUS

This edition published in 2014 by House of Stratus, an imprint of Stratus Books Ltd, Lisandra House, Fore St., Looe, Cornwall, PL13 1AD, UK.

www.houseofstratus.com

Typeset by House of Stratus.

A catalogue record for this book is available from the British Library and the Library of Congress.

ISBN 07551 4303 5
EAN 978 07551 4303 0

1

In a drab little back room of a third-rate boarding house an old man lay dying.

His fingers, the long, sensitive fingers of a musician, plucked lovingly at the worn pages of a loosely-bound sheaf of manuscript music.

In a corner of the room, wide-eyed, fearful, a young girl crouched over a book.

'Gretel, are you there, my child?' asked the quavering voice.

She dropped her book and hastened to the bed, her thin, tired little face lighting up with a look of passionate love and pity.

'Of course, Father. I wouldn't leave you,' she whispered.

'A good child, Gretel; a good child,' he said. 'It is getting dark. Light the gas, little one.'

She hesitated, her dark eyes seeking the window through which the afternoon sunshine of early June streamed cheerfully, lighting up every corner of the shabby little room and playing across the dying man's gaunt face.

'There are not many pennies in the jar, Father,' said the child at last with a wisdom beyond her years.

Old Franz smiled and nodded his head.

'Prudent child,' he said approvingly. Then he sighed. 'I am leaving you terribly at the mercy of the world, my Gretel, and the world is a hard and cruel place. There's no room in it for those who aren't successful, and to wring success from the hard stones of life you have to be hard yourself – hard and remorseless and unfeeling. You aren't any of those, my little one,' with a sad

1

smile and a shake of his head.

'I can be,' said Gretel, her small, pointed chin held high with a defiance which sat oddly on her childish immaturity.

'You'll have to be – you'll have to be!' sighed the old man. 'If only you could get Holmann to take the opera,' and he relapsed into that half-dreaming, half-unconscious state.

Gretel sat there with her hands working in her lap, fighting back the tears of weakness and sheer physical weariness which would fill her eyes and cheat her of these last hours for memory of all she had in the world.

Gretel's mother had died in giving her birth, and old Franz Baumer, who had been middle-aged when he conceived a mad passion for the frail little English governess whom he had married and brought back to her native land, had steadfastly refused all well-meaning efforts at parting him from the baby girl which was all he had left to him of that brief year of romance.

They had lived in this same little room ever since Gretel could remember, and this room had been their castle. Franz had taught music for their living, and when Gretel had passed her fourteenth birthday and left the school at which she had always seemed a stranger, she had been able to pay for her own little cupboard of a bedroom by making lamp-shades and fire-screens.

A step on the stairs roused her at last from the stillness which had been as intense as that of the old man in the bed, and she went softly across the room and opened the door.

'Oh, it's you, Mr. Wade. I thought perhaps it was the doctor. He said he would call in again.'

The young man outside the door hesitated and then he came into the room.

'How is he?' he asked, glancing towards the bed.

'Oh – just the same,' said the girl wearily, but Wade could see that the end was very near.

Together they stood looking down at the drawn face, creased by innumerable little wrinkles of age and kindliness. For once the restless fingers were still, though they kept their hold on the worn edges of the manuscript.

'Do you think – if someone were to take the opera – it could save him?' whispered Gretel, but the man shook his head.

'I don't think there's an earthly,' he said with brusque kindliness.

The old man opened his eyes and smiled.

'You, my friend? Gretel, go to your little room, *liebchen*. I would talk with this friend.'

She darted quick, uncertain glances at them both and then, swallowing a sob, slipped away.

The old man raised himself a little.

'Listen, my friend. This opera – you do not believe in it – no one believes. But I believe, I, Franz Baumer, who have seen so many operas come and go, so many fade, so many stay as they will stay for all time. This of mine, it will stay. I know it, here!'

Roland Wade tried to look sympathetic though he had heard of this opera for so long that he could feel no interest in it.

'You want me to try and do something about it for Gretel?' he asked.

'Yes—yes. That is it. For Gretel. She has nothing and no one. My Gretel has no need of relations or friends, but money she must have to keep her against the world. She is good, my Gretel, pure like the lilies. That is no good. A girl who is not pure has a better chance when she is left alone. See then, my friend, there must be a little money for her, and if you go to Holmann he will give you money. I did not tell the child, but he offered me money – fifty pounds! Fifty pounds for my life-work, my masterpiece! I would not bargain with him, but if Holmann will give fifty pounds, then be sure it is worth four times that much. You will go and bargain with him, my friend. You are young, strong, and you do not fear. You will go to him and make a bargain with him, but it is to be for royalties, no matter how little they are. Do not let him buy for his fifty pounds, or for a hundred and fifty pounds. There must be royalties, for so will my Gretel have a little that may be more. So you, my friend, will get for her all that can be got from this one thing of beauty that

I have done. You will do that for me, for the little one, *nein?'*

And Wade, cursing the weakness which had led him during the past few months to show sympathy in these two, the queer old German and his odd little girl who was not even pretty, could do no less than signify his willingness, and he was both relieved and annoyed when the doctor came and prevented any further discussion on the matter of the opera.

He flung a casual goodbye to the white-faced child as he passed her on his way out, shrugging his shoulders with a wry smile at the realisation that he, who prided himself on being the most selfish man in existence, had saddled himself with an unsaleable musical composition as the only protection of a young girl against the preying world.

Roland Wade at twenty-three might easily have been taken for thirty. There was a certain hard brilliance about him, a look of experience, of the man of the world, and he affected a cynical outlook on life which added years to his age. He was a climber, and though he did not appear, as the pianist in a little-known dance band, to have climbed very far, only he himself could look down and see how many rungs of the ladder lay beneath the feet which he planted firmly on each step.

Gifted with the art of mimicry, he was able, after close observation of a desired objective, to present a very passable imitation of that thing. In such fashion he had been able to impress upon the other members of the dance band the idea of his own social superiority, and it was not beyond the bounds of belief that he was what he represented himself to be, namely, a product of public school and University. It would have been much harder to credit the actual truth, which was that he had been born in Hoxton, and in one of its meanest streets at that, had picked up a precarious education at such times as his mother had been unable to restrain longer the activities of the School Board officer, and only shaken the dust of the East End off his shoes when his father had been committed to a long term of hard labour for almost murdering his mother in a drunken brawl. That lady having lost no time in taking up her residence with the man who had been the primary cause of the quarrel, George Wade, now become Roland George Wade, took his final leave of Hoxton and by sheer cheek had pushed his way to his present status.

He had always been able to pick a tune out of any kind of instrument and had spent hours amusing himself and a dirty crowd of his fellow young ruffians improvising on mouth-organ or penny whistle or on the cracked old piano which the landlady of the 'Bull and Bear' allowed him to tinker with when she was in a good humour.

He had caught at a chance of filling a gap left by the sudden fainting of the pianist at a tenth-rate performance at that same 'Bull and Bear', and at the end of the evening had pushed himself into the job, regardless of the protests of the now recovered pianist. After a few months of such work, travelling about London and sleeping in any corner which presented itself, existing on the generosity of inebriated audiences rather than on the few shillings doled out to him by the leader of the party, he pushed his way into a cheap dance band, and thence, by many small steps, to the position he now held. 'Micky's Merry Men' had already won some reputation for themselves by the time that Roland (the 'George' had now completely vanished) joined them, and his tall figure, clean-shaven, good-looking face, and perfect manners added considerably to the tone of the band. He had acquired the veneer of manners and speech which enabled him to pose as a Varsity man, but his uphill climb to reputable dance halls via all sorts of public-houses had brought him in contact with many who were going down the hill even faster than he was going up. He had been quick to recognise such from amongst his audiences, and when, after the show, the artists had been invited to sit and drink with those who remained, he had chosen shrewdly and taken note of every inflection and mannerism which would always betray the gently born and nurtured, no matter to what depths they might sink.

And at twenty-three he was by no means prepared to sit comfortably on the rung of the ladder which had made him a member of Micky's Merry Men.

He had posed and pretended so much, in fact, that he had almost come to believe himself that product of public school and Varsity which he simulated, and as such he felt he could well afford to feel superior to the clerks and typists who came to dance on Saturday evenings in the hall which had engaged Micky's for the season.

He was superficially brilliant, and he had the wit to recognise the superficiality and to cover it carefully. He was an expert copyist, but he had not an atom of originality in his make-up. He never thought a fresh thought nor composed a new air, and he chafed inwardly against this curb to his ambitions. If only he could write songs – dance tunes – a symphony – a musical play – anything!

It was whilst he was poised temporarily on the rung of the ladder which held Micky's Merry Men that he came into contact with the Baumers and became the unwilling custodian of the opera.

He was thinking about it with annoyance as he dressed for the evening. He had secured a temporary engagement for an hour or two at a popular restaurant, joining Micky's at a later hour, and it was when he was boarding his bus for the West End that an idea came to him suddenly. He could perhaps place old Baumer's opera, if there were actually anything in it, and do himself a good turn at the same time. On the front seat of that very bus sat a figure hunched up in a thick overcoat, for all the warmness of the June night, and it needed no second glance to verify Wade's first impression, which had given him his idea.

He made his way to the empty half-seat, tucked his roll of music between him and his neighbour, and smiled his pleasant, attractive smile.

'I thought no one but you would be huddled in an overcoat this weather, Mr. Cornwall,' he said cheerfully.

The older man started from a reverie, stared, and then smiled. He had spoken to this young fellow more than once at the restaurant which was so conveniently near his office, and he liked him – liked his pluck, too, in doing such work as came to his hand even if it was not the sort of thing that a well-educated young fellow of good breeding ought to have had offered to him as his only chance of earning a living. 'Ah, my boy, those years in India will never finish taking their toll of me, you know. I've learned wisdom at last, and what the devil do appearances matter, eh?'

'I've had to come to that conclusion myself, sir,' laughed Roland cheerfully.

'I know you have, my boy, and I honour you for it,' said the older man more soberly. 'Damn shame to see all you fine young fellows, well-born, well-educated, having to scratch a living anyhow and be thankful for the chance. Wish I could help you, Wade. That's a fact.'

And as this was exactly the opening Roland had desired, he lost no time in stepping in. Cornwall had promoted and managed a number of successful shows in London and the provinces, and Wade had cultivated an acquaintance begun casually, always with an eye on the chance of making a further rung of the ladder. And his perspicacity had been rewarded. His first sight of Cornwall on the bus (he had two cars but often chose to travel by bus) had reminded him that in Baumer's opera there was a part which could only be played by a genuine pianist. Old Franz had insisted on outlining the story to him many times, illustrating it by snatches of song or a running commentary on the piano, and Roland's brilliant idea was that if Cornwall could be persuaded to produce the opera he himself might take the part of the pianist.

'Well, as a matter of fact, Mr. Cornwall,' he began with just the right touch of diffidence, 'I believe you could help me, or rather a friend of mine.'

'Oh? In what way? Want a job behind the footlights?' asked the older man with his quiet smile.

Roland laughed.

'I might not be much good there,' he said. 'It's a sort of musical play which a friend of mine has written – calls it an opera, but it is hardly that, too light, but quite tuneful.'

Cornwall pulled a wry face.

'Like pouring money down a sink to produce anything operatic in these days, my boy,' he said.

Roland shrugged his shoulders elegantly.

'I know. I'm not pressing it or making a personal matter of it, but – well, will you look at the thing? It would satisfy him and ease my conscience about it.'

Possibly his indolence was a little overdone, for Cornwall caught his eyes and smiled shrewdly.

'Dabbling in that sort of thing yourself, eh?' he asked. 'Well, we won't probe too far. I'll have a look at it and give you an honest opinion. No frills, you know?'

'I don't want them. What's the use? When may I bring the thing along? Or shall I send it?'

'No, bring it along. Tell you what. Tomorrow evening I'm throwing a party. Nancy Morn will be there and some of the nitwits from that show at the Vanity. Like to meet them? Amusing until you get bored stiff with them. We'll try some of the numbers of your play on them and see how they take it. Any dancing?'

'Well, very little, though there is room for it if necessary.'

'Take it from me that it will be necessary if the show is to go down at all. There's one thing in which the public never loses interest, and that's legs, my boy,' and he rose with a chuckle.

'I've got to get off here and see a chap. Don't forget tomorrow night. Here's my card. Come late – not before eleven. They have to finish the show at the Vanity before any of them can get along,' and he was gone, with a friendly nod.

Roland Wade fingered the bit of pasteboard with a sigh of satisfaction. Even if old Baumer's play turned out a frost, it had brought him this invitation to Cornwall's fine house overlooking the park, a house which most people knew by repute.

The anticipation of it lingered pleasantly with him all the evening, and he went to bed to dream of future glories, sleeping so heavily that he heard nothing of the coming and going, of swift footsteps up and down the stairs, of the hushed voices and a girl's heartbroken sobbing which ushered in the new day.

When at last he went down the stairs, he paused on the landing at sight of a strange woman coming from the Baumers' room, which was heavily shuttered.

'Is he . . . ?' he asked, shrinkingly.

The woman nodded.

'Five o'clock this morning. You a relation?'

'No. My name's Wade. I—know them a little. I live here,' he said.

He was uncomfortable and would have liked to rush away, but common decency prevented him.

'Oh, you are Mr. Wade? The little girl left something for you,' and she went back into the room with its silent occupant, brought out a bulky package wrapped in brown paper and addressed to him in Gretel's writing, and put it into his hand.

He took it with a feeling of reluctance, almost as if it were something potent for evil.

'Where is she?' he asked.

'The Jews over the road took her,' and the woman went on her way.

Roland went slowly back to his room, a spartan enough place, dominated by the piano which he had scraped and saved to purchase. The rest of the furniture consisted of the barest necessities provided by the landlady. Some day he would live in wide and lovely rooms, furnished with the gracious beauty which only wealth can achieve. At present, with so many rungs of the ladder still above him, this humble, comfortless dwelling sufficed.

He had never actually handled the manuscript of Franz Baumer's opera, and such attention as he had paid the various readings to which he had been subjected had been scant and half-hearted. He had only a dim conception of it as a whole without having any clear detail in his mind. Now, with a few hours to waste and a disinclination to meet the moment when he supposed he would have to go and seek Gretel Baumer, he sat down at the piano and began to scan the music, giving it his close attention, a vision of Cornwall in his mind. How would the thing strike him? Was it utterly hopeless, or were there possibilities?

He took one of the songs at random and played it softly, having due regard to the fact that a dead man lay in the house, but as the scrawled notes took meaning beneath his fingers he forgot everything save that here was life, lightness, melody, that indefinable touch of the creative mind which we call genius.

He turned over the pages, played a few bars here, a whole passage there, hummed the words which were as melodious and original as the music, sometimes gay with a quaint joyousness which he found it difficult to associate with Franz Baumer, sometimes wistful and haunting. Yes – that was it! Haunting. The whole thing was haunting. Here were a dozen melodies which, in as many nights, might be turned into dance tunes, comedy numbers, ballads which could be dissociated from their context and yet seem complete in themselves. People would remember the melodies and hum or whistle them, would go home and pick them out on their pianos or whatever instrument they fancied. Records would be made of them, they would be flung across the world by the broadcasting stations.

As he played, his mouth grew bitter and his eyes hard with envy. Quite certainly Holmann had never given the thing his serious consideration, or he would not have let the old man turn down his paltry offer and go away.

He rose at last, pushed away the thick pile of manuscript, and went to find Gretel, disliking the necessity but disliking still more the thought of the criticism which might well be levelled at him by the other occupants of the house if he failed in what was clearly his duty. His nature was such that he must always live in the sun of approval, even if the approvers were as negligible in his scheme of things as the nondescript inhabitants of 15 Earl Street.

On the opposite side of the road, beneath three golden balls, stood the furtive little shop behind whose crowded windows sat the Jew, Josephs, spinning his golden web. Gretel, looking many a time into the dirty, crowded windows, had felt a lump rise in her throat as she realised the heart-breaking tragedy of the miscellaneous assortment of articles displayed for sale. Not one of them was new. Not one of them, she felt, but bore in scratch or dent or stain some story of its past. She could never bear to look at a baby's rattle that had been in one corner almost as long as she could remember the dents and tiny teeth-marks' eloquent testimonies, nor could she look unmoved on the tray on which lay a jumble of wedding-rings, most of them very thin and worn.

Old Josephs had always been kind to the child, and his fat, untidy wife had been the first to go to her when the news sped across the road of old Franz Baumer's passing.

'You kom back vith old Hannah, my leetle Grettle,' she had said, drawing the desolate child to her ample, not too clean bosom, and though at any other time the disorder of her dress and the oily smell of much frying which always clung to Mrs. Josephs slightly repelled her, in those first alarming moments she clung there gratefully enough.

So it was in the stuffy little parlour behind the shop that Roland Wade found her, her eyes red and swollen with weeping, her thin little form hopelessly engulfed in a black dress which belonged to one of the many Josephs who came and went unceasingly, whispering and watching with curiosity which held nothing but the purest good nature.

'Oh, Mr. Wade, it's really true, isn't it?' she asked him pitifully. 'They—they didn't make a mistake, did they?'

He shook his head and took one of her small, cold hands in his, thinking the while how deadly unattractive she was and what a pity it should be so. It was so much easier for a pretty girl to get along than a plain one. Her eyes, dark almost to blackness, seemed like deep, desolate pools in a face too small for them, and her fair hair was dull and lifeless, hanging forlornly about her shoulders.

'Afraid not, dear,' he said gently, for no one could have been anything but gentle to this forlorn little creature. 'Have you thought at all what you will do now?'

She lifted wide, blank eyes to his and shook her head.

'I can go on with the lamp-shades, but I cannot earn enough to keep the room. There is nothing else, is there?'

'There is the opera,' suggested Wade with an odd reluctance which he did not then analyse.

Gretel lifted her thin little hands in a gesture of dismissal.

'It isn't worth anything,' she said sadly. 'Father always loved it and believed in it, but he tried so hard to sell it and never got anyone even interested in it. No, I'm afraid that's no good, though right at the last he managed to tell me to give it to you. You got it?'

'Yes. I could try and do something with it for you,' he said with that same curious reluctance.

She shook her head.

'It's kind of you, Mr. Wade, but I know it would only be a waste of time. I'd like you to keep it as—as a remembrance. You have been so kind to us.'

He felt impelled to do something for her, which to Roland Wade was a most extraordinary impulse. So far he had never desired to serve anyone except Roland Wade.

'You can't stop here, kiddie,' said Wade. 'For one thing I don't suppose they've got room, and you wouldn't like it, anyway, would you?'

She hesitated between honesty and gratitude.

'They're so kind to me. They really want me to stay, I think, though I don't know why they should do anything for me. But – no, I don't think I could possibly stay,' with a little frown as her eyes travelled round the overcrowded room and her nose wrinkled at the pervading odour of hot oil and humanity.

She was a dainty little person, for old Franz had loved cleanliness and had managed somehow to achieve it through all the struggling days in the one room in which they had lived, cooked, washed and slept until Gretel was able to rent her own little cupboard of a place. Either of them would rather have gone hungry than unwashed, and their one window had always been open to all the winds of heaven. She felt she would either suffocate or be sick in this frowsy room.

'Have you any idea what you are going to do?' he asked anxiously, his impulse to help already beginning to fade a little.

She hesitated and then spoke diffidently.

'There are the nuns – at the convent, you know. Perhaps they would let me go to them – teach the little ones or something.'

'That would be a very good idea,' he said. 'How old are you?'

'Seventeen,' said Gretel.

He was staggered for he had thought of her as a mere child, so small and immature she seemed.

Before he could say more the door burst open and a rabble of Josephs of all ages and sizes burst into the room, arguing loudly and admitting in still greater force the odour of boiling oil.

From the shop came Mrs. Josephs, settled two of the arguments with a hefty right and left, and bundled the lot of them outside the door again, its final bang wafting the oily vapour in a thick bluish eddy about the room again.

Gretel pushed her hair out of her eyes with a childish gesture.

'Could we go quite soon and see the nuns, do you think?' she asked, and he perceived how near to breaking point were her nerves.

He glanced at the row of clocks on the mantelpiece. They were all going, all slightly different, but they gave a rough idea of the time, which was as near as ever mattered in this happy-go-lucky household where tomorrow was as good as today and the day after even better.

'I could spare an hour now if you like,' he said, and she assented gratefully.

They went through the shop with a murmured excuse to Mr. Josephs, and each drew a breath of relief as they filled their lungs with the comparatively fresh air of the street. They made an odd pair, the immaculate young man and the thin child in her voluminous black, but she was too much wrapped in her grief to be aware of it.

At the convent the nuns were placidly kind, and one of them took Gretel away whilst Wade had a long and slightly uncomfortable talk with the Reverend Mother – uncomfortable because he felt that her clear, deep eyes were looking much further into his thoughts than he cared.

'There is, then, nothing on which the child can live except her own small earnings, and she has no relations of any sort?' she asked at last when his explanations were over.

'Gretel does not know of any, and the people at the boarding house say no one has ever visited them or taken any interest in them.'

'And there are no effects? No property or belongings of any sort? I am obliged to ask these questions, you understand, Mr. Wade.'

'Oh, quite, quite!' agreed Roland. 'No, there is nothing. The piano belonged to Herr Baumer, but it would probably fetch very little if it were sold.'

And in the end it was agreed that the nuns would take charge of Gretel for the present, and she could complete her schooling with them, giving in exchange such lessons as she could.

'I must go back and say goodbye to Mr. and Mrs. Josephs,' said Gretel with quiet obstinacy when Roland would have gone away and left her there. 'Also I think they would like me to stay with them until after—after they—take him away.'

'You'd hate staying in that dreadful hole, Gretel,' he reminded her, amazed at such an unnecessary piece of quixoticism.

'I am sure they would be hurt if I didn't,' she persisted. 'They were so kind to me.'

Her reiteration of people's kindness irritated him, but the voice of the Reverend Mother broke in placidly.

'Gretel is right to go back if she feels like that,' she said. 'You will come back to us in a few days, my child?'

'Please, Mother, if I may,' and the oddly assorted pair were on their way again.

He left her at the door of the pawnshop and she held on to his hand a little fearfully.

'I'll come and fetch you—after, dear,' and he was gone. He felt that he had conducted a difficult bit of business with credit to himself and to Gretel, and when his mind reverted to the opera, he felt no need to stifle his conscience. That accommodating part of his make-up had long been trained to react decorously to the demands made upon it, and he swung along with the comfortable assurance that in all probability there was no value in the manuscript at all, and even if there were he could easily explain to the Reverend Mother that he had not thought it worth mentioning as an asset.

2

There seemed at first sight nothing but girls – girls in every conceivable colour and style – perfumes, flowers, the thin sound of a fountain drifting in between the chatter, music being played somewhere in the distance merely as a background for all the talk and laughter and not in any way interfering with it.

Trying not to feel ill at ease, though he had never penetrated such a gathering before, Roland threaded his difficult way to where cigar smoke and the popping of corks and a sudden roar of masculine laughter suggested he might find his host, and there he found him by a cocktail bar, sunk in an armchair with a girl perched on one arm and another bending over to light a cigarette from his cigar in spite of his protests. She had a mischievous face alight with laughter, and when she turned it to Roland at the sound of their host's greeting he recognised her with a little shock of pleasure as Nancy Morn, the popular leading lady at the Vanity Theatre.

'Ah, Roland boy, glad you got here. Make way for your betters, some of you impudent young hussies, and prepare to meet a young man whose name is not really Adonis, but Roland Wade. Miss Nancy Morn, Avril Henshaw, Betty Carslake – oh, take it that you know them all. And now perhaps, having spoiled my cigar for me and ruined your own frock, you'll have the grace to leave me to a man's life for a few minutes, Nancy sweetheart,' and he lifted her by the elbows and set her down a foot or two away.

She made a face at him.

'Great brute,' she laughed and slid a hand through Roland's

arm. 'I like the look of you, so come and let's tell the story of our lives, shall we?'

'Give him a cocktail first,' suggested Cornwall.

'*With* a pinch of salt in it, darling,' came another laughing voice. 'Wait for her to start and cap everything she says, Mr. Wade!'

'We'll have an Amy highball, Downing,' said Miss Morn serenely to the trim maid behind the improvised bar. 'That do for you, Mr. Wade?'

'My favourite,' said Roland, who had never even heard of such a thing.

By the end of the evening, or rather by the middle of the night, he had heard of enough things to make his head swim, and it said something for his strength of mind that by one o'clock he was still sober, even if unusually gay and talkative. He kept rigidly before him the knowledge that he had a great deal to hide, a great deal that he would rather bite off his tongue than give voice to in that assembly. Mr. Cornwall watched him with approval. The young man had his head screwed on the right way.

Wade struck exactly the right note with this theatrical crowd, was modest without appearing self-conscious, friendly without overstepping the bounds for a newcomer. Nancy Morn was charmed with him, and when dancing was suggested it was she who slid a hand beneath his arm to lead the way to the great empty drawing-room whose polished parquet floor was kept sacred to such events and to private auditions conducted by James Cornwall himself from time to time.

'What do you do, Mr. Wade?' asked the actress frankly as they danced.

He had been a little stiff and nervous at first, for most of his experience of dancing had been that of the onlooker from the musicians' dais, but her supple, yielding loveliness in his arms soon gave him courage and went slightly to his head.

'I'm a musician of sorts.'

'Really? What do you play and where and when?' she asked, but he was relieved of the embarrassment of an answer by someone who, with a mock bow, whirled his partner away from him and left him feeling rather a fool in the middle of the floor.

He snatched at another partner, since that seemed the thing to do, but after a few turns with her he found his host at his elbow.

'Park Odette and come and chin wag with me, Wade, will you?' he suggested, and the girl laughed and slipped away.

'This music affair of yours, Wade. Bring it with you?'

'Well, I did, but it can wait.'

Cornwall waved the suggestion aside.

'Not a bit. These young things will go on like that until they drop and they won't even know that I'm not there. That's the best of present-day hospitality. One's guests ask nothing but to be fed and wined and left to amuse themselves. Come along. Stebbs will get what you want if you tell him what to look for.'

The staid butler listened gravely and went away, following them in a few moments to the quiet little room shut away by double baize doors from the tumult of the dancers.

Cornwall took the roll of manuscript from him, nodded dismissal, and turned lights on and off until only the grand piano in the middle of the floor stood in a pool of light.

'Want to play the things yourself?' he asked, running his fingers through the sheets with their worn edges.

Wade shrugged his shoulders, aware of an extraordinary excitement surging through him.

'As you like, sir,' he said and the older man sat down at the piano and began to play, picking out bits here and there, pausing to read the words now and again, and gradually becoming utterly unconscious of the tall young man lingering in the shadows of the room. From selecting a few bars and then a few lines he began to play whole numbers, and then, flinging back the pages, he started at the beginning and crashed into the opening passages again, his notes not always quite accurate and with now and then a particularly complicated passage merely indicated, but Wade realised that the magic of the thing had caught him just as he himself had been caught by it the day before.

Suddenly Cornwall flung himself from the piano stool, crossed to the baize door and tore it open.

'Stebbs! Miss Morn to come here at once, please,' and he took no notice of Wade whilst he waited for her to come, returning to the piano stool and devouring the music again.

Nancy Morn came on her swift light feet, her face flushed, her gay blue eyes starry, her voice frankly curious.

'What's up, Corny? Found a sixpence in the pudding?' she asked him gaily.

'May be a sixpence, but looks uncommonly like half a sovereign. Like this?' and he played one of the lighter numbers, a gay, tripping little thing, singing the words to it in total oblivion of the curious effect of his deep bass upon the trilling melody.

Nancy laughed, made room for herself on the piano stool, and began to sing it herself in a small, sweet edition of the lovely voice which had brought London to her feet when first Cornwall had given her a part.

Wade listened enchanted. He had tried that very song over himself, had recognised its attraction, but had utterly underestimated the appealing charm of it until Nancy Morn sang it.

At the end of it she sprang up and clapped her hands in childlike glee.

'Corny, it *is* half a sovereign. Any more like that? What is it, and whose? Ah!' as Roland moved forward almost unconsciously and she saw him for the first time. 'Why—it's you! You!' and she came to him and took the lapels of his coat in her slim fingers with their sparkling rings, looking up into his face with a dawning excitement in her eyes.

'You – Roland Wade!' she repeated, her silky voice caressing his name. 'A musician of sorts!'

'That what he said he was?' came Cornwall's voice from the other end of the piano, and in it, too, was that hint of excitement.

She laughed exultantly.

'Of sorts! I suppose you do realise, don't you, that you've written a winner? What's it called?' and she let her hands drop from his coat and came back to Cornwall, who was turning the manuscript over to find the title.

'Good Lord, that won't do!' he ejaculated when he had found it. '*Summer Storm.*'

Nancy shook her head.

'No, that won't do,' she agreed. 'Too quiet. Not striking enough. We shall have to find another. Mind if we do, Mr. Wade? No, Roland. I shall never live it up to the Mr. Wade. Rather a good name for the bills though. Roland Wade. It will look well. Not too long. We must certainly think of another name for your play though. Let's have some more of it, Corny. Was that at random or did you select it?'

'More or less at random. Listen to this, though,' and he turned over the pages and sat down again, Nancy perched on the stool beside him, humming or singing with him.

'There will have to be more dialogue, of course, and a dance or two, and the stage directions want looking over.'

'That scene in the forest where the trees dance is a bit too much like panto, isn't it?'

'Yes. Listen to it again.'

'What about a solo there, ballet effect? Savina? Or that new dancer, Viladoff? Savina's getting a bit heavy.'

'Cut that bit of business at the inn and let Wilson meet Joyce in the wood. Makes that one scene instead of three and gives Clare a chance to change her costume. Plenty of clothes!'

The two voices rambled on. Wade standing in the background without attempting to follow it, his mind whirling with the whole astonishing business. They had both jumped to the conclusion that he had written the thing, and there was nothing on the tattered cover to suggest otherwise. Once or twice he cleared his throat to disclaim the honour they thrust upon him, but neither of them took any notice of him and he relapsed into meditation again.

They rose at last, and each caught an arm as they came to

where he stood, Cornwall's rather heavy face flushed and excited, Nancy's delicate little features alight with eagerness and pleasure.

'We're going to make you, my boy, with this!' said the older man and Nancy pressed his arm and lifted her dancing blue eyes to his.

'If there's one thing I adore,' she said, 'it's man in the making!'

Cornwall disengaged her hand from Wade's arm firmly.

'You're likely to do more unmaking than making at this stage, Nancy,' he said. 'At the moment, this is definitely my show, so hands off, young woman.'

She laughed, blew him a kiss from her fingers and began to dance, humming an air from the score they had just been reading. Seized by an impulse to do exactly the right thing, as usual, Wade sat down at the piano and began to play it for her, his admirable memory standing him in good stead even if he did not play it as Franz Baumer had so lovingly and carefully written it. She clapped her hands as he added a few meretricious frills to the rather dignified score, ended her dance in front of Cornwall and flung an arm about that stolid gentleman's rather thick neck.

'Darling, he plays!' she said eagerly. 'He could take the part of Revere!'

'And play a sloppy love-sick swain to you, I suppose?'

She laughed across at Wade, who still sat at the piano watching them, aware that he was faintly struggling to tell them the truth and equally aware that he was not going to do so.

'But, Corny, what a thrill! Clever young composer and playwright acts in his own first production and plays his own music!'

'Quiet! Quiet! What about if it's a failure? How will he stand the three hours of torture? If the fate of the play hung in the balance, he'd absolutely certainly push it over the precipice to join the hosts of other never-nevers.'

'But it isn't going to fail, Corny. It isn't even going to hang anywhere near the balance. With that music? And the fresh ideas in it?'

'My dear, when you're as old as I am (which heaven forbid should ever happen!) you will realise that no one on this earth can tell what will go down with the great B.P. Musical plays, as such, have had their day and it's only because this has a darn good story mixed up with reasonably tuneful music that I think it'll take. What do you feel about it yourself, Wade? After all, it's your play and if you want to take a part in it, that goes.'

The thought of acting in it with Nancy Morn certainly had seemed attractive at first thought, but he was wise enough to realise that the fate of the thing was almost entirely in the hands of Cornwall, and he would throw his best into it so long as it were left to him. It would be foolish to go against his better judgment right at the outset.

'I think you know what is best for the play, sir, and what you say goes every time,' he said.

The older man pressed his arm.

'Good boy,' he said approvingly. 'Anyway, I'd almost forgotten I've got a party on. Shall we go in? Come and see me tomorrow, Wade – or better leave it till after the weekend. Make it Monday? Ten o'clock, here?'

'Any time you say, sir.'

'All right. Eleven o'clock perhaps, and I'll probably get Hughes here. Is this the only copy?'

'Yes, I'm afraid so.'

Cornwall went across to a dictaphone which stood across the corner of the room, pressed a button and set the cylinder revolving.

'Miss Bateson,' he dictated into the mouthpiece, 'please have six copies run off quickly of the roll of manuscript at present entitled *Summer Storm* by six o'clock tomorrow evening.'

He shut off the power and hung up the mouthpiece, slid an arm through Wade's and the other round Miss Morn's shoulders and led them from the room, his businesslike air slipping from him as if it had been a cloak once they were outside the double baize door and making towards the music and laughter from the other end of the house.

Nancy slid away almost at once, and Cornwall frowned a little as he realised that in the wake of her came a trail of arrested conversation, quick glances towards where Wade still stood beside him, a concentration of interest on the tall, good-looking stranger who certainly looked as if he might be 'someone'.

'Confound women and their chatter,' muttered Cornwall, turning away, but to Roland the glances and the quickening of interest were as the wine of the gods. He held his head high and stepped purposefully towards one of the most important-looking women in the room, a middle-aged woman with a thin shrewish face and wonderful pearls. He remembered he had been presented to her in the off-hand way of the modern generation, though he had not noticed her at the time. Now his instinct warned him to take advantage of the rousing of her interest in him.

'Will you dance, Mrs. Hesketh?' he asked her with that slight and charming air of diffidence which he knew how to assume when occasion demanded.

She smiled, softening the shrewish look at once.

'That's charming of you, Mr. Wade. I should love to think it is disinterested.'

He bowed.

'May I suggest that such a condition is very unlikely when one asks an honour from a woman?'

Mrs. Hesketh laughed at that.

'You're a fraud, but a sufficiently attractive one to make me pretend I believe you,' she said. 'We'll dance.'

Amazingly, she danced like a fairy, and he said so without expressing his surprise, and she glanced up at him with speculative interest.

'Are you an absolute newcomer to the stage and stage folk, Mr. Wade?' she demanded.

'Absolutely. You would find me out immediately if I tried to pretend otherwise,' he said smilingly.

Her eyes, the one agelessly beautiful thing about her,

narrowed a little.

'I wonder why you asked *me* to dance?' she asked him.

'Because you are quite the most interesting-looking woman in the room,' he told her promptly.

'As Mrs. Hesketh – or as Maria Ludovini?' she hazarded.

Wade caught his breath sharply. Why—of course . . . !

'Madame, forgive me! I really had no idea,' he said, chagrined beyond all telling that he had not recognised her.

But the dancer who had once thrilled Europe and held it spellbound at the points of her twinkling feet and who now, with chill pride, insisted on being no longer anything but Mrs. Hesketh, laughed.

'Why should I forgive one of the most exquisite compliments that have ever been paid me? Maria Ludovini is enchanted because Monsieur invited Mrs. Hesketh to dance,' and he suddenly realised what quality in her had kept her audiences in love with her long after her form had lost its lissom grace and her feet their fairy lightness.

'Had I known, I should not have dared to ask you, Madame,' said Wade, and never had his pseudo-culture looked nearer the real thing than in his grave courtesy to this old woman, as he now realised she was. 'Mortals do not ask favours of the gods so personally.'

'I like you,' she said with an approving nod. 'You know what to say, and what is more to the point, you know how to say it! But I rather gather that that is your forte. You've written a play, I understand, and Cornwall is thinking of producing it for you?'

'Well – not exactly a play. I would rather call it a musical comedy, or a light opera,' he said deprecatingly. 'Mr. Cornwall has been very kind about it.'

'Kind, has he? Let me tell you, young man, that James Cornwall is kind to one person only, and that person's name is James Cornwall. If he offers you anything for your play, treble it before you begin to think about it! If he isn't certain he's going to make money out of it, he wouldn't touch it with a bargepole. Stand out for all you can get, and then try and get a bit more!

Anyway, I'll have a word with the old rascal about it,' and as the music stopped, she tapped his arm with one of her thin, jewelled fingers, smiled up into his face and moved away from him with the sinuous grace which she would never lose.

Nancy Morn came to dance with him again and teased him about what she called his 'conquest'.

'So frightfully clever of you to go up to her straight away like that, my dear,' she said approvingly. 'She's got oodles of money and you might do worse, you know, than make up to her! She must be seventy, if she's a day. A tempest of young love would kill her off in no time and leave you with all the boodle!'

He laughed down into her gay blue eyes and pressed her slender, boneless little body more closely to him.

'A tempest of young love demands youth and life, not old age and the doubtful boodle!' he told her.

Miss Morn nodded approvingly.

'Very nice! I see you've got distinct possibilities, but at the moment I'm still hopelessly tied up in an affair which won't be ready to join the great majority for at least – let me see – six weeks, I should say! Come round and see me in six weeks' time,' and she flung him a laughing challenge and slid from his arms into those of some other man waiting his chance.

He found plenty of other willing partners and flirted with them all, showing a nice discrimination between the types, and he was near the door when a little stir and something in the nature of a procession heralded the departure of Mrs. Hesketh. She paused at the sight of Wade and a little regal gesture beckoned him.

He hastened to her, holding up the procession.

'Come and have tea with me tomorrow afternoon, Mr. Wade,' she said graciously, her clear voice audible to the little group gathered about her, its marked favour duly noted. 'I have a flat in Emperor's Gate. You will find it in the telephone book,' and it was characteristic of the dethroned queen that she did not wait for a reply nor feel the need of one.

He was wise enough to take his own departure soon

afterwards, and was conscious of anti-climax when he was waiting in a fine drizzle of rain for a bus in which, at length, he had to stand, swaying and jostled by his fellows, the perfumed air of James Cornwall's drawing-room replaced by an odour of mingled humanity and damp clothing.

In his heart he was savagely determined that not much longer would he consort with the bus population, nor live in the comfortless little room which at the moment had to shelter him. He had been ambitious before. He had had his dreams all the time he had been laboriously climbing the ladder. Now. quite suddenly the dreams had burst from the nebulous cloud which had enwrapped them, and he saw them in all the dazzling brightness of James Cornwall's house and the jewelled, perfumed, utterly sophisticated women who had thronged it. He envied the men who had been there, able to meet these women on equal terms, to speak their language, and he formed an iron determination that before long he would be one of them. Even tonight, on this first venture amongst them, he had acquitted himself well, and women like Mrs. Hesketh and Nancy Morn had liked his company and told him so. Yes, assuredly he had made a good start, and in the warmth of that reflection he could almost forget the extreme discomfort of the journey and the distastefulness of his fellow-travellers.

In his room once more, he took off his evening clothes carefully, looked them over for any possible speck of dirt, and hung them in the shallow cupboard, covered with an old sheet which he had purloined from the bed long ago for that purpose. The shirt would do one more turn, he decided, with a mental note that a clean shirt a day would be part of life as he was resolved to live it before long. Then he got into bed and slept dreamlessly, his rest untroubled by any uprising of the ghost of old Franz Baumer, or any reminder of the pale, sad child tossing miserably in a fraction of a bed on the other side of the street.

3

Morning brought the inevitable reaction, and Wade got up in a thoroughly bad temper, which was not assuaged by a message that 'Miss Grettle wanted him to slip over and see her'.

He dressed impatiently, lost his collar-stud twice, discovered that the only shirt he could possibly wear with his new blue suit to Mrs. Hesketh's that afternoon had not come back from the laundry, had more than a suspicion that he was going to have a lumpy spot on his chin, and finally made his way down the stairs and across to the sign of the three golden balls. Of course Gretel had sent for him to discuss *Summer Storm* and of course he would have to tell her that Cornwall proposed to take it, and heaven alone knew what course the thing might take after that.

But Gretel held out her hand and lifted innocently grateful eyes to his when he went through to the room behind the shop.

'Thank you for coming, Mr. Wade. I hate to bother you, but— it's about the funeral. They have been here to see me, the men, and Mr. Josephs said he would pay everything, but I thought perhaps, there might be enough,' wistfully. 'I should like to be able to pay for it myself, for *him*, you know. Do you think perhaps if the piano were sold? You see, there isn't anything else, is there?'

He let his face relax into a smile. She was still entirely confident of the worthlessness of the score which, at this very moment, was being copied for James Cornwall, and her calm acceptance of this belief made him aware of a rush of generosity towards her.

'I'll tell you what I'll do for you, Gretel,' he said. 'I'll take the

piano into my room and use it. It's better than my own, and I'll
lend you enough on it to pay for everything. Then if you can pay
me back some day, you can have your father's piano, and if not
– well, you'll know it is in safe keeping with a friend. That do
for you?'

'Oh, Mr. Wade, will you really do that? I may never be able
to buy it back from you, you know, but I'd love to think you
have it, and I should feel I was paying for—for the last thing I
can do for him,' with a gulp and a threat of fresh tears.

He patted her shoulder condescendingly, feeling intensely
openhanded and generous.

'That's all right, kiddie. It's little enough to do for a friend,
and I'm glad to have the opportunity. That all you wanted me
for? I'm rather busy today, you see.'

'Yes. That was all. Thank you so very much, Mr. Wade. You
don't like me to say you're kind to me, do you?'

He smiled.

'It's a new experience to me to *be* kind,' he said indulgently,
speaking more truly than she had any idea.

'That's what you say, but I know differently,' she said shyly.

'That's all right, then. Tell the undertakers to send in their bill
to me and I'll see to it for you. Goodbye, kiddie,' and he was
gone, with a deep breath of relief.

He was glad that he had had this opportunity of paying
something to old Baumer. It would salve his conscience a little.

He decided to buy a new shirt, and added tie and handkerchief
and socks to match. It might be very important to retain the
impression Maria Ludovini had formed of him, and he was
aware that he had looked his best last night. It behoved him to
be extremely careful the first time she saw him as an ordinary
everyday working man.

Mrs. Hesketh's flat was small but luxurious, just as exquisite in
its way as James Cornwall's mansion, and the soft-footed, soft-
voiced maid who opened the door to him added to the general
air of costly ease.

'Mrs. Hesketh is expecting me,' murmured Wade, in his best Oxford voice, and the maid smiled her agreement and opened the drawing-room door to him.

The dancer was alone, and trailed across the room to meet him, her pale lavender draperies shapeless and yet caught round her supple form with a languid and charming grace. A faint perfume of violets moved with her, and the mauve shadows beneath the beautiful, restless eyes seemed rather as if they had been placed there by design than by the relentless hand of time.

'Age has many compensations, Mr. Wade, and amongst them the ability to receive a young man quite alone and to show him that he is a very welcome guest,' she said, with her tired, slightly bitter smile. 'Let us sit down and talk. What will you drink? You see how I bow to the trend of the age!'

'I will wait to take tea with you, Madame,' said Wade, with the little bow which did not seem out of place in the presence of this delicate survival of a bygone age.

She nodded her approval.

'I like you quite as much as I thought I did,' she said. 'Now tell me about yourself – your life – your people – your ambitions and, if you will, your ideals.'

He swept into the fray undaunted. He had told and retold, added to and embroidered the story of his life so much that it might almost have been true, and he was too perfect in detail to be afraid of his memory betraying him later.

'My life and my people – they're easy,' he said, taking a chair near the one into which she had sunk with the grace which attended her every movement. 'Shall I begin with the latter? Actually I haven't any people now. My mother was a Frenchwoman, one of the Berthelmys, but they disowned her when she dared to marry an ordinary English Captain of Hussars. She used to tell me of the very great marriage which had been arranged for her with a member of the real old French nobility, though she would never divulge his name even to me. I can remember my father only faintly. He used to come home for leave, and we had a marvellous time, my mother and I. Then my father was killed, and with him went the whole sunshine of my mother's existence. There was very little money, but we lived on her pension until, when I was fifteen, she simply faded and died. Then I found, quite by chance, an uncle of my father's, the only relation he appears to have had, and the old boy took over my education, spent royally on that and on the Varsity later, but was inconsiderate enough to die during my last term without making any provision for me.

'It's like looking for a needle in a haystack to look for a job without influence. I couldn't do anything but play the piano, and I took a chance that offered to play in a dance band, and that's how I've kept myself going ever since.'

The recital was told with a delightful mixture of diffidence and bravado, and he could see that he had made a good impression by it.

Mrs. Hesketh smiled with a new warmth.

'I admit quite frankly that the definitely-idle young men bore me,' she said. 'I should have thought far less of you if you had been presented to me under the wing of Marie Berthelmy, who was once a very good friend of mine.'

Wade caught his breath a little at that. He must walk very warily in that direction, he could see.

'Anyway, that disposes of my people and my life, doesn't it?'

'Yes. And the rest? Your dreams? Your loves?' pursued the curious little lady.

He laughed.

'Of loves I have none. I cannot afford them – as yet.'

'You will – you will! There can be no life without its loves, nor can any nature fulfil its needs without at least one unhappy affair. Oh yes! I have had legion,' as he glanced at her with a smiling question in his eyes. 'Some day I, too, will reminisce. Just now it is of you we will talk and think. You were going to tell me of your ambitions.'

'I wonder whether I can dare to be frank?' he murmured.

'Why not? I am old and discreet.'

'I want wealth and all the power that it brings!' said Wade, his head flung up, his eyes shining. 'I want always the best of everything, the most expensive – houses and cars and clothes, food, wine – even possibly women, so long as they are expensive!' with a laugh.

'In women, the best are not always the most expensive, and vice versa,' she told him with a smile. 'Oh yes, I have been *very* expensive, my friend, but I have also been a great artist.'

'No one could possibly challenge that, Madame,' he murmured, but she waved aside as negligible an observation so trite.

'That is why I sent for you. It is a definite loss to the age that the beauty of the ballet should be allowed to be forgotten. These exotic, shivering, loathsome modern dances which are nothing but sex orgies are neither beautiful nor edifying. They are definitely degrading. I spoke to James Cornwall last night about this musical play of yours, and this morning he has been to see me and played some of the score to me. That surprises you? I have never found any advantage from letting the grass grow under my feet. They are a dancer's feet, you see,' with a sudden little flash of the whimsicality that made her so human and endearing when she seemed the least approachable.

Wade sat in silence though every muscle in his body wanted to twitch with his excitement.

'James Cornwall thinks the thing is good and, what is more to the point with him, believes it will make money for him – and for you, of course, though that is your affair, not his. He wants some of the music employed as ballet music, and I have offered to undertake the whole of that side of the play.'

She paused, and he caught her hand in his impulsively and carried it to his lips. He could have devised no more fitting or acceptable tribute, and her withered, carefully carmined lips softened.

'Madame, I am speechless,' he said. 'I never have dreamed of such an honour.'

She nodded, well pleased, withdrawing her hand as a tap at the door heralded a maid with a daintily equipped tea-wagon.

'Thank you, Simpson. I am at home to no one but Monsieur Lefetz.'

'Yes, Madame.'

'Lefetz is my choreographer,' explained Madame as the maid withdrew. 'He will discuss the scheme with us and compose the ballets to my instructions. You will, of course, be prepared to make some small alterations and additions if required?'

With a slight uneasiness of mind, Wade agreed as gracefully as he could, and a few minutes later the little ballet-master was admitted, walking daintily on sharp-pointed French shoes, his hands posed always as if in the dance, his manner mincing and effeminate. Wade found it difficult to believe that such a body held the brain which had helped not only Ludovini but several of her protegées to success by its fantastic, weirdly beautiful conceptions, but as the conversation between the two of them progressed, he himself being merely a listener, he began to realise that it was so.

Between them a dream of poetry and grace began to take shape to an imaginative mind, and first one,, then the other, would rise to illustrate some point, the years dropping from the woman and the eccentricities from the odd little man as they wove the magic of their web.

The preliminary discussion was finished at last, and Lefetz bidden to go.

'Cornwall has promised you a copy of the whole score tonight,' said Ludovini. 'Go through it tomorrow. Then we will discuss it again,' and she nodded to him casually, spreading out over the couch her lavender draperies and transforming herself in some odd way by her very gestures into Mrs. Hesketh again, an old and rather weary woman.

Wade took the hint and rose after a few minutes' desultory conversation which had no bearing on the play, bowing low over the hand she acceded him willingly enough.

'I cannot even begin to express my deep gratitude, Madame,' he said.

She waved it aside with an action of inimitable grace.

'There is no need, my young friend. I get my own satisfaction from it. My only regret is that the one relentless foe of mankind prevents me from dancing your Chloe myself.' She frowned a little. 'We shall have to let Viladoff do it, though she is like a poker and has never learned to smile with more than her mouth. I wish . . . ' and she lapsed into a half-smiling, half-sad reverie of thought into which Wade could dimly follow her.

She came out of her dreams and shook herself a little.

'Ah, well, everything passes, but for you, my friend, they are but beginning. No, do not thank me again. We will consider that all finished with. You are giving me a new thrill when I thought there was nothing left but my very last bouquets to which I cannot make my bows! That is enough. See to it that you drive a hard bargain with Cornwall. He is not nearly as benevolent or kindly as he looks. Show me your contract before you sign it, and tell him that you are going to do so,' and she dismissed him with a smile and a little friendly tap on his arm.

Wade had occasion to appreciate that last bit of advice, for she drove a far keener bargain with the astute Cornwall than he had at first had any intention of making.

The crowded, heady events of the next few days left Wade little time for anything outside his work, though the leader of the band released him generously from the usual morning rehearsals for the time being, having been taken into confidence.

Wade tried to salve his conscience by finding time to attend the funeral of Franz Baumer, pretending to himself that he was going to tell her about the play when the sad business was over and Gretel left alone with him. Though he despised himself for such weakness, he could not rid himself of the superstitious fear of something supernatural all the time he stood or knelt with the weeping girl in the empty, gloomy church dominated by that long wooden box in which reposed all that was mortal of the old man who had trusted him. He eyed it, repelled and yet fascinated, and even when it had slid at last into the cold earth, Gretel's simple bunch of flowers and his own rather showy wreath laid on the roughly turned clods which would soon be heaped upon it, he could not shake off the feeling of the accusing spirit which no man could lay aside and cover with earth.

'Come along, dear,' he whispered to the girl who stood forlornly by even after the last words had been spoken and the clergyman was waiting a little impatiently for them to release him from a task too familiar to have much effect on him.

She lifted her white, tragic face to his as if she scarcely understood and the clergyman stepped forward.

'His spirit goes with you, my child. It is only the useless and mortal part of him which we leave here,' he said with mechanical kindness.

Wade shivered a little and checked himself in the very act of looking round as if he almost expected to see an accusing finger pointed at him. Then he hurried the child away, paid the church dues with trembling fingers, and sank back with relief in the cab which was to take them straight to the convent.

Just as they reached the gates, he sat up and began to speak almost desperately.

'Gretel, I want to . . .'

She shook her head, her eyes filling with tears again.

'Not now, Mr. Wade. I—I can't talk or—listen sensibly. I just want to—be quite quiet. You meant to be kind, I know, but—I can't bear any more kindness just now. I—shall only cry again—please!'

He held her hand, conscious of a feeling of reprieve. There was plenty of time, after all. Why force the issue now?

When the great double door had closed on him, shutting out even the sound of Gretel's little feet and those of the gentle nun to whom he had handed her over, he drew a deep breath of relief. What, after all, had he to reproach himself with? He had seen the old man buried decently and reverently, charged himself, via the Reverend Mother, with the care of the child, and fully intended, all in good time, that she should reap the benefit of the hard work he was putting into the play.

He returned to his room to find a telephone message waiting for him, brought over from the baker's, whose number he had been permitted to use.

'Would Mr. Wade please call at the Vanity Theatre before five o'clock to see Mr. Lester?'

Lester was the leader of the orchestra at the Vanity, and he found his black mood evaporating as he changed his sombre tie for one more in keeping with the new occasion.

He found Cornwall in consultation with the man he had come to see, and they greeted him with the casual welcome which was as nectar and ambrosia to him.

'Madame Ludovini wants the score altered in the second act to admit of a flower ballet, Miss Morn being the central figure with the rose song,' said the great man, coming to the point without preamble.

Wade had already discovered that though the dancer might be Mrs. Hesketh in private and social life, no one dare refer to her as other than Ludovini in her professional capacity.

He hesitated, realising the need to walk warily. So far he had been lucky. The score of *Summer Storm* was so complete, worked out with such a wealth of detail and loving care, that the alterations so far had consisted in cutting rather than adding. The thing had been too long even without the ballets which had added to it, and Wade had been canny enough to make provision in his contract for any numbers cut out. These were still his property, or rather reserved to 'author', so that he held several money-makers even after Cornwall had taken all he needed for his production, which was now being called *Night in Gale*. The addition of anything to the score was another matter, and he watched points with the utmost caution.

'You mean you want to turn that second overture into ballet music?' he asked at last when the two men had amplified their idea.

'Partially, but we have already repeated quite a lot of that for the water scene. How long will it take you, Wade, to let us have a new score suitable for the sort of ballet Ludovini likes? You know the sort of thing, light but very smooth and flowing with a decided rhythm to it, none of these ghastly blues with their speeches and discords. How long do you want?'

Wade thought furiously. What could he do? Anyway, he must ask all the time possible.

'A week?' he hazarded.

'Rubbish, man! We've got to have it in rehearsal within that time. Tomorrow? Day after? It need not be finished off, you know. Lester will see to extra band parts and that sort of thing. Just the simple score – piano score will do, you know. Day after tomorrow?'

Wade had to capitulate and he did it as gracefully as he could.

'I'll do my best, but remember that the rest of the thing has taken years to write, not a few hours. A composer isn't a tap which you turn on in the certainty of an outflow of suitable music, you know!' and he smiled deprecatingly.

Cornwall laughed a grim little laugh.

'That's where you make a mistake, my boy. That's just what a composer's got to be if he's going to get anywhere these days. He's got to be a penny-in-the-slot machine. The public put the penny in and when they turn the handle they've got to have what they want come grinding out the other end. Your business is to see to it that they do get what they want. Run along now, my boy, and mind and make the music tuneful and easy. Put in plenty of sugar for the ladies!'

Wade went away uncomfortably, aware that Lester's beady eyes, the eyes of a disillusioned and disappointed man, followed him with a curious expression in them, almost as if he *knew*. It was beyond the bounds of possibility that he could know, of course, and yet in the midst of all the adulation and flattery and froth of congratulations which he had received all round in these past few days, Lester seemed to have stood aloof. Damn the man, what was he, after all? Nothing but a blasted stick-waver, directing a lot of other stick-wavers and blowers to do what such men as he, Roland Wade, decreed they should do! At that moment he almost believed that he had actually written

Night in Gale and his despondency gave way to a swagger as he left the theatre and went across to the practice-room which the Merry Men hired and which he knew would be vacant at this hour of the day.

He sat at the piano and ran his nimble fingers over the keys, trying to improvise some new theme, the sort of sparkling, lilting thing of which old Baumer had known the secret. Try as he might, his fingers wandered off again into old, well-worn themes, given a new turn perhaps, but the old air just the same. Now and then he thought he had caught what he wanted, only to realise that he was remembering part of Franz Baumer's music, after all. He dropped his head in his hands over the piano, burying his fingers in his dark hair, his eyes frantic with fear and despair. What could he say to Cornwall? How explain the fact that he could write so prolifically as to have composed a score which was almost enough for two musical plays, and yet be unable to produce at will one simple, tuneful melody?

He struggled for another hour and then, realising that he would be late for his evening's work, he went out again, his head a whirl of despairing misery.

Incredibly early the next morning he was up and at the piano again, but a succession of worried dreams had not helped him in any way towards the needed vision, and his fingers seemed as clumsy as his mind.

Suddenly from amongst the raucous cries of street vendors and all the turmoil of a busy, cheap little street came floating up the strains of a violin, an old and wheezy one, played by a tremulous hand, the notes sliding into one another with a certain suggestion of a master hand which was faltering.

He went to the window, driven by some unexplained impulse, and pulled the curtain aside to look down at the player. He was an old man walking with trembling knees along the gutter, a cheap yellow violin tucked beneath an unkempt beard, but Wade obeyed that strange impulse and listened to the tune he played, picking it out from the multifarious noises which threatened to drown the uncertain sound. What was it he was playing? Nothing that evoked any memory, though it was possessed of something haunting and vaguely sweet.

He dropped the curtain and went back to the piano and began to pick out the air, embroidered it a little, listened again until the wheezy notes were lost in the street noises, and played the haunting melody again, more certainly this time.

He paused to wipe little beads of perspiration from his face. It would do. It could be made to do. Given the central theme, it was within his scope to turn it into at least the semblance of what Cornwall wanted. He worked at it furiously, scribbled the score down as he went, altered and polished and elaborated it, and at last rose from the piano and took at a gulp the coffee which had been standing outside his door on his breakfast tray for more than an hour. He did not even realise that it was cold and nauseous. He was saved! And by what a fluke! He began to wash and dress, shaving with his usual meticulous care, and came gradually to the conclusion that he was one of the favoured of the gods and being specially looked after. What other reason could one possibly find for the timely appearance of the old man with his wheezy fiddle?

It was ten o'clock by the time he was ready. Lester, he knew, would be at the Vanity at quarter-past for a rehearsal, and at half-past Wade strolled into the theatre with a casual nod to the stage doorkeeper.

'Oh, Lester!' he called carelessly, sauntering across the front of the stalls and leaning over the rail oblivious of the fact that a number was in process of rehearsal.

The conductor gave the signal to stop, the slightest possible expression of annoyance flitting across his face.

'Lester, this is the piano score Mr. Cornwall asked me to let you have to orchestrate,' and the manuscript was handed over the rail to him.

His look of surprise was not lost on Wade. He had the ghastly fear that that theme played by the old man and 'borrowed' by him was not original, after all; that it was something well known to Lester, an old master perhaps – possibly Purcell or one of those.

Then Lester looked up, and the relief was almost intolerable. The surprise was still there, with a little bewilderment added, but there was no accusation or derision – rather a hint of added respect. The older man had scarcely known what he had felt about *Night in Gale* and its composer. He had had a life's experience of music and musicians, and he would have been prepared to swear that *Night in Gale* was written by a man of vastly different type from this immaculate young blood. Yet Cornwall seemed satisfied, Ludovini had accepted the position without question, and the whole company was rapidly nearing completion, from Nancy Morn down to the humblest of the chorus, and seemed ready to fall down and worship at this new shrine.

'I'll get the work done as soon as possible, Mr. Wade,' he said. 'Now, gentlemen, please!' and the rehearsal was in full swing again.

Cornwall frowned a little when the fully orchestrated number was played over for him. It was not up to the standard of the rest of the thing, and everyone knew it. It was tuneful and rhythmical, and Lester had added a certain spice and fire to it, bringing out the air cleverly and subordinating the other instruments to the woodwinds which suited its particular style – and yet it lacked the verve and charm of the other numbers.

'It was done hurriedly and to order,' Lester reminded him.

'Yes—yes—of course. Oh well – if Madame is satisfied,' and he shrugged his shoulders and passed on to the next question.

Madame was not inclined to be critical. She had openly fallen in love with her young protégé, as she liked to call him, and so long as the ballet numbers had the necessary lilt and swing to them, she was satisfied.

During the weeks which wore into the months required for such an ambitious production, Wade made one or two half-hearted attempts to see Gretel and clear his not too troublesome conscience. The first time she had been ill, giving way at last to the burden of her grief and letting her undernourished little body take its fill of rest and ease and care. He had left flowers and fruit and gone thankfully away.

The next time he had been allowed to see her, but Reverend Mother had counselled him against saying anything which might distress her, and especially not to mention either directly or indirectly the loss of her father. They had talked disjointedly for some ten or fifteen minutes and when he did not go again until after the production of the play, it was manifestly too late to tell her.

Meantime she wanted for nothing. She said she was happy, though she was still too sad at heart to feel anything beyond a passive acceptance of the quiet, convent life and the gratitude which was an essence of her warm nature. She spent her time learning from the nuns and giving lessons to some of the tiniest children in the convent school, and seemed to ask nothing more of life.

4

Long before the *première* of *Night in Gale*, Roland Wade discovered that quite the least important person connected with a production is its author and composer.

In the first thrilling, disappointing weeks of rehearsal he was seldom absent from the theatre or one or other of the dingy, unimaginative rehearsal rooms where the smaller scenes and those involving only the principals were frequently tried out. At first he had tried to assert himself, offering criticisms and suggestions, but he was given scant attention and bare courtesy and his offerings cast aside as negligible. The big noise was James Cornwall and, in hardly lesser degree, Fawcett, his manager. The great Ludovini herself swept down occasionally at a specially appointed time, little Lefetz in obsequious attendance, and everybody listened respectfully to what she had to say, but at other times she appeared to take no active interest in the affair. It would have utterly delighted him to display before that small world the graciousness and interest which the great dancer showed to him in private, but she never gave him the opportunity, and as the weeks wore on into months and the thing began to take definite shape and cohesion he retired in high dudgeon and 'left them to it', as he told himself disgustedly. Anybody would think he were a mere outsider and had nothing to do with it instead of having written and composed the thing!

By this time he had almost made himself believe that that was true.

Two days before the date of production, Cornwall rang him up and invited his attendance at a full rehearsal. On the strength of his prospects, and to accord with the new importance he felt, he had moved from 15 Earl Street to a small top flat in a house which kept a telephone for the use of its boarders.

'You'd better come along this morning, Wade. We're going right through with full cast on the stage, eleven o'clock. See you there?'

'All right,' said Roland a trifle sulkily, considering that the acknowledgement of his part in the affair was coming rather late. 'If I can manage it, I'll get along.'

Cornwall chuckled. He knew exactly what was the trouble, but he had been in the game far too long to worry about trifles like authors' little vanities.

'Don't get hipped, my boy. Your turn's coming on Thursday when I get a chance of a rest on the back seat. So long. See you at eleven,' and the receiver clicked into place.

By five o'clock that day Wade felt that the bottom had fallen out of his world. By no wildest stretch of imagination could he conceive of the hopeless conglomeration of the day becoming a coherent, smoothly running, sensible production capable of being performed before an audience on Thursday. Nobody seemed to have any idea what to do; scenes were pulled to pieces by the ruthless hands of Fawcett and Cornwall and apparently never built up again; dances were altered and cut until the girls, looking like nothing on earth in their nondescript rehearsal shorts, were rushing about like a flock of silly sheep. Cornwall was curt and rude to everybody. Fawcett tearing his shock of untidy hair and perspiring visibly, Lester coldly furious and cutting, little Lefetz running hither and thither like a lost and half-demented monkey, gibbering in half a dozen languages to anyone who would stop and listen. Mrs. Hesketh drifted in, the one calm and unmoved figure in all that welter of confusion, stood in a box and watched for half an hour, nodded as if everything were all right, and left again without speaking to anyone. To Wade's salutation from the opposite box she gave but a nod and a friendly, detached smile, and he was still too much in awe of her to join her uninvited.

When Cornwall reached home in the early evening he found Wade waiting for him, white-faced and anxious.

'Stebbs, two very long drinks and then peace, perfect peace. Mr. Wade will doubtless join me in both,' said the great man, flinging aside coat and hat and sinking down in an armchair in the last stages of exhaustion. 'Don't begin to talk yet, boy. Have a drink first.'

Five minutes later they both felt better, and the older man looked across at the younger with a smile.

'Well, went fine, didn't it?' he asked.

Roland stared at him as if he had suddenly gone mad.

'I—what did you say?' he asked incredulously.

'I say it went fine.'

'B-b-but—all that confusion—nobody knowing what to do—everything upside down ...' stammered Wade, thinking Cornwall was pulling his leg and not knowing quite how to take it.

'Oh, that? Nothing, my boy, nothing at all! Must get it into reasonable length, you know. Too long now, but we'll try it out like that on Thursday and then cut again. I think we'll take it like this for the first night and see what the critics say. I've got Millis of the *Daily Post* looking in tomorrow and Dancy of the *World* has promised me he'll see the show right through. That's the beggar with these newspaper men. They look in for an hour, half of which time they spend in the bar, and probably miss the best of the show, which doesn't in the least deter them from writing and downing the lot! Routh of the *Morning News* doesn't know it, but a pal of mine's taking him out to dinner before the show on Thursday, and if Garret chooses the wines discreetly Routh may mingle a little honey with his poison. That man's got the most vitriolic tongue in Fleet Street and he doesn't mind who knows it!'

'Then you really think the show's going to be all right, Mr. Cornwall?' asked Wade nervously. Somehow he had never been able to bring himself to drop the 'Mr.' when speaking to James Cornwall, though he despised that fact as a little weakness which he must overcome before long. Even the negligible Lester called him plain Cornwall, and that unspeakable little Lefetz actually called him 'Jeemy' at times!

When Thursday night arrived Wade hesitated whether or not to take one or two chosen friends with him to the box assigned to him, but he decided against it in the end. For one thing, he had no really intimate friends. A climber cannot afford to twine the tentacles of friendship about him as he struggles upward. They have an annoying habit of clinging round one's feet just as the next rung of the ladder is in sight. The people he knew best were Michael Dent, the 'Micky' of the dance band, and a Mrs. Allister, an elderly widow, who occupied the rooms below his and whose acquaintance he had cultivated when he discovered that she had once been 'someone' and known 'everyone' until too obvious indiscretions had cast her out of the charmed circle.

Wade had no intention of forming Clare Allister into a tentacle, and he was glad that her age (she was over sixty) enabled him to establish a purely platonic relationship with her. He realised, however, that her undoubted culture, her breeding and perfect manners, her knowledge first hand of most of the best-known 'society' people, might stand him in good stead in his upward climb, and the top of his ladder had now reached such dizzy heights that it was lost in the clouds.

He decided that he might well spoil his chances of entering high social circles if his first public appearance were made in the company of Mrs. Allister, whom undoubtedly people would recognise. No, taking everything into consideration, it would be better if he went to the Vanity quite alone. It would even add to the piquancy and romance of the situation – young, handsome, unknown author of successful and novel production, alone and friendless in his empty box!

He dressed with even more exquisite care and at the last moment tapped at Clare Allister's door. She was perfectly well aware of his reason in not inviting her company, and accepted it without bitterness.

'I am just going, Mrs. Allister.'

She opened her door, revealing a room which, in spite of its obvious poverty, could only have belonged to a woman of culture and refinement. Roland had learnt much from that room already.

'Let me look at you, you young Adonis,' she said in her soft, beautifully modulated voice.

He followed her in, smiling, well pleased with himself, but she frowned a little as she cast a critical eye over him.

'Not the flower, Roland. That's a mistake,' she said.

He looked down at the malmaison with its tiny frond of maidenhair which he had chosen with such nicety an hour ago and fastened in the lapel of his faultless dinner-jacket.

'Oh, don't you like it?' he asked, disappointed.

She laughed with a little tender note in her laughter. Older women always liked him. He could be so charming to them.

'Not with a dinner-jacket, and not tonight in any case.' She took it out for him, smoothing the cloth into place again with her beautiful, blue-veined fingers which had no longer any rings to wear save the narrow band of her wedding-ring.

He laughed with a touch of embarrassment and then, with a charming gesture, took the flower from her fingers and fastened it in the soft folds of lace at her withered throat. Her eyes grew a little misty as she smiled her appreciation, and for a moment she held his hand in both of hers.

'Roland, don't be a fool and throw away the substance for the shadow, as I have done,' she said. 'Shadows are poor things to live with when you are old.'

He was not sure what she meant, which the substance and which the shadow in his life, but he carried her fingers to his lips in that graceful, easy way of his and prepared to take his leave.

'Goodbye, Mrs. Allister. Wish me luck,' he said.

'I do, my dear, with all my heart. Come in and tell me how it went, no matter what time it is.'

He went 'behind' for a few minutes, finding everything in a confusion which to his unaccustomed eyes looked chaotic but which was really a confusion of perfect order and intention.

'I shouldn't stay here, Mr. Wade,' counselled Fawcett, calm now and no longer perspiring and tearing his hair. 'You'll only get a bad impression and feel depressed. Everything's quite all right.'

He wandered off and encountered Nancy Morn outside her dressing-room. He had seen very little of her since the play went into production, but there was a pleasant friendliness between them.

'Don't worry, old boy,' she said. 'Everything in the garden's lovely. If I were you I'd go out to a show at another theatre and come back here in time to take the frantic calls for "author" about eleven o'clock.'

'I couldn't possibly do that! I must be in at the death,' he told her, trying to smile though he felt wretched.

She laughed, patted his shoulder, and went into her room, closing the door firmly behind her.

Back in his box, he found the indefatigable Cornwall waiting for him with a little knot of men whose names conveyed little to him, though he greeted them with his charming, rather diffident air and knew he was making the right impression.

The orchestra was tuning up with little unconnected bursts and ripples of sound, and the men drifted away from the box to their stalls one by one, Cornwall going with the last with a whispered word of encouragement to Wade as he went, and once more he was alone, looking down at that blur of faces suddenly blotted out by the dimming of the lights, and knowing a moment of utter panic when the orchestra struck up the first notes of the opening chorus and the curtain rose on the exotic Eastern garden in which much of the action was set.

Suppose it failed! He had counted on it so much, lived in it and for it and with it for all these months, woven such dreams about it, hung them to the stars so that the web covered all his universe! What if it failed!

But it was obvious from the very first that it would not fail; further, that it would be not only a success but a tumultuous one. Old Franz Baumer must have culled in his quiet existence a far greater knowledge of human nature than one would have thought possible, for he played on it as a violinist plays on the strings of his violin, touching the heights and depths. Sentiment and humour, romance and colour, melody and harmony – he had woven them into the fabric from which Cornwall and Fawcett and Lester, Ludovini and little Lefetz had spun the thing they had called *Night in Gale*.

Half-way through the first act Wade, daring to look about him, saw the great dancer in the royal box opposite him, and with her some Very Great Persons indeed, paying court to her and receiving her own homage which held nothing obsequious, a queen herself and aware of her royal status. She smiled across at him when the curtain fell on the first act and a tumult of applause followed the flashing of the lights in the auditorium. He bowed, aware that she was making his whereabouts known to her distinguished companions, and then everything was forgotten for the moment as Cornwall and a dozen others crowded in on him, shaking his hand, paying him compliments, some genuine, some fulsome, all exciting and acceptable in that magic moment.

Nor were the second and third acts anti-climax, and it was an astonishing and noteworthy fact that scarcely a seat in the row reserved for the Press was empty until the curtain had fallen on the final chorus and only the curtain calls remained.

Nancy Morn, a vision of loveliness in the bridal gown she wore for the last scene, came again and again, alone and with her leading man, Bruce Tenby, and at length came the shout for 'author' which had been ringing in Wade's ears, sleeping and waking, for months, and which was at last a veritable fact.

As if in a dream he made his way down the stairs and into the wings, a dozen hands meeting him to pull him forward and send him on, and suddenly he found himself between the footlights and the great satin curtain, the storm of applause bursting out again and then dying into silence as they waited for him to speak.

He acquitted himself well, and the few words which he had chosen long ago and carefully rehearsed in front of his mirror came clearly to his mind. He spoke them with becoming diffidence and charm, and when, returning to the wings after making his bow, he found Mrs. Hesketh waiting for him, he took her hand and led her back before the curtain, presenting her with a deep obeisance to the vast crowd who had loved her so well and had already had their memories stirred by her name on the programme.

She was a regal figure that night, dressed in black velvet, unrelieved save by the diamonds glittering at her throat and in her silver-grey hair and on the black velvet which sheathed the feet which could no longer charm save in memory. She smiled at them with misty eyes, presented to them the slim young man at her side, and then enchanted them by lifting her face to his and kissing him, laughing as she did so and sweeping him a curtsey before he led her off the stage again.

He stood in the wings for a moment, still holding her hand.

'Madame, I am overwhelmed by your graciousness,' he said, feeling slightly light-headed.

She laughed and tapped his arm with the fan she liked to carry whenever possible.

'Nonsense! I am never too old to enjoy the wine of success, and it is you who have provided the cup, my clever young friend. Ah, James! We win again, then,' as Cornwall joined them and slipped an arm round the younger man's shoulder.

'The divine Maria! That was a touch of inspiration, my boy, though I have not the slightest doubt in the world but that Madame herself planned and invited it! And now, what about supper? The company go as my guests tonight. I have a room at the Clair de Lune. You will honour us, Madame?'

'Thank you, James, but no. I am taking my own guests back to my house for supper. Another time we shall arrange for you to come, Roland. Tonight – perhaps better not. You go with James,' and she gave him a friendly nod, another for Cornwall, and went back to join her very important guests.

'Clever of her to have got them here tonight,' observed Cornwall as he slipped an arm through Wade's. 'She must have been damn sure of a success, though! I wouldn't have risked it, but Maria has never yet met the situation she could not carry off. That means there will be royalty itself here within the next week or so, of course. Nancy! Here he is!' as the leading lady, still in her bridal gown, popped an enquiring head out of her dressing-room door.

'Come along in whilst I dress, both of you.'

A wooden partition extending not quite to the ceiling cut the room in two, and from behind it she talked to the two men as she dressed, chattering excitedly, flinging them questions, comments, gay forecasts for the future, entirely in love with herself, with Wade, with life.

'Now come along,' she said, emerging at last in the beautiful, sophisticated evening gown which turned her at once from Baumer's sweet, unworldly heroine into the more comprehensible product of the age. 'Is the great Maria coming, Corny,'

'No. Entertaining the great ones of the earth herself, my dear.'

'Cheers. She's a bit too circumspect for my tastes nowadays, and one has to be careful what's said, though if one is to believe half the stories told about her stage days—my hat! Give me my cloak, Roland. You're leaning on it. Have I got too much lipstick on? Never mind. I shall probably have used it all up by the time the evening's over!' and she flung a laughing, provocative glance at Wade as she turned to let him wrap her in a marvellous cloak of silver and ermine.

Wade never had a very clear picture of the rest of that evening, for success had gone to his head even before he began to add Cornwall's champagne to it. He had a confused idea of eating and drinking and dancing, of making and listening to incoherent speeches, of going with Nancy Morn in her car when she insisted on going home, of kissing her most of the way and finally of being deposited, very muddle-headed, on the pavement outside the house where he lived, in the early hours of a chill autumn morning.

5

Since the devil looks after his own and the Lord helps those who help themselves, it is not surprising that with two such redoubtable allies, Roland Wade climbed with amazing speed that ladder whose narrowing rungs stretched upwards to infinity.

When both critics and gallery applaud a play, the cast can settle down comfortably to at least a good many months' steady employment. With *Night in Gale* they settled down to two years before there was talk of taking it off and adding to the number of companies already on the road. During those two years, money had poured in like the rain of an English summer.

James Cornwall rubbed his hands and congratulated himself on his perspicacity; Nancy Morn added a crown to her previous triumphs, for the part suited her perfectly; the leading man found himself for once not overshadowed by the feminine element of the show, but with a definite and powerful characterisation to carry through; and Roland Wade had moved from his modest top flat in Bloomsbury to a luxurious little service suite in Jermyn Street with a 'man' at his disposal.

He discovered that not only were there second and third crops to be harvested from *Night in Gale*, but that people were falling over one another in their anxiety to pay him money and yet more money. Excerpts from the play were broadcast; records were made of the songs and dance numbers; the ballet scenes were 'borrowed' at large sums of money to embellish future pantomimes once the London run was over; a world-renowned producer bargained for the American rights of production and within the first year, Wade was in Hollywood selling the film rights for a sum which might have raised the hair on any less sleekly brushed head than his.

For fifteen months he lived on his laurels, too busy retaining his balance on the dizzy height of his ladder to worry seriously about his future. Even in his secret thoughts, he never paused to remember now that he was not the author and composer of *Night in Gale*. He had salved his conscience in the first few months by going more or less regularly to see Gretel at her convent, had taken her all sorts of extravagant presents which he could see only embarrassed her.

'It's darling of you, Mr. Wade, but really I don't need anything,' she would say, shaking her head of tow-coloured hair with its long, neat plait hanging sedately down the middle of her navy serge back. 'You see, we live so simply here, and there's no possible opportunity for wearing such a frock as that,' fingering the filmy chiffon which foamed out of the gilt-edged box bearing a famous name.

He frowned, his conscience stirring uncomfortably from its sleep.

'But it isn't natural,' he objected. 'Don't you ever go out? No dances or parties or anything? After all, you're nearly eighteen, aren't you?'

'Perhaps I'm made differently from other girls. I'm happy here, living this sort of life. It suits me. I don't want anything else, really.'

After that, he had brought her less intimate things – books, pictures, a very expensive watch – but she had accepted them under protest so that finally he was driven to offering a cheque to the Reverend Mother.

'Gretel won't take things,' he had explained, rather annoyed. It would have been such a satisfactory salve to his conscience if he could have spent lavishly on her.

The calm-faced woman smiled serenely with that remote look in her eyes which always made Wade feel unpleasantly low in his own estimation.

'She is happy and content with the humble, simple things

which are really all we need, Mr. Wade. I am glad that it should be so. I think perhaps she will find she has a vocation, but she must discover that for herself and be quite sure. Meantime it would be the truest kindness not to bring her these presents for which she has no desire or use. Believe me, she has all she needs.'

'Then, will you let me give a donation to—to something or other on her behalf?' he asked, irritated.

'We are not permitted to accept anything for ourselves, of course, but we never refuse for our poor and needy,' she said in her calm way.

Wade wrote her out a cheque, stung to making it far more than he had intended. She was not profuse in her thanks, according him perfect courtesy, but leaving him with the idea that she did not really desire the gift any more than had Gretel wanted the platinum and diamond watch. He strode away feeling angry and uneasy, and after that he was seen no more entering the great gates and enquiring at the little postern for 'Miss Baumer'. He wrote to her desultorily, received from her formal, stilted little notes in reply, and finally even such a frail link was allowed to break. After all, he had done his best and if she refused to accept what he privately termed her 'share' in the success of *Night of Gale*, what could he do?

And with the second year of the play almost over, Cornwall began to fidget about a successor.

'We might run this into a third year,' he said doubtfully, 'but it's not good policy. It's the greatest mistake to let a successful show wear itself out. One or two of the understudies would, I think, take the chance of going on a first-class tour as principals if the London run were over, and I've found that a good working scheme. You've had your holiday, my boy, and played around quite a lot both here and in the States. Now you've got to settle down and put your best into a successor to *Night in Gale* and a good one, too. You've established a reputation which requires some upkeep, and no second-rate goods will go over with a public to whom you have given such a show as this. Wire in, my boy, and when you've roughed the thing out, let me have a look at it so that I can begin to wind up the present show.'

'What terms?' asked Wade in a tone which he certainly would not have used to Cornwall a year previously.

The older man's eyes narrowed a little. He had been somewhat disappointed over his young friend, realising that there was something not quite sincere beneath the charm of manner which had first attracted him. He could not define the lack, but he felt it, and this first suggestion of bargaining with him got him on the raw. He was a keen business man, but he was scrupulously honest in his dealings and he felt that, after two years of close association with him and his methods, Wade should have known better than take just that tone.

'I'll draft out my suggestions,' he said rather curtly.

'I shall expect a much higher percentage than I've had out of this show, you know,' said Wade.

'I should expect to offer a higher one, certainly,' agreed the other, 'but I don't know about a "much" higher one. After all, the success of one show is no guarantee that the next will succeed, and I am the man taking all the risks.'

'You've done very well for yourself out of *Night in Gale*,' Wade reminded him.

'Agreed. So have you. So have we all. In my position, however, I stand to lose just as much as I've made if I put on a show which fails. I've got to protect myself.'

'You suggest that my next show might fail, then?' asked Wade, and there was a distinct edge to his voice.

Cornwall shrugged his shoulders.

'I don't suggest anything. If you've been able to write such good stuff as *Night in Gale* once, I see no reason why you should not be able to do it again. On the other hand, there are dozens of cases where a man has produced one good play, one good picture, one book that's a best-seller, and has never been able to follow it up. Possibly he has put everything of which he is capable into that one effort, and he is left like a dried-up spring.'

Wade made no rejoinder. He resented Cornwall's doubts of his ability the more because of the anxious forebodings which of late had been filling his own mind. What was the next move? How the devil was he going to produce a successor to *Night in Gale?*

Back in his luxurious little flat which represented nearly all his dreams of comfort and beauty, he flung himself down in one of the deep leather chairs and buried his hands in his pockets, those white, shapely, well-tended hands which for two years had done nothing more useful than sign contracts and cheques and hold the willing hands of women.

Cornwall had not raised a new question. It was only that, in voicing it, he had increased a thousandfold the anxious worry which had gradually been creeping over his mind once so ecstatically filled with assured success.

He had more than once taken out the original manuscript of *Summer Storm*, ruthlessly cut by Cornwall for the evolution of *Night in Gale*, but the numbers which he had cast out were disjointed, the music lacked cohesion, and his brain absolutely refused to provide any sort of story which would link up the delicate, romantic idylls so oddly born of old Franz Baumer's mind. Who would have thought the old boy capable of such fantastic, airy delights? Certainly it was much easier to credit Roland Wade with them.

He sat down at the piano and pulled the worn manuscript out from the bottom of a pile of music, opened it and began to play some of it with fingers which irritated him with their stiffness and ineptitude. He played the notes correctly, but the soul of the music had fled. For an instant he knew horror. Was he losing the one thing he had ever been able to do?

Frantically he exercised his fingers, played scales and arpeggios, worked at every joint with frenzied zeal and at last returned to Baumer's manuscript and heaved a sigh of relief as he found his old skill returning.

'Must work at least an hour a day,' he told himself, and then caught at the basis of that thought with a sudden constriction of his breath. What did he mean by that? Was it possible that he would have to go back to the old life, the eternal dance music ground out hour after hour, night after night? He had been living up to his income, living lavishly and foolishly. The bare rent of this flat absorbed more than his total earnings as a pianist in the old days. Then there was Wrenn, his man, to keep and pay and provide with the expected perquisites in the way of suits and shoes and shirts cast off long before they had had adequate use. He had spent several hundreds on the furnishing of the suite, small though it was, and the huge wardrobes were filled with expensive suits for every conceivable occasion.

He had, of course, indulged in a car, a small, rakish sports car which was expensive to run but which added to his 'tone'. In addition, he ran up huge bills for the hire of luxurious saloons when evening occasions demanded a closed car, or when some influential acquaintance of the fair sex might possibly accept his escort. He never let his mind wander from the main chance, and on his upward climb he had no time to cultivate the friendship of people who could not help him.

He was aghast at the insidious introduction into his mind of that thought that he must not neglect his piano-playing. Was it really possible that he might have to go back to that sordid, grinding toil for a bare subsistence?

Frantically he played over Baumer's delicate, haunting airs, rejected the lilting words which belonged too obviously to the story of *Night in Gale*, but could replace them with no others. He rose at last, flung a half-coherent message to Wrenn and made his way out into Piccadilly and, without realising where he was going, found himself in Charing Cross Road and halted instinctively at a furtive little bookshop outside which were portable shelves offering for a few pence secondhand books on every subject under the sun.

He had gone in there once for an old book giving period illustrations for one of Ludovini's ballet settings, and he had been queerly attracted by the girl who had served him. She had the face of an artist's dream, a delicate oval in which were set features which might have been modelled in alabaster, clear-cut, sensitive, highly bred. Her skin was naturally pale, and the dim interior of the dusty little shop accentuated its ivory whiteness. Eyes dark enough to be almost black were startling in their relief, and above the wide, white brow was smooth-banded the hair as black as night.

Wade had been surprised and intrigued at the sudden vision of her. Then she had come round the corner of the counter with its load of magazines and foreign papers, and he had understood why the dark eyes had seemed laden with tragedy and the beautiful mouth embittered. She was hopelessly deformed, with a hunched back and a sideways lurch which told of a diseased hip.

They had talked about the illustrations he wanted, and she had found them for him, astonishing him by her wide knowledge, and they had gone on talking, the girl losing her diffidence and forgetting as she talked the blight which had clouded all her young life.

Since then, Wade had gone to the shop several times, ostensibly to consult one or other of the old books which, for a few pence, became accessible to a customer, but actually because he found her interesting and unusual.

Her dark eyes softened as his tall figure blocked up for a moment the narrow doorway, and he noticed that she made no attempt to come round her protective counter towards him. He guessed her poor little rag of pride.

'Hullo, May. How's things?' he asked, in the friendly voice which had become music to her ears.

'Much as usual, Mr. Wade. It's a long time since you came in,' she said softly, leaning over her counter.

'Call that lazy young brother of yours in and come for a ride with me,' he said abruptly, the idea suddenly born. He loved to do a kindness if it could be done at no cost to himself, and just now he found her adoring admiration of him particularly acceptable. It might restore that faith in himself which Cornwall had shaken that morning and which had had an even ruder shock when he found himself contemplating the possibility of a return to the old life.

The girl flushed to the roots of her hair, and her eyes gazed at him in incredulous wonder. For her the heavens had opened.

'Oh, Mr. Wade, do you mean it?' she breathed.

He was touched.

'Of course. The fresh air will do you good. Have you a warm coat? It's cold, and the car's open.'

'Oh yes, if you can wait just a minute,' and she flashed her rare and lovely smile at him and lurched away through a door at the back of the shop, to return some five minutes later wrapping a shabby fur coat about her and driving before her a grubby and reluctant youth of some seventeen or eighteen years.

Wade turned the battery of his smile upon him.

'Hullo, Joe. You won't mind letting May have an hour or two off, will you? Here,' slipping a ten shilling note into his ready hand.

The boy grinned, pocketed the note, and the hunchback sister knew that she need have no fear for the shop whilst they were out.

Wade helped her into the low-sided car with a gentle concern for her which reduced her to a state of slavish adoration of him. It was so easy to be kind to children and animals and such poor things as this. It gave one such a comfortable feeling of well-being.

'Comfy?' he asked, glancing down at her.

'Beautifully,' she said.

He eyed her shabby coat distastefully. Her hat, a soft little knitted affair pulled down on one side of her head, was exactly what every other girl in London was wearing, rich or poor, but he felt that the coat did not do him credit. She was so lovely, too, and her deformity was quite unnoticeable as she lay back in the low car.

He pulled up at a smart little shop at which he had already paid various bills – for services rendered.

'Mind waiting a moment?*' he asked with a smile, receiving a dazzling denial.

Some minutes later he came out with a coat flung negligently over his arm, a thing of pastel blue cloth, thick and soft, with a deep cape and cuffs of moleskin. He dropped it over the side of the car into May's lap and went round to his own side.

'Like it?' he asked, starting up.

She was bewildered.

'I—you mean—you've bought it for someone?' she stammered.

'For you,' he said. 'Can you slip it on in the car or shall I run up a side road and stoShe was crimson. No one ever gave her expensive gifts, and certainly no man had ever given her anything in her life.

'You—you can't really mean that, Mr. Wade?' she asked unsteadily, and then horrified him by bursting into tears.

'Here, you can't do that, not out in the street!' he told her. 'Whatever will people think? I shall be arrested for abducting you. Don't, my dear, for the love of Mike! The police will stop us and accuse me of seducing you!'

She smiled through her tears, a bitter, haunted smile.

'Not once I was out of the car,' she said. 'Oh, I'm sorry! It—it just got me for a moment. No one has ever been so kind to me before.'

That's all right. Slip it on, there's a good girl. Sure you can manage? Stuff the other round your feet.'

He would have hated to touch her and was glad that circumstances provided him with an excellent excuse for keeping his hands on the wheel.

She wriggled out of one coat and into the other, snuggling her chin into the soft fur which framed her delicate beauty to perfection.

'I feel like a queen.' she said, and her dark eyes told him, if he had cared to see, 'I love and adore you!'

He drove for miles through the countryside, and May, cuddled down in her blue coat, pretended to herself that she was straight and comely and that this young god at her side was her lover.

'Happy?' he asked her once, and her dark eyes flashed an

answer.

'Happier than ever in my life,' she told him.

He took her to a comfortable old inn to tea and had it laid in the garden, with a rose arbour for a background and a vista of fields and woods rolling endlessly before them.

During the past months he had learned how to treat many kinds of women. He did not consciously make her fall in love with him, but after the pseudo-clever, sparkling women with whom he had come so much into contact, this modest and thoughtful girl amused and intrigued him.

They drove back through the starlit enchantment of the evening. At first it was Wade who talked, but gradually he let her monopolise the conversation, her huskily sweet voice weaving the magic spells of her mind. She began to turn her disjointed little dream pictures into a story, fanciful and delicate, with heroes and heroines and noble steeds and enchanted castles.

They had laughed at first, Roland putting in small absurdities now and then, but gradually he, too, was caught in the spell of the quiet and the night and the beauty of the girl beside him, and he let her talk on uninterrupted.

'You'll come again?' he asked her as he helped her out of the car outside the little shop which looked dingier than ever now.

'Oh, if I may!' she told him longingly.

He nodded and held her hand a moment, smiling down into her glorious eyes and thinking for the hundredth time what a pity it was that her body did not match her face.

'One day soon. Good night, May,' and he was gone, leaving her in a whirl of wild happiness and passionate regret.

It was not until after he had reached his rooms and was luxuriating in the bath that he realised that May had given him the story he needed to link together those disjointed songs of old Baumer's. Of course the setting would have to be altered a little. The more he thought of it the better were its possibilities, and as soon as he could he slipped back to his piano and old Baumer's manuscript.

He remembered for the first time a parcel of papers and

books which the landlady at 15 Earl Street had given him at the last moment before he moved out. They had been lying neglected in the attic for years, and it was only when the men came to mend the roof that the bundle had been turned out. Would Mr. Wade take charge of it for poor little Gretel, as he would probably be seeing her?

He had agreed and promptly forgotten it, but suddenly he remembered it and dived to the bottom of the trunk which had formed a part of his luggage in all his various moves. Most of the contents were disappointing. But mixed up with the rubbish were odd sheets in Baumer's careful notation. No words had been written, but many of the sheets contained music obviously intended for ballad settings. The lilting melodies almost suggested the words.

With Baumer's music and that fantastic, romantic story which the hunchback girl had given him, he knew he had all the elements of another successful play of the type which, in *Night in Gale*, had taken a blasé London by storm.

For days he struggled to find those words himself, but the task was utterly beyond him. His verses were mere doggerel, foolish and childish.

And at the end of a week he went to the dingy little shop in Charing Cross Road again.

'Come out with me?' he asked the girl, watching the haze of happiness which seemed to hover about her at the very sight of him.

'I'll get the blue coat,' she said, and laughed.

It was the first time she had laughed for a week.

6

He knew, of course, that she was in love with him, but he felt that that could not possibly matter, she being as she was. He told himself that it was pure kindness to give her such happiness as probably would never come her way again.

The second ride was followed by others, and after tea came dinner, a little intimate meal at that same old-fashioned country inn where visitors were few and far between and no one took much notice of the pair, save to throw a pitiful thought towards the pathetic little hunchback with the beautiful face who obviously adored the good-looking man who was so kind to her.

Gradually Wade spoke of his projected play, told her of the difficulty he found in setting suitable words to the music.

'I can write reams of music, hear the songs whilst I compose the tunes, know so exactly the sort of thing I want to put into words – but somehow the words won't come,' he told her.

'They came in *Night in Gale*,' she reminded him with pride in her voice.

Since she had known who he was she had been half a dozen times to see the play at the Vanity.

'I know, but it took about ten years to evolve that,' he said, with some amount of truth. 'I can't take another ten years for this one. I am being worried right now to offer a successor to *Night in Gale* and the ideas won't come!'

She glanced at the piano at the other end of the room. They had been dining together for the second time in the little country inn, and her first feeling of shyness and something tinged with awe had worn off. She felt at home with him.

'Play some of them to me now and I'll tell you what they suggest to me,' she said.

He hesitated.

'I'm such a fool,' he said. 'Do you know, although I wrote the things, I can't play them without the manuscript? Look here. I'm not going anywhere tonight. Come back with me to my rooms and let me play them to you there, will you? It's quite all right. My man, Wrenn, will be there and he's a most efficient chaperon!'

Her lovely mouth drooped a little.

'I don't have to worry about things like that,' she said.

He took her hand and held it in his for a moment, warmly, comfortingly.

'I wish you wouldn't spoil things between us by talking like that,' he said gently. 'You're the loveliest pal a man ever had, May.'

She raised haunted eyes to his.

'A pal – yes,' she said quietly, and added no other comment.

There was a few minutes' silence between them and then he moved.

'Well, what about coming back with me?'

She got up, an odd little smile hovering about her mouth. He could not know how he crucified her by such an invitation. Had she been other than she was, had she had a straight and sound body, not necessarily even a beautiful one, he would not have made that calm suggestion in that calm voice. There would have been a suggestion of all sorts of things behind such an invitation. As it was – he would play the piano to her!

'All right,' she said, and he did not trouble to try and read the thought behind her dark, fathomless eyes.

They drove back almost in silence, he pausing once on the way to put through a telephone call to Wrenn to expect him 'and a lady'.

Wrenn was perfectly well aware that his master lived the usual life of the young man about town with independence and a sufficiency of money. His little affairs were conducted in such complete secrecy that not even his personal servant could have named or described any of his partners in such affairs.

When, an hour later, Wade assisted May Carter from the lift which opened immediately opposite the door of his suite, Wrenn was dumbfounded.

She caught the fleeting expression of amazement on the man's face, and wished passionately she had not come. Life could hold nothing for her. Why had she not stayed in the dark little shop where she could hide herself instead of coming out into the light like this, offering her hideous body to the criticism of servants?

Wade, noticing nothing, motioned to her to go into the sitting room, and she lurched in, her nervousness making her limp even more pronounced.

'Cocktails, Wrenn.'

'Yes, sir,' and the man glided away. Queer business. She must have money, he decided, and began to select the bottles with his customary precision.

May felt nervous and embarrassed. She had never been in such a room as this, and instinctively her modesty took fright even whilst her reason told her how absurd was such an attitude.

Wade caught the look in her eyes and smiled.

'Sizing this up as a den of iniquity?' he asked teasingly, aware once more, now that she was seated in one of his deep chairs, of her amazing beauty.

She flushed and met his glance candidly.

'I've never been in a room like this before, and never in a man's rooms,' she said.

'See how I am enlarging your experience and outlook,' he laughed, standing looking down at her with unveiled admiration in his eyes.

'Play to me,' she said, and he laughed and went across to the grand piano which dominated the room.

He played a medley of well-known melodies at first, running one into another with the meretricious skill of the experienced pianist, but presently he began to drift into the music of Franz

Baumer, and she sat forward a little, realising that these were the songs whose words had so eluded him. He had told her the story, admitting that her own fanciful imaginings had been its inspiration, and now he interspersed the music with a few words to indicate what point in the story should have been reached.

He swung round on the piano seat at last.

'Well, that's that. Like it?' he asked.

Her eyes shone.

'It's beautiful,' she said softly. 'The music sings – tells its own story without words. One knows so exactly what is going on.'

He lifted impotent hands.

'But the words! There must be words – words to songs – dialogue to thread the music together – words, words, words!'

She laughed .

'Let me write them,' she said, half-jesting, half in earnest. How marvellous if he would let her serve him like that!

His surprised stare was well done, though this was what he had hoped for.

'But—could you?' he queried uncertainly.

'I don't know. I'd like to try, though! Play that first song again, the one where Briony is regretting the marriage arranged for her. Give me a pencil and paper first, and I'll jot down just what the music suggests without bothering about rhyme or anything.'

They worked together until far into the night and at last, after a respectful cough, Wrenn appeared to know whether anything else would be required.

'What's the time? Good Lord, May, do you realise it's just on two o'clock? You go, Wrenn,' and the man withdrew.

May had jumped to her feet.

'It can't be as late as that, Mr. Wade?'

'Afraid it is, my dear. Will they be worrying at home?'

Her mouth took the bitter line which it had forgotten during these magic hours.

'Oh no. There's only my father and Joe, and they never worry whether I am in or out. Why should they? They know I'm safe enough.'

He was filled with a sense of exultation. He realised that her brain was just what was needed to provide the text for old Baumer's music. She had only roughed in the few songs at which they had worked, but he knew that she had caught the spirit of the music in her unerring choice of words, in phrases which were harmonies in themselves, in imagery both delicate and forceful.

He caught her hands and looking down into her exquisite face, forgot her unlovely body.

'May, you've been wonderful,' he said, and she held her face very still there beneath his own until he bent and kissed her lips. She closed her eyes and wished that in that moment she might die. Then, very gently, she drew away from him, lurched clumsily against the table, and broke the spell.

'I must go now,' she said, and he made no attempt to restrain her, finding her coat for her, helping her into it and trying not to show the distaste that he felt as she shrugged her malformed shoulders into it and drew it about her closely, almost as if she defied him to forget that humped back.

'I'll come with you, of course,' he said, but she shook her head very definitely.

'Please don't. It will look odd, and I am perfectly safe in Piccadilly at night.'

He frowned.

'May, I wish you wouldn't keep saying things like that. They only hurt you – and me.'

'Perhaps I have to keep on hurting myself in case, for one mad moment, I forgot what I looked like,' she said and was gone.

When he came in the next afternoon from a luncheon engagement, she was there in his room, pages of manuscript scattered about her, her pencil and notebook busy.

She looked up with her grave and lovely smile.

'Did you mind?' she asked. 'I couldn't get on without reference to the music, and when I rang up and found you were out, I thought you wouldn't mind.'

'Of course not,' he said rather stiffly. She looked worn,

hollow-eyed from want of sleep.

Wrenn brought in tea and May dispensed it nervously. As they talked, he began to thaw, and by the time the little wheeled table was removed again, he was in the mood of the evening before.

She read to him the lyrics she had now perfected and polished, and he sang them softly to the music, charmed more than he thought it wise to say and worried only by that irritating speculation as to what she would require as recompense. He hated the thought of sharing the honours with anyone or having to include another name on posters and programmes.

'You think they'll do?' she asked.

'Very well indeed,' he said.

'I can link them up with the dialogue now,' she said, rising from the chair which he had set near the piano for her. 'I see you've made a start,' referring to the manuscript in which he had written his rather clumsy and stilted effort.

'Look it over and see if it wants any little alteration, will you?' he asked.

'Of course. You won't mind if I alter a word or two here and there? After all, it's your show, you know,' with a little laugh.

'Is it? In spite of all you've done for it?' he asked, and her ears caught the tinge of jealousy in his voice. He was only a little boy, after all, she thought tenderly.

'I've done very little,' she said.

'Enough to make a lot of difference,' he ceded grudgingly. 'Like to see your name on the bills when we put the show on?'

She loved him, and her love was that utterly selfless thing which is content to give all and receive nothing. In that giving lay joy which lifted her to the stars.

She laughed.

'My name on the bills? Whatever for? It doesn't sound a name for show-bills, either. Whoever heard of a May Carter in the limelight? No, I'm perfectly happy helping you and knowing I have helped,' she said, her voice dropping to a whisper.

'But I must do something for you in return, my dear. It

wouldn't be fair otherwise,' he said, enormously relieved.

She lifted her eyes to his, her ravaged face beautifully tender.

'You have done more for me already than anyone in the world has ever done.' she said. 'For the first time in my life I have known what it is to be happy – really happy.'

He was inexpressibly touched. He could be ruthless in his upward climb, but he was aware of that streak of tenderness in him which might at any time cause his downfall. He hated to hurt anything, especially such helpless things as this little hunchback. He was reminded, too, of Gretel and her gratitude. There was something that appealed in exactly the same way about both of them. He had wanted to help Gretel, but she had withdrawn into her convent and made it impossible. What could he do for May? She refused her share of fame. He knew that she cared very little for money. How and on what could she spend it? Personal adornment could not count much with her, and she was debarred from much of the pleasure which other girls could buy for themselves.

He caught her eyes fixed on him again, and suddenly he knew. It was colour and romance she wanted, something to brighten if only for an hour the drab horror of her life. He spelled romance for her.

'You are very sweet, May,' he said, taking her face between his hands and looking down at her.

She caught her breath. How easy it was to stir her, he thought idly, and what a thousand pities that she should be as she was.

'I love you,' she said softly.

'I know, my dear. I wish you didn't.'

'Why wish that? It is happiness to me to love you. I don't ask or expect anything of you, so you don't mind my telling you, do you?'

He was troubled. He did not want anything really deep and emotional to develop.

'Don't love me too much, dear,' he said.

'With all that is in me, Roland. How odd that I can call you that, isn't it?'

'Why? Heaps of other people do.'

'But they are your friends, people of your own world. I am just a little bookshop girl and ugly at that.'

He laid his fingers against her lips.

'You're not to say it. To me you are very sweet and lovely,' he said.

He knew that every word he said was inflaming her more, but he could not help it. It was part of his nature to be nice to women, and he could no more have snubbed and chilled her than he could have kicked a dog which fawned on him or a cat rubbing round his legs.

She caught back a half sob and rose to go.

'Can you wait for this until tomorrow?' she asked him, fingering the manuscript. 'I'd like to take it with me. I'll bring it back tomorrow afternoon, shall I?'

He referred to his engagement book, usually flatteringly full.

'Not in the afternoon. I'm taking my leading lady to a *thé dansant* to discuss future plans,' he said.

'Nancy Morn? She isn't good enough for Briony,' said May firmly.

He opened his eyes.

'Do you mean that? Seriously?' he asked, rather startled. It had never occurred to him. It had seemed such a wonderful thing to have Nancy Morn in his play at first that he had never pictured anyone else as his heroine.

'Most seriously. She is pretty, of course, and she dances well, but her voice is thin and she relies on her figure and her clothes rather than personality and good acting. You want Iris Cavann for Briony.'

'But—I'd never get her! She only acts with Richard Myatt, for one thing.'

'Well, Richard Myatt would make a fine brigand chief.'

His head whirled with the daring suggestions, for Myatt and Iris Cavann were absolutely front-rankers. It would never have occurred to him to aspire to them. Beside Iris Cavann, Nancy Morn seemed a mere chorus girl.

'They'd never look at the play,' he said.

'Well, why not give them the chance?'

'Hallam produces for them.'

'Go and offer Hallan your play then. Suggest to him that he discusses it with Iris Cavann and Myatt before he turns it down. You can always go back to the Vanity with it.'

Wade had a vision of Cornwall's indignation were he to do such a thing. Of course, May had no idea of the circumstances in which *Night in Gale* had been produced, nor of the risk which Cornwall had taken nor the immense amount of work put into it by him and the principals before the rather crudely constructed play could take presentable shape. There was Ludovini, too. Would she still take an interest if Hallem were producing rather than Cornwall? Still – Iris Cavann and Myatt!

'Think it over,' she said. 'By the way, when am I to come if not tomorrow afternoon?'

He was to have gone to Cornwall's house for one of his popular 'crushes' tomorrow evening. Perhaps in the light of this amazing possibility it would be wiser to cut that out.

'Come in the evening. Have dinner with me here, won't you?'

She flushed and then grew very pale. She knew that she would have to suffer a hundredfold for all the joy she was snatching from life's reluctant hands, but she decided that it was worth it.

'I'd love to come,' she said steadily.

She dressed herself for that dinner with a desperate and pathetically futile attempt to disguise her deformity. She wore a dress of soft creamy lace, its deep cape-like collar designed to hide the ugly line of back and shoulders, and touched her mouth with a crimson lipstick though she hated both the feel and the effect of it.

Wade looked at her lips and smiled.

'I shall hate to kiss that lipstick,' he said.

'You don't have to kiss it,' but she looked away from his laughing, dangerously attractive eyes.

'Then wipe it off,' he suggested and opened the door of his

bedroom for her, sauntering into the sitting room opposite.

She hesitated and then went in, her breath coming quickly. The only masculine apartment she had ever entered before was that shared by her father and brother, and certainly that stuffy, untidy, unbeautiful little place had nothing in common with the almost feminine elegance of Wade's room with its Queen Anne bed on graceful cabriole legs, its ultra-modern dressing-table designed to retain something of an old-world grace without detracting from present-day utility, the great wardrobes which ran along the whole of one wall.

She ventured no more than a glance round the room and then scrubbed at her lips till every trace of the greasy mess had disappeared.

He appeared in the doorway as she finished and waited for her to join him. She was painfully conscious of her ungainly walk as she did so, but he did not appear to notice it. He took her face between his hands and kissed her, and she quivered beneath his touch.

During the perfect little dinner which Wrenn served to them, he was the most charming of hosts, deferring to her tastes and her opinions, making her drink strange drinks and laughing aside her half-frightened reluctance.

'Don't you realise that you're the heroine in the clutches of bold, bad villain?' he asked her. 'He always has to ply her with strong drink which she never suspects is drugged, the dear little innocent."

'Thanks for the warning!' she laughed.

'Oh, this isn't drugged. You've got a job of work to do before I get you in my power, madam,' he assured her and filled her glass again with the potent, amber wine.

After coffee, served with old cognac in tiny crystal glasses, they settled down to work, though tonight neither felt in the mood and he played desultorily, breaking off to talk to her and at last shutting up the piano altogether and drawing two chairs close to the fire which a sudden cold spell made welcome.

'I'm not in the mood tonight. Come and talk to me.'

The weeks of strain, the last few nights when sleep had refused her even that relief from her thoughts, had sharpened May's perceptions to a fine point, and she watched his every movement, his least shade of expression, with a too keen appreciation of the thoughts which actuated them. She did not miss the slight frown with which he watched her cross the room in her awkward fashion, and she was acutely aware of the fact that in helping her into the deep chair he avoided touching more than her arm and her hand. He had himself well under control for he felt profoundly conscious of the help she had given him, of her selfless devotion to him, but that almost imperceptible shrinking from her misshapen body was beyond his power to avoid.

She clenched her hands in her lap and began to talk, rapidly, feverishly, keeping her eyes turned away from him, and at last he reached for her hands and held them in his own, checking the spate of words to which he had scarcely listened. He knew how he could repay her, knew that even the pretence of love from him would feed her starved desires, and he was nerving himself to overcome that antipathy so that he could repay her in the only coin which she would take from him.

'Don't go on talking. You don't really want to talk, do you?' he asked.

She turned fever-bright eyes on his, and her fingers trembled beneath his own.

'No. Only—I've got to go on talking,' she said unevenly.

He released her hands to cross to the light switch and plunge the room into a darkness relieved only by the leaping flames of the fire. She sat very still as he came back to her and crouched on the rug at her feet, but when he let his dark head rest against her knee, she stroked his hair with gentle fingers. If only time would stay its course for awhile and let them be like this, he not able to see how hideous she was and she almost able to forget it!

He turned his head and looked into her face, searching its beauty, the deep, grave eyes, the tender mouth, the lovely curve of cheek and chin and throat.

'May, you're very lovely,' he said softly.

For once she did not thrust her deformity at him but pretended he had forgotten it. In her heart she knew it was only pretence.

'I love to hear you say that,' she said and smiled at him.

Desperately he gathered up his courage. If they could stay in the darkness, he might forget.

'Stay with me tonight. I want you to,' he whispered to her.

She caught her breath sharply. She had known that this might happen, had almost prayed that it would happen. She knew that she would never know the joys of being beloved, of marriage and children. How could it be wrong just to take this sip of the cup which thousands might drain but which would never be held to her lips for more than a fleeting moment? She was a woman and she loved him, and the twisted, misshapen body held the same desires and needs and passions as did the whole and beautiful bodies of other women.

She put her arms about him and held him, pillowing his head on her breast, then found his lips and kissed him with the starved, passionate kisses of a woman so that he did actually forget everything save the ardour of her love and the amazing revelation of a passion which he had never before experienced.

'I love you so,' she whispered. 'You are the sun and the moon and the stars to me, all the earth and all the heavens. You are all the Paradise I want, all I have ever dreamed of. Don't talk, my dearest love. Just let me hold you and keep you for this moment of life. It's only a bubble. With a breath of wind, it will burst and be just a spray of mist and then – nothing. Keep very still, my darling. We are in Paradise, you and I.'

He had sounded the lovely depths of her spirit, known from her work for him something of the beauty which dwelt in her twisted body, yet he had never guessed at the wealth of passion, of romance, of poetry which seemed in this hour to make her something more than human. Her love flowed over him, engulfing him, making him blind and deaf.

'You mustn't love me so much,' he whispered at last as her voice slipped into a silence which still seemed to throb with her words, with the close touch of her lips, with the pressure of her arms.

'Why not? You are all I have to love – all I shall ever love. Oh, my dear, hold me just once in your arms! Let's pretend that we are lovers, you and I.'

Swept away by her passion, he rose and lifted her bodily in his arms, crushing her against him – and as he did so, realisation was forced upon him. She was crumpled, twisted, shapeless in his hold, and his arms had hurt her, for she could not check the little cry that came from her lips. He set her down instantly, almost dropping her back in the chair, and at that moment the fire shot up in a sudden blaze and lit them both with its pitiless glare – the hunch-backed girl cowering ungracefully in the chair and the man across whose face had flashed helplessly a look of disgust.

The look was gone in a moment, but the girl had seen it and when after a few seconds he bent half-heartedly to take her hand in his again, she drew it away gently but unmistakably and rose to her feet, passing a hand across her brow with a little weary gesture.

'I am going, Roland, my dear,' she said quietly.

He was ashamed of himself, knowing how terribly he must have hurt her warm and generous spirit, anxious to make amends and yet aware that none could be made.

'Darling, I want you to stay,* he said miserably. 'I—I'm so terribly—sorry.'

'There's no need for you to be,' she said with an odd, strained little smile. 'I ought to have known better. I did really. It was just that it was—sweet to pretend for a little while that I could be like other women.'

'Dear—dearest – stay with me! I love you.'

She shook her head.

'No, dear. You don't have to pretend that sort of thing to me. You see, I know. I have been like this all my life, and when

73

you've seen people pity you and shrink from touching you or looking at you for twenty-two years, you—well, you know that's all there is in life for you really. I was born like this, all twisted and ugly.'

'Don't talk like that, May. Don't think like it,' he insisted, in a passion of pity for her. 'What is the body? You have such a rare and lovely mind, such thoughts, such dreams.'

She shook her head.

'A girl's mind doesn't matter unless she has at least a passably attractive body, my dear. You know that as well as I do. Let's not talk any more about it. I blame only myself for this uncomfortable moment. Let me go now, Roland dear,' and she went across the room and turned on the lights, all of them, scattering the last shreds of that web of dreams in which so short a time ago she had enmeshed them both.

He held her coat for her, miserably conscious that he was not showing up well in this horrible affair.

'You must let me do something for you, May dear – all the help you've given me – those songs . . .'

She shook her head with a smile which, sad though it was, held no self-pity or reproach.

'You've given me all the happiness I've ever had. If I've spoilt it by making a fool of myself, that's my affair. I came here tonight deliberately intending to stay if you asked me to, so you see you've nothing with which to reproach yourself. You haven't toyed with my innocent young mind or anything like that. I've— loved loving you, my dear. Shake hands and cry quits, shall we?'

He took the hand she stretched out to him and would have drawn her nearer, but she resisted him.

'No more kisses,' she said. 'That is—over. Goodbye, my dream lover,' and for a moment her voice faltered and her dark eyes grew misty with the tears she was too proud to shed.

'Not goodbye, dear. I shall see you again!'

She gave him a long, strange look as if she would engrave indelibly on her mind every tiniest detail of him. Then she drew away the hand he had been holding.

'Perhaps, some day. Who knows? Meantime, I thank you with all my heart.'

He stood quite still after she had gone, vaguely conscious that Wrenn had opened the door for her and bidden her his aloof, discreet good night. Then he crossed to the cocktail cupboard and poured himself out a strong whisky and soda.

For some days he did not venture near the little bookshop, nor could he bring himself to look again at the completed manuscript which still lacked its title. He felt that he could not bear to look at her firm, characteristic handwriting nor recall the memory of her in every skilfully turned phrase of the lyrics woven of her dreams. She had asked so little of him, and that little he had been too weak-willed to give.

At the end of a week, when no message or word had come from her, he pulled up his car at the dark little doorway and went purposefully in. He could at least take her for a run into the country, which she loved.

There was no one behind the counter, and after waiting a few moments he knocked at the door leading into the house. There was a clatter of footsteps and the head of the boy Joe appeared round the door. He stared a little as he saw Wade, and his young face hardened.

'What do you want here?' he asked rudely.

'I should like to see your sister,' said Wade with dignity.

'Yes. So should we,' said the boy, glaring at him.

'Why—what do you mean? Isn't she here,' asked Wade sharply.

The boy came into the shop and closed the door behind him, standing with his back against it.

'No, she isn't here. What's more, she isn't nowhere. She's dead,' he said, his struggle against tears making his voice gruff and harsh.

Wade leant heavily against the counter, his face very white. It was obvious that the news was a blow to him.

'Dead? May? You—you can't mean it?' he asked.

'Well, it's true. What's more, it's your fault if the truth came out,' said the boy truculently.

'I don't know what you mean,' said Wade with an effort at a sternness he did not feel. He realised that he was in the presence of a very deep and real grief, and the news had shocked him personally. Still, such an accusation as that could not be allowed to pass unchallenged.

Before the boy could speak again the door behind him was pushed open and he stood aside to admit his father, a little thin-faced man whom Wade had seen once or twice when he had emerged from the shed at the back of the shop where he pursued his business of repairing old books and manuscripts and valuable bindings and pictures.

'Dad, here's Mr. Wade,' said the boy sullenly.

The man came forward heavily.

'You're not welcome in my house, Mr. Wade,' he said, not without a certain dignity.

'I am sorry for you to say that, Mr. Carter, because you must be harbouring hard thoughts of me which I do not think are entirely justified,' said Wade. 'I have just learned with profound regret of the death of your daughter. I had no idea she was even ill.'

'She wasn't.' said Carter stolidly. 'She poisoned herself.'

'Good God!' said Wade, horrified.

'Yes, there may be a good God, but it's hard to believe it sometimes. My May was as good a girl as ever stepped, and no one could say different. She was happy and contented, too, in her way till you came along and unsettled her and gave her ideas that weren't no good to anyone like her. Why couldn't you have left her alone, Mr. Wade?' the little man broke off passionately. 'She couldn't have been no good to you, and all you did was to break her heart and make her want to die. You killed her. Mr. Wade, sir, as sure as if you forced the stuff down her throat!'

Wade shivered. It sounded horrible, and though he would not admit that as the truth, he knew that he was not entirely guiltless in the matter. Suddenly he remembered her words when she had left him a week ago, insisting on saying 'Goodbye' rather than just 'Goodnight'.

He had spoken of seeing her again.

'Some day perhaps.' she had said. 'Who knows?' and she had smiled in an odd, inward way as if at her own secret thoughts. She must have been thinking even then of this dreadful thing.

'When—was it?' he asked, his lips as white as his face.

'Last Thursday night. She had been out somewhere or other, perhaps with you, eh?' and the little man peered suddenly into the other's face.

Wade kept himself in hand and did not betray himself by the twitching of a muscle. Insinuations of that sort would never do. They might blight his life forever if they became whispered about in the theatre world.

'Certainly not,' he said stiffly.

'Well, she went somewhere or other all dolled up. I heard her come in some time after midnight, but she never answered when I called out to her. She never answered in the morning either, Mr. Wade. She was dead.'

'But – how did it happen? What did she do? Are you sure she took her own life?'

It seemed incredible. She had seemed so sane, so well-balanced, so sensible.

'Well, the doctor who's always looked after her made it a bit easy for us. She's always had sleeping draughts because of the pain, and that night she finished up the lot, enough for half a dozen, the doctor said. He gave a certificate with long words on it, but he knew as well as we did. She was careful with the stuff and only took it when the pain was worst in case she got so as she couldn't do without it. She knew the dose and she took that lot on purpose. Oh, Mr. Wade, why couldn't you have left people like us alone? We don't mean anything to gents like you, and it was cruel, that's what it was, cruel to unsettle our May like that.'

'But, Mr. Carter, I don't really see how any blame can be attached to me in the matter,' said Wade stiffly.

The little man's eyes gleamed vindictively.

'No. You wouldn't see. I tell you this, Mr. Wade, that if I could have fixed the blame on you for our May's death I'd a done it if it cost me every minute of my life and every penny I possess. If you hadn't come nosing about here, taking her out in your car, giving her coats and things, taking her to tea and meals at places she'd never seen the like of before, she'd a been alive today. That's why I say you killed her, Mr. Wade, and I shall always say it to my dying day.'

Wade felt that this had gone far enough. He was sorry about the girl's death and inexpressibly shocked, but, after all, it was nothing to do with him and he had to protect himself from little rats like this.

'Now look here, Mr. Carter,' he said firmly. 'I am very sorry about your daughter's death, very sorry indeed. What I did was done in the purest kindness, and she knew it as such and took it as such. She enjoyed the car rides and benefited from them, and my conduct towards her was in every way above reproach. Mind, I am in a position to prove that, and if I find that you have uttered or spread any slanderous suggestions about me, I shall not hesitate to invoke the law to protect myself. You understand?'

'Oh yes, I understand all right. You needn't be afraid,' said the man sullenly. 'I know the law as well as you do, and I know on whose side it would be if it came to words between anyone like me and a gent like you. They say justice is blindfold, but the bandage is wearing a bit thin and gold's a nice bright colour. Oh no, Mr. Wade, I shan't make any mistake. You needn't be afraid. The affair of my daughter is all over and done with for *you*. It's only us, Joe and me, who'll go on having to remember it every hour of the day, and every room we go into. It's only Joe and me it matters to that she's gone.'

There was still that dignity about the little man, a dignity which shone through a dirty suit of overalls and a questionable command of English grammar, and Wade was acutely aware of it.

He backed towards the door of the shop.

'Well – there's no more to be said, Mr. Carter, except that I am very sorry . . .'

The little man took a menacing step towards him.

'Don't say that word again, Mr. Wade,' he cried.

Joe put a restraining hand on his father's arm, and Wade turned and walked out of the shop, drawing a deep breath of relief when he had put a few streets between him and that most unpleasant interview.

7

The death of May Carter was a distinct and unpleasant shock to the complacency of Roland Wade. Naturally he did not take to himself any blame in the matter. Why should he? There had been nothing in their relations with one another which should have given her any reason to commit suicide, and any advances which had been made or desires shown had been rather on her part than on his.

No, certainly he could not be held to any extent to blame for what had occurred, but the thing did leave a nasty taste in his mouth, and he could not bring himself to handle the manuscripts which spoke so intimately of her. He thrust them down into the old trunk, piled things on top of them, and tried to forget them. Somehow or other he must find a means of satisfying Cornwall with a new script, though how he was to do so was at present a worrying uncertainty.

A few days after his visit to the Carters, Wrenn came to him with the information that a 'young person' wanted to see him.

Wade was feeling irritable and disinclined for conversation with anyone, least of all a 'young person'.

'What sort of person?' he asked peevishly.

'A young woman, sir. She has been several times before, but said she must see you yourself. She seems quiet and well-behaved, sir, but I think she will keep on coming till she sees you.'

'Oh, all right. Let her come in, but warn her I'm busy and can't spare her many minutes.'

A small and colourless girl, dressed in a cheap copy of a smart fashion-plate, came diffidently into the room and held out to him a bulky parcel wrapped in brown paper and loosely tied with string.

'This is for you, Mr. Wade,' she said nervously.

He took it gingerly.

'For me? What on earth is it? Who sent you?' he asked.

'May Carter gave it to me to give to you before she—died,' she said. 'She came very late on the night she died and put the parcel into my hand and said I was to give it to you myself if—if anything happened to her. She looked queer and she'd been crying, but she wouldn't say any more and I told her she ought to be in bed. I'd had to get up to open the door for her. She said she was going straight to bed then. I wish I'd a known!' and the common little voice broke off in a little wail of grief.

'What is in the parcel?' he asked stiffly, resenting this new intrusion of May Carter into his life just when he was beginning to get over the affair.

'I don't know. D'you think I'd look, and her dead?' asked the girl with a touch of indignation. 'All I did is what she asked – give it into your hands. And now I'll go, if you don't mind.'

Wade made a movement to take out his note-case.

'Would you—mayn't I . . . ?' he hesitated.

The girl flushed.

'I don't want your money, thank you,' she said. 'Folks don't have to pay me for doing what my pal asked me to do,' and she rushed out of the room before the tears could choke her and make her feel humiliated before him.

Wrenn was waiting, and a moment later the door of the suite had closed behind her, leaving Wade standing with the thick packet under his arm.

Slowly he undid the string, and a little pile of school exercise books slithered to the floor, with them a scrap of folded paper. He picked it up distastefully and opened it, knowing that he would see the firm, purposeful writing of the dead girl.

These are for you, Roland, with my love. No one else would

81

make use of them even if they could. With your name on them
they might be worth something. Goodbye.
I love you.
May.

He dropped the scrap of paper as if it had burnt his fingers, and it was a long time before he could bring himself to open the books at his feet. When he did he found that at least three of them, carefully labelled and numbered, formed the manuscript of a novel of some considerable length, written in May's legible writing, closely lined. This accounted for the thickest of the books. The others contained short stories, fantastic little poems, snatches of really beautiful prose, revealing almost indecently to the man who read them the soul of the girl who had written them.

Some might be saleable. He recognised that at once, even before he had read them right through. Her phraseology was vivid, her characterisation strong. He wondered why she had not tried to market them herself, and remembered the diffidence, the lack of belief in herself, which had frustrated all her efforts. It was only because his name was to be attached to the work she had done for him that she had been able to carry it through. He could well imagine that she had never actually intended these writings to be read by any eyes but her own.

It was nearly midnight when, with a deep sigh of satisfaction, he closed the last of those closely written books. The story had a tense and vivid charm of its own, and that charm was enhanced by the unerring choice of words, by the striking phrases, by the quick appreciation of the dramatic. For the twentieth time he wondered why on earth she had not submitted it to a publisher, and then he picked up again those few lines she had written to him, the words scrawled hastily and with none of the legible precision with which her manuscript had been written.

'With your name on them, they might be worth something.'

He screwed up the paper and flung it into the fire. Absurd. Of course he could not make such use of her work. He might have taken old Baumer's music, but he had done all he could to make Gretel accept her share. It was not his fault if she had refused. In this case, he could not imagine himself going to May's father with the story and handing over the proceeds. No, the only thing to do was to wait till the thing had blown over and been forgotten a bit, and then to go and see old Carter, hand him the manuscripts and suggest that there was money for him in them.

The poems and lyrics were different. These by themselves were probably useless, and he might be able to set them to music some day and give them the only value they were likely to possess. The manuscript of the novel was bundled into the trunk which held the new play, and the smaller exercise books found a temporary home in the drawer of his bureau. He would look them over some time or other.

He met Cornwall the next day by chance, but the situation between the two men was accentuated by the fact that both of them hesitated and then passed on with a nod and a brief word.

'Thinks he's got me eating out of his hand for the rest of my life, I suppose,' thought Wade savagely.

'Ungrateful young puppy. He'll see which side his bread's buttered if I let him alone,' thought the older man, half-amused, half-annoyed.

Wade was due at a dinner-party preceding the opera, and his irritation against Cornwall followed him into his taxi and up the ornate staircase which led to Lady Colley's sumptuous drawing-room.

His hostess tapped him briskly on the shoulder, her large, good-humoured face reproaching him playfully.

'You look out of sorts with life, my friend,' she said.

He managed to summon up a smile. She had been a good friend to him, for though she had execrable taste and flaunted her wealth almost to the pitch of vulgarity, she knew everyone who was anyone, and Wade owed to her introductions many an important dinner or weekend visit.

'I shall soon recover my balance here,' he said. 'Life has its pin-pricks for us all.'

'It shouldn't stick them very fiercely into *you*,' she said archly. 'By the way, I've heard a rumour that you have a new play almost ready to displace *Night in Gale*. Is it true?'

He hedged, his annoyance increasing. Why must everything be after him, pressing him like this? Damn it, genius could not be turned on and off like a tap,

'Rumour seldom tells the truth, but they say there is no smoke without fire,' he said lightly.

'Now listen, Roland. I've got this party together chiefly for you, and I want you to make the best of it. You're going to take Iris Cavann in to dinner, and later we're going to be joined by Hallam. We're dining at this ungodly hour partly to get to the opera house in time for the first act, and partly so that Iris can get to her theatre in time. You've met her, of course?'

'Casually once or twice, but never for more than a few moments,' he said, his spirits rising. How odd that so soon after that well-remembered conversation with May Carter he should be going to meet both Iris Cavann and Hallam in one evening!

'We'll go down to dinner now, good people,' said the hostess as they came near the little group. 'Iris, you know Roland Wade. He's going to look after you. I always think the old-fashioned way of partnering for dinner is so much more comfortable,' and she paired off her guests with that easy, friendly good humour which made her the perfect hostess.'

Iris Cavann was tall and dark, almost statuesque in her beauty and in the regal way in which she held herself. She was even more beautiful off stage than on, and Wade instinctively compared her with Nancy Morn, to the latter's disadvantage. His head whirled with the thought of having this regal woman to star in a play of his.

He found her delightfully easy to talk to, and though their conversation was naturally chiefly connected with the stage and stage folk and traditions, he found her interestingly well-informed on a variety of subjects when one or other at the large round table attracted her attention.

Towards the end of the meal, she referred very gracefully to his own play.

'I must confess that I very seldom go to see any other production, Mr. Wade. There are so few opportunities, though I always like to give my understudy a chance every now and then. I did go to see *Night in Gale* the other day, though, and I cannot tell you how much I enjoyed it and how sincerely I congratulate its author. I'll make a confession, I wanted to meet you again now that I've seen your play, and I suggested this very meeting to our hostess. Does that sound brazen?'

'It sounds almost too delightfully flattering to be true,' said Wade.

She shook her head.

'I never flatter. A woman has her mirror and a man his men friends, and those should stand for truth,' she laughed. 'And now I shall have to beg Lady Colley to let me go. I am on very early in the first act, and my dresser is indescribably slow.'

He rose with her.

'I regret very much that I did not bring my own car tonight, but will you let me take you in a taxi?' he asked.

'That would be charming of you,' she said, and it was characteristic of her that she dismissed her own car in order that he might do so.

He waited to see her make her first appearance, thrilled to the sound of her beautifully modulated voice, remembered phrases and speeches which May Carter had written into his manuscript for that very voice, and felt his head buzzing with speculations as he went to rejoin Lady Colley's party in her box.

Hallam was there, reserved and uncommunicative, and Wade felt his good spirits evaporate in that chill presence. After the confession which Miss Cavann had made to him, he had almost expected the great Hallam to come forward with a suggestion about his next production, but it was not until the opera was over and the whole party on the move that the producer showed any interest in him except as a fellow-guest.

'By the way, Wade, Miss Cavann is looking for a new type of play, and she has suggested that you might have something in your mind. Have you?' he asked in his abrupt unsmiling way.

Wade flushed a little. He would dearly have loved to tell him to go to the devil, but he conjured up a smile instead.

'Well, it is much in embryo at the moment, Mr. Hallam. but – well, in fact, I—er—I have put together a few ideas.'

'Come along, good people,' called Lady Colley from the door of the box, and Hallam moved towards it.

'Well, as soon as you have anything definite, perhaps you would care to let me know?' he suggested negligently, and followed his hostess out.

'Coming back for a drink and a gamble, Roland?' she paused to ask. 'You're coming, Mr. Hallam?'

In spite of the chance of keeping in the great man's company, Roland declined. He had some thinking to do, and he could only do that alone.

As he made his way back to his flat on foot, enjoying the night air, he told himself that that thinking was still to be done whereas in his heart of hearts he knew that it was done already. He knew that he would offer May Carter's lyrical setting to old Franz Baumer's music to Hallam in the course of the next few days.

And he did it.

Hallam was too cautious and too unemotional to show what he thought about *Maiden Errant*, but Wade departed with the feeling that an offer would be made to him. The thought of James Cornwall, who undoubtedly had engineered his former success, gave him a few uncomfortable moments, and he realised that production under Hallam would be a very different thing from the friendly, enthusiastic management of Cornwall, but undoubtedly Hallam's successes were of the big type and far more certain than Cornwall's. Hallam's shows were more dignified, on an altogether more elaborate and lasting scale, and even the chorus parts in them were not despised by people who would have expected something more than that in a Cornwall show.

Wade was kept on the rack for a fortnight, and at the end of that time he was invited to go and see Hallam in his office in Shaftesbury Avenue.

The producer came to the point at once and without preamble.

'I'll put on your show, Wade, if we can come to terms,' he said curtly. 'I have outlined what I propose. Look it over,' and he pushed across the littered table a typewritten agreement.

Wade read it, felt his head swim at the terms offered, toyed for a mad moment with the thought of pretending he had expected more, but at last put the typescript into his pocket.

'I'd like to take this and consider it, Mr. Hallam,' he said.

'Certainly. I don't bargain, though. I can't afford any more generous terms than that. You can't afford to take less. If you can get more, that is your own affair. How long do you want?'

'A few days?'

'All right. Friday afternoon of next week, not later than four. Thank you, Mr. Wade. Good afternoon,' and he pressed the bell to have the door opened.

Wade compared the businesslike atmosphere with the friendly methods of James Cornwall, and for a moment he felt inclined to throw Hallam aside and go back to his first friend and take the lower terms which he knew he would be offered. Then a vision of Iris Cavann's gracious beauty swept before his eyes. If he threw Hallam aside, he would lose his chance for ever of getting into intimate touch with her, and he desired above all things to find a secure foothold in the world to which she belonged. Iris Cavann had the entrée into houses far more exclusive than Lady Colley's, and already Roland Wade saw himself gracing drawing-rooms to which at present he could not aspire.

He reached his flat to find Nancy Morn seated waiting for

him. He wondered that he had ever thought her desirable. She was pretty, charming, rather sweet, but he no longer desired her.

'You wouldn't come to me, so I've come to you, my dear,' she said, taking his two hands in her small gloved ones. 'Roland, what's wrong between us?'

He pressed her hands and let them go.

'Wrong? Why, nothing, Nancy, is there?' he asked lightly. 'Have something to drink?'

'Nothing, thank you. It shows how very far we've gone for you to offer me cocktails in the afternoon between shows – or have you by any chance forgotten that we had a *matinée* this afternoon?'

'Good Lord, it's Thursday, isn't it? I had forgotten. That what you came to remind me of?'

'Not exactly, though I thought it was time somebody reminded you you *had* a show running in town,' said Nancy.

'But you can't expect me to be at every performance, my dear. Have a heart! I have other things to do,' he protested.

'I'd like to think so. You ought to be working, Roland. This show won't hold London much longer, and the memory of the great B.P. is short and its affections fickle – like yours.'

'Do you refer to the memory or the affections?' he asked, with a laugh, sensing the seriousness behind her light words and wishing she would go. For a brief while he had imagined himself in love with this girl. What a mercy he had never proposed to her as he had more than once been tempted to do!

'Both,' she said. 'When are you coming back to us, my dear?' To whom, Nancy?'

'Corny and me in particular – or perhaps, me in particular.'

He stalked across to the window, and stood there looking down. There was so much that was good and decent in him warring with his inordinate greed for advancement and gain. Cornwall had given him his first chance, had risked a great deal of money. He had been generous, too. Wade realised that, in not tying him for future productions as Hallam would have done, Cornwall had shown a belief in him which his present intentions did not justify. Even with this second composition, almost sure of success, Hallam had tied him for future work.

And Nancy, too, had given of her best, and it was all as much for him as for herself. Roland knew that. He had known it all along. She would have given more. He wondered how and why he had resisted her, but he was now thankful that he had emerged safely and at liberty.

He came back to her, but her tell-tale eyes showed him that she knew already that the game was lost.

'Don't know how to begin, do you, Roland?' she asked quietly.

'No, honestly I don't, Nancy. You make me feel rather a worm,' he said.

'We knew you'd go to Hallam. Somebody told Corny that you were in Lady Colley's box at the opera with him the other night, and she's never happy except when she's pulling strings. She pulled your string for you, my poor Roland, and you're dancing gaily on the end of it.'

He bridled a little.

'Why the "poor" Roland?' he asked.

She patted his hand, preparing to go.

'Because you think you're sitting in the cart whereas in reality you're between the shafts, my dear. Goodbye, Roland – and good luck,' and she blew him a kiss from her finger-tips and was gone.

He knew that with that kiss she had quite definitely gone out of his life.

He sighed, wandered about restlessly, wishing there were something he really wanted to do, some place which called to him. For almost the first time in his life he felt the need of roots, of a home, of some fixed environment.

'A rolling stone gathers no moss,' he thought to himself, and then, with a shrug of his shoulders, added: 'And who the hell wants to gather moss, anyway?'

But that night, oddly enough, he dreamed of Gretel Baumer, though she was mixed up with May Carter in some queer way.

They had the same soft, gentle eyes, and even in his dreams they made him uncomfortable. He woke, unrefreshed, still with that vague longing for roots of his own, for something more lasting and secure than the will-o'-the-wisp which he was forever chasing.

He signed his contract with Hallam, received a charming little note from Iris Cavann, and a fortnight later *Maiden Errant* went into rehearsal with Richard Myatt in the cast and half a dozen only slightly less familiar names materialising into human beings who were to speak the words of May Carter and sing the music of Franz Baumer to enhance the reputation and bank balance of Roland Wade.

He found it a much more difficult proposition to achieve any measure of familiarity with Iris Cavann than it had been with Nancy Morn. Outside the theatre, she was quite definitely 'Miss Cavann', and few people even knew where she lived. Certainly there were no hectic parties, no secret orgies, no scandals either open or hinted, in connection with her. She was charming to him just as she was to everyone, but even on the day of the final rehearsal, Wade felt he had come no nearer to knowing her than did the stage hands.

Maiden Errant was a success. It was bound to be with Hallam running it and such a cast to portray it. The critics were inclined to be a little supercilious about 'this remarkable young man who cannot achieve anything mediocre', but they gave the play their favour and sat back with an eye on Roland Wade which meant 'What next?'

The next was the production of a slim and very exquisite volume of *Ballads and Dreams* by Roland Wade.

Had his name been quite unknown, it is doubtful whether any publisher would have ventured to cast to the world such a web of fantasy, and the critics contented themselves with a tolerant acceptance of the little book as revealing the interesting personality of Roland Wade as something of a dilettante. He had inscribed it 'To M. C. in deep gratitude.'

After all, he had salved his conscience, and who would understand, even if they knew, what May Carter had to do with that little volume? A few days after the book had been placed with a graceful little note in Iris Cavann's dressing-room, she wrote to him on thick, expensive note-paper which bore an address in Queen's Gate, and asked him to call.

Directly he saw her in the setting of her own home, he realised how easy it must be for her to portray the great lady on the stage. The huge house was one of the few which had not succumbed to the heavy hand of time, which had turned nearly all other such houses into hotels or chambers or more or less uncomfortable and inconvenient flats. One felt the solid and impregnable dignity of the house as one ascended the spotless steps, inset with mosaic patterns, and rang the bell which was of gleaming brass and disdained its neighbours of chromium and nickel.

A butler with the face of a churchwarden taking up the collection admitted him, took his hat, and ushered him up an enormous staircase and into a huge, gloomy drawing-room whose Victorian grandeur could not be softened even by the wealth of flowers which stood in bowls and vases everywhere.

Miss Cavann introduced him to two elderly and ultra-sedate women – 'My mother and my aunt, Lady Rachel Herde, Mr. Wade' – and presently others drifted in, mostly women, with a sprinkling of men. All of them seemed so much at home in the overpowering room that Wade realised this was a 'set', and that in it Miss Cavann lived, moved, and had her being at such times as the theatre did not claim and absorb her.

'I expect you are surprised at the ultra-decorous atmosphere,' she suggested.

'Surprised a little, yes, but pleased and oddly at rest,' he said.

'You feel that? I should not expect restfulness to appeal to you at all. You seem to me so essentially volatile – winged – unfettered. I cannot connect you with anything fixed or rooted.'

That's just it. I'm not fixed, not rooted, but lately I have begun to feel dissatisfied with that state. When I am in a place like this, feeling that everything around me has been solid and immovable for generations before I began to flutter about like a distracted moth, I realise my—inadequacy.'

She smiled.

'I think it was the reverse of that which drove me into the theatre. I have always lived here. My father died before I was born, and there have always been just my mother and my aunt and myself in this great, quiet house. Part of me loves it, belongs to it, would shrivel up and die if I were taken out of it – but the other part of me craves excitement and light and movement and changeableness. With my work at the theatre and my private life here I am fortunate enough to be able to feed and satisfy both parts of me. Yet I know that I might be able to live without the theatrical side of me but I couldn't live if I were uprooted from this,' with a little gesture of her hand.

'I wonder what you are going to do with yourself and your life, Mr. Wade.' she went on with a sudden change of tone. She was interested in this young man, admired his brilliance and the modesty with which he carried off his success. 'There are so many possibilities ahead of you, but one feels you have achieved fame too soon. Most men have to work all their lives to get where you are at—twenty-four?'

'Twenty-five,' said Wade with a little smile, but at the back of that smile lay the anxiety which he could never entirely kill. What, indeed, was there in the future for him? He was comparatively rich, and there was still much gold to be mined from his two plays. He was careful with his money now, and did not intend to increase his living costs. He had contrived to put away in safe investments the bulk of the proceeds of *Maiden Errant*, and even his slim book of *Ballads and Dreams* had brought him in a nice little sum. Yet would he be content to live for the future on the modest and unaided proceeds of such investments, even if he could add substantially to them before *Maiden Errant* was a derelict mine?

Miss Cavann watched his absorbed face, wondered not for the first time that its clear-cut, good-looking features should show so little sign of the undoubted genius of his mind, and then rose with a word of apology to take leave of some of her guests.

She came back to him just as he prepared to leave, and something mischievous in her strangely varied mind set her thoughts dancing. It was high time that this romantic young man should fall in love, and she speculated on the result of bringing him into contact with the one person with whom it would be the height of foolishness for him to fall in love. Charming and modest though he always appeared to be, she felt that it was much too early for him to settle down to complacent success. Also it had been apparent in *Maiden Errant* that the passions of the writer of those lyrics and love scenes had never been aroused, had certainly never suffered the pangs of frustration. They were delicate, witty, graceful, but they lacked the sheer human element which might have roughened them, but which undoubtedly would have made them more powerful.

Yes, certainly this young man must fall in love at once – but hopelessly and impotently in love.

And that was how he came to meet Hermione Wakelyn.

8

There are some rooms which seem to absorb the very spirit and express in line and colour the personality of those who dwell in them.

Such a room was Hermione Wakelyn's drawing-room. The whole house, spacious, dignified, high of ceiling and wide of corridor, held that affinity with her, but it was in the drawing-room that one came to the very core of her. It was a long room with wide windows at each end, one set overlooking the broad street and the park, the other opening on a stone, pillared loggia whose steps led down to the paved walks of an enclosed garden.

The room was essentially calm and peaceful.

Each article of furniture in the room was perfect and beyond price, and though here and there the periods were at variance, everything was placed so that there was no jarring note. A beautiful Satsuma jar held great sprays of almond blossom, their delicate pink glowing against the creamy wall. A log fire burned in each of the two huge grates, and cushioned chairs were drawn hospitably towards them.

The room was exquisite – perfect – and comfortless.

It was empty on an afternoon in early May, but when the door opened to admit Lady Hermione Wakelyn, one felt immediately that the intangible lack of the room was filled. Tall, perfectly proportioned, *soignée* from the dark crown of her hair to the narrow, patrician arch of her foot, one knew that here was the perfect complement to that calm, beautiful room.

Her face was strangely serene in an age of worry and unrest. Beneath straight, level brows, eyes of clear, hyacinth-blue looked straight out at a world of which she had never known fear. A straight nose with sensitive, finely cut nostrils, lips beautifully modelled, a chin which was firm without losing any of its essential femininity, a flawless skin delicately touched with powder – all these went to make up the serene perfection of the woman whom, at twenty-five, one thought of as woman rather than girl. There was that air of repose about her, of poise and self-assurance, which one associates rather with the forties than the twenties.

Her life had been sufficiently unusual to produce such an effect. Born into the purple, the only child of parents whose family trees had their roots in the days before the Conquest, she had been surrounded from earliest days by beauty which had stood the test of ages, by meticulous care for both her person and her mind. Her father, precise, scholarly, retiring, had lived long enough to instil into his only child something of his passion for perfection, for truth, for honesty whether in dealings with his fellow-men or in the beauty which his wealth enabled him to gather about him. Nothing imperfect, nothing of doubtful antecedents, nothing not absolutely genuine, found a place in the home and the life which for eighteen years went to the making of Hermione.

Then the old earl died, and amazingly, within twelve months of Lord Fenley's death, his widow remarried, and the amazement was not so much a matter of the fact of marriage as the husband chosen. It would be impossible to imagine a greater contrast than Vance Croft presented. He was a man of the people, son of a country solicitor of no known antecedents, and not a very successful solicitor at that. Vance had become a wanderer on the face of the earth, never sticking at anything but always managing to make a living for himself and anyone who happened at the moment to be attached to his person and dependent on it.

Moreover he was a widower when he met Lady Fenley, and trailing at his heels was a schoolgirl daughter who adored him. The world which her ladyship had adorned for so many decorous years was amazed and aghast at the marriage, and no one, least of all the outraged Hermione, could understand how the laughing, careless, ultra-masculine Vance had captured the imagination of the woman who had appeared entirely content with life with her erudite husband. In her forties she flowered again, became suddenly human but so entirely a stranger to her daughter that to both of them it was a relief when Croft, irked after a few weeks in the great, treasure-filled house to which his bride had brought him, took himself and her and the small Diana wandering over the world again.

Meantime Hermione, mistress of a large fortune which, had been left to her by her father with no restrictions, mistress, too, of the great house which her mother had thankfully made over to her when she married Vance Croft, took up the reins of government at nineteen, and proved far too capable and self-respecting for the very natural criticism of her world to retain for long its barbs.

She searched for and found an elderly cousin of her father's, a widow of slender means and unimpeachable reputation, installed her in her home as a sop to the Cerberus of convention whom, in all essential respects, she faithfully served, and her beauty, wealth, and breeding soon established her as one of the most sought-after hostesses of the day once people had recovered from the shock of her youth.

A great marriage was predicted for her, and she was almost the fairy princess of the nursery tales in the number and variety of her suitors. Her mother, wrapped in the blissful dream of her own happiness, read of her and laughed with the gentle laughter of one who stands outside and is content.

'Hermione was always odd,' she said. 'She is so much more Fenley's child than mine, touched with just that same cold, unwavering perfection. Fenley would have made an excellent barrister if he hadn't been so unnecessarily rich.'

'I can't imagine how you endure life with me after so much perfection,' her husband said lazily.

'You want to live with perfection to know exactly what it means, my dear, nothing ever going wrong, everything thought out and prepared to the least detail – nothing to ruffle or annoy. Oh perfect life, how I hated it! I find myself hoping maliciously that Hermione will eventually choose herself a husband who drinks and gambles and keeps a dozen other women! The Fenleys need an antidote to make them human.'

'I must admit that Hermione scared me stiff, Viola. Was she always as perfect?' asked Croft.

'Always. As a small girl, she ought to have been a horror – tidy and clean and polite and excelling at her lessons, with glowing reports from the expensive schools to which we sent her. Yet somehow she never was a little horror. I believe there is something human in her underneath all that veneer. She's kind and just and unbelievably generous, not only with money (which doesn't matter to her) but also in her mind. She expects perfection of herself and the things that belong to her, but she is oddly tolerant of outside people and happenings.'

'Yet she hated our marriage and despised both of us,' he reminded her.

'Yes, because at the time I was one of her belongings. When she could dissociate me from her life and the memory of Fenley, I simply ceased to count. She and Fenley have always been like that over the valuables they have collected – if ever they got something which turned out to be fake, or even doubtfully genuine, they felt it a reproach to them but they simply cast it out, cut their losses and forgot about it as soon as possible. That's how she has made my defection bearable.'

Viola Croft lived only four years after that marriage which had brought love and passion to her starved heart. Torrential floods and the bursting of a dam in the little Indian village where for a while they had halted, sent them both to their death, held in one another's arms, and Diana, left for once at a school in Paris, found herself desolate and alone.

Hermione was twenty-three when the news of her mother's death was cabled to her. It was characteristic of her that she set herself at once to the business of caring for Diana Croft, whose address she ascertained by cable to India.

Diana was seventeen when Hermione swept down on the expensive finishing school for which her mother had found the fees. Croft had never been able to save anything in his happy-go-lucky life, and Diana was aware that she was practically penniless. She had retained a hazy memory of Hermione, and she was not at all prepared for the self-assured, perfectly poised woman of the world, complete with her chaperone, her maid, and her chauffeur, with whom she travelled in almost royal state. Nor was she prepared for the essential kindness of heart, the unassuming generosity of manner which held no patronage.

To Hermione herself Diana was something of a shock. She expected to find an older edition of the undersized, red-haired, freckled youngster who had for a few brief weeks drifted in and out of the great London house. She found instead a slim, attractive girl, her red hair subdued and tamed, her freckles concealed, her manner decorous and demure, and her eyes too red with weeping to dance and flash defiance as once they had done.

Hermione bore her off with her to London, gave her a suite of rooms which would have ravished the heart of any girl, and very wisely left her alone to find her balance, neither asking nor expecting that she should at once ally herself with a life which was completely foreign to her.

That was two years ago, and to the young, two years make an eternity. Never at any time had Hermione made the girl feel a recipient of her bounty, and gradually Diana had begun to fit into the comfortable, dignified, well-ordered life which had driven Viola Fenley to just that vagabond existence which she no longer regretted.

And it was into that calm and beautifully planned life that Roland Wade was precipitated.

The telephone rang in the little room adjoining the drawing-room, sacred to Hermione, and from somewhere or other came Mrs. Jeffson, fluttering grey moth of a woman, to answer it.

Hermione turned towards her as she came back.

'What is it, Louise?'

'Miss Cavann, my dear,' said Mrs. Jeffson hesitatingly.

Hermione smiled. She was always gently amused at the little woman's intensity and the serious way in which she took her work.

'More theatre tickets?' she asked. The theatre was the one passion of Mrs. Jeffson's otherwise rather spartan life, though Hermione had always to persuade her that she could safely be left for a few hours.

'No, dear, but Miss Cavann is coming this afternoon and she suggests bringing a—er—a young man with her.'

Hermione laughed this time.

'But, my dear Louise, why not?'

'Well – it's really so odd, Hermione. The young man is a Mr. Roland Wade, and—well—I don't know anything about him. He wrote the play in which Miss Cavann is acting.'

'What an odd thing for Margaret to do,' Hermione said doubtfully. 'Who is the young man, apart from the writing of plays?'

'I don't know. Miss Cavann doesn't seem to know either. She—she only laughed when I asked her.'

'Go and look him up in *Who's Who*, Louise, will you?'

She realised that her exclusiveness, her prejudice against admitting to her house those whom she did not consider her social equal, was pure snobbishness. She was ready to admit that patrician blood and breeding were not essential to the making of fine men and women, nor did she pretend that such attributes always produced the sort of people with whom she wished to associate. Yet inherent in her, deeply rooted by her antecedents, her birth, her training as a connoisseur of the fine arts and of antiques, was that love of things upon which the seal of the ages had been set, so long as the things remained true to type. She prided herself on knowing that anyone who came to her house and met others of her acquaintance met only genuine and desirable people, according to her own interpretation of those attributes.

And now Iris, who should know her as well if not better than anyone in the world, proposed to bring to her house this unknown young man from that odd theatrical life of hers, his only claim to interest being, it seemed, that he could write a popular and rather frivolous play.

Mrs. Jeffson came fluttering back, a book open in her hand.

'I could only find him in *Who's Who in the Theatre*, my dear. It says very little about him.'

Hermione took the book and glanced at the small paragraph.

WADE, Roland, born 6 May, 1907. *Night in Gale* 1929. Ballads and Dreams *1931*. Maiden Errant *1931*. *Short stories* and poems in magazines.

Hermione frowned and handed the book back. There was no mention of parents or any sort of forbears. Most extraordinary of Margaret. Surely she could not be so foolish as to contemplate marrying this young man? Why, he was only just twenty-six and Iris must be nearly thirty, though she still looked incredibly young on the stage.

'Ring up Miss Cavann and say it is not convenient this afternoon, Louise,' she decided.

In a few minutes the little woman came scurrying back.

'She is out, Hermione, and I rang up the theatre, but she is not there. I am afraid she will come straight on here with that very strange young man.'

'Well, it can't be avoided, I am afraid. I am expecting Sir Christopher Dunray so I cannot possibly go out. He promised to give me his opinion on that Weinardt miniature I bought the other day.'

The expert came early, and they were still wrangling amiably about the claims of the miniature when Miss Cavann and her escort were announced.

Roland Wade felt only slightly less excited than he had done on that memorable day, now so definitely relegated to the past, when he had taken his first manuscript to Cornwall's house. He remembered that occasion now with an inward smile of derision. How far he had come since then! The tall, comfortable old house had appeared to him then to be the last word in luxury and refinement, but how small and cheap it seemed now that he had become accustomed to such houses as Iris Cavann's!

He had come with her today with definitely pleasurable anticipation.

'I'm going to take you to see a very particular friend of mine, Roland,' she had said. 'You've never met Lady Hermione Wakelyn, have you?'

'No,' said Roland, discreetly hiding the fact that he had never even heard of her.

Miss Cavann smiled.

'You wouldn't, of course,' she said thoughtfully. 'Well, you're going to. I'll ring her up this very minute and we'll go today. She is one of the people who still hold regulation At Home days, and we shall find her there,' and she had lifted the telephone to deliver the message which had so perturbed its recipients.

Wade had had time to look her up in Debrett, and to confirm his impressions of a very great lady by reference to Richard Myatt, whom he had met as he left the Cavanns' house.

'Lady Hermione Wakelyn? Lord, yes. Very big stuff, my boy. Friend of Iris Cavann's, on the private side. Why do you ask?'

'Oh – nothing. I heard the name and wondered,' said Roland.

Myatt had cherished a hopeless passion for Iris for years, but he had never been admitted to her private life as Roland had been.

So it was with a swelling pride, if in some trepidation, that he followed Miss Cavann into the stately drawing-room of Hermione's house and was presented to the surprisingly young and beautiful hostess.

He felt at once the antagonism beneath her charming greeting, and something leapt up within him in his own defence. Here, he felt at once, was his ideal woman – here her perfect setting – here his own dream of what life should be.

She came to talk to him presently, and the little knot of

people to whom he had been presented and who had come and gone, drifting idly about to other groups, faded away and left them for a few moments alone. Hermione wondered how to entertain this unbidden and unwanted guest.

'I have just been discussing with Sir Christopher a miniature I bought the other day. I attributed it to Weinardt, but he seems so sure that it is not genuine that I am beginning to feel a little uncomfortable myself. Do miniatures interest you, Mr. Wade?' she asked.

He had risen when she came near him, and was glad that, tall as she was, he was half a head taller.

'I must confess that I don't know a thing about them, Lady Hermione, but I should very much like to repair the defect.'

They moved across the room to the shallow case, and she opened it and laid in his hand the delicate oval of ivory. She found herself looking at his hand as he held the miniature on his open palm. It was a beautiful hand, well-shaped, firm, artistic. He caught her look, and, to her immense annoyance, she found herself flushing slightly. 'I see they have called her "Spanish Lady", but I should have taken her for rather the French type,' he said.

She looked up, glad of the everyday comment which had served to restore her momentarily disturbed tranquillity.

'That's very interesting. What makes you think that?' she asked. 'I should have said she was purely Spanish, which makes me a little uncertain that it is a Weinardt. He is much more likely to have painted Frenchwomen.'

Roland leapt cautiously into the breach. He had early divined that he was under a certain amount of suspicion amongst these people, and he wanted to lose no time in establishing himself a little more securely upon this perilous rung.

'My mother was a Frenchwoman,' he said. 'One of the Berthelmys, though she was estranged from her family by her marriage and I am not personally known to them. I have portraits of her and of them, however, and some vague resemblance sprang to my mind when I first looked at this miniature though I scarcely see it now that I look more closely.'

Hermione was looking at him speculatively.

'That's very interesting, Mr. Wade – very interesting. Sir Christopher!'

The courtly old man came across to them.

'Mr. Wade fancies some resemblance to some old French portraits in my "Spanish Lady",' she told him with a little note of triumph in her voice. 'Have you met Mr. Wade, Sir Christopher Dunray.'

'I hate to disappoint you, my dear, but I feel convinced that Weinardt was not responsible for that hair. His always has that dull, rather flat effect.'

'Why should Weinardt not have learnt that trick from, say, Luglos?'

'H'm. I should like to see that French portrait to which you refer first,' said the old man drily.

Hermione, her usually unemotional face alight and eager, caught at his words.

'You shall. Shan't he, Mr. Wade? You will bring it, the one of which this specially reminds you? We will meet here, Sir Christopher, and confound you utterly!'

'I should be delighted,' murmured Roland, wondering how on earth he was going to get hold of the quite imaginary portrait but too experienced a campaigner to be nonplussed so early. His luck in having caught her interest so as actually to achieve a personal invitation to repeat his visit was almost too good to believe.

'When? Tomorrow? No, tomorrow I have promised Diana to go with her to some hospital affair in which she is interested. Friday then?'

'Monday or Tuesday would be more convenient,' said Wade playing for time and not wanting to appear too anxious.

Hermione smiled at him.

'Ah, I had forgotten you were a man of affairs. Tuesday then, in the afternoon? You, Sir Christopher?'

'Dear lady, I, too, am a man of affairs and the House is sitting.'

Hermione hesitated, and so anxious was she to force him to confirm her already uncertain opinion that for once she risked an invitation which she knew she would regret.

'Dine with me, then, on Tuesday evening. And you, Mr. Wade? I feel it would not be fair for me to have a private view of the portrait beforehand. Tuesday evening at eight?'

'I shall be charmed, Lady Hermione,' said Roland with a little bow.

'I dare say we shall be alone unless Diana brings anyone home. By the way, where is she?'

'Probably clearing away slums or championing a lost cause in some East End police court,' chuckled Sir Christopher.

Like many others who knew them well, he liked and admired Hermione but he loved Diana.

She came in as they spoke, and the air seemed on the instant charged with electricity. She wore no hat, and her blaze of red hair had blown loose in the wind which had whipped the colour to her cheeks. Hermione was like the moon, cold, perfect, impersonal, unflickering; Diana was like a flame, glowing, changing, blowing this way and that. People regarded the moon with wondering awe. They warmed their hearts at the flame.

'Hullo, everybody. Tea, for the love of heaven, and some of those little scrunchy, sugary cakes and blow my figure! Oh, Chris, you old darling, did you send me those millions of pairs of stockings from Freyne's? I do hope you did because I should have to drag my rag of pride from its hiding-place and refuse to take them from anyone else.'

She slid into a chair which the old man placed for her, patting his hand as she did so rather as if he were a nice friendly dog.

'After that, I should simply have to pretend that I did send them even if I didn't,' he said.

'Ah, but I know you did. Lovely, aren't they?' and she stuck out a slim leg for his inspection.

'Absolutely perfect,' he decided and everyone laughed.

It was odd how utterly the atmosphere had changed with her advent. Wade noted it – noted, too, the curious effect it had had on Hermione herself. She had greeted her young sister with a smile which held nothing but indulgent friendliness, and yet now that the centre of attraction had moved from her to Diana and her face was in repose. Wade divined a certain wistfulness, something almost of sadness, about her eyes and mouth.

He drew away from the circle which had closed about the younger girl, a circle which had not permitted him an introduction to her, and devoted himself to his hostess, exerting himself to interest her. It was a little difficult at first, but he soon had her talking and listening, and gradually the conversation drifted to the theatre, as was perhaps inevitable.

'I have not seen a play of yours, Mr. Wade,' she said. 'I don't care very much for the theatre, I must admit. The blatant artificiality of it will not allow me to enjoy the situations.'

'You miss a good deal.'

'Do I? I wonder. What, for instance?' she asked him.

'I think the theatre, more than anything else, opens one's eyes to other sides of life. One is permitted to enter into states of living, states of mind, which can in no other way reveal themselves.'

'Is that an advantage? One can only live one life, after all and one section of the community does not really touch another.'

'It should,' said Roland. 'You learn breadth of mind and of sympathy and understanding.'

He was only talking for the sake of talking, but Hermione was interested with that single-minded honesty which she brought to bear on anything which occupied her thoughts for the time being.

'They say women always apply general principles to personal ends,' she said. 'That should excuse me for doing so, being very much a woman. I think perhaps you are right. I think I could learn breadth of mind over some things.'

'But, believe me, I didn't suggest anything personal, Lady Hermione!' She smiled, and he saw how that smile warmed her.

'I know. I know. I chose to apply it personally, however. Sometimes I think I live in too small a circle, too much in the past perhaps. With Diana here, it should not be difficult to modernise my life and yet – Mr. Wade, I am a back number in so many ways!' with a laugh that held a little self-consciousness. 'I have a feeling I should like to see your play.'

'I cannot tell you how honoured I feel, or how humble,' he said, and meant it. She was so far above anyone he had ever known, a being from a world of which he had only vaguely dreamed and he was in awe of her. 'May I send you tickets?'

'I should like it of all things. I think, however. I should prefer to get tickets in the ordinary way. I am not one to take advantage of my friends, and, after all, there are two of them concerned,' breaking off to smile at Miss Cavann, who had broken away at last from her small circle of men and come to join them. 'Margaret, come and jeer at me. I have expressed my wish and intention to go and see this play of Mr. Wade's in which you are acting.'

Margaret Cavann threw a glance from one to the other. He had not lost much time, she thought a little derisively.

'I shall be much interested in your reactions to it,' she said. 'It is very modern. You may be shocked.'

Hermione smiled.

'Possibly. I have come to the conclusion that I am too easily shocked, Margaret, so it will be an experience and possibly a lesson to me.'

'Coming down the marble steps amongst the populace, so to speak? Do you know which night she is going, Mr. Wade? I want to make quite sure she misses nothing.'

'She will not let me send her tickets,' said Wade ruefully. He had felt the slight prick of her withdrawal from their intimacy in that refusal. It had reminded him that she set limits to her graciousness.

Margaret laughed.

'So like you, Hermione, darling, though Hallam would have loved to give you the royal box and I am quite sure they would have played the National Anthem for you when you came in.'

'Who's playing the National Anthem?' broke in Diana's

voice, and they moved to make room for her, her dancing grey eyes passing from one to another, her hand sliding through Hermione's arm in a caressing little gesture.

'Darling, you don't know Mr. Wade, do you?' asked her sister. Diana flung him her ardent smile.

'I know of him,' she said. 'You wrote *Maiden Errant*, didn't you?'

'I did. How did you know?'

'Martin Hale told me just now. I've seen it and I hated it.'

'Diana!'

'My dear!'

She nodded her head, laughing.

'I did. It made me cry, and I am too much of this century to like that.'

Wade was relieved.

'Oh, if that was all . . .' he began when she put up a hand to stop him.

'Oh, it wasn't all. I really did hate it. It's too sentimental and it isn't true to life,' she pronounced.

'In what way?' he demanded stiffly. There had been so few adverse criticisms on his production that he resented one from this young girl.

'Don't get high hat about it,' she warned him. 'That girl wouldn't have fallen for a caveman. Her whole upbringing, centuries of tradition and repression and false values, would have made her instinctively keep to her own kind.'

'But that is exactly the point.' said Wade. 'It was because of those traditions and her soul-sickness with them that she broke away when opportunity offered.'

Diana shook her red head.

'Don't you believe it. No, Mr. Wade, you overdrew her at the outset. She was too deeply buried in convention, too much plastered in forms and rituals, too firmly tied by the spirit of past ages, to do what she did. The rebels break out earlier than that. I might break out in such circumstances, but never Hermione, for instance.'

They all laughed at her sudden introduction of the personal, and Hermione rose.

'I must certainly go and see this play and decide whether or not I should have broken out,' she said.

'Do, darling,' said Diana. 'It'll be an education to you, but I'm not at all sure I want you to break out. You are so utterly and entirely perfect as you are,' and there could be no possible doubt of the affection and sincerity of the girl.

'Well, that rounds off the conversation too perfectly to spoil it by prolonging it,' decided Margaret. 'Roland, I'm going straight to the theatre. Can I drop you?'

'If you would.'

They said such farewells as seemed necessary, and very soon only Hermione and her sister remained and Martin Hale.

He was a tall, athletically built man. He had a military bearing in spite of wearing a false leg, and on the occasions on which he still appeared in uniform, a whole rainbow of ribbons stretched across his breast. At such times Hermione was definitely proud of him, but, as he said ruefully, a fellow couldn't go about the world in full dress uniform with a row of medals in order to keep a girl's attention. Martin Hale was such an essential part of her life that she would miss him.

He had been in love with her as long as he had known her, which was now some ten years. He was thirty-five and since he had left the Army, complete with his artificial leg and a good pension to add to his comfortable private income, his whole business in life had been Hermione. The fact that she repeatedly refused him did not daunt him. He was like that.

Diana liked him, teased him, consoled him, and called him 'The Faithful Heart', and could quite understand why Hermione refused to marry him.

'He'd be so comfortable as a husband; one would sit on him for life and not even notice he was there,' she said. 'I'd rather have something with a few knobs and prickles to add some fun to the horrible monotony of marriage.'

She came now and sat on the arm of his chair, ruffling his

carefully smoothed hair in a way he particularly disliked.

'Darling, I know that annoys you, but I feel irritating this afternoon,' she said, as he caught her hand and held it firmly.

He smiled amiably. It was really impossible to upset Martin, which fact probably accounted for his ability to remain friends with both the static Hermione and the dynamic Diana.

'What is the irritant factor today?' he asked.

'Oh – life in general and in particular. I've been talking to a man who has just been let off from a charge of theft, or of what in our mad civilisation goes for theft. He's been out of work for two years after having been with one firm for thirty years. He is fifty-four and he has two sons out of work and three children of school age. The two sons haven't qualified for the dole, and the whole lot of them have been trying to live on the man's thirty-three bob a week. Well, he's been let off because he has an exemplary character, but he's got to pay back the two pounds he's annexed within a month or go to prison and, presumably, come out again with even his thirty-three bob taken off. How on earth can the poor wretch find two pounds in a month when he had to steal it to eke out his miserable pittance before? If you could have seen his face, the stark misery of it! It amazes me how people stand it at all. Why don't they do something? Why don't all these babblers in Parliament *do* something instead of talking for hours on end or going for nice trips to Peace Conferences and so on? My God! I'm seeing red—red—red!' and she jumped up and began to pace the room like a caged lioness.

Hermione and Martin had seen too much of this to be at all perturbed though the former ventured a mild remonstrance.

'Diana dear, why get so upset? After all, what can we do, you and I? I'm terribly sorry for these poor people, but I don't see that I personally can do anything about it.'

'Darling, you can! Look at all the people you know in Parliament, both Houses. Get at Cheston, when he's not too busy killing poor defenceless birds. And you, Martin! Why don't you put up for the next empty seat and *do* something? You've seen war and suffered by it. These poor beggars have seen it too, and they and all they care for are suffering by it. Go in on their side and give them a helping hand! Oh, if only I were a man!'

'There's nothing to prevent you from putting up yourself,' suggested Martin mildly.

'What, at nineteen, with Hermione's name and wealth behind me? Nobody would take me seriously and can you see these old buffers listening to me even if I got in? They'd enjoy the look of me and wonder what it would cost to take me out, and never hear a word I said! Hermione, I'm broke and I want to borrow . . .'

'I know, dear – two pounds!'

'Three, please. I'm going to get him a job somehow, and he must have more boots. Well, lend me the three pounds, Hermione darling, will you? Take it off my next month's allowance.'

Hermione rang and instructed the maid to find Mrs. Jeffson.

'You can't go on trying to carry the world's burdens like this, my dear,' she suggested.

Diana spread helpless hands.

'Oh, I know, I know! But I can't sit tight and watch men like this, decent honourable men who ask only to be allowed to do good, useful work for the community, go to pieces whilst I buy Poiret frocks for the ultimate benefit of my maid.'

'Oh, Louise,' said Hermione as Mrs. Jeffson arrived in her usual breathless state, 'take this young firebrand away and give her five pounds, will you? Charge it up to her next month's allowance – if it will stand it!'

Diana gave her a hug before she sped away.

'You're a darling,' she said. 'Whoever makes the haloes in heaven will put an extra rim on yours!'

Hermione sighed when she was left alone with Martin Hale. Diana always left her a little exhausted whatever the topic of conversation.

Tired, dear?' asked the man.

'No, not that. It is only that—I'm feeling old, Martin.'

He laughed.

'At twenty-five?'

'Oh, not just years. They don't really count except as lines on your face. The lines are coming on my heart. Diana is so exuberantly young and vital. I don't think I have ever been as young as that.'

'It isn't good for you to live the sort of life you do, Hermione Since Diana's been here, you've been gradually letting yourself sink into the role of mother, which is absurd at your age. You subordinate yourself to her, let her take all the colour and light. It is as if she stood blocking up the one window in the room. I wish . . .'

She put up a protesting hand, though she smiled with the rare softness and gentleness which he alone could bring to her rather severe face.

'Don't, Martin dear. I know what you're going to say, but do face the fact that it is impossible. I like you better than any man I have ever known, but it isn't love. Sometimes I think love is an impossibility for me. I have never really loved anyone, not even my father, whom I admired and respected more than anyone else in the world.'

Then why not risk it with me, Hermione? Your life is so incomplete living as you do. You say you feel old. That is because you are not letting life fill you with all the things to which every woman is entitled. Come to me, dear, and let me give you the happiness I feel sure you will find. I don't ask for wild and passionate love. After all, I am thirty-five and have seen all I want of that sort of love from other people. Don't mistake me, Hermione. I haven't sown a crop of wild oats and come to you in the end.'

'It isn't many men who can offer a woman what you are offering me. I wish I could take it. I wish it with all my heart, but – it doesn't tempt me, my dear. I shall probably fulfil my destiny eventually in maiden-aunting Diana's children whilst she goes about reforming the world!' she ended with a smile.

He sighed and rose. Somehow since Diana's advent

conversations were apt to begin with her and end with her, no matter what irrelevant matter came in between.

'I'm sorry, dear. I always go on hoping and believing that one day you'll come to me. I shall be there.'

'Martin, you're such a dear!'

He held her hand a moment, smiled his kind, unprovocative smile, and limped away.

Hermione sat over the fire for a long time, realising at last that, though it had gone out, it was not the chill of the spring day that made her feel so cold and empty and futile.

9

In the interval which elapsed between his introduction to Hermione and his first dinner with her, Roland Wade worked harder than ever in his life before, and with more fierce determination to succeed.

He must either find some portrait which fitted his imaginary description of it or else disappear from the scene and lose for ever what he considered to be the greatest chance of his life now that mere material success and fame were his. Iris Cavann (he could not yet think of her as Margaret) had given him a taste of the dignified, orderly life which was an essential to the people of her world, and he was determined that he would consolidate his position on the rung of the ladder to which one hand now clung so precariously.

He combed the most likely parts of London for the portrait without success, visited numberless antique shops and art dealers in Chelsea, Knightsbridge, and the Kensingtons, spent hours in galleries searching for something which might aid him, made copious notes of names and periods, but without avail. Then he set to work on Greater London, raked the suburbs, and spent profitless hours going from one to another. At last, almost in despair, he remembered seeing a quaint little shop in Westerham, in the heart of Kent. He had seen a number of queer old portraits in the window, and thither he went.

The two gentle old ladies, who might have walked out of one of their own faded prints, listened to him, smiled at one another, and finally produced a sheaf of ancient Daguerrotypes.

'These are our own family likenesses,' one of them said. 'We did not mean to offer them for sale, but if they are of any value to you we might do so.'

Most of them were impossible, but Wade seized on one and studied it eagerly.

'French?' he asked.

'Yes, our great-grandmother,' he was told rather wistfully.

Wade drew a deep breath.

'I should like to buy this,' he said, and was disagreeably astonished at the business acumen which the faded old sisters displayed in clinching the bargain. Still, it was worth untold gold to him he told himself as he placed the portrait carefully in his pocket. Might it not be the key to a gate through which, only a few years ago, a few months even, he had never dreamed he could venture?

Diana Croft made the fourth at the dinner-table in the great house in Carlton House Terrace. Wade had looked round the huge, solidly furnished dining-room with swelling heart. Here one could breathe – expand – fulfil one's destiny. Nowadays the memory of his humble beginnings never troubled him. He had become the perfect mirror in which was reflected faithfully any environment in which it was placed. No one would have credited him with any association with Hoxton.

Hermione received him charmingly, and Sir Christopher, shown the Daguerrotype, was jocularly impossible of conviction on the subject of the miniature. Wade put it away at last. It had served its purpose, and they went down to dinner with the warming consciousness of friendship amongst them.

Diana was the irritant note of the party. Not only did she refuse to take the art discussion seriously, but she would not take Wade himself seriously, letting her needle-like wit torment him, her grey eyes dancing fun and yet holding something in their depths now and then which vaguely disquieted him. It was as if she were sizing him up and seeing through the veneer which he had now persuaded himself was rather the whole substance than the mere covering.

He was relieved when, after the elaborately-served, perfectly-chosen meal, a youth called for her and bore her off to a dance.

'I'm thankful it is anything as normal as a dance,' said Hermione drily, leading the way to her little sitting room which was so much less formal than the great reception-rooms. 'I am never quite certain that I shan't have to go and bail her out of prison or collect her from some hospital.'

Sir Christopher chuckled.

'She's like a fountain on a thirsty day to an old buffer like me,' he admitted.

'I shouldn't mind a neat little fountain with a marble pool,' said Hermione. 'Diana is more like a Niagara in one's garden!'

'She's intensely alive, isn't she?' ventured Wade, lighting a match and holding it to her cigarette, watching the lovely line of cheek and chin glowing in the little circle of light.

The flicker of something like regret passed in and out of the blue eyes again.

'Yes – alive, terribly,' she said, more to herself than to her guests. 'I've been to see your play.'

'Am I to be glad or sorry?'

'I liked it, quite definitely.'

'I sense the "but" which you did not say.'

She smiled at him.

'I'll say it then. I found it difficult to associate it with you – or shall I say, I must have learned very little of you when we met. It is the work of a dreamer of dreams, a seer of visions.'

'And you cannot visualise me as that?' he asked.

They had forgotten Sir Christopher, who had strolled away and was examining once more the 'Spanish Lady' which had been left on the table.

'I am trying to. My impression of you was rather of the worker, the determined straggler. I put it badly, I am afraid.'

'You put it beautifully. I am a mixture of both. I suppose at heart I am a dreamer. I must be, for all my work is naturally of that type. But I have had to struggle. One can't live on dreams, and the marvel of it is that in the struggle I don't appear to have overlaid entirely the dreams.'

'I marvel at that, too,' she said softly. 'Perhaps I shall be able to find you in your play when I see it again, as I intend to do. I liked your women. Diana says they aren't real flesh and blood women, but then she is such a realist!'

'Yes, one cannot imagine her playing with dreams.' agreed Wade with a smile.

'You have captured the hearts of your public, you know. That is surely a great achievement in these days when we dare not admit the possession of such worn-out commodities as hearts. Your Briony made me cry. That's a confession, isn't it? Next time, don't make your heroine so terribly human. She might almost have been devised by a woman. It is uncanny for a man to see into our inmost thoughts as you saw into your Briony's.'

'Hermione, I am absolutely convinced that this "Spanish Lady" of yours is a fake,' said Sir Christopher, sauntering back to them quite unaware that he had cut into a conversation which bordered on the intimate and personal. Both felt oddly relieved at the interruption.

'To be perfectly honest with you, I have come to the same conclusion myself,' said Hermione. 'You see how I have delivered my own head to you on a charger!'

'You are incomparable, Hermione. Only about one woman in ten thousand would have the courage to admit she was wrong with such generosity,' said the old man, patting her cheek affectionately.

'I hate pretence of any sort,' she said. 'If everyone were honest, what a lovely world it would be! Well, let's call it a fake and get rid of it,' and she held the beautiful little picture poised above the fire.

Wade caught at it instinctively. It seemed sheer vandalism to him.

'Don't destroy it!' he cried.

She withdrew her hand and turned enquiring eyes on him.

'Why not? It's worthless,' she said.

'To you, perhaps. But surely if a thing is beautiful in itself, its beauty has value.'

'Yes, if it is simply a thing of beauty. But this miniature purports to be something it is not. It is a copy, an imitation, and I've absolutely no use for fakes,' and she made another movement to drop it in the fire.

Driven by some irresistible impulse, he caught at her hand and she turned to look at him, their eyes holding one another in a startled way. It was as if this act of hers had some personal and terrific import to both of them. He could not bear that she should cast this lovely thing to destruction merely because it was not what she had thought it to be, whilst she felt oddly frustrated in his determination to save the thing which was not only worthless to her but definitely abhorrent.

'Give it to me rather than do that,' he said, and slowly she let the little miniature drop from her hand into his.

Sir Christopher cleared his throat noisily. He, too, had sensed drama in the little scene, and there was something about Hermione, a hint of awakening, of startled bewilderment, which made him feel he was a spectator at something which should not have been revealed to him.

'If you are interested in Weinardt's work of the French school, Wade, you ought to see my own collection. Bring him down to Whytelode, Hermione. I'd like you to have a look at my new arrangement of the Vandine plaques, too. I am not sure I have improved them. Why not run down for lunch one day?'

Hermione was aware of a strange reluctance even whilst her reason told her that it was unwarranted. Sir Christopher was the soul of hospitality, and what more natural than that he should wish this new apostle of art to see his treasures? What more natural than that in the circumstances he should suggest the three of them meeting again in that way?

'That would be very nice,' she said at last, and Wade felt his pulses leap. She had felt the obstacle of her own pride and surmounted it for interest in him.

The visit to Sir Christopher's lovely old country house, made in the Jaguar which had displaced Wade's little sports car, was an unqualified success. It was as if Hermione had determined to justify herself in having thrown down the obstacle which might have kept them apart. Also the absence of Diana made itself felt. Her intense vitality had the effect of devitalising others with whom she was in contact. Alone, Hermione's natural graciousness and serenity showed itself in her smooth and finished phrasing, her calm smile, her slow and lovely laughter.

They strolled in the autumn glory of the gardens which gave work to an army of men, and Hermione became gently reminiscent, admitting him to her confidence, speaking of her early life, of her father and, more reticently, of her mother.

'I think perhaps I have understood my mother better since Diana came to live with me. She was faintly imbued with the same sort of radiance which Diana sheds, and in the quiet, decorous life she led with my father she must have been fading and wilting for years.'

'I don't think it has been the right atmosphere for you either,' said Wade.

She raised her eyebrows.

'What makes you say that? It has suited me perfectly for as long as I can remember,' she said.

'You think that because you have grown up with it, become so accustomed to it that you think it is your proper setting. You have lived far too much in the past, I think,' he said, greatly daring in his criticism of this regal woman.

She was not offended, though she reflected afterwards that she might easily have resented it from a number of people. For almost the first time in her life she was enjoying the luxury of discussing herself and her reactions.

'You think I am out of date? Diana sometimes terms me Victorian,' she said with a smile.

'I don't think that, but I do think you have never been allowed to be really young and irresponsible. This counsel of perfection of yours – it must preclude many legitimate pleasures. There are many things one can enjoy by merely accepting them at their surface value which would vanish into thin air if one examined them for the possible imperfection beneath.'

She shrugged her shoulders and laughed a little.

'You may be right. I admit I have never been able to enjoy lots of things which other girls of my age enjoy just because I must be assured of their intrinsic worth. You think it a fault, this "counsel of perfection" as you call it?'

'Not a fault, but rather a pity. I find it hard to realise that you are younger than I am, not really much older than Diana, but I know how old you are. I looked you up to see!' and she had to join in his ingenuous laughter at his confession.

'Make me young, then. You have made me feel that I must be a prig. Am I that, I wonder?'

'I'd like to tell you what I really think of you, but I daren't he said softly.

She looked at him with that look of a startled fawn which he had brought to her eyes more than once in their short acquaintance. She seemed poised with one foot hovering over the step she dare not take, that step over the barrier which each of than felt would someday be crossed.

'I think we'll go in,' she said a little breathlessly, and he followed her without a word, nor did their conversation touch even remotely on the personal during the drive back to town.

During the months that followed, they seemed to have dropped out of one another's lives. Wade heard of her, saw her name occasionally in the society columns of the papers, caught a glimpse of her once at an important Charity Matinée, but otherwise she seemed to have ceased to exist for him save in the tormenting memory of her.

And in September his book, *The Silken Tassel*, was published.

The publishers had made the most of his name and reputation, played skilfully on the public interest and imagination beforehand, and launched the novel to a certain success. Even the critics who had predicted great things for the young playwright were surprised at the book, at its brilliant technique, its rapier-like wit, its fantastic, highly improbable plot which the characterisation made to appear natural.

'This brilliant young author,' they wrote, 'has served up to whet our jaded appetites a new dish – not an old one freshly garnished, but something different, piquant, intriguing to the palate.'

Hermione sat for a long time with the book in her hands. He had sent it to her with a graceful little note begging her acceptance, and that vague, intangible fear which she had felt for him almost from the first began to take more definite shape. She did not want to be reminded of him. Quite definitely she did not want him to come back into her life – and yet here he was between her fingers, bound in these green and silver covers, his mind searching out hers, his thoughts – those delicate, fantastic, unreal and yet strangely human thoughts – echoing through her own.

Diana came in and surprised her in a brown study.

'Hullo, darling—oh!' as she caught sight of the book.

Hermione looked up and there was an odd light in her blue eyes. She could not so quickly recapture herself.

'I was reading it,' she said, half to herself. 'It's beautiful. A lovely mind.'

Diana looked at her searchingly.

'Only that? A lovely mind?' she asked in her quick way.

Hermione came back to herself and flushed.

'Why do you ask that?'

'Hermione, you aren't falling in love with this Roland Wade, are you?'

'My dear, I scarcely know him!'

'That doesn't prevent people from falling in love. In fact, it is almost essential to their doing so,' laughed Diana.

'You are such a cynic, Diana. Is there anything at all in which you believe?'

'Myself – and generally you, my sweet. Hermione, don't dwell on that young man and his book too much. I have a hunch that neither of them is going to be good for you.'

'I do like him, quite a lot,' came the half-reluctant admission.

There is something terribly attractive about a mind which can think thoughts like these,' her fingers tapping the book she held.

'Hm. People don't always write what they think by a long way. They write what people think they ought to think. After all, Roland Wade writes to make money just as every other author does, whatever high-falutin' reasons they may give for writing.'

'I feel the man who wrote this is sincere, Diana.'

The younger girl shrugged her shoulders and prepared to go on her way.

'I don't think any man is sincere,' she said, 'especially men with the *beaux yeux* of this particular one. Remember the gipsy's warning!' and she was gone.

But the seed she had sowed took root in soil more than ready to receive it, and during the days that followed, Hermione realised that it had done so. Was Diana right? Was she falling in love with Roland Wade? She had been quite right when she said that she scarcely knew him, for they had met only three times, and the last occasion had been months ago. Yet she felt that she had never known anyone as closely as she did the writer of *The Silken Tassel*. Just as in his play the personality of the author had gripped her mind and heart, so had the written words revealed to her something to which every fibre of her being leapt in response. It was as if all her secret dreams, unexpressed even to herself, unrealised even, her ideals, her hopes and fears, had been given words and meanings. In the self-repressed, fear-haunted girl in this novel she saw herself as she had never realised she was.

She sat down at her desk at last, took up her pen, and wrote quickly before she could repent in a second thought.

Dear Mr. Wade,
I have read with the greatest interest and pleasure your book.
I appreciate very much the thought which prompted you to send me a copy. I seem to have met in its pages a friend whom I had lost. Come and see me. I should like it so much.
Yours very sincerely, Hermione Wakelyn.

Roland Wade caught his breath in a sharp little sigh of relief when he had torn open the letter and run his eye over the few lines. Who was the friend she had lost – herself as seen in the book, or him? His pulses quickened.

After some deliberation, he answered her letter.

Dear Lady Hermione,
Your note warmed my appreciation of myself far more than have the kindly critics. Is it abusing your generosity to ask you if you will dine with me one evening? If you prefer it, I will ask Miss Cavann and some other man to join us, but I should like you to choose an evening first.

Yours most sincerely, Roland Wade.

He was not satisfied with it, but as it represented about the twentieth attempt, he decided that it had better go.

Hermione answered it by telephone, her voice hesitating a little, but warm and personal.

'Mr. Wade? This is Hermione Wakelyn. I had your note this morning and I should like very much to dine with you. Will Thursday of this week suit you? I am going down to Whytelode on Friday. Sir Christopher is my godfather, you know, and I usually act as his hostess when he gives a housewarming.'

He had the impression that she was talking to cover a certain embarrassment.

'I can, of course, be free on Thursday. Shall I ask Iris?'

'Do you want to?'

'Not in the least.'

She laughed.

'Thursday, then. When and where?'

'May I call for you? About eight?'

'That would be delightful.'

He spent much care and thought on that dinner. It must be at exactly the right restaurant, a place which could afford to be exclusive and yet at which they would be seen. It was no part of his plan to have any hole-and-corner friendship with her. Yet it would not do to flaunt his acquaintance with her at this early stage, so he chose the restaurant with discretion, gave careful orders for the table, the flowers, the food, the wine, and left the rest on the knees of the gods. They had been so kind to him so far that he felt safe in trusting them in the matter of Hermione.

He had not realised how beautiful she was until she came to him across the room in which he had waited for her. Her gown of maize-coloured velvet was absolutely plain and moulded to her slender, perfectly proportioned figure. Her dark hair was waved in close, classical lines about her head. There were diamonds in her ears and on her fingers, but the white column of her throat and her beautifully modelled arms were bare.

The evening held enchantment for both of them, for it took them into a new world. Wade was tasting for the first time in his life the delights of companionship, open and accepted, with a beautiful woman of the world in which he longed so ardently to dwell, and Hermione was drinking with every moment the heady wine of love. She recognised it for what it was. She was glad to be alive, glad to be with him, glad to let this clamouring stranger come in and take possession of her heart. What did tomorrow matter? For almost the first time in her life, she lived in the moment and thrust from her every other thought save of its joys.

They spoke of his book, and she told him, haltingly at first but with quickly increasing confidence, the impression it had made on her.

'How do you know so much of a woman's mind?' she asked him.

'Guess-work,' he told her with a smile.

She shook her head.

'I can't believe that, and yet – I can't any more believe that you have been able to delve into a colourful past.'

He laughed.

'No, nor that. I can't claim the blameless life of a saint. After all, I am a man and I have lived a man's life, but I did not find

Angela in my past, I assure you.'

'No. If you had done, you would not be here with me,' she said gravely.

He leaned towards her.

'Perhaps that is why I am here,' he said quietly. 'Because—I had not found her when I wrote that book about her. Most men have an Angela in their secret hearts. Not many of them find her.'

She looked at him, her eyes deep and soft, eyes which seemed to him for the first time the eyes of a young girl.

'Do you think *you* will find her?' she asked.

'I wonder,' he said very softly, and they were silent for a while.

It was still early when they left the restaurant, and he suggested going to see a film which had excited comment. She agreed, as she would have agreed to anything which kept him with her for that enchanted hour, and afterwards he took her back.

'You will come in for a cocktail or something?' she asked.

He refused, knowing that he was wise. She would want to talk to him again. That film had been provocative, for one thing, and they had only touched on it on the drive home.

'I may see you again, very soon?' he asked.

'I am going to Whytelode tomorrow,' she told him regretfully. 'Why not come down there on Saturday? There will be a crowd, and Sir Christopher always gives me *carte blanche* in the matter of invitations. Come in the afternoon, and there will be dancing after dinner.'

'I should like it above all things. Till Saturday then?'

'Goodnight.'

Her eyes lingered on his.

'Goodnight – Angela,' he said, and was gone almost before he heard the swiftly caught breath.

10

Wade motored back after midnight on that first Saturday, at peace with all the world, and on the following Saturday he went at Hermione's invitation, to spend the weekend, lengthening it out until Tuesday evening so that he could take her back to town.

Inevitably there was talk, for she had been a lodestar to so many men ever since she came out, their endeavours to interest her seriously being so unsuccessful that her marked favours to any particular man could not fail to arouse conjecture. Like a bolt from the blue, this young man had arrived amongst them and seemed about to take her by storm. He had been judicious in the spreading of information about himself, and the few bare facts had been seized on by gossip and, for want of anything more tangible, woven into what was almost a shroud of mystery about him, adding subtly to his attractiveness.

Everyone knew his reputation as playwright, poet, and author, and Hermione's position made it practically impossible for anyone to cold-shoulder him.

She herself was in a turmoil of doubt and unrest, a state quite foreign to her nature. It would not be true to say she had fallen in love merely with the writer of *The Silken Tassel*, but it was unquestionable that every conception of him was coloured by thoughts of that book, by the gracious and tender mind which it revealed. She was not a woman easily to be won. She would demand too much, be prepared to give too much, to allow of a mistake. It was against every principle, every instinct, all her upbringing and the tradition in which she had been reared to take a husband outside her own accredited social class. And yet, with every hour she spent with him, with every re-read page of his novel, she knew she was breaking up tradition, preparing to make holocaust of all the inhibitions, the principles, which before his coming had seemed an essential part of her life, a controlling factor of her future.

Wade was under no delusions about her feeling towards him. He knew that he attracted her, that she admired him for his genius, that she was physically drawn towards him, but he recognised as well the struggle she made to resist the attraction. She was not his for the taking, and the difficulty whetted his desire for her. He did not blink facts. He was not in love with her, though he admired her calm beauty, her poise, as he would have admired an impersonal work of art. He realised his position, however. His plays had been gold-mines to him; his novel was still being translated into other languages; he had sold distant serial rights, dramatic rights, film rights. Later there would be cheap editions, according to the trend of the sales. But after that – what then? He had nowhere to turn for further material. His abnormal luck in the past could not by the furthest stretch of imagination continue in the future. There was nothing for it but a wealthy marriage, and he felt further favoured of the gods in that they should have placed before him, surely within his reach in due time, a woman so abundantly able to satisfy his luxurious tastes and beautiful enough to make such a marriage desirable from quite other points of view to a normal man.

He began to feel an almost superstitious dread of failure as he fought against her frequent withdrawals from him, her alarms and fears. So far everything he had touched had turned to gold. Failure had seemed impossible. Time after time, when he had seemed pushed into a corner, the way out had been made radiantly-plain. He felt that his first failure to achieve that on which he had set his heart would be the signal for a fall down the ladder of success, complete, final, irremediable.

He remembered the anxieties of the weeks immediately preceding Hallam's offer for *Maiden Errant*, and he had no desire to experience them again.

No, certainly there could be no doubt as to his course, but he had that superstitious dread of courting disaster by failure in anything he attempted.

So the autumn months ran on into winter, and he had become an habitué of Hermione's house, her accepted escort to all sorts of functions, his *entrée* into her particular circle made easy by her friendship with him. At last, with the passing of the old year, he resolved to take his last tilt at fortune.

They were dancing at the house which Martin Hale's widowed sister looked after for him, and it was understood that the whole party would go on to a night club to see the old year out. This frequenting of night clubs and midnight cabarets was part and parcel of the new life into which Hermione had been born with the coming of Roland Wade, and she wondered sometimes if she had ever really been alive before.

She was dazzling that night, for Diana had insisted on her wearing white and her diamonds. Against its gleaming purity, her dark hair and warm colouring glowed like a jewel, and when the younger girl saw the effect, she wondered unhappily whether she had been wise. She too, knew, that Hermione had come to life, and she could not thrust from her mind the fear which always possessed her when she thought of her sister and Roland Wade. Still – she shrugged her shoulders and went her way. After all, Hermione's life was her own.

Wade was glad when he saw her that he had decided to put his luck to the test. He felt he would have been either less or more than human to have resisted the temptation tonight, and when they were all making a move about eleven o'clock to go on to the night club, he thrust his arm through hers and held it closely.

'Do you want to go to this place with the crowd?' he asked her in a whisper, his head bent to hers.

She shook her head, laughing rather breathlessly.

'What else is there to do?' she asked.

'See it out with me—alone, will you, Hermione,'

It was the first time that he had ventured to drop the title to which he had meticulously adhered, and her face coloured delicately.

'Wherever you like,' she said.

'You trust me?'

'You know I do.'

'Come along then. I put my car where I knew I could get it out quickly,' and he led her down the stairs and out at a side door to the street at the back of the house.

They said nothing at all whilst he steered skilfully through the night crowds of Piccadilly, past Westminster, and out through London into the quiet country where no one seemed to care about the passing of time, and only the lamps of some shuttered farmhouse or the lowing of cattle in their warm stalls broke the darkness and the silence.

He stopped the car at last, wrapped her white fur cloak about her, and got out, giving her his hand.

She stepped from the car, her face pale and serene, but her eyes like the stars in the frosty sky above them.

'Where are we?' she asked, and scarcely knew why she whispered, for they might have been the only two in the world, so still and dark and empty of life was it.

He set his arms about her and held her within their circle.

'At the gate of Paradise, beloved,' he told her, and felt that in that moment it was so. She was so lovely, so fragrant, so altogether desirable. And she was his for the taking. He knew that now, however much he might have doubted before, knew it in the quiver that ran through her at his touch, knew it in the starry eyes and trembling mouth so near his own.

She did not speak, and he drew her closer within his arms.

'Darling, do you know why I've brought you here? So that for just this one hour I can forget everything but you, pretend that we can really enter into Paradise, just you and I, Hermione – Hermione. I love your name.'

'I had rather it were—Angela,' she said, and her voice quivered as she spoke.

He held her motionless, scarcely daring to break the spell of that magic moment. Then, with the tiniest movement, she lifted her face and he set his lips to hers.

'Hermione, I love you.'

'Oh, I've wanted you to say it,' she breathed, her eyes closed, her whole being swept with the surging joy that was within her. This, at last, was life, her flowering, her awakening. She knew it, and rejoiced.

'Say it to me, Hermione.'

'But you know. I have loved you from the very first, I think. Oh Roland, what a proud fool I've been! I tried to fight against it, but in my heart I knew.'

Somewhere in the distance a village clock struck, and they listened to the strokes, counted them until the twelfth had died away, and then she put up her arms and held him.

'The new year, Roland – ours – the first year of my real life. Oh, I am glad, glad!'

'Darling, how can there be anything for us? I daren't ask you to marry me.'

She stared at him, amazed, bewildered, her world rocking on its base.

'Not—marry me, Roland? What do you mean?'

'The Lady Hermione Wakelyn – and the poor playwright? Queen Cophetua and the Beggar Man?'

She silenced him with her lips against his.

'What do those things matter when we love one another? Come back, my dearest dear, and let us tell them. I want to share my happiness with the world – but you with no one,' breaking off suddenly into sweet surrender which was the more sweet coming from such as she was.

He held her long and passionately, and then almost thrust her into the car and got in beside her, jabbing furiously at the starter.

'My dear, what's the matter?' she asked.

'Only that I am a man and you are the most desirable woman in the world,' and he bent all his energies to turning the car in the dark little lane whilst Hermione, with a sigh of pure happiness, lay back against the cushions and watched him.

Diana was home by the time she let herself into the house and went softly up to her room, her lover's kisses warm on her lips, the memory of his arms still about her.

'That you, Hermione?'

'Yes, dear. Are you in bed?'

'In bed, with you roistering about the countryside with a man?' and Diana trailed into the room, a bizarre wrap over her green satin pyjamas, a hair-brush in her hand.

'I found Germaine half asleep over your fire, so I told her not to wait up,' she said.

'Oh, I am so sorry. I quite forgot to tell her not to stay up,' said Hermione contritely, slipping off her wrap and crouching down by the fire.

'I rather think you've been forgetting a lot of things lately, my beautiful,' said Diana, dropping into a chair and preparing to stay.

Hermione lifted a flushed face.

'Diana . . .' she began.

'I know, my dear, I know! You've got a girlish rapture written all over your face. "Hermione, I love you!" "Oh Roland!" . . .'

'Di, don't.'

The teasing look faded from Diana's face, leaving it unusually serious.

'Sorry, dear. Is it really serious, Hermione?'

'Deadly serious, Di.'

'You mean you're going to marry him?'

'Yes.'

Diana frowned, but she wielded her hair-brush in silence for a few minutes whilst her sister made her slow and methodical preparations for bed. Then she suddenly threw down the brush and came across to Hermione, setting her hands on her shoulders.

'Darling, are you sure you're in love with this man? Or do you only think you are?'

'Of course I'm sure. Is it likely that I should have reached my present age without being able to recognise mere infatuation?'

There was a touch of hauteur in her tone, but Diana disregarded it.

'You will probably be mortally offended at what I'm going to say, Hermione, but I don't believe you could seriously fall in love with Roland Wade. He isn't of your world, to begin with. He hasn't had your antecedents, your dignified upbringing, isn't clothed in tradition as you are. No, please hear me out,' as Hermione would have checked her. 'He's got a sort of fascination. I realise that fully, though it would never attract me. You can't exist on fascination though, not *you*, Hermione. You will want to dig beneath it and test the solid substance on which marriage must be founded to be a success.'

'Don't you think one finds solid substance in his work, in his book particularly?' asked Hermione proudly.

Diana seized on the point eagerly.

'That's just it. You're marrying the mind of the man – but you've got to live with his body.'

'You needn't be coarse about it, Diana.'

'It isn't coarse. It's simple, everyday sense. Come to that, marriage *is* coarse if you regard sex matters as coarse, because it's my belief that happiness in ninety-nine hundredths of the marriages today is dependent on sex and sex alone.'

'Diana!'

'I know what you're thinking. I'm only a kid compared to you, and at nineteen you think I am, or ought to be, just sweet innocence, scarcely out of the gooseberry bush stage. Believe me, darling, you're far nearer the gooseberry bush stage than I am. I have lived a life nearer to nature, seen and heard things that would turn your hair green. I wish—oh I *wish* you didn't feel it necessary to marry Roland Wade!'

Hermione had listened to this diatribe with mixed feelings. It was impossible to doubt Diana's sincerity. Also the older girl had to admit to herself that doubts and fears had found an echo in her own mind before that magic hour which had swept away everything save the wonder of first love. A year ago, a few months ago even, she would have scorned as outside the limits of possibility such a marriage as she now contemplated. She had always imagined that her married life would be a continuation of her serene, dignified, ultra-conventional existence with a man entirely in accord with such a life, a man indisputably of her own class, her own birth and standing, a man steeped in tradition, the bearer of a name which she would be calmly proud to perpetuate.

And now she was to give her life, her dreams, her hopes, her ideals, everything in which she had been nurtured, everything in which she believed, into the hands of Roland Wade.

Whilst she sat on the edge of her bed, hesitating over her reply, there swept over her suddenly the memory of that hour with her lover, and she turned to Diana with her eyes misty and her face aglow with a new loveliness.

'Diana, I love him so!' she said very simply, and she might have been a village girl rather than the Lady Hermione Wakelyn in the simple and tender sincerity of that admission.

The younger girl bent swiftly to kiss her. She felt that there was nothing more to be said after that little speech, after the sight of the transformed face, the sound of the warmth and lovely tone of her voice.

'Darling, all I want is that you should be happy. Good night. Bless you,' she said and was gone, leaving Hermione, in her cobwebby veil of dreams.

Roland did not come to her until the next evening, though she had waited for him expectantly.

He was both exultant and dismayed at the accomplishment of his purpose. He had never been quite sure of success until that moment when he had taken her in his arms, but he was a little afraid of the extent of his victory.

Capable of honesty with himself in spite of the living lie on which his whole existence was founded, he realised how little he would be able to give of what Hermione expected. He had been aware of a certain strain of romanticism in her, but it was not until she had lain in his arms, until she had begun to reveal something of the intimacy of her thoughts, until all that talk of 'Angela', that he realised how essential a part of her feeling for him was her memory of the book she believed to be the mirror of his mind.

Could he possibly live up to that? What would she expect of him?

He wished it had been Diana who was the heiress. He doubted whether he could have achieved marriage with her, but at least he would have found his match, diamond to cut diamond. He was a little afraid of her penetrating mind, her rapier-like thrusts, the devil of laughter of which he was always conscious in her eyes even when she seemed kindest – but they would have met on common ground and fought out the battle of marriage on it. Diana would have expected more of his body and less of his mind, and seen that she got it. He was more than a little uncomfortable as to exactly what Hermione would expect and to what extent he could give it.

So that it was not until the evening that he could bring himself to test the impressions of the night before.

She came to him with a faint reproach in her eyes, and at sight of her some of his dismay fled.

He took her in his arms.

'Hermione, how lovely you are!' he said, and rejoiced in the leap of his pulses at the touch of her, at the faint, elusive fragrance which clung to her and seemed a part of her.

'Yet you waited a whole day to come to me!' she accused him softly.

'I was afraid.'

'Of what, my dearest?'

'Afraid that I should find last night only a dream.'

She laughed and gave him her lips again. What else had life left to offer her? It was utterly as she would have it.

'You believe it now?' she asked.

'If I am still dreaming, I hope I never wake. Hermione, you're going to be mine, my wife! Dare I really believe it?'

She slipped from his arms and picked up a sheet of paper which she had brought down with her.

'Will this make you believe it?' she asked, and he read an announcement for *The Times*, neatly typed by Louise Jeffson who had learnt, heaven alone knew with what anxious toil, to use the typewriter which her beloved Hermione had installed for her.

'A marriage has been arranged, and will shortly take place, between Hermione, only daughter of etc. etc., and Roland Wade, only son of the late Captain George Wade, Tenth Hussars, and Mrs. Wade (*née* Berthelmy). Indian papers please copy.'

Roland read it with a feeling of acute discomfort. It was one thing to aspire to marriage with anyone like Hermione, but it was quite another to have to exhibit his credentials like this in the cold light of the columns of *The Times* for all the world to see and discuss and fail to verify! Rumours could always be amended, quelled, explained away. Who could explain away this sort of announcement in the most dignified and veracious journal in the world,

Hermione was puzzled at his expression and slid a hand through his arm.

'What's the matter, darling? Don't you like it?'

He still frowned.

'Is it really necessary, Hermione?'

'Well, dear, it's usual and expected, isn't it? One always does do that sort of thing, and it's the best way of letting people know,' she insisted gently.

He became aware of the steel within her gentleness.

'It's usual with you and your sort, dearest,' he said slowly. 'I wonder if you realise how far apart we really are, though? All this,' tapping the paper he held, 'seems so artificial and senseless to me. Why make a ceremonial announcement of it? Couldn't we just tell people, or slip away and get married and let them find out?'

She laughed, but there was a note of regret in her laughter. She did not want to be reminded of the difference in their stations just then. She wanted, fiercely and determinedly, to be proud of him and of the marriage they were going to make.

'We couldn't do that,' she said decidedly. 'It would look furtive – as if we were doing something we were ashamed of. And we're not, are we, my Roland? We're terribly proud of it!'

'Darling, I am terribly proud of it and I love to think you are as well, but . . .'

He hesitated and she pressed the arm she held.

'Say it, dear. We don't want to start with half-uttered sentences and inconclusive "buts", do we? Tell me anything you like. I'll try to understand, whatever it is.'

'It's all the—embroidery. I don't want you to marry what I've come from, my parents, their achievements and position. I want you to marry me, Roland Wade, myself – Roland Wade and not just the son of two other people who died long ago. I wonder if you understand?'

She knitted her brows in some perplexity.

'I don't really. You see, one's people do matter whether they are alive or dead. They are one's credentials to a certain extent. They are what make me different from my housemaid and my butler.'

She had no idea that she might be regarded as a snob when she made such statements. She had been born and bred in the belief of her essential superiority to her housemaid and her butler, and she made the simplest statement of fact when she expressed that belief.

Roland moved impatiently. Quite clearly, this announcement could not be allowed to stand. Discovery was inevitable, and though people would hesitate to attack a rumour, they would most certainly not hesitate to expose such blatant lying as those publicly printed words. He would lose not only Hermione, but also every other hardly won achievement.

'We shall never see eye to eye on such things, dear,' he told her. 'People say that the secret of a happy married life is the ability to agree to differ. Shall we agree to differ about this?'

She hesitated. She had been an undisputed queen for so long, her slightest wish law, that she resented being thwarted in any chosen project. Then the essential sweetness of her nature triumphed and she smiled.

'If that will make you happy,' she said. 'Does that mean that the announcement is not to go in at all? That will give rise to a good deal of comment and far more publicity than the conventional statement to the Press, you know.'

'Let me alter it, may I? Prove to me that you want really to marry me, Roland Wade, and not just the son of my father.'

She picked up a fountain-pen, unscrewed the cap and handed it to him with a smile, and he bent down to write at her desk, putting the altered paper in her hands a few moments later. He had left untouched the words relating to her, but after his own name he had erased everything and written instead merely 'author and playwright'.

Hermione read it and then laid the paper thoughtfully down again.

'Do you know, I rather like that,' she said at last. 'It sounds sincere and dignified somehow. You are quite right, Roland. It is the author and playwright I want to marry – not the son of Captain George Wade.'

'You're generous, Hermione.'

She looked at him swiftly.

'I love you,' she said softly, and before he could do more than flash his attractive smile at her, the door was flung open to admit Diana.

She marched up to Roland, her hand stretched out.

'Hullo, brother-in-law,' she said coolly, and he felt the odd magnetism of her touch as her hand rested in his for a moment. He felt suddenly thankful that it was Hermione he had had to choose and not this flame-like girl. With Hermione he could be quiet and at peace. With Diana he would always be living on top of a volcano.

'So you know?' he asked her.

'Of course. Hermione came home at an ungodly hour last night with all her banners flying and the sound of drums in her ears, and I was not long arriving at you. I congratulate you,' and her eyes met his with that uncomfortable hint of mockery in them.

'I deserve congratulation on such amazing good fortune,' he said stiffly.

'You certainly do,' said Diana calmly.

Hermione looked up from the paper which she had been studying again.

'Entertain one another whilst I go and give this to Louise to retype and send off, will you? You'll dine here, Roland? I thought it would be more comfortable to stay at home this evening.'

'May I see the announcement?' asked Diana. 'I guess that's what it is.'

Hermione handed it to her without a word, but her face told them nothing as she read both the original announcement and Roland's alteration. She handed it back and did not speak again until she and Wade were alone.

'Your alteration, of course?' she asked.

'Yes.'

'I wonder if that was being terribly clever – or just honest?' she hazarded, looking at him speculatively.

'Just honest,' said Wade, unable to cure himself of the stiffness he was feeling. He was never able to decide how much she guessed about him. 'I want Hermione to feel she is marrying me, myself, and not merely the product of a bygone generation.'

Diana nodded thoughtfully. Then she looked at him intently.

'I should like to ask you an unpardonable question,' she said.

'Shall I ask it for you? Just why am I going to marry Hermione? '

'Yes.'

'I am in love with her.'

'But you don't love her,' said Diana coolly.

'As far as I am capable of loving, I do,' he insisted.

She shook her head.

'You can't tell that. I wonder if you would want to marry her if she were poor and a nobody – if she were Diana Croft, for instance?'

He flushed.

'You're being horribly downright,' he said.

She crossed the room and sat down on a couch, patting it in invitation to him.

'Sit down and let's talk,' she said. 'I rather like you. How do you feel about me?'

'Enormously relieved to hear you say that. I like you, too, Diana, though I'm a little afraid of you.'

'You don't have to be. Last night I was definitely not on your side. I thought Hermione was making a hideous mistake and I will admit quite honestly that I tried to make her change her mind. Today I've watched her and I've come to the conclusion that, whatever you feel towards her, she's terribly in love with you. I know Hermione. Since she feels the way she does about you, it would be a tragedy to her to lose you. Mind, I'm not saying you're very good for her. The thing is, are you going to be good *to* her?'

He felt braced by her outspoken and not unfriendly attitude, relieved to know that he had this very vital young person as, at worst, a neutral.

'I'm going to try to be,' he said sincerely, and she nodded.

'All right. I don't often gush, but I'm going to tell you here and now that I think Hermione is the finest person I know. She's sound right through, and all this high-falutin' business of social position and ancestors and so on is only a veneer which she can't help. The fact that you've pierced the veneer so that she actually intends to marry you shows that you've got very deeply into her affections. Still, she'll have to go through it a bit with her friends and relations. You might as well recognise that and be prepared for it. If it had been me, nobody would have troubled about it. I've actually no more place in this grand world of theirs than – well, than you have, dear brother-in-law, since we're being candid. I'd marry a duke or a crossing-keeper if I felt like that about him, and I should consider myself as no more aspiring to the duke than condescending to the crossing-sweeper. I'm built that way and my father was a rebel against convention and class prejudice. He never at any time felt that Hermione's mother was socially his superior, and when she had got used to the idea of being just Mrs. Croft, she didn't either. But Hermione will always be the Lady Hermione Wakelyn whatever her legal surname is. You remember that, Roland, and don't expect to be engaged to one woman and married to another. See?'

Roland smiled.

'Yes, teacher,' he said meekly, and they both laughed.

'There's something very likeable about you, young feller-me-lad, though I wouldn't marry you if you were the last man on earth!'

Hermione came back to find them still laughing, apparently on the best of terms, and she slid an arm within one of each.

'I want you to be friends,' she said. 'You're both so dear to me.'

Diana gave her a bear-like hug.

'I've been telling him that if he isn't good to you, ma mie, I'll cut him in quarters and fling them to the four winds of heaven!' she laughed.

11

Diana was right when she predicted a storm of disapproving criticism from Hermione's family and friends at her proposed marriage to the young playwright. Everyone was frankly aghast, for she was the very last person whom they would suspect of a misalliance.

She held her head high, took her fiancé proudly into the inner circle of her life, showed by every look and gesture that this was a considered and final decision, and, Hermione being who she was, the family felt that they and not she would be the losers if they persisted in their disapproval. Roland played his part creditably, walking warily along the bridge which separated his former life from that into which his marriage would precipitate him.

Whilst they waited to see the attitude of the present holder of the title. Hermione's bachelor uncle, they probed and peered with discreet thoroughness into such meagre facts as they were given of Wade's origin and history. He had been clever enough in choosing his father to make sure that there had been a Captain of Hussars called George Wade, and further that he had died without apparently having achieved marriage; also that he had been providentially lacking in relations, so that there was no one to give the lie to that side of his claim. His unpremeditated claim on the Berthelmys, however, gave him a good many bad moments and he wished profoundly he had not been so foolish in that flight of imagination. However, it was admitted that the family had been scattered during the war and that many strange things might have happened in those chaotic times. Since the young man claiming kinship with them was about to marry into such a family, however, the Berthelmys were not too insistent on their denials and old Madame Marie, whom Roland had rashly claimed as a grandmother, went so far as to admit that she would like to receive a visit from the young man.

'My daughters were brought up strictly and as well-born French girls should be brought up,' she said in her dignified way. 'The war broke up everything, however, and who is to say what secrets went to the grave with my Marie, who was killed in the British Red Cross Hospital, or my Blanchette who, they say, perished in an air raid in Paris?'

What the old lady really thought or believed was shut up in her clever, scheming brain and since she died before the projected visit was more than a vague suggestion, no one ever knew how it would have resulted. Suffice it that the Berthelmys were apparently prepared to accept this fiancé of Hermione's, and in the face of that, little more could be done though a great deal could be said, and was said, privately.

The seal was put on the affair by Fenley himself. He invited the pair down for the weekend, looked Roland over with his rather gay, bachelor eye, and gave his approval, even if he qualified it slightly to Hermione and rather more definitely to himself.

'He's the last person in the world I should have expected you to cotton on to, Hermione,' he said candidly. 'I always thought you'd make a match of it with Hale in the end. However, I think the more of you for taking a mike out of the lot of us. For the first time in your life you're almost human.'

'Uncle Greg!' she protested laughingly. There had always been a comradeship between the two.

'Well, it's true. My advice to you, m'dear, is to humanise him a bit, though, before you throw him to the wolves out there,' with a vague gesture towards the terrace and the grounds which at that moment were populated with as many of the Fenleys and Wakelyns as could find any sort of excuse for calling during that weekend. 'Get someone to teach him to sit a horse and shoot and hunt and so on. It'll make him more according to pattern.'

'But, Uncle Greg, he's an artist – a musician – a genius. He doesn't have to ride horses and shoot things,' said Hermione, her eyes wandering to where she knew that Roland, in a little knot of her relations, was being probed and dissected under the microscope for their edification.

Fenley laughed his bluff, good-humoured laugh.

'He can be all that – but I should teach him the recognised parlour tricks for his own sake, if I were you. Get Hale to teach him!' and he chuckled mischievously at her rising colour.

Yet he was prepared to be neutral, if not altogether approving, and since it was obvious that nothing anyone could do or say would prevent this marriage, the rest of the family decided to accept it.

The marriage took place, with due pomp and ceremony, three months later, Hermione a fairy princess of romance in her frosty white and the famous Fenley pearls which her uncle had insisted on her wearing. Roland had realised a substantial part of his capital to buy pearls for his wedding gift to her, and these she wore bound about her head to hold the misty white of her veil.

'I shall have to wear the family pearls or offend my uncle hopelessly,' she had said to him when he had given her the long, flat case. 'Those I shall wear round my neck, but yours will be my crown, my beloved.'

He had gone through that tremendous day as if he were playing a part in one of his own plays. It all seemed so unreal and, surrounded by her family, her friends, all the fashionable and wealthy crowd which seemed to take a delight on that day in displaying their importance, their cars, their jewels, their elaborate gifts, he felt oddly lost and depressed. He had looked forward to that day as the crowning point of his life, as his ultimate triumph – and he found it oddly disappointing.

For a time he and Hermione had stood side by side beneath an arch of flowers in the centre of one of the great reception-rooms, receiving the guests and their gracefully spoken felicitations which to Wade rang hollow and insincere but which Hermione seemed to accept happily enough. Then, when they had greeted the whole throng one by one, she was engulfed by a crowd of her own particular friends, and somehow separated from him so that he found himself wandering on the fringe of the charmed circle, a stranger in a strange land.

Diana, exquisite in the green and gold of her bridesmaid's gown, found him and stood with him to watch the elaborate, jewelled, perfumed scene.

'Well, how does it feel?' she asked him with her mocking smile. 'Going to like being one of them?'

He had a moment's revelation and he turned to her impulsively, feeling her friendliness in this world of strangers.

'I shall never be one of them,' he said, and she nodded her agreement.

'You'll feel outside it, just as I feel,' she said, the mockery dying for once and a rare earnestness and gravity taking its place. 'They're artificial, purposeless, useless, most of them. Hermione's brought me amongst them, but I'm with them and never of them. It doesn't matter two hoots about me feeling like that, but you've got to be of them to make Hermione happy, Roland.'

'Do you honestly think I shall ever be that? Or that any of them will really accept me? I shall always be Hermione's husband,' he said, and there was a flavour of bitterness in his tone. He had only just realised that truth, and he did not like the taste of it.

'I'm rather afraid you will, my friend. You see, Hermione's something of a queen amongst all this. She admires you tremendously and you've stirred her young heart – but you'll have to bow down and worship her as well.'

'Suppose I don't?' he asked suddenly.

She laughed.

'You will,' she said and turned away to greet a friend.

Hermione, lovely as a dream in her bridal white, flushed and radiant, came to find him and surprised the lingering shadow of his talk with Diana still on his face.

'What is it?' she asked him smilingly.

'I am—afraid, I think, my dear,' he told her simply, and just then there was no pretence about him, no reaching after effect.

She came close to him, her eyes dewy and soft.

'Darling, no regrets today, and no fears,' she whispered, and he would have been churlish to resist that appeal of eyes and voice.

'There could be none whilst you are with me,' and his voice shook.

During the remaining hours of that almost interminable reception he let neither his bride nor their guests see that gnawing, persistent fear which was robbing him of the supreme content he had confidently anticipated.

And at last it was over and they were alone, he and Hermione, in the Pullman which had been reserved for them on the late boat-train. Hermione had made all the arrangements – or rather, the little army of servitors amongst which her life seemed to be set had made them for her. There was no lavish or vulgar display of the money which had made all this luxury possible, but Roland was conscious of it as an undercurrent to everything. Hermione's money! He was a rich woman's husband, beyond any doubt in the world.

They were to go to Paris first and then on a protracted tour of France and Italy, returning in the autumn to take up life together as Hermione visualised it.

'There will be such lots to do to the house,' she had said when suggesting at least six months abroad. 'I want everything to be quite perfect for you. I owe that to my temerity in marrying a genius! There has always been a lot of waste space in the house so I am having the rooms on the top floor turned into a haven of refuge for you, a place that will be absolutely private and soundproof! The only way of reaching it will be by a private lift from your own suite next to mine, and even I shan't come without an invitation.'

'Believe me, I am not used to working in luxurious comfort and silence,' he had protested laughingly, hiding the dismay with which he heard her plans. He had never imagined that she would take his 'work' as seriously as all that!

'Then you will work all the better,' she said contentedly. 'You don't know how glad it makes me feel to know that I can give you the peace and beauty and freedom from anxiety which you must absolutely need to create all the lovely dreams that are born in your mind.'

He had stirred restlessly, looking away so that she should not see what lay in his eyes, that thing so oddly akin to shame.

'You idealise me, Hermione,' he had said rather brusquely.

'Why not, since you yourself are an idealist?' she had replied in her serene, assured way.

And so the plans had been discussed and made and approved for the suite which he would occupy after the honeymoon, a suite which connected with hers at one end, and which, at the other end, led by an electric lift to the two soundproof rooms at the top of the house, the larger to be fitted with everything of which a musician might dream, the other to be his study. The windows of both rooms could be opened to a stone balcony which was to be large enough to accommodate a small roof garden.

'Women like your Briony, or the Angela of your book, would never be able to struggle to life without a garden,' she had said. 'I have given Carter's *carte blanche* with such space as the builders can spare them, and they will create a dream of delight for you.'

'For us,' he had demurred.

'For *you*' she had insisted. 'I shall come there only by invitation, and if ever I get jealous of Briony and Angela and all their successors, I shall invite you to desert them for a holiday with just me!'

'You will make me too comfortable to work, my dear. What then?'

'That won't be possible. Anyone who can write as you have done, either books or music or songs, must be so much wedded to the gods that nothing can divorce you from them. Roland, I'm so proud of you, so proud to be marrying you. Make me prouder still!'

And now he was definitely embarked on this vast adventure, marriage with the Lady Hermione Wakelyn, now become Lady Hermione Wade. 'Change the name and not the letter,' someone had quoted to her jestingly, but she had brushed aside the mere suggestion that happiness would not be her portion. If she could choose so unerringly a chair, a picture, a length of silk, a gown or hat, why should she be mistaken when it came to choosing a husband?

Roland was rather quiet on the swift journey to the coast, caring for her perfect comfort, pathetically anxious to find something left for him to do, and she found unnecessary things, divining his thought.

'Find me a magazine or paper or something that doesn't shriek my own photograph at me, darling, will you? Did I really look like that when we came out of the church? You look terrible in that, too,' and she made room for him to sit on the softly cushioned lounge beside her.

He laughed ruefully.

'I look as if I hadn't shaved for a week,' he said. 'Hermione, do you realise that we are married? That you are my wife and I your husband? That you may actually see me when I haven't shaved?'

She shook her head.

'I don't want to see you when you haven't shaved if I can help it – not if you look like that!'

'I do.'

'Then don't let me see you, any more than I intend you to see me other than beautiful. I think one of the tragedies of marriage is the contempt bred by familiarity. Husbands and wives so soon rub the bloom off by not caring about the little things enough. We're going to care, Roland, you and I. Let's try and keep the loveliness of today all our lives. I want our marriage to be— perfect.'

He held her to him and kissed her desperately. If only she

would take this more lightly and easily, demand less of life and of him! He was determined that, if it lay in his utmost power, he would make her marriage the perfect thing she desired. But was it in his power? His very life was founded on a lie, and throughout this wonderful holiday which she had planned and made possible for him, the shadow of that top floor of her house would be flung across him.

He tried to express something of his thoughts.

'Don't aim too high, Hermione, darling. I am only human, and so few marriages are perfect. I doubt if any of them are really that.'

'Ours is going to be,' she said, lying in his arms in utter content.

'But I myself am so far from perfection, my dearest, that it isn't logical to expect perfection to come out of me. Make allowance for my faults and for the failures I am so sure to make. Don't let us found our marriage on impossibility.'

But she shook her head.

'Perfection *is* possible,' she said. 'There have been perfect marriages. My mother's odd marriage with Diana's father was perfect, I believe, though I could not have made such a marriage.'

'Why not?'

'My dear, he was really impossible! He made no pretence at being gently born or bred, and my mother exchanged the lovely, orderly, dignified life we lead for a sort of caravan existence. Not actually a caravan, of course, but life in furnished houses, hotels, queer little rooms even, and meals cooked and served anyhow. I have learned a lot about it from Diana and I simply cannot imagine my mother, as I knew her, living like that.'

'I have lived like that, Hermione,' said Roland abruptly.

She smiled in her serene way.

'I know, dearest. You don't belong to that sort of life, though. You wouldn't choose it. That is one of the joys of marriage with you – that I can give you a physical environment to match your beautiful mentality, your spirit.'

He was uncomfortably silent. Had she been other than

147

Hermione, her words might have sounded ultra-sentimental. Said in her quiet, sincere fashion, they were the expression of her thoughts in the intimate confidence of their married life and he realised unhappily the pedestal on which she had placed him. For how long could he maintain that precarious position?

And exactly what would happen to both of them when he tottered and fell?

A courier in uniform met them at the quayside and conducted them to the boat and to the one luxury suite which it boasted. Hermione disliked air travelling, and as her life had no need of any of the modern rush and bustle, she could afford to travel as she liked.

'Shall I see about the luggage or anything?' Roland asked her as he followed her on board.

'Oh no, the courier will see to everything,' she told him negligently. 'Give him your keys, dear, and tell him what luggage you have and we need not trouble any further. I expect Germaine has already given him mine. He is going to Paris with us.'

Such travel was a revelation to Roland, who, even on his trip to Hollywood, hitherto the most important journey of his life, had had to scramble for places and look after his own luggage and tickets and other necessaries. Hermione had had simply to wave the magic wand and every slightest difficulty was smoothed from their path. It was certainly very delightful and easy.

Their suite consisted of two communicating cabins, and Hermione announced her intention of lying down directly they got on board, short though the passage was.

'I am a terribly bad sailor, Roland, and I always make it a practice to lie down immediately I get on the boat and stay there for the whole of the crossing, whatever it is like. Germaine knows exactly how to look after me, and tomorrow, after a few hours' sleep in Paris, I shall be presentable again,' and she flung him a smile and a nod and disappeared, the French maid like a darting shadow behind her.

Germaine shepherded her mistress on deck when the boat

had berthed at Boulogne and nearly all the other passengers had disembarked, and the courier came to usher her ashore.

'The luggage is on the train, my lady, and everything in readiness," he said, and they followed him across the busy noisy station with its blue-bloused porters and officials looking to English eyes so untidy and unbusinesslike.

There was a drawing-room on the luxurious Paris express for them, and Hermione came back to her husband from the adjoining compartment with her travelling dress changed for a wrap of soft, furred satin, her feet in blue mules to match.

'Won't anyone come in?' he asked a little anxiously.

She laughed.

'Why should they? Germaine and the courier, Watts, will see to everything. That is why they are here,' and she dropped into a deep armchair and smiled an invitation to him to take the opposite one.

It was the same when, after the smooth, swift journey to Paris, a car met them to take them to a hotel of which he had heard only vaguely and reverently.

By some miracle of transport, one of the miracles which Roland speedily learned to accept as part of Hermione's environment, Germaine was already in their suite, smart and neat in her uniform and looking as though she had been there for days.

He came back to their sitting room to find a perfect little meal ready for them, a discreet waiter ready to materialise or fade away at the least gesture.

'I'm terribly tired, Roland, and I'm going straight to bed,' said Hermione, flushing a little when the table had been whisked away and they were alone again. 'Tomorrow I am ready to be quite charming to you, but tonight I'm not fit company for anyone.'

He held her in his arms, gently, possessively, realising how that little speech of hers accentuated their position with regard to one another, though he knew that such a thought was infinitely far from her mind. She saw herself always the leader, always the queen, with him the follower, the slave.

'Tomorrow we begin life together, dearest,' she whispered.

'Why tomorrow, my sweet?'

The nearness of her, the soft, supple body in his arms, the faint fragrance of her hair caught at his senses and made them swim. She sensed, with a quick shaft of fear, his rebellion against her edict and he felt her stiffen a little in his hold.

'Don't let us spoil the—ultimate perfection,' she said, and in her voice was that little quiver of fear.

He laughed and swept her up into his arms, holding her closely against him. Today had been hers, her world about them, claiming her, disclaiming him. Tonight, with the world shut out, was his!

'This is the ultimate perfection,' he said, his lips against hers, and, as once before on that night when he had first spoken to her of love, she felt her senses sway, and only this overwhelming passion of desire left. 'The day has been yours. The night is mine, beloved – mine and yours.'

Long after he slept, his dark head crushed into one of the silk pillows of her bed, Hermione lay awake and stared out into the darkness. So this was that strange and secret thing which men called love. It was oddly disappointing to her, disquieting, disturbing, frightening even. She had always been so sure of herself, so calm, so self-possessed. An overthrow of her plans had been cause for annoyance and she had never welcomed the unexpected in anything.

And now, against all her careful preparations, this wild, unleashed passion had come to bewilder and amaze her. She had been innocent but not ignorant. She was no untutored, stupid girl, and she had entered into marriage with full realisation of its obligations. The prospect had been slightly distasteful to her, as it is to a great many sheltered girls, but she had been sensible enough to accept it. It had not entered into her wildest imaginings, however, that she, Hermione Wakelyn, could be so swept away, so overpowered, so obsessed by a passion which she had scarcely realised existed.

She leaned on her elbow and watched her husband, this stranger, this *man* who had made himself the one man in the world who would henceforth be different from all other men. He looked so peaceful, so young and untroubled, so undisturbed by that cataclysm which had overwhelmed her. He was Roland Wade – her husband – and yet a stranger, clad in strange garments. The collar of his silk pyjamas was undone and had fallen back revealing the white skin of his chest in contrast with the slightly darkened skin above it. By the revealing light of the shaded lamp which still burnt by the side of the bed she saw that already his chin and cheek wore that slightly bluish tint which by the morning would be that of an unshaven skin.

She was oddly repelled. She had not wanted to see him like that. She wanted him always as she had known him, immaculate, perfect, well-groomed, prepared for her.

She remembered suddenly something Diana had said to her about Roland.

'You're marrying his mind but you've got to live with his body.'

She had not realised that, had even thought it coarse and unnecessary of Diana to say it. But it was true. She had married Roland Wade because she had admired his work, loved his mind, his genius, the beauty which he had been able to create, the beauty which still lay within his soul waiting for birth. Yet tonight, within these last amazing hours, what was it she had loved? Was that love at all? Where in those transports had been her memory of him as a poet, a musician, a genius? She had remembered only his body and hers, his arms, his kisses.

And now he was lying in her bed, asleep on her pillows, unaware of her even, his chin unshaven. She knew that it was ridiculous, childish, hysterical, to mind that last foolish little item, but she could not forget it. In some women it would have roused tenderness. In Hermione it roused a faint but positive repulsion. She had loved his mind, married his mind, wanted to live with his mind – and it was true what Diana had said – she had to live with his body.

She slipped out of bed, flung a wrap about her and crouched down on the wide window-seat, pushing aside the heavy velvet curtain so that she could look out on Paris, the city that never sleeps.

Roland stirred, opened his eyes, blinked them uncertainly and at length sat up and stared at his bride in some perplexity.

'What's the time, darling?' he asked sleepily.'About four o'clock,' she said in an odd, chilly little voice.

'What on earth are you doing out there in the cold?'

'Just—thinking.'

'But heavens, what a time to get up and think! Come back to bed, dear, and go to sleep.'

'I—I don't want to, just yet,' she said, refusing to turn and look at him.

He got out of bed and came to her, slipping an arm about her shoulders and aware at once of her slight withdrawal.

'Darling, what's the matter? Do tell me,' he urged.

'Nothing,' but her voice was not reassuring.

Then come back to bed. You'll get so cold out there.'

She stood up and slid from his arm.

'I—Roland, will you—I'd like to be alone now,' she said in a breathless voice.

He flushed, stared at her, frowned a little and then turned away.

'Of course, my dear,' he said, picked up his dressing-gown and stalked through the communicating bathroom into his own room, uncertain whether to be annoyed or indulgent. Surely he had not married a prude? Yet he remembered her surrender of a few hours ago, its unexpected passion and abandon. He reflected that women were always an unknown quantity, climbed into his cold bed, shivered for a few moments and then dropped asleep again.

In the morning they met with slight embarrassment, Hermione offering him a kiss at which he ventured to do no more than peck, so cool were her lips. He noticed that she was fully dressed, although it was early and breakfast was served in their private sitting room.

'I ordered an English breakfast for you,' she said. 'I prefer the continental one, but men usually despise them.'

'I should be desperately hungry by the middle of the morning on just rolls and coffee,' he agreed lightly, and thereafter conversation languished until, with the table removed again, they stood awkwardly before the fire.

Roland took one of her hands in his.

'Hermione, what's wrong between us? Isn't it better to have it out now? Don't hold some secret grudge against me, especially after—last night.'

She raised troubled eyes to his.

'That's just it. I—I didn't know marriage would be like that. I don't think I want it to be,' she said slowly.

'But, darling, that's what marriage is, happy marriage, anyway. Else why do people marry?'

'For heaps of other things, surely – companionship, mutual interests.'

'One can have those without marrying nowadays. We married for love, Hermione, didn't we? There could not have been any other reason for you to want to marry me.'

'That was my reason, Roland. I did love you. I do still,' but there was a curious little note of wonder in that last reflection. It was true. She did still love him. That was somehow unchanged, though she could not bear to remember the events of the night before.

He laughed tenderly and drew her into his arms, slightly reluctant though she was.

'It seems strange and disturbing to be a wife after having belonged only to yourself so far,' he said, his voice gentle and persuasive. 'You don't really regret marrying me, do you?'

'No. No, of course not. Only . . .'

'Yes? Only what?'

'Oh, my dear, it's so difficult to explain what I feel. I love you so, the real you, the essential part of you, the immortal, intangible part, the God in you. It is the best love, the love of the spirit. We don't want to—belittle it, smirch it, make it just a thing of the senses. Darling, am I talking rubbish?'

He kissed her gently and laughed a little.

'Utter bosh, my sweet. Have you done?'

'I knew I couldn't make you understand,' she said.

'You make a mistake. I do understand, Hermione, but you've got this all wrong. Anyway, it's a gorgeous day and all Paris lies before us and I've never been here in my life before and I don't know a dozen words of French now, so I'm utterly dependent on you – unless you'd rather I found the obliging Watts?'

She could not but catch his mood, for she was really in love with him and wanted to be happy with him.

'Of course I'll go with you myself. I do love you terribly. You know, don't you?'

'Bless you, yes. Let's leave all worrying thoughts out of our calculations for the moment and go out! Sufficient unto the night?'

She nodded, flushed a little and rang for Germaine.

During their weeks in Paris, Roland was tender and considerate, keeping his passion in leash the more easily since he knew that he was not deeply in love with her. He never ceased to marvel at his good fortune, at the colossal success which had crowned the years of struggle, and he was sincerely determined that Hermione should not regret having married him. Seeing that she felt as she did about the physical aspect of their lives together, he found new cause for thankfulness that he was not so passionately in love with her that restraint would be intolerable. As things were, all was most convenient and satisfactory.

Either alone or under the guidance of the ever-discreet Watts, they 'did' Paris, from the shops and the opera to the Montmartre of the regulation tourist, and Hermione enjoyed it the more because of her husband's enjoyment, seeing things anew with his inexperienced eyes and revelling in her power to satisfy his every whim.

Roland found himself unexpectedly embarrassed at her

generosity, and had to argue against it many times. He had certainly wanted a rich wife and an unassailable position in the world he had set out to conquer, but he had not expected to feel like a gigolo, and he told Hermione so frankly when he found a set of links and studs in black pearl displayed on his dressing-table one evening.

He took them into her room, knocking first with his punctilious observance of her right to privacy.

'Darling, I don't want these, really,' he said.

She dismissed her maid with a nod and turned to him, closing his hand on the open case.

'It's much nicer to have the things one doesn't really want than just to possess necessities,' she told him laughingly.

He did not join in her laughter. Somehow he had hated himself when he saw that case.

'I'd much rather have just the necessities,' he told her, and the tone of his voice made her own face grave and a little wistful.

'But if it is my joy to give you the unnecessary things?'

He laid the case down on her dressing-table and closed it with a little snap.

'I'd rather you didn't,' he said shortly. 'You give me too much as it is,' and he walked out of her room, leaving the case there.

Yet the next day she persuaded him to take it back, and he shrugged his shoulders and accepted the inevitable, wondering what sort of man he really was. Before this marriage of his, he had had no doubt. He was quite simply and honestly a climber, if it could be either simple or honest to climb as he had done. Now, married to Hermione, he began to wonder whether, after all, the struggle had been worth it.

She was a little more careful and judicious over her gifts after that, wrapping them up less obviously, but both knew that the early charm to both giver and recipient had somehow been dimmed.

From Paris they went on to the Italian Lakes, dismissing Watts and adding Germaine's cousin, Louis, to their train as personal valet to Roland.

'I certainly feel a little less like a travelling prince now that the urbane Watts is no longer ready to do my slightest behest,' he laughed. 'Perhaps I may be allowed to do something for my wife myself.'

'Why bother?' asked Hermione lightly. 'I think we shall miss him and would have been better advised to let him stay until we have decided to go home again. He was so useful.'

'Well, make me useful,' he suggested.

'My dear, you couldn't possibly be as useful as a man like Watts. After all, that was his job.'

Wade had already discovered that his wife was sublimely indifferent to the amount of trouble she caused to her employees, accepting service from them as her right. She paid them generously and expected her path through life to be perfectly smoothed before they allowed her feet to tread it. Her husband had several uncomfortable moments before he became sufficiently accustomed to her methods to accomplish the ease and luxury which had hitherto appeared to surround her by magic. Not only had the best trains of the day to be selected, but private suites had to be reserved in advance at any place at which they had to break their journey for more than an odd hour, and these always at the best hotels, which Roland early found were not necessarily the showiest or the most expensive. Flowers had to be ordered, and cars in readiness at the station so that Germaine, with the most important of the luggage, could be hurried to the hotel first to get everything ready for her mistress.

Hermione was mildly amused at his anxious endeavours.

'Darling, why bother so much? Find Cook's place and tell them we want another courier. It will all be done for us then and you can enjoy life.'

'I prefer to do *something* for my living,' he retorted, leaving her whilst he went to telephone about the trains and cars for the next morning.

But once they had reached their objective, a tiny village on the grassy, wooded slopes above a sapphire and diamond miniature lake not yet discovered by the tourists who had thronged Como, Roland found himself able to relax. They had a chalet to themselves, with Germaine and Louis and an old Italian couple to look after them, and here they drowsed away the magic days of early June, climbing down the rough path to the edge of the water, swimming in its icy coldness and lying afterwards in the sun-hot grass to bake themselves brown. The scramble up again for lunch was a thing of laughter and breathlessness, but it was worth it when, dressed and neat again, they sat on the open, wooden terrace of their chalet to do justice to Elizabetta's tempting fare. In the afternoons they walked for miles, a flat picnic case slung over Wade's shoulder and a camera over Hermione's.

They were utterly happy, though each felt that this was an oasis in a yet uncharted and unknown desert. Before them stretched a life which would be new to them, would hold strange possibilities and certainties. Just now they willed themselves to forget and just be happy.

In the blue and gold days and the quiet, star-filled nights, Hermione showed him the essential woman beneath the glamour and wealth which in normal life enfolded her. He came to know the steadfast, honest soul of her, plumbing its depths and finding only sweetness and beauty and truth there. He came to know himself, too, and to despise that which he had become. In the silence and simplicity of mountain and lake, in the sanity of their life there, he came to wish with a passionate intensity that he could be frank with her, could cleanse his soul by confession, could show himself to her as he really was. She made no secret of her worship of what she believed him to be, and at such revealing moments he was intensely miserable. Then his elastic nature reasserted itself and he forced himself to forget everything save that he was on his honeymoon with a beautiful and loving woman, and found that ephemeral happiness again.

Of the passion of that first night, little seemed to remain. Roland was always gentle, considerate, self-effacing, and it was easy for Hermione to believe what she wanted to believe, that their love had risen above the purely physical and mundane plane. They kissed as lovers, lay in one another's arms in peaceful contentment, but that wild abandonment of passion seemed to have gone from them. If Roland had his thoughts about it, he kept them to himself, content in her contentment and in his own knowledge that what he felt for her was rather tenderness and friendship than the turmoil of love.

With July came the tourists and even their sanctuary was no longer inviolate, so as they had rented the chalet from Elizabetta on a weekly basis, they decided to move on.

They went lingeringly, staying on for yet another week, then an extra weekend, and one day longer on the excuse of wanting to see a religious festival and procession in the little village in the valley below, but at last they were actually on their travels again, to Germany this time and the lovely, wooded valleys of the Rhine. They wandered back to the cities, consoling themselves for the loss of woods and lakes and trees by revelling in luxurious hotels, in the shops and theatres and cabarets where Hermione displayed her marvellous clothes and Roland caught reflected glory from her and the reputed possession of her.

They danced night after night. She had never cared greatly for dancing before her marriage. With Roland, whose dancing had become a very perfect accomplishment, she discovered an unexpected delight in it.

Through Germany they passed into Holland, wandering slowly and luxuriously over the flat, industriously cultivated country with its busy waterways and its comforting air of prosperity and freedom from the restless anxiety which racked the rest of the civilised world. They spent a month where they had intended to pass only a week, finding such genuine kindliness and hospitality wherever they went that they were charmed into lingering. Letters followed them, however, and amongst them a somewhat disjointed one from Diana to the effect that she proposed to take over a half-share in a hat shop somewhere in Chelsea, with a flat over it.

'You'll want to bill and coo, my darlings, without my restraining presence for one thing,' she had written, 'and for another, I feel it is the time for me to cease to be a mere parasite. I think we can make the thing pay if we can get rid of the mortgage. That is where I come in and, if you will, Hermione, where you come in too. It can be done for six hundred pounds, and we (Stella Brent and I) propose to borrow the money from you, have the deeds put in your name, and repay you in chunks as and when we can. Think this over and let me know, my love. If you insist, we will allow you a discount on your own hats, but we hope you won't insist as you will probably be our most distinguished and wealthy customer.'

Hermione smiled and passed the letter across the breakfast table to Roland.

'Going to let her do it?' he asked when he had read it, catching a glimpse of Diana herself from the breathless, hastily written sentences which, with all their haste, held enough sound sense to show that she had given time for thought before writing.

'I don't know. Won't people think it rather odd for her to have a shop?'

'Because of you, you mean?'

'Yes. There is really no need for her to do anything like that, is there?'

'I agree with her if she objects to being a pensioner on your bounty,' he said suddenly – so suddenly that she looked up, startled.

'Roland! You sounded so—strange when you said that. Why should she not be a pensioner, as you call it?'

'Isn't her own creed that those who don't work shan't eat?' he asked.

'Yes, I suppose it is. And of course, no one ought to live on anyone else, ought they?' asked Hermione simply. 'Well, perhaps I will let her have her head. Telegraph to her, Roland, will you?

And to my solicitors to put the thing through for her?'

'Without waiting to see the place or anything?' he asked.

'Why should I? It is evidently what Diana wants, and I can trust her implicitly.'

'But this other girl, this Stella Brent,' referring to the letter. 'Suppose she's not quite all she should be, not quite straight in her dealings. Six hundred pounds is a fairly substantial sum, you know.'

Hermione waved aside his objection with her usual indifference to money.

'I always trust people until I find they have deceived me. Then they are finished as far as I am concerned. Send the telegrams for me, there's a dear, and then we'll go out. Ring for Germaine as you pass, will you?'

He went out slowly, her words unpalatable to his mind. What would happen in the event of her finding out that he had deceived her?

And in September they definitely turned their faces towards England, with Germaine and Louis left to follow them by a later boat with all the luggage which had mounted to colossal proportions during their six months of travelling.

'I shall be glad to be home again, after all,' said Hermione, as they stood on the deck of the steamer. The sea was so calm that for once she had yielded to his persuasions to stay on deck.

Roland made no reply, and she looked at him quickly.

'Won't you be glad, dearest?' she asked.

'Yes.'

She was troubled. She had sensed the difference in him ever since they had discussed their return journey. It was almost as if he went back with her reluctantly.

'What is it, my dear one? You don't regret anything? Or feel anxious or worried about anything?'

'Hermione, I owe you so much,' he said abruptly.

She breathed a sigh of relief. She had imagined something much more devastating than that, though she had no idea what.

'Is that all? My dear, you owe me nothing – or if you ever did, you've repaid it a thousandfold in the happiness of the last six months.'

He laid his hand over hers as it rested on the rail.

'I should be glad to believe that, Hermione,' he said quietly. 'You have been happy?'

'Don't you know that?' she asked him, her voice warm and sweet.

His hand gripped hers convulsively. He wished with all his heart that he could wipe out those months, wipe out all the time there had been since they met, wipe out even that meeting. There was sorrow and disillusionment ahead for her and he knew himself powerless to avert it.

'I wish I could keep you happy all your life,' he said in a low voice, and she was silent, sensing something beneath all this which she could not understand.

12

Their home-coming was a ceremony and Roland could not help the impression he had of a theatre setting, the flight of marble steps, the great doors flung open, the glittering lights, the servants all smiling. Then Hermione, glowing and happy and gracious, greeting each in turn, saying just the right thing; lastly himself, a little nervous and awkward, unable to rid himself of the feeling of unreality and artificiality. This, then, was to be his life, this his setting, this the keynote of all his actions.

He followed his wife up the wide staircase, past the reception-rooms which he knew and through a swing door to the most important of the bedrooms, strange ground to him. Hermione had not wanted him to see the house and his own rooms until they were altered and made ready for him, and he could see how proud and pleased she was now that she could take him to them.

'These are my rooms,' she said, 'my bedroom and dressing-room and bath, and yours are opposite,' opening a door and showing him the perfect little suite of rooms which contained everything the heart of man could desire. He wondered for a moment of amusement how he would have accepted this division of rooms if he had been the traditional lover-husband of this beautiful wife of his. He had a sudden and unpremeditated vision of his home-coming with a wife of his own class, a comfortable, sensible; affectionate little middle-class girl whose eyes would have opened wide with amazement at a suggestion of two rooms with their own dressing-rooms and bathroom! Somehow that vision was attractive. He brushed it aside and followed Hermione back from the gleaming black and white marble bathroom to the big, airy bedroom.

'This is my *chef-d'oeuvre,'* she said, crossing to a corner and turning the handle of what appeared to be a large wardrobe, panelled in dark mahogany to match the definitely masculine furniture and fittings of the room. The door opened to reveal a little electric lift which was lighted automatically by the opening of the door.

'Did you chant "Open Sesame" to it?' he asked following her into the tiny compartment and watching her manipulate the electric buttons which would send them up to the top floor or down to the hall level. 'I feel as if I had walked into a fairy tale.'

She laughed delightedly, like a child springing a surprise on its elders.

'You wait,' she promised him, and a moment later they had stepped out of the lift again and were in a long, narrow room which he saw at once was designed for a music-room.

The roof had been raised so that the sloping ceiling should not detract from the sound, and the walls and floor were of some light, hard wood, probably teak. One or two exquisite Persian rugs broke its polished splendour, and their soft, indeterminate pinks and blues were repeated in the faded, time-softened tapestry which covered the divan and the two or three deep easy chairs which constituted all the furniture of the room save for the gleaming grand piano which dominated everything from its raised dais at one end.

'Do you like it, Roland?' asked Hermione as he stood taking it all in.

'Am I going to hold concerts here?' he queried, not knowing quite what he felt about all this splendour, though sure of extreme discomfort in any case.

'If you like. It is yours. Your own very private room, this and the one next to it,' opening a door in the panelling and showing him a small room fitted as a study, a businesslike desk flanking the low-silled window, and one wall devoted to tier after tier of shelves, quite empty at present. Here, as in the music-room, everything had been planned for the comfort and convenience of a worker. Lights had been placed thoughtfully and prodigally; a smaller table held a typewriter and a telephone; there was a dictaphone, a cupboard fitted with trays and many shallow shelves above its deep drawers which ran on noiseless bearings, an electric fire stood ready for service when needed, and a deep, leather-clad easy chair supplemented the more utilitarian swing chairs which stood at each desk.

It was the sort of room of which every writer dreams but which probably very few actually achieve.

Hermione walked across to the window and turned a handle which swung a double window across the glass of the other, shutting out every sound from the street below.

'There is a ventilating shaft in the ceiling,' she said, and showed him how it worked. 'There is the same arrangement for the windows in the music-room so that either room can be made absolutely soundproof.'

'My dear, I am far too much overwhelmed for speech,' said Roland, his dejection increasing with every moment. How on earth could he justify this elaborate setting for his 'genius'?

'These are for work,' said Hermone, 'but this is for pure joy,' and she flung open the French windows and led him out to the roof garden which she had planned with such care and delight.

It was a place of infinite peace and beauty, created by artists to delude with the belief that it was the heart of the country rather than the heart of a great city. From amongst fern-set rocks a tiny stream fell and gurgled. In a shallow basin brightly coloured fish darted about the clear water.

Hermione sat down on a stone bench and looked up at her husband with eyes that were soft with love and pride.

'You like it, Roland?'

'It's beyond my most marvellous dreams, and I can hardly believe that I am awake and not dreaming a fairy tale,' he said, dropping down beside her and drawing her closely within the circle of his arm. 'And yet, I'm—a little sorry.'

She turned puzzled eyes on him.

'Darling, why?'

'Because you—you are making a sort of little tin god of a quite ordinary man, my dear,' he said, desperately realising that if ever he had had an opportunity of confessing to her, that opportunity had gone now that he had been faced with all these elaborate and slightly bizarre preparations for him.

She pressed more closely to him, happy and a little excited and inclined to sentimentalise about it all.

'No. What I've tried to do is to make a temple for the little tin god,' she told him laughingly.

'Hermione, I'm not worth it. I'm not a god at all. I'm not an idol. I've got feet of clay.'

'Even if you have, I never want to see them,' she told him. 'Roland, do you realise that I've never even heard you play? Come and play to me now,' and she rose and pulled him to his feet, turning to go back to the music-room.

'Do *you* realise that after six months my fingers will be like clothes-pegs?' he objected, but he went obediently to the piano, opened it and began to exercise his fingers on the keys. They were certainly stiff but would still do his bidding, more or less, and after a few minutes he began to play to her, glad that she had gone back to the garden after opening the two sets of French windows wide and drawing back the heavy velvet curtains.

He was glad that this, at least, he could do for her, and as his fingers found easily enough the old, well-remembered, dreamy music of Franz Baumer, he thought it might have been written for just such a scene as this – the long room and the windows opening on that peaceful little garden, Hermione herself the princess of a fairy tale as she sat motionless on the high-backed stone seat with the last gleams of the sunset aslant over her dark and lovely head.

Presently he became aware that she had come in from the garden and was standing framed in the doorway, watching him, and the sheer beauty of the picture she made brought him down the long room to stand at her side, swift desire pulsing in him and not for ever to be denied.

He took her in his arms and held her closely, the faint, elusive perfume which always clung about her mazing his senses.

'Hermione! Oh darling!' and he caught her up and carried her back into the shadowed room, holding her against his heart as he had held her so seldom.

She trembled and her breath came in quick, painful little gasps.

'Roland, I don't want it to be like this!' she whispered in an odd, strangled voice.

'Why not, my dearest dear, my wife?' he asked triumphantly.

'It—it can't be right. I hate to feel like this!' and she struggled to free herself.

Some of the mad passion within him died, and though he held her closely, he was more restrained in his kisses.

'Of course it's right, Hermione. Aren't you mine and I yours? Isn't this the beginning and end of all creation? Isn't this why you were made woman and I man?'

'No! No! Roland, it can't be. It isn't—what I believe in—or want,' she repeated.

He set her free but stood facing her, his eyes searching her, his mind in a tumult. Whither were they tending with this strange, unreal marriage of theirs? Was she really cold?

'Do you mean that, Hermione? That you don't want our marriage to be like that? That you want us to be just—friends?'

'But can't we be friends?' she asked pitifully. She understood herself no better than he did. She had been so certain that she loved him. She still did love him. Of that she knew no doubt. Only . . .

'You mean as we have been during these months – excluding that first night?' he asked her quietly.

'Can't it be like that?'

'You mean it is always to be like that, Hermione?'

'Well, for—for the present,' she pleaded.

His face hardened.

'Hermione, I wonder why you married me?'

'I loved you, Roland. I love you still. Can't two people love one another – purely, not just like—like animals?'

He gave a short laugh.

'What are people but animals, dressed up?' he asked. 'You've got a queer notion of marriage, but I'm not exactly in a position to object, am I?'

She frowned a little.

'I don't understand,' she said.

'Don't you? Look round you. Take that natty little lift and go downstairs and look round again. Listen to your friends and watch their faces. You'll understand all right why I can't object to anything you choose to do,' he said bitterly.

She turned to go, her head held high.

'I hate you when you talk like that,' she said. 'I hope by dinner time you will have come to your senses.'

But at the door of the lift she paused irresolute. He had not moved but stood in the centre of the room, a dim outline in the shadows.

'Roland.'

'Yes.'

She came back to him swiftly, her hands on his arms, her face lifted to his.

'Don't let us quarrel on our first night at home. These months together have been so wonderful. Don't quarrel with me.'

He took her in his arms and kissed her gently, unemotionally and set her free again.

'I don't want to quarrel any more than you do, my dear,' he said.

'Then you won't say those things any more, about your position here, I mean?'

'No.'

'Nor think them?'

'You can't control my thoughts. They, at least, are my own,' he said. 'Anyway, isn't it time you were dressing for dinner? You thought one or two people might call later.'

Long after she had gone he stood there, motionless, brooding, in the gathering darkness, seeing this wonderful marriage of his in ruins about him, wondering just what was left on which any sort of happiness could be built.

He went down to his rooms at last to find Louis waiting for him, his evening clothes laid out, a bath drawn for him in the black and white bathroom with an electrically warmed mat for his feet and towels spread on the hot rail. Downstairs there would be a perfect dinner, perfectly served, Hermione herself lovely and dignified, the perfect wife and hostess and mistress of all this splendour.

Perfection! Already he had come to hate the word, the thought. He had a wild desire to rise up in his wrath and smash things, run berserk through the house, shouting and tearing up things as he went.

Then he laughed aloud, to the mild astonishment of the quiet little French valet.

'Louis, my cabbage, if ever you see signs of my going stark, staring mad, shove me in that overwhelming bathroom and turn the cold water on me and keep me there by force until you see sanity returning.'

Diana relieved the tension when he and Hermione met again, for she had rushed in to welcome them, intending to go out again and leave them alone for their first dinner.

'There's absolutely no need, my dear,' Hermione was telling her laughingly when he came into the room. 'Roland, Diana is being discreet and going out to dinner, but I disclaim the discretion seeing that we have had six months alone already.'

'Please stay. You might even sell me a hat,' he said. He realised, faced by Diana and her glowing youth, how sedate and 'settled' he and Hermione had become.

'Darling, you'd look priceless in the latest little Air Force caps. You really invite me to stay? I shall get a much better dinner here than if I have to go out and buy one.'

'*Buy* a dinner, Diana?' asked Wade incredulously. 'Whatever has become of all the young men of the town that you should be reduced to buying your own food?'

'My dear, I've positively had to cast the lot of them in this furious reconditioning of Stella's shop. We've taken the other half of the shop and are papering and painting it ourselves in between customers, who are, alas, few and far between at present.'

'Why not put the young men on to assist?'

'I regret to inform you that the young man of today is purely ornamental,' said Diana in her best 'maiden aunt' manner, her eyes sparkling deliciously. 'Why don't *you* lend a hand, honoured brother-in-law?'

'Right. I will,' he declared to the astonishment and amusement of both and he did actually turn up the next morning at the little shop, finding Stella Brent, tall and dark and ethereal-looking, balanced on the top of some steps pasting up a gay border to the grey wallpaper of their 'annexe', whilst Diana, in an overall and gloves which could be slipped off at a second's notice, knelt on the floor with a pot of bright green paint.

He was surprised to find how glad he was to be busy again, even if the work was new and uncertain, and the two girls chaffed and made merry at his expense whilst they kept him at it, putting up shelves, fixing mirrors and laying linoleum. It seemed so curious to him that Hermione's sister should be scraping to save a few pounds like this that he commented on it to Stella as they were laying the last square of linoleum.

Stella, who proved to be not at all as ethereal and unworldly as her looks suggested, raised her delicately pencilled eyebrows.

'But Di hasn't any money, and why should she use Lady Hermione's?' she asked.

'Well, she's her half-sister and Hermione has always done everything for her and would give it willingly and without a second thought,' he said.

'She's already helped us out of the wood, and neither of us wants to exist on charity. Whilst Di was so young and everything was strange to her, it was different, but one doesn't go about taking things for ever. We're determined to make this pay and get rid of our debt to Lady Hermione as soon as we can. Di!

We've finished this job. What's the next?'

'Oh, food, food!' sang out Diana from the shop. 'I've just sold that blue feather hat to such a pretty girl. Isn't that luck? And we were so doubtful about buying anything as expensive. Dare we shut the shop and all go out together?'

'I ought to go back to lunch,' said Roland awkwardly, and there was an odd little silence which Diana broke in her inconsequent way.

'The call of the bride is heard in the wilds of Chelsea! You'd better go, Roland, or Hermione might not like it. She hates people to be unpunctual or casual, though she's had to swallow a lot of it from me, I'm afraid. Call at the ham and beef shop and ask them to send in two club sandwiches and a ginger-beer as you go, will you?'

He went back to Carlton House Terrace feeling that he had stepped into another life, and it was with a feeling of something like panic that he found himself thinking of chains and fetters. The whole atmosphere of the place, the thickly carpeted floors, the silent-footed servants, the ease and luxury, the quiet voices – everything contributed to that feeling of a weight hung about him. It was unnatural to him. He had not been bred to it, and the atmosphere which had been a heady delight to him when he breathed it as a visitor from another sphere was becoming stifling now that he actually lived in it.

There were guests to luncheon, charming, insincere people who bandied superficially clever nothings to one another by way of conversation, talking of things beyond his knowledge and experience. He was well aware that all of them had come with the intention and for the purpose of taking stock of him and putting through his paces the husband which Hermione had foisted upon them.

He felt he owed it to his wife to make as good an impression as possible, but he was aware all the time of the futility of it all. He did not belong to these people nor did he feel that he would ever make them his own.

In the weeks that followed, however, it seemed that the

dismal predictors of disaster to the amazing marriage would have to eat their words. The pair were scrutinised in public and freely discussed in private, but nothing appeared to justify the forebodings almost universally felt at their wedding.

Hermione the lovelier for the added charm of maturity and wifehood, was an even more popular hostess than she had been before her marriage, and Wade, immaculate, debonair, charming, was always at hand to complete the picture, the perfect cavalier, the attentive husband.

Martin Hale, still the 'Faithful Heart', though he scorned to wear that heart on his sleeve now that Hermione was another man's wife, was now the intimate friend of both. His chief concern was that Hermione should be happy, and since apparently this decorous young genius whom she had married was essential to her happiness, he must be helped over the dangerous places.

It was he who, at the country estate which Hermione had purchased, taught Wade to ride, to handle a gun and a rod, and to acquire at least the rudiments of the requirements of a country gentleman. Wade liked him but secretly despised him, which proved how little he really appreciated the quiet determination of the man who, watching and waiting and possessed of eternal patience, was content to bide his time until this ridiculous and unsuitable marriage should fall to pieces.

And of all those either intimately concerned or merely looking on at the marriage, only two realised that at the heart of it already lay the possibility of disaster.

Those two were Hermione and her husband.

Even to herself Hermione refused to confess failure until the months, gradually turning into a year, forced it home to her and made her sit down to reflect on life in general, her own and Roland's in particular.

Exactly whither were they tending, she and this charming young husband whom she had so romantically loved? She might have held him, might have averted the final catastrophe, might even have won his real love and laid her own on more solid foundations had she been able to rid herself of her romantic dreams for him and given way to the physical desires which she so strenuously repressed. If she had had a mother, an elder sister, a very wise married friend even, she might have been made to understand that no marriage, save between extraordinary and abnormal persons, can thrive on the sort of fare she had decreed for herself and her husband.

Her only tangible grievance against him was that he showed no sign of fulfilling that high and proud destiny for which she had designed those rooms, for which, though she could not realise it, she had actually married him. After the first few weeks when they had been a novelty, he seldom even went in his work-rooms, as she had termed them. The piano was never touched except on such occasions as he conducted a laughing, chattering, frivolous throng of girls and young men into the tiny lift, letting them loose in the roof garden whilst he played jazz to them as an accompaniment to their noise and laughter.

Hermione had intended that for their Holy of Holies, a place sacred to them, where only he and she should walk. She felt that it had been defiled, though she never spoke of it. He treated it as a show place, allowed press photographers there with their cameras and gossip-writers with their adjectives and inquisitive eyes.

'Mr. Roland Wade with a party of friends in the delightful roof garden created for him by his artistic wife, Lady Hermione Wade.'

'The gifted young playwright and author entertained some of the younger set in his beautiful music-room this afternoon, giving them tea on the roof garden.'

Roland, growing desperate in the artificial, unsatisfying life he led, went sometimes to absurd lengths, secretly sneering at those who were only too ready to accompany him in whatever childish scheme he devised to make the time pass. He knew even better than did Hermione that this marriage could not last unless they could place it on a different basis. Beneath the pretence lay something inherently decent, deny it as he might, and now that there seemed no longer any need to climb and struggle, he realised how unsatisfying were all the things for which, all his life, he had craved.

If Hermione had given him a chance, had made any attempt to put aside her rather absurd worship of her own ideals and dreams for him, he might even have told her the truth and, since their love was still young enough to survive a shock, out of it might have come something more natural and enduring. There was no other woman in his heart, and he still believed her the loveliest and most desirable woman he had ever known. He had not lost his original attractiveness for her, his charm of manner, his capacity for delightful companionship. Here were surely all the ingredients out of which real love might have been made – and yet the months went by and they knew they were missing it, drifting away from it slowly but surely until soon it would be out of their reach.

Meantime the paragraphers kept busy with their names, the photographers with their photographs, and rumour began to suggest that it was time a new play appeared from the hand of this versatile young composer, a new book – something, anyway, to justify the elaborate work-rooms whose existence were public property.

The immediate and practical result of such rumours was the appearance of Hallam, who presented himself one day at the house and was shown without ceremony into one of the smaller rooms off the hall which were used for casual and unimportant business callers.

The famous theatrical manager looked round him with grim amusement, perfectly well aware that in the house of Lady Hermione Wade he was of little importance. It was characteristic of him that he had chosen to call like this rather than make an appointment and so prepare Wade for the interview. He wanted to be able to judge for himself whether or not anything further was to be expected from a young man who had never impressed him with a sense of responsibility and power. Wade came to him rather guiltily, trying to disguise his embarrassment with an airy bonhomie, but Hallam ignored such an attempt and came straight to the point.

'Anything in this, Mr. Wade?' he asked rather brusquely, handing him a newspaper cutting.

Roland took it and glanced at it. It was written in the usual style of a newspaper gossip-writer.

'Talking to Mrs. Charles Ferrisser today, I mentioned the name of a successful young playwright who seems to have forsaken the muse for what rumour states is a remarkably felicitous marriage. Mrs. Ferrisser, who is a great friend of the young couple, however, assured me that the little bird who whispers of a new musical play is not necessarily a cuckoo. I wonder if Hallam knows any more about it than I do?'

'What tripe these people do write,' commented the younger man carelessly, handing back the slip.

'Is it all tripe? Or are you going to be in a position to offer me the refusal of anything further?' asked Hallam curtly.

He had made a comfortable sum from the production of *Maiden Errant*, even if it had not raised the furore of *Night in Gale*, and he had no intention of allowing a breach of the contract which obliged Wade to offer him his subsequent script.

'If and when I have anything else ready for production,' said Wade coldly and uncomfortably, 'I will let you know.'

'The public memory is short and its affections fickle,' Hallam reminded him. 'If you are going to offer them anything else, you would be wise to do it before they have lost the taste for your particular brand of stuff. It isn't everybody's meat, you know, and it doesn't follow that it will always be acceptable to the theatre-going public.'

'Are you telling me, Hallam?' asked Wade with a slight insolence born of his life of ease and flattery.

'Yes, I am,' he said. 'People are wondering whether you are Roland Wade the playwright, or merely Lady Hermione Wade's husband. If the former, you should consolidate your reputation with a new production. If the latter, I need not waste my time.'

'You are impertinent, Hallam,' snapped Wade.

'Possibly. I came here on business. If there is nothing doing, I won't take up your time.'

'I have told you that when I have anything to offer you, I will let you know.'

'Do,' said Hallam, picked up his hat, made a formal leave-taking and went his way, uncertain whether to be angry or pitiful.

In the hall he passed Hermione who eyed him uncertainly and acknowledged his hesitating bow with a courteous little smile.

Roland joined her, and she could see that he was ruffled.

'Who was that?' she asked as they went up the stairs together. 'Anyone I ought to have recognised?'

'No. Only Hallam, the theatrical manager,' he said carelessly.

She turned to him, interested at once.

'Roland! Not about a new play?' she asked.

His frown deepened. He had been annoyed by Hallam's visit, and Hermione's interest in it made him the more annoyed.

'Asking for news of one, yes,' he admitted shortly.

They had reached her own sitting room, a room which even he never entered without express invitation. She opened the door now and turned with a gesture which he could not ignore without rudeness. He followed her in and began to play restlessly with the little brass animals and ornaments which stood on a low Benares table.

Hermione came to him and put an arm round his shoulders, a caress from her being rare enough to mark some special occasion in her thoughts.

'Dear, tell me about the play,' she said, and her voice was

warm and friendly.

He resisted an almost overpowering temptation to shake off her hand.

'There is nothing to tell,' he said, trying not to sound too curt. 'There isn't a play.'

'Then why should Hallam come?' she asked, not understanding.

He straightened himself suddenly, and her hand fell from his shoulder at the movement. She made no attempt to touch him again, quite well aware of his lack of response and too proud to invite a second rebuff.

'He, in conjunction with a good many other people, think it is high time I ceased to be merely Lady Hermione's husband and show the world Roland Wade again,' he said deliberately, his lips curling into a sardonic little smile.

Hermione was silent for a moment. Then she began to speak quietly, thoughtfully, every word chosen before she uttered it.

'It hurts me that you should be thought of merely as my husband, Roland. I know it must hurt you, too. That is why I understand the bitter note in your voice. Dear, when such a thing need not be, why not alter it? You know how I have believed in you, in your destiny, loved your genius, almost worshipped the mind which has already conceived such beauty. Sometimes I am afraid I have—despoiled you, Roland. I thought if I made things easy for you, gave you loveliness and dignity and freedom instead of the struggle you must have had before we were married, it would smooth the way for you to greater heights. Instead I seem to have made it harder – taken away your ambitions – spoiled your dreams. Oh, Roland, have I? Have I?'

He could not resist the appeal she made to him. Gradually, if very slowly, the essential decency within him was stirring, making its claim on him, and it was to that man that Hermione appealed.

He caught her hands and held them to his lips. It was an act of homage – but it was also an act of contrition, of remorse that he had no power to alter things, to make her happy, to stem the torrent which some day must engulf them both. This deception could not last forever, though when he married her he had been so incredibly foolish as to believe that it could.

'Darling, you've brought me heaven,' he said, and that other self of his stood and mocked the words.

'I wish I understood you, Roland, but I don't suppose any woman who married a genius can expect to do that,' she said.

His arms closed round her suddenly, almost roughly.

'You're not to say things like that, Hermione. They make me feel—a worm. I'm not a genius. I don't seem to be anything anymore. Can't you see me as a man, understand me as a man, love me as a man? We could be happy, but we're not. You aren't any more happy than I am, are you?'

She met his eyes steadily, her own calm and clear, his tortured.

'No, I don't think I am,' she said slowly. 'Is everyone always reaching up after—the unattainable, I wonder? I scarcely know what I want. I love you, but . . .'

He caught up her words.

'Dear, that's just it. You can't forget that "but". You admit yourself that you are reaching after the unattainable. Can't you take life as it is, accept what offers and try and be content with it? I know I'm a disappointment to you, Hermione. You expected such great things of me, idealised me, thought far more of me than I deserved or could ever hope to live up to. Darling, can't we start again? Won't you try and see me as I am, just an ordinary mortal?'

It was a desperate appeal, and yet he knew that it would be useless. How could she see him as an ordinary mortal when her whole conception of him was of the minds of old Franz Baumer and poor, crippled May Carter, wrapped up in the body of Roland Wade?

She smiled, and if he had needed proof of the uselessness of his plea, that smile would have provided it. It was frankly disbelieving.

'I know you better than you do yourself,' she said. "I have read about men of genius before. They all have these fits of depression, of unbelief in themselves, of certainty that they will never create anything again. I'm not going to despair. I believe in you, my dear, and I'm going to make you believe in yourself again – or wait in patience until you do. Once the divine spark is lit, it can never be quenched.'

In a last desperate clutching at a straw, he held her to him, kissed her with a hungry passion, tried to force forgetfulness on both of them.

'Hermione, love me! Let me love you! We're drifting so far apart, and soon there will be no return for either of us. Doesn't it make you afraid?'

He felt her instinctive defence yield to him gradually, and her lips were warm beneath his own.

'Don't go out tonight, Hermione. Stay with me here,' he said, and she made no attempt to stop him as, with one arm still around her, he stretched out for the house telephone and sent a message down to Mrs. Jeffson.

That night they seemed to have recaptured something of the idyll of their honeymoon months. As if by mutual consent, both of them avoided the subject of their earlier conversation. They ordered dinner to be sent to them in the sitting room of Hermione's suite, and she came to him there, a wrap of white lace and dark fur replacing her usual evening gown. In it she seemed infinitely more approachable, more intimate, less remote, and for a few hours they played the old game of love – but each knew it for a game, a brief respite, a truce which tomorrow, or the next day, must give way to warfare again.

Nothing had been altered. She still expected a new flight of genius from him. He knew how impossible it was.

Yet this one night was theirs for forgetfulness, theirs for memory.

13

And it was then that Gretel Baumer came back into his life.

He had almost forgotten her very existence, and if he remembered her at all it was as a thin, uninteresting child with great sad eyes and a mat of tow-coloured hair. He had supposed vaguely that she had become a nun, which he considered an excellent solution to the life-problem of a plain girl. He was, therefore, astonished and a little perplexed by a letter which, after being readdressed several times, eventually found its way to the breakfast table in Carlton House Terrace.

> *'Dear Mr. Wade,'* the Reverend Mother had written, and he could conjure up a vision of her from the stiff, angular, precise writing. *'Since it was you who originally placed Gretel Baumer in my charge, I feel it right to inform you that she is leaving the convent and taking up work in the office of the father of one of our pupils. We have decided that she is not likely to have a vocation, as we had hoped, though the convent is always open to her if she chooses voluntarily to return and enter on a novitiate. I should be glad to have an opportunity of seeing you before Gretel leaves my care, and shall esteem it if you will call at your convenience.'*

He saw himself with some amusement as the arbiter of a young girl's fate, but he could scarcely refuse so simple a service, reluctant though he was to meet again the daughter of Franz Baumer. Also he could not but be a little disturbed at the prospect of having her at large again, no longer a timid, heartbroken child but a girl of twenty odd.

Realising that a good deal of time had already been wasted in the readdressing of the letter, he decided to go that day, and duly presented himself at the remembered iron-studded door and asked for Miss Baumer. As he had half expected, it was the gaunt figure of the Reverend Mother who came to him, her black robes sweeping the ground, her piercing eyes seeming the only human thing about her.

'You are Mr. Wade?' she asked. 'I think I remember you, but it is a long time ago.'

'Over four years,' murmured Roland. 'You wrote to me about Gretel Baumer. I really have no authority with regard to her, you know. It was only that she was—well, rather a waif and I had known her father.'

'I understand that and remember the circumstances perfectly. Gretel has always remembered them, too, and thinks of you very kindly and gratefully,' said the emotionless voice.

Poor little kid, thought Wade, cast among such impersonal beings!

'Is she still with you?' he asked.

'Yes. I preferred to see you and talk to you before I let her go. She is a very capable and intelligent girl, Mr. Wade, but of course she is young and inexperienced and unspotted by the world.'

'Quite,' agreed Wade politely.

'I wish I could place her in the charge of some woman who would watch over her, but I know of no such woman, and Gretel herself is rather fiercely independent.'

For a second something almost human gleamed from the deep-set eyes and the thin lips softened to a smile.

Wade was half inclined to mention the fact that he had a wife, but he could not visualise Hermione and Gretel together.

'I should like to see her. I might be able to suggest something,' he said gravely, and the Mother tinkled a little bell which brought an elderly nun shuffling in her felt slippers to the door.

'Ask Gretel to come, please,' she was told, and shuffled away.

They sat in constrained silence until a light step and a quick tap at the door made them turn.

'Come in, my child,' said the grave voice, and Gretel entered, looked across at Wade in a moment's uncertainty, and then smiled.

He stared at her. In an instant the vision of the shrinking, tow-haired child fled forever and in her place was this slender, graceful girl, her ash-blonde hair brushed severely back and coiled in the nape of her neck, her face a little pale and dominated by a pair of wide, dark eyes. No one by any stretch of imagination could have called her pretty. She was not even good-looking, judged by the accepted standards of regular features and consistency of colouring. Her hair was too ashy and lustreless, her features not clear-cut, her mouth too wide and generous, her eyes so black that, set in her pale face, they were startling and disconcerting. Yet it was a face at which one would look and turn to look again, a face about which one would conjecture and wonder.

She was dressed so simply that the navy blue, high-necked frock with its spotless collar and cuffs were almost conventual, and it was this as much as anything which gave her an air of virginity, of essential purity and innocence.

After that smile, which irradiated her whole face and gave it a sudden charm of its own, she came across to him, walking lightly, assuredly, and held out her hand.

'Mr. Wade!'

Her voice was quiet and soft and warm. It seemed to embrace him as her smile had done.

'Gretel – a most unexpected Gretel,' he said, and it was impossible to resist that smile and handshake.

She laughed, and there was that same warmth and charm in her laughter.

'But really Gretel,' she said. 'It has been four years, you know. Four years do a lot to scraggy and frightened little girls.'

The Reverend Mother watched them with her calm, impersonal gaze. Gretel had been useful to her and was beloved of the pupils in the convent school and by most of the nuns –

too much beloved. There was too much of the rebel in her, too great an independence, too definite a personality to be altogether acceptable in a place where humanity had to be moulded into pattern.

'What have you been doing all the time?' he asked.

He had forgotten the silent onlooker, so amazed and intrigued was he with this unexpected Gretel.

She turned to flash a smile at the woman at her side and then looked back at Wade.

'Learning and teaching and being very happy,' she said simply.

'Yet you want to go away from here, out into life?'

'Yes. Reverend Mother agrees that is best. I have no vocation.'

'What exactly does that mean?'

'No desire or aptitude for the life of a nun.'

He looked at her, at the wide dark eyes, at the generous mouth, at the vigour of her erect young body, and thought of the quiet, creeping figures of the nuns with their strings of beads and their downcast eyes.

'So you are going boldly out to a job,' he commented. 'Can you hold one down? Are you qualified?'

She smiled again.

'Why, yes. I told you I had been learning. Reverend Mother has had me taught shorthand and typewriting and bookkeeping, and I have acted as secretary to the convent for a year. I am going to into the office of a shipping company in Leadenhall Street. It is arranged that I shall start next Monday – that is, if you agree.'

He made a gesture disclaiming responsibility as he smiled back at her.

'My dear, where do I come in?' he asked. 'I haven't any right of jurisdiction over you!'

The quiet voice of the Reverend Mother broke in on them. He noticed how cold and lifeless it sounded after the girl's warm tones.

'Your name is recorded in our books as Gretel's guardian, Mr.

Wade,' she said.

He laughed.

'I wasn't aware I had that honour,' he said.

'It was necessary before we could accept a girl of her age,' said the Mother. 'The guardianship ended when she became twenty-one, of course, but I felt it would not be right to let her leave our care without notifying you. Am I to consider that you agree to her doing so?'

'Why, of course. I couldn't very well object, seeing that I have ignored her very existence for so long. Is there anything for me to do about it? Any—fees or anything?' he asked a little awkwardly.

'No, nothing. Gretel has more than earned her living for some time, and she will have a reasonable salary from Messrs. Garner.'

'I see. She—she will have to find rooms, of course?'

'Mr. Garner has arranged that. She is going to a girls' hostel in Kennington.'

The conversation seemed to have ended, and Wade rose, rather at a loss what to do or say. It was impossible to suggest, under the forbidding eye of the Mother, that they should meet again, and yet he had an odd reluctance to part from this Gretel.

She solved the question herself in her direct, fearless way.

'I should like you to know how I get on, Mr. Wade,' she said. 'You were so kind to me that I have never been able to feel quite a stranger to you.'

He glanced at the older woman and sensed rather than saw her disapproval of Gretel's outspoken manner, and it gave an added warmth to his own reply. They seemed linked and outside the cold life of the convent.

'I shall most certainly want to know about you,' he said. 'Will you telephone me one day? This is my number,' writing it down on a page of his notebook and tearing the slip out for her. He scarcely knew why he did not give her his card except that he had an unreasoning desire to keep her apart, even then, from his life in Carlton House Terrace. She seemed part of his real life, of himself, and not of Lady Hermione Wade's husband.

She tucked it away and held out her hand.

'I shall certainly do so,' she said. 'Goodbye.'

Eyes and hand met him warmly, frankly, and he felt again that link between them.

'Rather *au revoir*, isn't it? I've been too negligent a guardian as it is.'

As if by mutual consent he and Hermione had declared a truce, and neither of them, by word or look, reminded the other of what lay in their secret thoughts. Wade hoped she had either forgotten or accepted the situation, and Hermione cherished the hope that he would find the long-delayed 'inspiration' now that she had shown him her earnest desire.

They had spent much of the year in England, either in London or at Heseldene, on which much money and thought had been expended, but she suddenly decided that she wanted to go in search of sunshine.

'The Murray-Lisles have asked us to join them in Cairo and go up the Nile with them,' she said, looking up from a letter she had been reading when he came in a day or two after his visit to the convent. 'Would you like to go?'

He hesitated. It would mean a renewal of the companionship which of late had been embarrassing to them both, so far had they drifted in their thoughts from each other. It was as if a barrier had been erected by her ambitions for him and his inability to fulfil them. He knew that the Murray-Lisles never lost consciousness of his social inferiority to them, and that fact added to his dislike of accepting further hospitality from them.

Hermione saw his hesitation and was quick to place on it the construction she desired.

'You are thinking it will interfere with your plans for work?' she asked.

He caught at that chance of escape.

'Well, any sort of work would be impossible if I were touring Egypt, especially as Mrs. Murray-Lisle's guest,' he agreed.

'Would you mind terribly if I went without you, Roland? It

would only be for about three months, and I should make a point of being home for Christmas,' she suggested.

Not even to herself would she admit that she would be relieved of a certain amount of strain if they parted for a while, but she let a little sigh slip from her as he agreed in his easy way.

'I think that would be the best plan,' he said. 'After all, you have been chained to England all the year and we haven't had much sunshine. You go, dear. I shall be all right.'

'The servants will be here to look after you, of course,' she said. 'I can picture you with bachelor parties, too,' with a laugh that hid a slight embarrassment. Neither dare admit that the parting would be welcome. That admission would fling aside a curtain behind which were hidden unnameable things. They must go on pretending, even to themselves, lest the curtain so much as quiver.

'I don't suppose I shall feel very gay without you,' he said, but the words did not ring true and he wished he had left them unsaid.

A fortnight later she had gone. It was like the departure of royalty, he thought with a grim smile. First had gone the luggage, piles of it, with one of the footmen to superintend it. Then Germaine had gone with a dressing-case, Hermione's jewels, in a flat leather case, strapped to her wrist. Next had gone Martin Hale, who was going to Marseilles on business and had persuaded Hermione to make that part of her journey by air. He was to meet them with the tickets and passports, after seeing that all the arrangements were complete.

Lastly, in the Bentley which was to go overland and be shipped to Alexandria, went Hermione and her husband, his sole job being to look after her and see her off. She wanted to add his own sports car to the retinue to take him back from the aerodrome, but he decided against it.

'We look like a royal procession already,' he had told her laughingly.

'But how will you get back?' she asked.

'Darling, how many times have I to remind you that there *are* people, quite a lot of them, who manage to get about without private cars? There are such things as buses, and I have also a quite useful pair of legs.'

'Oh well – all right,' she surrendered with a smile. 'You know, I am feeling quite sentimental about leaving you, after all. Sure you wouldn't like to come?'

'Just imagine the chaos it would create if I said "yes",' he teased her. 'No, my dear, let's be thoroughly modern and go our separate ways for the time being.'

'I shall be terribly in love with you when I come back, Roland.'

'That suggests something which gives one to think!'

'That I'm not in love with you now? You know I am. Only...'

'Only you're disappointed in me?' he asked.

'I want you to prove to me how wrong I am,' she said in a low voice. 'I think, for lots of reasons, we are wise to be parted for a little while. You can work in utter peace, just as you did in your bachelor days and I shall feel much kinder when I've had a little sunshine! Here we are at the airport, with Martin waiting.'

'I don't see the red carpet and the band,' he said.

She flushed and laughed.

'Darling, it's just the way I'm made,' she said.

'Not a bit of it. It's the way other people have made you,' he said rather grimly. He wondered if he could have loved her, really loved her, if she had been rid of all this panoply of her wealth.

He toyed with the idea of deserting the great house in which he had lived a life which had begun to pall. He had still a few hundreds of his own money left, for during the eighteen months of his marriage he had had no expenses save for clothes and very small personal necessities. Even his cigars and cigarettes had been provided for in the liberal budget of Hermione's housekeeping, and as he had always been an abstemious man, his club expenses were small.

On those hundreds he could live at least in freedom from the thrall of Hermione's money and the position he had to maintain as her husband. He would be glad to be rid even of Louis, whose quiet and efficient service often got on his nerves.

Then he remembered that he was expected to work at a new masterpiece in those rooms he had come to hate, and that although Hermione herself would not be there, plenty of her friends would be on the watch. Also he had undertaken to supervise certain alterations which were to be carried out in the larger reception-rooms. In fairness to Hermione he could not neglect what was almost the first service she had required of him. No, everything considered, he would have to remain in the place of his bondage for sleeping purposes, at least.

He lunched at a cheap little eating-place which he had frequented in his working days, finding considerable pleasure in the experience and chatting with one and another of his onetime acquaintances who had not even known his name, but who remembered his face as he remembered theirs. It was refreshing to realise that they did not know him as the husband of Lady Hermione Wade, but merely remembered him for himself.

He drank his coffee in leisurely enjoyment and then strolled out into the wintry sunshine again, feeling very much his own man. There was a new film being shown at a converted theatre and he went to see it for the sheer pleasure of staying away from Carlton House Terrace hour after hour without even ringing up to say he was doing so, and a girl in the picture reminded him of Gretel Baumer, the new Gretel with her deep eyes and warm smile.

She had not telephoned him as he had expected her to do, and, on an impulse, he went into a telephone box when he left the theatre and looked up the shipping firm whose name he remembered.

A man's voice answered him and he asked for 'Miss Baumer' rather self-consciously, but the next moment he heard hear voice.

'You, Gretel? This is your guardian speaking. Why have you never rung me up?' he demanded with a mock sternness.

She laughed. He remembered her laughter, too. In fact, he

was surprised at the impression she had made on him in those few minutes of their interview.

'Forgive me, Mr. Wade. I've been so busy and it has all been so strange. And – I wasn't really *quite* sure that you meant it.'

'Of course I did. What time do you leave tonight?'

'Five o'clock.'

'It's nearly that now. May I come and call for you?'

'Heavens, no! It simply isn't done. I'll meet you outside the Mansion House at quarter-past, if you like,' she said.

'I do like, most emphatically. Are you a punctual person or a fashionable one?'

'Have you forgotten that I've lived, moved, and had my being to the sound of bells for four years?' she laughed. 'Quarter-past five,' and she rang off.

'What do we do? Have tea first, or shall we make it dinner in an hour or so?' he asked when they met.

'I've never been out to dinner in my life,' said Gretel. 'I'd like to do that.'

'Splendid. A cup of tea first?'

'We have that in the office. I still feel frightfully thrilled at talking about my office,' she admitted with her warm laughter. 'I think you would like me to change my dress if I am going out with you, wouldn't you?'

'You look very nice as you are,' he said, contrasting her almost unconsciously with the girls to whom he had become accustomed. Gretel was like a breath of country air to a town- dweller.

She looked down at herself deprecatingly.

'Not nice enough to go out with you,' she said. 'Will you come with me and wait whilst I change? I bought myself a frock with last week's money.'

'For me?'

'Well—yes,' she admitted, and their friendship strode forward with the laugh that confession raised.

'Will they let me in at a girls' hostel?' he asked as they walked to the bus stop.

'I've moved from there,' said Gretel calmly. 'I didn't like it. I have taken a furnished room, a bed-sitting room.'

He stared at her. She was a most unexpected person.

'What about the Reverend Mother? Surely she doesn't approve of that.'

She looked at him in some perplexity.

'But I don't have to ask her, do I? I didn't think of that. It was horrid at the hostel. The girls stared and had bad manners and it was not quite clean, so I just went.'

He gave a shout of laughter. He realised he need have had no concern for her ability to take care of herself, for all her convent life.

'You're great, my dear.'

'Did I do wrong, Mr. Wade? Ought I to have asked anyone?'

'Of course not – though you might have told me, seeing that I have so recently surrendered my guardianship.'

She looked at him with grave enquiry in her dark eyes. Then she laughed again.

'You're teasing me,' she said. 'Look, here is our bus. We go to Victoria Station.'

Her room was in one of the many streets of 'has-beens' in the vicinity of the great station, and he frowned as she opened the door and invited him to follow her. There could be little doubt as to the type of house it was, and every door they passed on their upward way looked as if it had a furtive secret.

She was at the top, in a large attic which caught all the light and air obtainable through its wide-opened window, but even so it was dark and stuffy.

'This is my room,' she said, 'but you'll have to wait outside whilst I change. I'll give you a chair.'

He thought about her a lot whilst he waited, and by the time she opened her door to him again, a little fluttered and excited by the new frock, he had made up his mind.

'Gretel, you can't live here,' he said.

'It isn't awfully nice, is it? A girl at the office told me about this room being to let, and I thought it would do whilst I made up my mind where I want to live. I simply had to get away from that awful hostel. This house is at least clean, and I can keep my own room as I like.'

'I'll find you something better,' he said. 'Got your coat? It's cold out.'

She gave a little sigh.

'What's that for?' he asked.

'Oh, just—you give me a feeling of belonging,' she said. 'It seems so long since I belonged to anyone. At the convent no one owns anything and no one belongs to anyone, except to God – and I never seemed even to belong to Him. I was really a misfit there though they were so kind to me and I loved some of the nuns. I shall have to wear this coat. It's all I've got, but it's warm if not very beautiful.'

He helped her into the serviceable tweed, and followed her down the stairs.

He took her into Soho, to one of the little restaurants where one goes solely to eat and talk, and he liked to watch her taking stock of everything, commenting now and then in her own rather dry fashion, sipping her wine and smiling across the rickety little table at him.

'You're spending a fortune on me, Mr. Wade,' she said. 'You haven't told me a thing about yourself, what you're doing and how you're getting on. Are you still playing in the dance band?'

He realised with a shock that she still visualised him as he had been before the production of his first play, and with that thought came the memory of how he had acquired that play.

'No,' he said slowly, as she waited for him to speak. 'I—I left that some time ago.'

'What are you doing now then? Another band?'

'No. I—as a matter of fact, I am not doing anything at the moment,' he said.

Her face expressed concern.

'I'm so sorry. I ought not to have asked. But I shouldn't have come with you and let you spend money on me like this when you're out of a job. Oh, why did you let me?'

He smiled at her anxious face.

'My dear, that's nothing. I'm not broke or anything like that. I can quite afford it, really.'

'Oh, Mr. Wade, are you sure? I feel terrible about it.'

'Please don't. Everything is all right. And do you really have to call me Mr. Wade? I call you Gretel, you know, and it makes me feel terribly old to have you call me by my surname. I've got a Christian name, you know.'

'I know, but – you see, I've thought of you all these years as Mr. Wade and I can't imagine calling you anything else.'

'I'm flattered to think you've remembered me at all,' he said, filling her glass again. The wine was making her eyes bright and flushing her pale cheeks.

'Remembered you? After you were so kind to me? You're all I've had to remember, you see, except my father. How could I possibly forget all you did for me?'

He wished he could forget the way he actually had treated her and her dead father. Well, now that she was out in the world again, he must do what he could to make it up to her. First and foremost she must be found some decent place in which to live.

He spoke of that again when he took her back to the furtive street near Victoria, she having refused his invitation to a theatre on the score of expense whilst he was out of work.

'Will you let me find you a better place to live in, Gretel? This is a beastly hole and not the sort of street you should be in at all.'

'I can't afford a lot of rent,' she said hesitatingly.

'You shan't pay any more than you do here. Will you let me? I've got more time than you.'

'Why should you bother?' she asked.

He took her hand in his.

'Just now you said something very sweet to me. You said you had a feeling of belonging. Well, you do belong to me, don't you?'

'I don't really – but I'd like to pretend I do,' she said, and her voice shook a little.

He realised that she felt deeply those things which she

allowed herself to feel. She was a woman who would live strongly but probably unhappily. It doesn't do to feel anything overmuch.

'Then pretend it, my dear, will you? And promise me that you will let me get you away from here?'

'All right. It's terribly nice of you—Roland. But you're not to let it cost you anything. I do so hope you'll get a job soon.'

'You're a very nice person to know, Gretel. Good night, my dear.'

'Good night. I'm so glad I belong,' she said breathlessly and slipped into the house quickly and closed the door behind her.

14

When Hermione went away, the very last thought in her husband's mind was of another woman. Yet within a month it was an impossibility to consider an existence which did not hold Gretel.

He had found her another room in a tall, old house in Chelsea. He had passed it on the way to Diana's shop and more than once had let his imagination picture the sort of people who had chosen the gay chintz curtains with little Dutch figures on them and who always kept bowls of fresh flowers on the window-sills. In the spring there were bowls of hyacinths and daffodils growing on the ledges, and in the summer the front door was usually open to let one catch a glimpse of old oak panelling, a carved, age-blackened treasure chest and some pieces of dully gleaming pewter. A fat black cat was usually sunning himself at one or other of the windows and periodically a family of puppies, assorted, clambered up and down the steps, where a guard of wire-netting limited their activities.

Curtains – cats – puppies – flowers – all looked perpetually clean and bright and comfortable, and when, a day or two after his first evening with Gretel, Roland saw a small notice 'Room to let' pinned to one of the chintz curtains, he stopped his car and climbed the spotless steps.

Mrs. Dormer matched her house, for she was clean, bright, and comfortable, and the next day he brought Gretel, bag and baggage, to occupy the large back room which the good lady, a little tremulous and apologetic, had said they had decided to let as 'times are so hard with *him* out of work and never likely to get anything else at his time of life', with a succession of nods towards the kitchen regions which they translated as being also in the direction of Mr. Dormer.

'The young lady can always use my front sitting room if so be as she has visitors, sir,' she explained with a meaning look at him and a smile which suggested romance.

They laughed and looked at one another.

'Well, she probably will,' agreed Roland, and he was tactful enough to leave all the money matters to Gretel, already aware of her fierce independence.

Thereafter came many small matters to engage his attention on her behalf. There was a shelf for her books, of which she had a number, most of them her father's and beloved for his sake, a few religious books given to her by the nuns and a dozen or more cheap editions of famous novels which she had bought herself.

Together, and with Mrs. Dormer's admiring consent, they turned the room into the semblance of a sitting room, disguising the bed with covers which Gretel made and building at its head a rough bookshelf made after a design which Gretel had found in a magazine.

'This is exactly what I want, Roland, though it looks very posh in this picture,' she had said on the second evening of her occupation of the new room. He had called to see if she were comfortably established, and Mrs. Dormer had made coffee for him and served it in the 'parlour'.

He came to bend over the book with her, and he was glad that she could not see his face at that moment.

'It says that this is a room at Heseldene, the country home of Lady Hermione Wade. She's got your name. Of course I don't expect we shall make anything that looks like *that*, but we might get near enough to it if you could cut down that little old bookcase Mrs. Dormer says I can have. I expect that's a cupboard underneath the bookshelf,' observed Gretel, not noticing his distrait manner. 'I wonder what's kept in it?'

Roland could have told her that there was whisky and cigars.

Instead he laughed and turned the page, but there were more photographs of the house and even one which showed Hermione herself walking by the lily pool.

'Isn't she lovely?' asked Gretel, but there was no sound of envy in her voice. She was much too sensible to indulge in any wistfulness about Lady Hermione Wade and was engrossed for the time being in Gretel Baumer. 'Turn back to the bed arrangement, Roland. Do you think we could do it?'

'Probably. May I take the book and work it out?'

'Yes, do,' and he rolled it up and tucked it safely away in his overcoat pocket, afraid of what the letterpress might say, nor did he make an occasion for producing it again.

He could not have said what was his reluctance to tell Gretel of his marriage. At first he had scarcely realised that she did not know of it, and as the days went by it became increasingly difficult to tell her, and every day added to the difficulty of confession. She accepted so naturally his position in her own social class that it would be a shock to her to discover that he had been grafted into a world that held Lady Hermione Wade. It simply never occurred to her to connect the similarity of names, on which she had commented merely in passing.

And day by day she wound about him the strange fascination of her personality, her quiet, good sense, her simplicity of heart and manner, the warmth of her friendliness. They forgot that she had only pretended that she 'belonged'. It seemed that they had always belonged.

She talked to him frankly, as she had never talked to anyone in her life.

'In some ways I'm horribly ignorant of life, Roland,' she said as they sat and had their first supper in the now converted room, which Mrs. Dormer agreed was so much like a sitting room that there could be no harm in her entertaining a man in it. 'I don't mean I don't know the elementary facts. I know babies don't grow under gooseberry bushes and that marriage isn't a necessary preliminary to their arrival, and I had to learn to take care of myself long before my father died. What puzzles me is the way girls think of that sort of thing. In the office none of the girls seem to think it matters going away for weekends with men and forgetting all about them afterwards. It seems pretty awful to me but it must be because, as I say, I'm ignorant and behind the times.'

'I like you that way,' he said. 'Do you know, Gretel, I never cease to wonder how you existed within convent walls for so long. You're not the type to be meek and complacent and credulous and obedient.'

'I wasn't any of them, I am afraid. It used to puzzle and grieve them so that I just had to pretend to believe and to be devout, but—will you be terribly shocked, I wonder?'

'Nothing could possibly shock me, my dear,' he said. 'Go ahead.'

'It all seemed so silly and futile and impossible to me. I could never have become a Catholic, though I often wish I could. It must be very nice to light a candle in the real belief that the bit of burning wax would do all the priest says.'

'Why not believe it, m'dear, if it brings you any pleasure?' he asked in his indolent, charming voice.

'I couldn't get any pleasure out of something I knew to be false,' said Gretel.

'Oh, Lord, you too?' he groaned, half in mockery, half in bitterness.

'Why me *too*?'

'Oh – nothing. Let's go out, shall we? What about that film at the Empire?'

'No. You can't afford it, Roland,' she said decidedly.

'Oh, have it first and afford it afterwards. Come on.'

But as the time lengthened out, he became more and more oppressed by the knowledge of the things he hid from her, his marriage and, even more, his theft of her father's manuscript.

The actual hiding of his marriage from her worried him only because he hated to deceive her. The fact itself could not matter, for Hermione was hundreds of miles away and he was fulfilling the letter of his obligation to her by overlooking the house repairs and writing discursive, charming letters to her in reply to her own.

The real canker at his heart was the knowledge that he had stolen from Gretel, defrauded her, built the very fabric of his life on a lie which placed him where he was and left her working for a few pounds a week. Even had he been able to conceive a method whereby he could repay her, in actual material fact it was impossible. The thousands he had received from that and his subsequent production and from his novel, had melted like snow in June. Somehow Gretel's life must be made easier and smoother, though her independent spirit made it look a superhuman task.

As their friendship deepened and she came to look for his visits evening after evening, his voice on the telephone, his tall form on the pavement outside her office waiting to take her to lunch, it became obvious that he could not keep up this pose of being a man out of employment. Also that pose made it more difficult for him to help her, and she even began to insist on paying her half of the expenses of any outing they had, though such insistence gave rise to bitter strife between them and threatened to break a friendship which had become a part of their mutual and separate lives.

A fantastic solution came to him when, in reading his paper one morning, his eye strayed to an advertisement and remained fixed on it.

'Pianist required for Abe Sumpter's Masked Band, four afternoons and occasional evenings during winter months.'

Wade rang up the number quoted at the end of the advertisement.

Abe Sumpter offered him an interview, and he slipped a mask over his face before that shrewd Hebrew came to him. Briefly he gave his reasons, reasons which he knew would appeal, for the engagement was in an orchestra in a newly fashionable restaurant. He was a man well known in society, he explained, and his bearing and accent gave credence to the statement. He was temporarily embarrassed and also he would enjoy the fun of the thing. He must insist on being allowed to retain his incognito, however, and wished to be known merely as 'Mr. B.'

The young Jew caught at the idea as good publicity. Wade played to him in that superficially brilliant way of his, and at length he was engaged to play for the band at Domenico's on four afternoons a week at a salary of eight pounds with an extra pound for any evening on which he was required to play.

He rang up Gretel to tell her, and they dined at their favourite Soho restaurant to celebrate it. He told her of the ruse of the mask, though not his real reason for such secrecy.

'They'll be all over you if they take you for a real nob, Roland,' she laughed. 'I think it's a priceless idea and you're likely to make much more out of it than if you went simply as Roland Wade. By the way, your name must be quite a common one. It's always cropping up. Miss Alson at the office says that a man called Roland Wade has produced two successful musical comedies, though of course that was during the term of my incarceration! Odd that it should be your Christian name as well, isn't it? I suppose you haven't been getting famous behind my back, have you?' with a sudden, darting suspicion. He was always so well dressed and he had certainly acquired an air of affluence and well-being.

He laughed the question away.

'My dear, you know quite well that I could never compose even a nursery-rhyme tune! You must remember.'

'Yes, I do. Still—well, if you haven't, don't begin now.'

'Why not?'

She looked at him in her frank way with those deep, clear eyes of hers.

'Because that would take you so far away from me,' she said slowly, and he looked away, startled at what he saw flicker for a moment in her eyes.

'I don't want to go far either, little Gretel,' he said.

His new duties gave him an excuse for seeing less of her for a time, but he was restless and dissatisfied without her, and in the end he took up the broken habit of spending his evenings with her, sitting in her room with her, reading and smoking or just talking whilst she knitted endless garments and was supremely content to have him there – or else taking her to cheap seats at a theatre or a picture palace.

One evening he took her to a cabaret show, but she frankly disliked the atmosphere and was disgusted at some of the turns.

'Why don't you like it?' he asked.

'For one thing, we don't belong,' she said. 'You look as if you did, but I both feel and look like a fish out of water. I loved my frock until it displayed its deficiencies here, and now I shall never like it again and it's got to last me for the rest of the winter at least'I'll buy you another.'

'You can't afford it on eight pounds a week, and even if you could, do you think I'd take it?'

'Why must you be so darned independent? After all, I never bought your frocks when you were my ward, so why shouldn't I make up for it now?'

'If you really yearn to buy a girl a frock, there's one dancing on the stage now who could do with it,' she said.

He looked and laughed. He enjoyed her little pruderies, though he would not have had her different.

'I wonder how it is that, try as we may, we English can never succeed in capturing the spirit which makes the liberties of the Folies Bergères amusing in Paris but merely slightly vulgar here?'

'Indeed? What do you know about Paris and the Folies Bergères?' she demanded.

He made a grimace. He must be more careful not to give himself away. He hated lying to her, but when he made a slip it had to be done.

'I went there with a band once,' he said.

'I don't want to come to places like this again,' said Gretel calmly.

'Mademoiselle has only to speak!' he murmured mockingly, and she flushed and smiled her irradiating smile.

'Roland, how rude and ungrateful of me! I was always getting into trouble at the convent for saying what I think.'

They had risen to go, and he was slipping round her shoulders the simple little evening cloak which she had made for the occasion. His fingers touched her bare shoulder, and he knew that she quivered at the faint contact. He was playing with fire, but he could not resist it.

'I want you always to say what you think to me, my dear,' he said in a low voice.

Her eyes met his, a little afraid, a little excited, and she caught the collar of her cloak together with a convulsive gripping of her hands. Her breath came quickly from between softly parted lips.

He slid a hand beneath her arm and turned towards the door.

'We'll have a taxi, dear,' he said unsteadily. 'I've got two evenings with the band this week.'

She made no demur. There was something almost dreamlike in the way she followed him, let him help her into the taxi, heard him give the driver her address, and made room for him beside her.

He slid an arm about her and held her lightly, but he could feel her slender young body trembling, see the slight sway towards him of which he knew she was totally unconscious. It made him newly aware of her utter innocence and his own experience. It would be so terribly easy to take the sweetness of her.

Suddenly he tapped on the glass and motioned the driver to stop. 'Dear,' he said in a quick, rather breathless way, 'I'm going to send you home alone. I've—just remembered something I've got to do, a man I must see. Do you mind?'

The cab had already stopped, and the man was looking round enquiringly.

'Why, no – of course not,' said Gretel, startled. 'Take the taxi and let me go by bus, though. It will be quicker for you.'

'No. You go on.'

He opened the door of the cab and stood for a moment on the step, bending his tall head so that it was on a level with her own face.

'I wonder if you understand that I'm a mere man?' he asked her, and jumped out, closing the door on her amazed expression and the question which she had no time even to frame.

He paid the man for the journey.

'Set her down at the very door and wait till she's gone in, will you?' he asked, and the man, grinning to himself, nodded his agreement.

Gretel went slowly up to her room and sat down on the edge of her bed, her thoughts still a whirl of perplexity. What on earth had Roland meant?

She undressed and got into bed, and her last thoughts were of him and he wandered through her dreams, a figure of romance, the hero of adventures which, in her daytime thoughts, would have brought a flush to her cheeks and an incredulous denial to her lips.

And Roland paced his room for hours after she slept. He had never in his life been seriously in love, though his feeling for his wife had come so closely to it that he had believed it the real thing, chiefly because he was so anxious to believe it. He could not bring himself to believe now that this disturbing impression he had of Gretel meant that he was falling in love with her.

Gretel Baumer was just a nice little girl, sweet and unspoilt, and by way of making a hero out of him because he was the one and only man on her horizon. When Hermione came back, which should be in another three weeks' time, he would have to tell Gretel the truth as gently as he could and leave her to find other friends and a suitable romance of her own.

Yet the thought of Gretel with another man, Gretel engaged and married, Gretel with the babies she quite frankly admitted she longed for, gave him an unpleasant feeling which he knew was sheer jealousy. Why should he feel like that if Gretel were nothing but the 'nice little girl' he tried to think her? He told himself sternly that she must not be encouraged to go on falling in love with him as undoubtedly she was more than ready to do, but the mere recollection of her deep eyes, of her smile, of the quality of her voice when she spoke to him, of the way she looked at him, stirred his pulses.

This thing must not be. He had taken Hermione, with her wealth and position and the love which he knew that, in her own way, she gave him. He would not add to his perfidy by complicating their lives with Gretel.

He took from a drawer his wife's last letter, beautifully written in her clear, characteristic writing, every sentence turned and rounded, every word correctly chosen and conveying exactly what she meant it to convey. It was the letter of a close friend rather than of a wife, though she began it 'My dearest Roland' and ended it 'With dear love to you, Hermione'. Between those two more or less conventional expressions of sentiment ran only the concise, graphic account of her travels, with one or two anecdotes concerning the rest of the party, a witty commentary which was never malicious. She made no mention of her return, though she should be starting now to reach England by Christmas, as she had intended.

He sat down and wrote to her on the impulse of the moment, scarcely realising that he was asking her to throw him a lifeline.

I am lonely for you, he wrote. *Your letter gives no hint of your return, but the house is finished and very empty without you. I need you, Hermione darling. Send me a wire that I may begin to expect you and count the days.*

There was little else in the letter, and it was more simple and sincere than any he had so far written her, but by the time it reached the last address she had given him the party had moved on. Hermione had not greatly cared about the idea, but she was a guest and as such felt she could not embarrass her hosts by a refusal. The proposal was to spend at least a fortnight with the super-caravan which had been fitted out for them, but finally the period was lengthened out to a month on the invitation of a wealthy Arab who had been educated in England and was glad to offer the lavish hospitality of his oasis to the English party.

Wade's letter followed them to the edge of the desert and

was then flung into a post-bag with a number of others to await the return of a post-messenger employed by the party. When that worthy did finally return, however, he was so heavily laden with 'baksheesh' that he forgot entirely the little matter of the post-bag, so, that Hermione did not receive her letter until, months later, it was unearthed and forwarded to her in London.

Her own letter, apprising him of the desert scheme, reached him only a week before Christmas and he realised that it would be at least another month before she came home. He stood with the letter in his hand, staring down into the fire, seeing two faces – his wife's, calm, serene, beautiful and cold – Gretel's, not even pretty, but warm and glowing and vital, instinct with life and, if he dare to let it be, with love.

He crushed the letter and flung it into the heart of the fire where the flame leapt up and devoured both those faces he had conjured up.

During the past fortnight he had purposely seen little of Gretel. The hurt look which he knew would be in her eyes haunted him and he had to keep away from her by main force. Fortunately Abe Sumpter made increasing demands on him, and he could fill up every afternoon and every evening if he so desired. That provided him with an excellent excuse for not seeing Gretel, but he hated the weekends when he knew she must be watching and waiting.

At length, two days before Christmas, he saw her. She had come to the restaurant where he was playing, and his eyes were drawn irresistibly to where she sat at a table near him, quite alone, her plain dark suit and indifferent manner discouraging any unwelcome attentions which might be expected by a girl dining at such a place alone.

He knew she was watching him, and he felt suddenly that he must see her again, must talk to her, must see the light deepen in her eyes and hear the warmth of her voice, that low, throaty, infectious laughter of hers.

There was a pause between the numbers, and his fingers ran lightly over the keys in soft arpeggios for a moment. Then, lifting his head slightly and turning it towards her, he began to play. The other members of the band stopped tuning their instruments to 'give him a show', as was their custom now and then, but he played softly, the music almost drowned in the hum of conversation from the diners.

Gretel set down her glass, which had held lemonade, and let her hand stay on the table, arrested by the melody he played and by the memories it evoked. It was a song her father had written, part of that beloved opera of his which she had almost forgotten. She herself had penned in the words when he had laboriously translated them from the German in which he loved to write.

'Sweet, I never tried to make you
Just my own;
For I knew I must forsake you,
Leave you lone.
Could we not just live a little,
Smile a little,
Love a little?
We must only give a little,
Ask a little,
Take a little.
Sweet, I do not dare to make you
All my own.'

Playing softly, he watched her, saw her hand clench slowly and then open and lay inert against the white cloth whilst she lifted her head and turned it towards him. Her eyes were like deep pools, shadowed and still.

A few minutes later the band played their concluding number and rose with relief to pack up their music. Wade saw Gretel move, watched the waiter hurry to her with her bill, and then he turned to the 'cellist.

'Stuff my music into your case, Bennet, will you? I rather want to get away.'

'Sure. Cut along,' said the other, and Wade jumped down the

low platform and hurried to the small dressing-room at the back.

He caught Gretel just as she let the door swing behind her. Her face expressed no surprise. She had known, after he played that song, that he would come.

'Taxi!' he called, and the next moment she was seated in it, Wade beside her.

'Gretel! My dear,' he said, and laid his hand over hers. He felt it tremble for an instant. Then she turned her palm over so that her fingers curled into his.

'Did you mean—that song?' she asked him in a low voice.

'Yes, Gretel.'

She caught her breath sharply and then sat quite still, her fingers quiescent in his, and he watched her face in the flickering, changing light from buildings and from cars which passed them. She was pale but quite calm, and he saw that her eyes had shadows beneath them. They made her seem older, more of a woman than he had seen her until now, a woman who had already entered the borders of her heritage of pain.

He would have spoken, but she checked him with a quick word.

'Don't let's talk now, Roland. Let's just think what we want to say to one another and how to say it and presently we shall be—home.'

Without a word or a look, they knew that they had crossed the border of friendship and that henceforth and forever it would be impossible to recross it and stand where once they had stood.

She fitted her key into the door whilst he paid the driver, and she had already gone up to her room when he entered the house.

Mrs. Dormer came bustling out to greet him with a smile which held a faint reproach.

'We thought you'd forgotten us, Mr. Wade,' she said archly.

'Sorry. I have been very busy. May I pop up?'

'Oh, yes, of course. Shall I bring you coffee or anything?'

'No thank you,' and he was up the stairs in a few strides and behind the closed door with Gretel, facing her, their thoughts coming too quickly for utterance.

He came to her at last and took her hand in his.

'Dear, forgive me,' he said quietly. 'I didn't mean to hurt you.'

She lifted her candid eyes to his.

'Then why did you?' she said simply.

'I had no right to come,' he said in a low voice. 'I still have no right.'

She frowned a little.

'Was that why you played my father's song to me? You say you meant it. Why?'

He still held her hand in his, but it was listless and unresponsive now. He realised that she was feeling so acutely with her mind that her body scarcely felt the contact of his. He knew that he must tell her. The truth could not any longer be withheld.

'I've got to tell you why, and—it's going to hurt horribly, Gretel, my dear,' he said gently.

'I'm afraid I've given you the power to hurt me, haven't I?' she asked, smiling bravely though he heard her voice quiver.

'Gretel, you mustn't care like that – you mustn't. I'm married, Gretel.'

He could not look at her. He felt he could not bear to see her pain. Bitterly he regretted the uncontrollable impulse which had made him come to her again. She would have suffered in any case, but during this past fortnight she must have begun to get accustomed to it, must have been trying to persuade herself that whatever had been between them was ended.

He heard the caught breath, the quick step of involuntary recoil from the blow, and then there was utter silence in the little room which had framed their comradeship. The ghosts of it crowded about them and laid cold fingers on them.

It was Gretel who spoke first, and from her voice all the warmth and colour seemed to have fled. It was chill and dulled.

'Why had you to do that to me, Roland?'

'I didn't know you were going to care like this,' he said, and hated himself.

'Couldn't you have waited for me?' she asked. 'No, that's stupid, too. I think something in my mind has got muddled up. I am not being very sensible, am I?' and she conjured up the ghost of a smile, infinitely sad.

'I'd have given anything to spare you this, Gretel,' he said wretchedly.

'Never mind. You didn't make love to me, did you? You haven't anything to reproach yourself with. You don't love me, do you?'

He was silent, his mind busy with the crowded turmoil of his thoughts. What was the true answer to that question? He did not know. For perhaps the first time in his life he was being utterly honest with himself, struggling to be honest with her. He knew that he was strongly attracted to her, that she stirred him as no other woman had ever done, that he thought of her constantly when he was away from her and longed to be with her, that he was entirely contented when he was with her. He realised how deeply her pain had affected him, how bitterly he reproached himself for being the cause of it.

Was all this love?

'Dear, I don't know,' he said at last, very slowly, his eyes meeting hers at last.

She gave him again that brave ghost of a smile.

'Then you don't,' she said. 'You see, I know. Just let me say it to you this once and then not any more. I will lock it away. I don't belong either to the age or the type that swoons or goes into a decline through unrequited love. I shall get over it. Only—just at first it—hurts rather a lot.'

'Gretel, I'd better go,' he said abruptly.

She shook her head and walked across to her own chair, inviting him to take the one which had come to be regarded as his.

'No. Let's sit and talk and be friends again. Light the fire, please, and would you call down to Mrs. Dormer that we should like some coffee if she has any made?'

Amazed at her courage, loving her for her gallant bearing, he did as she asked him, lighting the gas-fire and then going to the door to ask for the coffee.

'Talk about something else for a little while, Roland – anything will do,' she said, and he realised how near breaking point she was.

He plunged into talk, aware that she heard only part of it, choosing a subject at random, embroidering it in a quick, amusing way he had caught from Diana and her friends until at length he had caught her attention and won a gleam of laughter from her sombre eyes.

Mrs. Dormer bustled in with the coffee, beamed on them as she set it down on a little table near Gretel and would have stayed to gossip at the slightest encouragement, which neither of them gave.

When they had finished it and Wade had carried the tray outside and come back to her, Gretel began to speak quietly and almost unemotionally.

'Shall we talk about it now, Roland, and find out just where we stand? Whether any sort of friendship is possible, or whether this is—the end?'

'Are you sure you want to, Gretel?'

'Yes. I've got to know. I couldn't stand being left to wonder and picture it and—make up all sorts of stories about it. Do you love her, Roland? Are you happy?'

The temptation to give way to the old, hackneyed tale of the neglected husband, the unhappy marriage, came to him, but he thrust it away. He would not stoop to that when Gretel was taking it so gallantly and finely.

'I think we are happy in our fashion, Gretel. Hermione is wonderful to me and I owe her more than I can ever repay.'

'Hermione?' She was startled, her memory catching at a half-forgotten scrap of information. The similarity of names had been sufficient to register an impression which otherwise she might never have noticed. 'You mean . . . ?'

She felt it too incredible to voice, but he nodded his head, his mouth twisting a little in bitterness.

'Yes. Lady Hermione is my wife – or rather, I am Lady Hermione's husband,' he said.

'Why do you say it like that? What is the difference?'

'Don't you realise that that is the inevitable result of anyone like me marrying into that class of society?' he asked curtly.

Gretel frowned. He was a stranger to her when he talked like this. He seemed to have gone far away from her and she did not know how to call him back. Neither could she begin to understand this marriage which had overturned her world.

'Why did you marry her, Roland? You don't love her,' she said at last.

He looked straight into her eyes, his own hard and cold, his mouth curved into bitterness. He meant to drink to the dregs this cup which he himself had mixed.

'She was very rich and the Lady Hermione Wakelyn, daughter of an earl. I was ambitious and I wanted her wealth and position,' he said.

Gretel drew a sharp breath of pain.

'No, Roland, no! Not like that!' she cried and made a little movement with her hands as if she could hold the idol which was trembling on its base, keep it from smashing into atoms at her feet.

'Just exactly like that,' he told her steadily.

She gripped her hands together and he saw the white of her knuckles, saw her eyes close and her face whiten, but she sat straight and stiff in her chair, summoning up all her forces, struggling with this horror. Then she opened her eyes and the tension relaxed.

'That is a hard knock to take, Roland,' she said quietly.

'You don't have to remember it, Gretel. You can forget it along with all the rest of me. You see I'm not worth the pain you've borne for me, am I?'

She gave him her frank, direct smile.

'Women seldom count the cost. If they did, none of them

would ever let themselves love,' she said.

He rose quickly from his chair and began to pace the room, afraid of her nearness, of her gentleness, afraid most of all of himself.

Thoughts of Hermione came too, crowding, insistent. All his life he had used women for his own ends. Hermione he had used more than any of them and had given her nothing for all he had been prepared to take. She, too, must come into his scheme of things; she, too, must have her share in the strange, new being which was evolving from all this strain and unrest.

He turned suddenly, his face very pale.

'Gretel, I'm going to make you hate and despise me,' he said.

She smiled at that, though the shadow did not lift from her eyes.

'That would be impossible,' she told him sadly enough.

'Then listen. Someone told you at your office that a Roland Wade had written two successful plays, musical plays. I denied that they had anything to do with me. I lied to you, Gretel.'

She opened her eyes in amazement.

'You—you mean you did compose them?'

'No. I never composed a note or a line in my life. Your father wrote them, both of them. I stole them. He entrusted to me with his dying breath a manuscript which he had tried to sell, his life-work, the opera he had spent years in writing, the opera he believed in. I sold it, Gretel. There was enough material for two productions in it. He called it *Summer Storm*. I called the two of them *Night in Gale* and *Maiden Errant*. I made money out of them, lots of money – your money, Gretel. Do you understand? They bear the name of Roland Wade. There is a book of poems, too, exquisite little things – and a novel. I did not write those either. A cripple girl wrote them, a girl with a twisted, deformed body and the mind of an angel. She loved me. I made her fall in love with me so that I could steal her mind, get her to work for me and publish her songs in what I called my play. She died. She committed suicide because I was coward enough to funk giving her the mere travesty of love which would have satisfied her. She was deformed, you see, and the delicately nurtured, highly bred, high-minded Roland Wade could not bring himself to touch a deformed girl. So she died – and sent me before she died the writings which afterwards became songs, poems, and a novel by Roland Wade.'

Gretel gave a little moaning sound and crouched back against the table, her hands gripping its edge, her body shrinking away from him as if the words that poured from him were whip lashes about her defenceless body.

'Don't—don't!' she whispered, scarcely aware that she spoke.

'You are beginning to understand me at last? Your father and this cripple girl made me what the world, including my wife, believes me to be – the young genius, playwright, author, poet! You out of all the world know me for what I am. Even I have never faced myself before. Believe me, I don't like the look of myself any more than you do!'

His voice broke on a note of bitterness, and for a moment there was no sound in the little room save the queer, jerked breathing of the girl who cowered against the table.

He came closer to her and stood looking relentlessly down into her suffering face.

'Is that enough? Now do you hate me enough to—let me go?'

She could not speak. She could do nothing but stare at him in that tragic fashion, stunned and helpless.

Wade turned on his heel and left her without another glance.

The strange, new being that was Roland Wade returned to his wife's house to find Diana waiting, impatient as ever at the waste of her time. She always maintained that, if she lived to be two hundred, she would not have found time to do all that she had in mind for a life's experiences.

'Hullo, Diana,' he said casually, scarcely knowing whether to be glad or sorry not to be left alone that night.

'Hullo yourself. Look here, brother-in-law, I'm throwing a party here New Year's Eve. OK with you?'

'Good heavens, Diana, you don't have to ask *me*! You've got much more right here than I have,' he said.

She laughed. He was always candid and at ease with her, and she appreciated it and probably understood him better than anyone else did. She could not explain satisfactorily his former reputation as a genius, but she shrewdly suspected that he had lost whatever powers he had possessed and would never regain them, whatever his wife's attitude or ambitions.

'We won't argue on that, seeing that today's nearly tomorrow. The fact of the matter is that I've had so many invitations to make merry on New Year's Eve and say goodbye to a most satisfying year that I've hit on the plan of turning the invitations back to the givers and having them all here.'

'Do the servants know, and approve?'

'No, but they will. I've got Jarvis on a bit of string and what he says goes. Give me a drink, there's a love. A very pale whisky. You look as if you wanted a strengthener yourself, old son. What's up?'

'I've had—a bit of a jerk,' he said, turning away from her probing eyes to open the cocktail cupboard.

'Worrying about Hermione?'

'And other things,' he said, measuring out the very small quantity of whisky which she considered a drink.

She took the glass from him and continued to regard him contemplatively. Rumours had reached her ears, rumours which she had been too loyal to trouble about, but which had not come and gone without leaving a slight trace in her mind. It was impossible for him to go about with Gretel as he had without someone seeing him.

'I've always rather liked you, you know, Roland,' she said conversationally.

He smiled and raised his own glass to her.

'I thank you, small sister, and reciprocate the sentiment,' he said.

'I still don't think you're good enough for Hermione, but you're better than some people would have been. You've played the game with her although, for some extraordinary reason, you've never really loved her,' she said calmly.

His lips opened for a disclaimer, but the next moment his mind pushed aside the broken pieces of the plaster cast and stood clear of them.

'No, I don't think I have,' he said slowly.

'Yet she must be terribly attractive to a man. She's so lovely.'

'She's—too perfect, I suppose, for anyone as imperfect as I am,' said Roland. 'Still, we can't sit here and discuss her, can we? And I'm very fond of her. You don't doubt that, do you? And grateful to her for more than I can ever repay.'

'That's all the wrong way round, you know. Roland, can't you really bring out another play, write another book or something?'

'No.'

He made no attempt to enlarge upon that curt monosyllable and she was not the type to seek to force a confidence. She believed too profoundly in the right of the individual.

'All right. I'd better go, I suppose, or tongues will begin to wag. They're never still quite, you know, and it's been a dull season for the scandalmongers.'

She met his eyes very fully as she spoke, and he wondered whether she meant to convey a warning by that measured little speech.

'I agree with you,' he said steadily.

'Come and see me off the premises? And call in and see Stella and me next time you're out Chelsea way, won't you?'

He reflected on that parting speech, when she had gone, linking it up with her previous one, sure now that she had heard rumours and was warning him. She was friendly towards him, but her passionate love and loyalty were, as they always had been, Hermione's. She would stand for nothing that might even remotely hurt her half-sister.

And Gretel would hurt Hermione, he knew that – not consciously nor intentionally, but by reason of her very existence.

Well, he had definitely prevented any possibility of that hurt by his confession to Gretel. She could never forgive him, and he knew well enough to be quite sure that his secret was safe with her and would never be given to the world.

He sat brooding until long after the servants had gone to bed and the house was quiet. Step by step he reviewed his life, saw it in all its nakedness, its scheming, its lies, its grasping greed, and he did not like the vision. Seen from its lowest standpoint, what had it brought him? The empty life with Hermione, her gradually growing distrust of him, a distrust which he could do nothing to dispel – the ever-present fear of discovery – the need for more lies, more scheming and planning, the elaborate rebuilding of the sham which the world knew as Roland Wade – either that or the breaking up of his life with Hermione.

He had been sincere in his desire to repay her for her generosity and her love towards him. He realised now, in his self-abasement, that the only thing he could do for her was to replace the plaster, remodel the cast, cover again the man who had stirred to life and whom, he knew, would never now lie dormant and quiescent again.

It was with bitterness of spirit that he at last turned off the lights and went up through the silent house to the luxurious room which Hermione's love had made possible for him.

He could not make up his mind to relinquish his position with the masked band, though the primary reason for it, the need to keep up appearances to Gretel, had gone. He realised that he would be in a quandary if he did not free himself before Hermione came home, and yet he clung to those hours as the one thing in his life of which he was not ashamed in this new, struggling soul of his. In spite of the aura of romance and legend which had gathered about his intentionally mysterious person, the other members of the band had come to meet him as one of themselves, looking on him as a good fellow, expecting no more of him than had Micky and his Merry Men in the old days. He enjoyed the work, and the few pounds he drew on Friday afternoons were sweeter to him than any of the great sums which he had received from his stolen plays or from the lavish hands of Hermione.

When a cable from her told him that she expected to be at home within a week, flying from Alexandria, he made up his mind that he would have to give Abe Sumpter notice. Before he could carry out his purpose, however, something occurred which drove every other thought from his mind and left him stunned. .

He had come in from an evening engagement with the band to find Jarvis waiting for him with a message.

'There is a man waiting to see you, sir, in the library. He has called twice before when you were out, but this time he insisted on waiting, though I said you might be late.'

'Who is it?' he asked indifferently, divesting himself of coat and silk muffler and handing them to the butler.

'Says his name is Carter, sir.'

Wade's hand paused in mid-air and he forgot to let it drop again.

'Carter? What sort of a man is he, Jarvis?' he asked quickly.

'Smallish man, sir – not a gentleman at all, sir.'

Wade drew a deep breath and his hand dropped slowly to his side.

'I don't want to see him, Jarvis,' he said.

'I am sorry, sir, but I don't think he'll go away. I could have him put out, of course, but . . .'

'No, no. You can't do that. All right. I'll see him,' and he walked across to the library door his mind in a turmoil. What on earth had brought May Carter's father back into his life? He had no possible doubt of the identity of the unwelcome visitor.

'Well, Mr. Carter?' he asked briskly, once inside the room with the door shut and the pale-faced little man rising to face him.

'It isn't well, Mr. Wade. It isn't at all well,' he said, and there was no mistaking the aggression in his voice and attitude. This was no longer a father stricken with grief, but a man with a purpose, and a purpose that boded no good to his listener.

'I am sorry to hear that,' said Roland courteously, biding his time. 'Anything I can do for you?'

'Oh yes. There's something you can do all right. Ever seen anything like this before, for instance?' and he pulled from the voluminous pocket of his bulging coat a bundle of papers, loosely fastened at the corners and frayed at the edges as if they had been in existence some time. Wade noticed that the pages had been crumpled and carefully smoothed out again. Then he bent more closely, caught a word or two here and there, a name, a remembered phrase, and slid out a hand to take the papers.

Instantly the little man caught them back, a nasty sneer on his face.

'Oh, no you don't, Mr. Wade – *Mr. Roland Wade*, the famous author. I happen to know you a bit better than I did last time we met, and you don't lay your hands on these. You can look at them, though, if you want to. Perhaps you've seen enough, eh, *Mr. Roland Wade?*'

Wade knew what they were. They were the original draft of the book May Carter had written, the book of which the fair copy had come to him, the book which he had entitled *The Silken Tassel*, the book which, on one of the shelves of the very room in which they stood, bore his name in silver lettering beneath the title.

'Kindly explain yourself and this extraordinary visit, Mr. Carter,' he said, his throat dry and constricted.

'I'd have thought these papers explained both, Mr. Wade. You'd better take another look,' and he held out the bundle, gripping them with offensive firmness between his finger and thumb whilst he flicked over the pages, pausing long enough to let Wade read here and there. He did it with a sickening consciousness of Nemesis come upon him.

'Well?' he asked, still waiting for the other to take the initiative. He did not intend to give himself away, though he had no hope of being able to avert catastrophe. The little man had mean and crafty eyes, and he had moreover a real and bitter grievance against the man who was in his power.

'My daughter wrote these pages, my daughter May, Mr. Wade, my daughter you were so kind to, taking her rides and giving her swell dinners and things.'

'Well? What if she did?' fenced Wade boldly. 'What has that to do with me?'

From another pocket the little man brought out a book and laid it on the table.

'And who wrote *those* pages, Mr. Roland Wade? Eh? Look,' and he opened it at a page whose corner had been turned down, thrust it into Wade's hand, and turned feverishly over the loose sheets he held until he found what he sought, and began to read, slowly, carefully, letting every word have its full significance.

Automatically Roland followed the words on the printed page of the book which bore his name, and when Carter's voice ceased on a triumphant note, he laid the book down with fingers which trembled slightly.

'You're in a nasty position, Mr. Roland Wade.'

'Merely because you happen to have become possessed of a rough draft of my novel?'

'Written in my daughter's handwriting with her corrections and alterations? How do you explain that, Mr. Roland Wade, author?'

The reiteration of his name in that contemptuous tone had become maddening, and Wade had much ado to keep his hands off the man.

'You know that your daughter did secretarial work for me, surely?' he asked, playing desperately, even though he knew in his heart that the game was up.

'Perhaps I do. These papers of hers are dated though, and I've got a diary of hers, too, that refers to them and mentions when she'd finished a chapter. *And* those dates begin before she ever met you, Mr. Roland Wade. Can you explain that away, eh?'

Wade decided to give it up and make the best deal he could.

'Well, I don't admit anything, but, as you know quite well, I am not in a position to have unpleasant rumours attached to my name. I have my wife to consider.'

Carter smiled nastily.

'Ah yes, your lady wife. I am quite sure she wouldn't like to hear about poor May Carter, apart from this book, would she, Mr. Wade?'

'How much do you want for those papers?' asked Wade curtly.

'I'm not selling them. My poor dead child's own writing, that's not for sale. Oh no,' and he put the papers back safely into his pocket, ostentatiously closing the flap on them.

'I see. Blackmail,' commented Wade, furious and helpless. 'Well, I may as well be frank with you. I am not a rich man, Carter. I doubt if I have more than a hundred pounds to my name at this moment.'

'Your wife, the Lady Hermione, is a very wealthy woman, Mr. Wade.'

'Kindly leave my wife out of it,' snapped Wade.

'Certainly, if you arrange for me to do so,' said Carter smoothly.

'You damned hypocrite, with your posing and your pretended grief about your daughter's death!' burst out Wade. 'You're nothing but a dirty blackmailer trying to make a living out of her.'

'I don't think we'll start calling one another names. I've got a few I could use for you, stealing a girl's honour and then making money out of her once she's done herself in.'

'I never stole her honour, and you know it,' said Wade furiously.

'Do you think I believe all a doctor says, especially when important people like Mr. Roland Wade have an interest in what they say? Pah!' and the man almost spat on him in his scorn. 'Now enough of this. I want five hundred pounds, and I want it at once.'

'And if I don't see my way clear to letting you have it?'

'Then I'll start an action against you for stealing my daughter's novel, and don't forget that I've got proof. I don't know how much you made out of that book, but five hundred'll do for a start.'

'It will have to do for a finish as well, I am afraid,' said Wade curtly. 'I doubt if I have as much as that all told now.'

'You'll have to get it then. I want that five hundred, in Bank of England notes, by ten o'clock tomorrow or these papers and my daughter's diary go to my solicitors.'

Perhaps he saw murder look out of Roland Wade's eyes at that moment, but he only smiled and faced him without a tremor.

'It'd be no good to do me in, Mr. Wade, either. My boy Joe knows all about this, and he knows what to do if I meet with any accident,' and he turned to pick up his hat from a chair. 'I shall be in the shop tomorrow morning myself. Good night, Mr. Roland Wade,' and he went out, treading lightly like a cat and leaving his victim silent and desperate.

What on earth was he to do? He might possibly rake up the five hundred pounds, and there were still a few royalties on foreign editions due to him, but what of the future? Carter had as good as admitted that this was only the start, and his demands would probably increase as time went on. He dare not go to the police for protection, for there still remained the boy Joe, who, not having been a party to the blackmail, would at once tell all he knew to the papers, or to his publishers, who, in duty bound, would have to investigate the whole business.

In the morning he did what he had known from the first he would have to do. He drew out five hundred pounds from his bank, leaving himself with little more than ten pounds in hand, and went again to the dark little shop in Charing Cross Road which he had never thought to see again. The pale ghost of May Carter haunted it, peered at him with her great dark eyes from behind the counter, touched him with her thin, delicate hands as he passed the bundle of crisp notes over to her father, and he could have sworn that eerie laughter followed him as he turned and almost ran from the shop into the icy January morning.

Terrified of being left penniless and hating with that new self of his to draw on the joint account which Hermione had always kept open for him at her bank, he decided not to withdraw from the masked band. That money at least was not tainted; it was

219

clean and his own beyond anybody's right to question.

Towards the end of the month Hermione returned, gracious and lovely and yet oddly aloof. During her absence she seemed to have built a wall behind which to hide herself, an intangible thing which he sensed during their first hour together and which grew more impregnable as the days went by.

The house was filled with life and movement again, with dinner-parties and dances and bridge, with the coming and going, the plans and the endless ringing of the telephone inseparable from the life of a society hostess. Little Mrs. Jeffson trotted about like a fussy hen, her feathers often ruffled, her one chick more than she could manage at times.

To Wade himself Hermione was charming, but he was a stranger and she evidently intended that he should remain so. In her calm, inscrutable eyes he could read nothing, and not even when they were alone did she give him any clue to her real feelings towards him. It was as if she had with intent placed this separation between them to mark the end of one phase of their life together and the beginning of another.

Only once did she touch on the subject of his 'work', and then so indefinitely that only he could recognise the implication.

'Margaret joined us for a weekend in Malta,' she said. 'She is on holiday until Mr. Hallam recalls her to begin work on her new play. I understand that Redruth Miller has been asked to write one specially for her.'

'He understands her technique perfectly, I always think,' said Roland gravely.

There were others present, and for a moment their two pairs of eyes met and then parted again. It was as if Hermione, in that speech, had released him from his obligation towards her, had accepted it and withdrawn herself.

She had been home some three or four days when they met outside her bedroom door. She had been out but he, required to fulfil an engagement with his band, had made an excuse which she had accepted indifferently, too indifferently.

'I am rather tired. I shall read for a little while in front of my fire and then go to bed,' she said when they met like that.

'Hermione . . .'

He longed to be on the old footing with her, to be able to talk to her, to meet her mind and not just her body in that aloof, unresponsive fashion.

She smiled enquiringly at him as he paused on her name, but he could read no softening, no interest or desire.

'You were going to say something?' she asked.

'Hermione – may I come in and talk to you?'

She lifted her eyebrows almost imperceptibly and turned to open her door, leaving him to follow her.

'You may go, Germaine. I'll ring,' she said to the waiting maid, took a cigarette from a silver box, and turned to Wade for the light he at once offered her.

'We haven't seen much of each other since you came back, my dear,' he said rather awkwardly.

'I am naturally busy after having been cut off from my friends for so long,' she said. 'Won't you sit down?'

She might have been inviting a casual caller to take a seat in her drawing-room, he thought rather bitterly. He scarcely knew what he wanted of his wife. Certainly he did not desire to claim her as such, to force upon her attentions which he knew would be utterly repugnant to her and which he himself did not desire. His life was so chaotic, his future so uncertain and clouded, his days and nights so beset with fears, his mind so scourged with the self-reproach to which he was not yet accustomed, that he was stretching out his hands for help, help from anyone. Where could he more surely get help and strength and courage and reassurance than from Hermione, so calm and stable and undisturbed?

'How have you amused yourself?' she asked conversationally. 'Your letters have told me little.'

'There has not been much to tell. I have been living a quiet life, with Diana as my chief visitor. I have not cared to go out much whilst you have been away. I have been seeing to the alterations, too.'

'Oh yes – of course,' she said indifferently.

'You're tired,' he said, rising abruptly. 'I was forgetting.'

'Would you ring for Germaine, Roland? My head aches a little and she will brush my hair.'

'Let me do it,' he suggested.

She looked at him in surprise and smiled.

'You haven't Germaine's touch,' she said.

He crossed the room, pressed the bell, and came back to her. She looked very lovely sitting there in the blue and gold chair, her cloak of sapphire velvet and white fox making a frame for her. Yet he knew that she made no appeal. Unconsciously he was seeking Gretel, Gretel with her soft mouth, her deep, velvety eyes, her quick and eager youth – Gretel as he had seen her last, too, with the softness gone, the youth quenched.

He turned suddenly and went without even a conventional good night.

During the months apart from her husband she had done some strenuous thinking. Once away from the physical charm of him, from his attractive voice, from the smile which she had remembered after their first meeting, from the disturbing nearness of him, she found she could marshal her thoughts and see them in their true perspective. Ruthlessly she surveyed the eighteen months of their marriage, discounted the abnormal conditions of their six months' honeymooning, and looked with searching eyes at their real life together, weighed up what each had brought to it, what each had taken from it.

She had no petty thoughts of mere material gain, of money or its value in possessions. That side of their marriage never entered into her consideration of it. She was concerned rather with the spiritual side of it. She accepted without question the fact of Roland's love for her just as she believed in her own. What troubled her was the recognition of the fact that their mutual love had brought ruin on her husband's creative genius, had dulled his brain and, by making his dreams materialistic, had destroyed the faculty of inventing others.

Roland seemed content with the life she had given him. Where she had so ardently desired to open the doors of a fuller, freer life to him, she had only succeeded in making him so comfortable that the wide-open doors had no lure for him. She did not lay the blame entirely on him. She apportioned to herself her own share and, those long, deep thoughts over, she made up her mind that when she returned to him it should be on a different footing. Since her love had failed to raise him to the heights on which she still believed he could dwell, she would withhold it from him, leave his body free that his mind might soar.

She wondered now whether she had chosen wisely. Roland seemed distrait, worried, unhappy. She resolved to sound Diana on the subject, for she was too thorough and conscientious to persist in her line of conduct whilst there was any reasonable doubt of its wisdom. She did not wish to alienate her husband from her, bitterly disappointed though she had been with him. She hoped by restoring his own self-respect and her swaying faith in him to bind them in a new and more enduring bond. Surely the utter freedom from her and the demands of her life on him must have the effect of driving him back on the creative genius which had formerly controlled his existence?

Diana, questioned, was evasive.

'Darling, he's been the most exemplary husband whilst you've been away, if that is what you're hinting at,' said she in her direct way, scorning polite subterfuges and innuendos. 'He's been alone here such a lot, superintending the alteration of the rooms, or wandering like a lost soul through various people's receptions. I've danced with him and dined with him just to keep his pecker up!'

For one wild moment Hermione wondered if Diana were the trouble. She was so gay and sweet, so full of attraction for men.

The thought gave her pause. How much would she mind? She was appalled to realise that what she would mind most was the scandal, the parting from Diana, all the beastly rites of divorce. It showed her very plainly the stage she had reached in her love-life with her husband. It was ended, and she did not even grieve beside its grave.

She was kinder to him after that. It was almost as if she were trying to absolve herself, seeking his forgiveness for this thing which she had never dreamed would happen. She had been so sure that she loved him, that she would love him forever, that nothing he could do or leave undone would make any difference. And now, whilst he was guiltless towards her, love had fled.

15

Whilst Hermione was busy setting her life in order, Wade felt it incumbent on him to do the same.

He could not altogether understand her attitude to him, though he could find little fault with it apart from her entire disregard of any desires he might have as a husband. She never locked her door against him, but a mere lock would have been less far effective than her aloof, ice-cold friendliness. He had never been a man to whom women, merely as such, were a necessity. He had had the usual experiences of a normal young man before his marriage, but they had left him either quite indifferent or else slightly disgusted with himself. Hermione's withdrawal of herself from him puzzled him a little because she had seemed deeply in love with him at one time and there appeared no definite reason why she should have changed. However, her beauty had always been too cold, her poise too perfect, her whole personality too complete in itself, for him to have desired her overwhelmingly. He would not have been a man had she not in the early days stirred his senses, but since their separation and her return, he found that he had no insistent need of her.

But of necessity his thoughts turned back to Gretel, dwelt with her, found how deeply she had pierced his life, how impossible it was to cast the memory of her from his mind. In the artificiality of his life with Hermione, in the ever-present need to watch himself, to keep up his pose before her friends, to act the perfect husband and host when he knew that he was but a figurehead in either capacity, he found himself remembering

Gretel and the supreme naturalness which had been possible with her. There he had been in his own element, amongst the people to whom he was Roland Wade instead of Lady Hermione's husband and the young genius so inexplicably disappointing to his admirers.

He longed to have news of the girl, conjured up harrowing pictures of her ill, unemployed, lonely. He could cherish no hope of forgiveness from her, but he felt he must know how she was and whether she needed anything.

Finally he went out to the Chelsea house, interviewed a hostile and silently accusing Mrs. Dormer, and asked for news of Gretel.

'You've got rather a nerve to come and enquire, if you ask my opinion, Mr. Wade,' said the woman.'

'I know it looks bad, Mrs. Dormer, but you must believe that I was helpless in the matter. Is she well?'

'Yes. I look after that,' was the uncompromising answer.

'Then – Mrs. Dormer, I am worried in case she is ever ill or in need. I've written down my telephone number. Mrs. Dormer, will you promise me that if ever she needs anything or—anyone or—well, if anything happens in which I can help, that you'll ring me up and tell me?'

Mrs. Dormer had her own ideas on the subject, but she took the slip of paper reluctantly and placed it for safety in one of the many little vases which stood on the parlour mantelshelf. She thought it very unlikely that she would have recourse to it. She had come to care for Gretel almost as if she were the daughter she had never borne, and she had no intention of allowing this man to wreck the girl's life if she could help it.

'Very well, Mr. Wade. I think your best way will be to let her alone, if I may say so,' and the meaning look she gave him showed him that she had a shrewd suspicion of the truth.

'I intend to. Only she must never be in need, and I want to make sure of that,' he said, and as Mrs. Dormer made movements as if she wanted to get on with the work he had interrupted, he took his departure.

And in less than a month that slip of paper was searched for and found, but not by Mrs. Dormer's capable fingers.

Influenza, so-called, had scourged the country again, and amongst the first of its victims was Gretel. The good woman nursed her assiduously, though she had only a mild attack, but in a week Mrs. Dormer herself was stricken down and when pneumonia followed, Gretel insisted on getting up to help with the nursing, in spite of feeble protests from the patient and half-hearted ones from a scared and helpless husband.

Finally came the doctor's orders that Mrs. Dormer must be taken into hospital in a last attempt to save her life, and after the ambulance had taken away its pitiful burden, gasping, and unconscious, Gretel collapsed on the kitchen floor and there remained until Mr. Dormer returned.

It was obvious that she was seriously ill, and his hazy mind recalled something his wife had told him about Mr. Wade and a telephone number on the parlour mantelshelf. After the experience he had just had with Mrs. Dormer, he was terrified and rushed off to a telephone once he had managed to lift the girl and cover her up warmly on the old kitchen sofa. He was fortunate enough to find Roland in.

'Right. I'll come at once,' said the reassuring voice, and the man rushed back to Gretel, mopping his perspiring brow.

Hermione was giving a rather important dinner-party. Two cabinet ministers and their wives were to be present, and the affair savoured of an incursion into politics from which until now she had held sublimely aloof. Diana, red-hot socialist and almost communist as she now avowed herself to be, had wheedled from her half-sister an invitation of which Hermione was secretly nervous, and she had departed from her usual custom far enough to discuss the affair with Roland and confide in him her scruples. The talk they had had was more friendly and intimate than any since her return from Egypt, and both were inwardly pleased at being on a little better footing with each other.

Now, just as Hermione was leaving her room, lovely as a

dream in one of the pale oyster shades which best suited her clear, dark beauty, she was amazed to meet Roland with a coat on over his evening clothes.

'Roland! You're not going out?' she asked incredulously.

'My dear, I'm terribly sorry. I ran up to tell you. I simply must go, but I'll be back before dinner is served. I swear it, Hermione!'

He looked worried and anxious, and Hermione's smooth brow wrinkled in a frown. Their semi-detached existence had made it possible for him to come and go more freely than before, but she could not be quite unaware of his mysterious disappearances nearly every afternoon and occasionally in the evening too. He had sometimes amused himself by picturing her horror had she discovered him playing the piano in a restaurant which she and her friends frequented! He had actually seen her there two or three times.

'I think you are behaving in a rather curious fashion, with these mysterious appointments, Roland,' she said, an edge on her voice. 'I really must ask you to make a special point of getting back before we go into the dining-room. I want you to look after Mrs. Pakeney, you know.'

'I'll be back, Hermione,' he said, and ran down the stairs, leaving her to look after him thoughtfully.

Hermione's car had just been to fetch Diana, and Wade crossed the pavement just as the chauffeur got into his seat again.

'Oh, Barter!' he called.

'Sir?'

'Run me out to Chelsea, will you? Top of Oakley Street as quickly as you can,' and he jumped in and slammed the door as the car moved off.

Almost without exception, Hermione's servants liked their new master. He was unassuming with them, gave little trouble and was not afraid to show his appreciation of their services. Hermione they revered and regarded almost as royalty, but to Roland they told their troubles. Unconsciously they realised that he was one of themselves.

'Don't wait for me, Barter. I'll get a taxi back,' he said as the car slowed down and he jumped out.

'Her ladyship hasn't given me any orders till I take Miss Croft back tonight, sir, so I can easily wait,' said the man, but Roland smiled and shook his head. 'No thanks. I'll get a taxi,' he said and walked rapidly down the street.

Dormer admitted him with obvious relief.

'She's real bad, Mr. Wade, sir, and I've been for the doctor but he hasn't come yet,' he said, leading the way to the kitchen.

Gretel lay back on the sofa, two tell-tale patches of red in her white face, her breath coming painfully through parched lips.

'Where's Mrs. Dormer?' demanded Wade at once. 'She ought to be got to bed.'

The man told him tearfully.

'What about your neighbours, then? Any woman we can get?'

'Afraid not, sir. Mary's always been for keeping herself to herself, as the saying goes, and we don't know the neighbours.'

He seemed so helpless and unreliable that Roland, desperate at the sight of Gretel's condition, bade him curtly to get a hot-water bottle ready and then picked up the girl in his arms and carried her to her room, thankful for the unconsciousness which saved her from the embarrassment of knowledge of his ministrations.

By the time Dormer ushered the doctor in, she was in bed, the hot-water bottle to her feet and cold cloths on her head.

'I haven't the least idea what to do, Doctor,' he said. 'Is this right?' relinquishing his position by the bed.

The doctor glanced keenly to him and then back to his patient.

'Get a fire and open the window wide, Dormer. Better put something round the bed to keep off the actual draught, but she must have all the air she can get. We shall have to have a nurse, if we can get one, though it's almost impossible just now with so much of this sort of thing about. Are you a relation?' turning to Wade.

'I was her guardian whilst she was under age,' he told him,

meeting his suspicious eyes so steadily that the doctor nodded, satisfied.

'She ought not to be left, and she may want oxygen before the night is out. Can you get a cylinder? Take my card to the chemist's in the main road and ask for one and bring it back. I'll stay till you get back and then try to send you a nurse.'

Wade took the stairs three at a time, raced up the street, found the chemist just shutting up for the night and rushed the cylinder of oxygen back in a taxi.

For half an hour they watched her together, Wade and the doctor in the room. Dormer pottering in and out with whispered offers to do this or that, with fresh hot water, with coal for the fire, and then the doctor rose reluctantly.

'I can't do any more for her,' he said. 'I'll send you a nurse if I possibly can, but if I don't, you understand how to go on with the oxygen? Not too long at a stretch, but when the breathing is fairly strong again, leave off the pump. I'll come back in a few hours' time, before I turn in. I've got to go to three or four other people tonight. No woman I can send along to you? Sister or aunt or anything?'

'She has no one in the world except myself,' said Wade quietly.

The doctor, who had never lost his keen humanity, put a hand on his shoulder.

'People get better after a much worse attack than this, you know," he said. 'Sorry to leave you, Mr. Wade, but I must. I'll send that nurse if I possibly can.'

It was an eerie experience for the two men who were left, almost strangers to one another, to watch beside the sick girl, and at length Wade suggested that Dormer should go to bed. The constant, sibilant whispering and the shuffling feet and occasional, furtive sniff got on his nerves and he knew that Gretel herself would hate to have him there in her bedroom.

The man demurred half-heartedly and then went thankfully away, for he was already worn out with broken nights in attendance on his wife.

Moving softly, Wade set the room in perfect order, enjoying the service for her, his heart contracting painfully as he caught her laboured breathing, knew that in that quiet room, unconscious of his very presence, she was fighting her battle with death.

When he could do no more, he sat down by her side with a book, but he could not read it. He watched her with his whole being concentrated on her, aware in this hour of agony that the girl he watched meant everything life held for him. He prayed in thought, as the prayers of our childhood come to the memory of most of us in our hour of anguish for those we love, scarcely believing in them but knowing that we have no other hope to which our fainting souls can cling.

Every now and then her breathing grew so faint that he reached for the oxygen tube, but she rallied again, perhaps subconsciously aware of his mind fighting with her. Towards midnight she stirred and opened her eyes. He saw in them the faint flicker of recognition and he drew back instinctively lest the sight of him disturb her. He need have had no fear. She was too near the borderland to be moved by the memory of quarrel or bitterness on this side.

He bent to catch what she said, and her voice came to him in a thread of sound.

'Don't leave me,' she whispered and closed her eyes again.

'I'll stay with you, dear,' he said unsteadily, joy surging up in him in spite of that dread shadow which lay over them.

A few minutes later she opened her eyes again and moved her hand as if to seek his. He let his own close over it and she smiled.

'Roland, am I going to die?' she asked him, finding her voice with difficulty and gasping for breath.

'No, darling. I'm going to keep you here,' he said, and she sank back on the pillow again with another faint smile, closing her eyes but keeping her fingers curled within his.

Towards morning the nurse came, starched and efficient. 'I can stay until eight,' she said. 'If no one can be sent to relieve me, can you do so? Are you a relative?'

'Her only one,' said Roland quietly. 'I'll stay in the house in case she wants me.'

The woman eyed him keenly and noted the signs of strain, but he was of the type to help rather than hinder, or she would have sent him right away.

'Very well. You go and get some sleep and I will call you if necessary. No woman in the house or available?'

'No. Her landlady was taken away to hospital this morning. There is only another man in the house. You will be sure to call me if she wants me?'

'Quite sure – but she won't,' with a professional eye on the girl.

He slept in uneasy snatches, with dreams through which wandered Hermione and Gretel inextricably confused, and before seven o'clock he was creeping to the sick-room again, a tray of tea and biscuits in his hand for the nurse, who was thankful enough for them.

'How is she?' he asked.

'About the same, which is the best we could expect,' he was told briskly but kindly. 'You had better get more oxygen as soon as you can, and telephone to this number to see if they are sending another nurse to relieve me.'

Vaguely in and out of his mind drifted thoughts of Hermione, of the dinner-party at which he had failed her, of the possible consequences of all this, but nothing seriously counted with him at that moment but Gretel – Gretel whom he loved with the first real love of his life – Gretel who might die there in that quiet room.

He learned that a nurse was on her way and returned to find the doctor already in the house.

'She has the sort of constitution which fights pneumonia,' he told Wade when he had drawn him outside the room again. 'She is splendidly healthy, and if she has proper care and attention, there is no reason why she should not pull through. What exactly is the financial position, Mr. Wade? The hospitals are full, but she will have to have a nurse with either a second one or else very competent help.'

Roland, wretchedly aware of the way in which May Carter's father had stripped him of almost all he had, loathing the thought of using for such a purpose Hermione's money, did some rapid thinking. He was earning, and it was never difficult to get two evenings' work in addition.

He discussed the question, decided that the money would pay a nurse for the day, with a woman to help and to stay late in the evenings if he himself came to relieve her later. Was such a thing possible? Could it be done without Hermione's knowledge? If the thing was absolutely forced on him, he must use Hermione's money, but there was a certain pride in the thought that he could earn this sum for Gretel.

The matter was arranged in that way provisionally, and by nine o'clock Wade had let himself into Hermione's house, utterly tired but with the heartening knowledge that at last he was justifying that belief in him which Gretel had once cherished. He was working and planning for another human being than himself for the first time in his life.

He found Louis, imperturbable and wooden-faced as ever, laying out day clothes in readiness for him, and his face expressed nothing when his master came in in evening clothes and crumpled shirt. He had valeted gay young husbands before, and what would you?

'Her ladyship up yet, Louis?' he asked, stripping thankfully for the bath which was already steaming in the adjoining bathroom.

'Non, Monsieur. Germaine say she does not yet wake. I bring Monsieur's breakfast in 'ere, yes?'

His master realised all that was being conveyed to him. Hermione was not awake and therefore ignorant of the fact that he had only just returned. Further, Louis would himself bring up breakfast to give the impression that his master was only just getting up.

He nodded and went across to the bathroom, returning later

to find a liberal and appetising breakfast under a range of silver covers on a table by the fire. He had no appetite, however, and picked half-heartedly at a grill, washing it down with copious draughts of black coffee and confirming Louis in his belief that his master had been indulging in a 'ver' theeck night.

A meeting with Hermione was inevitable, and he had no idea what explanation he could give her of his inexcusable behaviour of the night before. To tell her the truth just now was impossible. He could not picture in detail the line she would take, but he was sure that she would find means of preventing him from going near Gretel again. He knew that the one thing she hated and feared was scandal, and it had never touched her name. She was not cruel, but she would not consider that the sickness of an unknown little typist could possibly warrant the risk of scandal. The future was too vague and clouded for any plan to form in his mind. He could only live from day to day until Gretel was better. To contemplate any other outcome of her illness was too intolerable pain.

When he had finished dressing, he went up to the music-room, partly because he had a private telephone line there but largely to put off as long as possible that uncomfortable interview with his wife.

She came to him there, an exquisite wrap of rose satin and lace trailing about her, bringing with her that atmosphere of queenly serenity which seemed always to cling to her. Amazed, he realised that there was an unusual kindness and softness in her face, and it echoed in her voice when she spoke to him.

'Dear, why couldn't you have told me the truth about last night?' she asked, not waiting for the apology he tried to frame. 'Don't you think it would have been kinder to give me a chance to understand?'

He stared at her. How on earth could she know? What was he to say to her?

'I dare not tell you, dear,' he said awkwardly. 'In any case I had hoped to arrange matters so as to get back for your party.'

'I know you did. I knew all the time that you had really

meant to come back, but it was not until afterwards that I discovered the reason for your going off like that so suddenly. I must have been blind not to have understood before. It must have been going on for a long time. I suppose it all started whilst I was in Egypt?'

Her voice was still gentle and friendly, and he wondered if he had suddenly gone mad, or if he were still dreaming that chaos of nonsense in Mrs. Dormer's best bedroom.

'Yes,' he said, 'it started then.'

'I don't like it, Roland, and I don't want you to go on with it – but why couldn't you have trusted me?'

'How did you find out,' he asked, the question refusing any longer to be denied utterance.

She smiled.

'So very simply,' she said. 'I had seen you several times and was struck by the similarity, by the way you sat, by little gestures you have. You always had your back to me, though, and you were never without your mask. Then after everyone had gone last night, I went up to your bedroom, wondering whatever had become of you and scarcely knowing whether to telephone the police or not. Quite by accident I saw something poking out of a drawer. It was the little tassel on the end of your mask string, Roland. I didn't realise I had even noticed it until that moment, but I remembered seeing that tassel. One of them was still whole, but the other had most of its silk ends broken off, leaving only the little gilt cup that had held them. I opened the drawer and found the mask – and then I knew. I suppose you have another which you wore last night? Dear, I feel—well, I don't quite know what I feel about it. What gave you such an extraordinary idea in the first place?'

He had listened to her in an amazement which had gradually turned to a vast relief. He was reprieved. Whatever action he took in the future, he was not to be forced into one now, and he felt almost sick with the relief, putting out a hand to clutch the back of a chair and gathering together his scattered wits to answer her.

'I—I was just living on you, Hermione,' he said.

She smiled and came to him, slipping a hand through his arm in a way she had not done for months.

'It isn't that. You don't imagine for one moment that that was why I kept urging you to write, to compose something, do you?'

'No, dear.'

'It isn't anything to do with money. Money's nothing – just an accident, though its possession makes life a lot more pleasant. It wasn't a case of money between us. I don't want you to earn anything. Why should you? It was only that I wanted to go on believing in you, admiring you, loving your wonderful talent. I didn't want it wrapped up and hidden and neglected. Dearest, don't you understand?'

He turned to her in a sort of desperation. If only he could make her understand! Yet that new self of his was still too weak, too fluttering and uncertain, to tell her the truth. Also he dare not risk being cast off by her now that Gretel was so ill and might need more than he could earn for her. He hated the thought, but love is ruthless and cares nothing for any other code.

'Hermione, it is you who don't understand,' he said. 'I *can't* compose. I can't create. I can't write. It's all—gone from me. I shall never be able to do it again. All I can do is just play the piano, play what other people have written. Don't *you* understand, Hermione?'

She drew her brows together in a frown, but she did not relinquish her hold on him.

'I think you only imagine that you can't do it, Roland. I still believe in you. I still hope that you will justify my belief and my—love, Roland. I do love you. You don't doubt that?'

He hesitated.

'We've drifted rather far apart lately, haven't we?' he asked her slowly.

'Then make it possible for us to draw near again,' she said almost passionately. 'And give up this absurd piano-playing business, dear, won't you? What's the use of it?'

'It doesn't make me independent of you, Hermione. One can't live in your style on a few pounds a week . . .'

She laughed.

'My dear, it's so ludicrous. It really is. Besides, what on earth would our friends think if they found out? And they might, you know. I found out.'

'They haven't access to the drawers in my bedroom, you know,' he reminded her with a smile which he tried to make natural.

'Dear, do give it up and be sensible. Why, you're wearing yourself out at it and not giving yourself a chance to create something original again.'

'I tell you, Hermione, that I *can't* create.'

'Well, I believe you can if you like.'

'Don't insist on my giving up the work which you find ludicrous, Hermione. Don't you realise that a man doesn't want to be dependent on his wife for even the cigarettes he smokes and the socks he wears? Let me keep some vestige of self-respect, even if I do have to go on being known as Lady Hermione Wade's husband!'

She could not ignore the bitterness behind his speech and she gave in with a good grace, though she smiled wryly over it.

'If you really feel like that, go on with it, of course. Only I do hope nobody finds out! Whatever should I look like?'

'No one will find out, my dear. I'll double my precautions, and I always have the piano so that I sit with my back to the people.'

She shrugged her shoulders and walked across to the corner which held the lift, flinging him a laughing glance before she left him.

'I really never thought I should be the wife of a restaurant pianist!' she said, and he could not but admire her for the sporting way she had taken it, for there was more amusement than contempt in her voice.

He sank down into a chair with the feeling of reprieve strongly within him again. Not only was he rid of the fear of her

237

discovering that particular deception, but he could now come and go more freely and be at greater liberty to be with Gretel.

16

For a fortnight Gretel's life hung in the balance, the longest fortnight Roland Wade had ever known. Yet now that it was over and she was gradually becoming conscious of her surroundings, conscious of him and (he could not doubt) of her memory of him, he knew fear of a strange and paralysing nature. In her weakness and utter dependence, she had become a hundredfold dearer to him. No human being had ever been dependent on him before. To none had he been necessary. And now, for that nightmare fortnight during which he had lived as an automaton through the hours of the day, this beloved woman had been in his care, helpless, dependent, unconscious of all the devotion he had lavished upon her.

The day nurse, a cheerful little person with a romantic soul, wove marvellous stories about them, her patient and the quiet, devoted, good-looking man who came, often in immaculate evening dress, to watch over her through the weary hours of the night.

She would never find him asleep when she came in the morning, as many unofficial 'watchers' were found. He was not even drowsy, though as the days wore on he grew thinner and more haggard and there were deep shadows under the eyes which scarcely even glanced at the romantic young nurse.

Then came the night when, waking from the lethargy with which the heat of fever had left her, Gretel moved and spoke to him, spoke in her own natural voice, weak and husky though it was.

'Is it you, Roland?' she asked.

He put down his book and came to her swiftly, bending over her.

'Yes, Gretel, dear. Do you want anything? A cool drink?'

'No. Only – sit nearer to me.'

He moved his chair, and she lay resting after the effort of speech. Presently she spoke again.

'I've been ill, haven't I? Very ill.'

'Yes, dear, but you're going to get better now.'

'I must have been terribly ill because I've imagined that you've been with me all the time, right through the nights,' she said, the words coming haltingly and with an effort, but quite coherently. 'That must have been because I was ill.'

He held a glass to her lips, the iced champagne which had been keeping her alive, and she sipped at it thirstily.

'It's very nice,' she said drowsily and slept again.

When she woke he had gone and the bright little nurse was moving briskly about the room. She lay and wondered. It was so difficult to separate her dreams from what might possibly be real.

'Nurse, have you been here all night?' she asked at last.

'No, dear. I've only been here about half an hour. Why?'

'Nothing, thank you.' and she lay very quiet again.

Before the nurse went that night, she thought it well to give a sleeping draught. Her patient had been increasingly restless as the day wore on and there were signs of a rising temperature.

'Does it give me dreams?' asked Gretel hazily, settling down on fresh, cool pillows, glad of the night.

The nurse laughed.

'Maybe,' she said. 'Do you like dreams?'

'Some of them – so very much,' she murmured, her eyes closing already.

'You'll be careful not to excite her in any way, won't you?' the nurse warned Roland when he came to relieve her and found Gretel asleep.

'You don't think I'm—bad for her, do you, Nurse?'

'I don't think so. Don't you let me find her with a temperature in the morning, though!' laughed the girl as she gathered up her case and gloves.

Hour after hour only the ticking of the clock or the soft thud of a falling cinder in the grate broke the silence, and it was with something of a shock that Wade looked at Gretel to find her eyes wide open and staring across at him.

'Gretel, you're awake!' he said softly, going to her.

'I have been for a long time. I've been trying to discover whether you are real or still part of a dream,' she said in a whisper.

'Have you decided?'

She smiled and found his hand with her own weak one.

'I can't explain how it is, but it's really you, isn't it?'

'Really me,' he told her, smiling, his fears strangely slipping away. They two, in that darkened room, with the silent world shut out, seemed to be quite alone, isolated, belonging to each other. Fear had no longer any place there.

'Has it been you the other times, Roland?'

'Every night, darling.'

She closed her eyes at that, and he bent over her in some alarm.

'Gretel, are you all right?'

The lids fluttered open again to reassure him.

'Yes. I was only—remembering that you called me that,' she said and lay with her eyes closed again, though her fingers held his tightly.

After that, she made rapid strides, wanting to be well, a docile and gentle patient.

It had not been altogether easy for Roland to come to her night after night, and he had had in some measure to let Louis into the secret.

'It is a little friend of mine who is very ill, Louis, and I help with the nursing. I owe—him—a lot and this is a way to repay. Her ladyship might worry because I lose so much sleep, so she need not know.'

The man had nodded his head, his face as expressionless as ever.

'Monsieur may rely on me,' he said gravely, and he had proved a staunch friend.

Yet Hermione herself distrusted the arrangement which she believed to have been made. She had no idea that Roland slipped out of the house every night, sometimes soon after dinner, at other times going first to keep his band engagement and going straight on to Chelsea. Yet she could not fail to be aware that he was out a great deal, for he was seldom available as host at her own dinner-parties and never as her escort to those of other people. The fact was being remarked, and there were many people who would have been only too glad to turn the matter into matrimonial disturbance. The success of the marriage had irritated those who had foretold disaster, and they were quite pleased to be able to nod their heads in confirmation of their own wisdom.

Apart from the inconvenience and her fear that his 'band' engagement would be discovered, Hermione could not overlook the effect on Roland, the signs of strain and fatigue. Also he had taken to having long sleeps in the morning hours, often not putting in an appearance at all until luncheon, Louis constituting himself a veritable dragon on guard at his door.

Hermione blamed herself a good deal. Had she not been so insistent on his producing work of some sort, he would never have had such an absurd idea. That being the case, she must make it her business to put an end to it and get him to lead a normal life.

Her renewed attack on him made him realise that these magic nights must come to an end. He dare not, for Gretel's sake, risk discovery, for though she was definitely on the way to recovery, she was in no fit state for such trouble as Hermione could and undoubtedly would cause them.

He spoke of it that night, sitting in the dim little room which had come to represent all he had or desired of happiness.

'Darling, you're so much better, aren't you?' he asked.

They had never spoken of how he came to be there, night after night. At first she had been too ill and weak to wonder about it. She had just accepted it as part of the upheaval and strangeness of the first illness she had ever had. Then later she had been afraid to talk of it, afraid to know her own thoughts, afraid to know his. He was there. That was enough.

'Yes,' she said, and there was almost a sigh on the word.

'Sorry?'

'In some ways. It's been—so sweet, hasn't it?'

'So sweet, my dear,' he said in his deep voice, a voice which no one but Gretel had ever heard.

'You sound sorry, too, Roland.'

'Only because—all the loveliest things must end,' he said very sadly.

'You mean that this must end?'

'Yes.'

She lay a long time without speaking, her eyes closed, the deep fringe of their lashes dark against her pale cheek. She had acquired a delicate, almost transparent fragility which gave the illusion of beauty in that soft, pink-shaded light. Wade watched her with his heart in his eyes. She was so small, so defenceless, so terribly alone. What were they to do?

She began to speak again, quietly and composedly, but her hand sought his and held it close within her own.

'Darling,' she said, 'I've learned a lot whilst I have been ill. I suppose I have been so near the other side that I have learned to see things in their true perspective here. I have learned that love, real love, is the greatest thing in the world. It doesn't forgive because, when one loves, there simply isn't anything to forgive. You just—love.'

'You mean that you can forgive me, Gretel?' he asked in a low voice.

She turned on him her lovely smile.

'Haven't I said that there isn't anything to forgive? You see, I love you, Roland, and in some magic and wonderful way, you love me too, don't you?'

243

'More than my life, my dear.'

'I know. I don't know when I began to realise it, but it's gradually worked down right into my mind and heart and you don't have to tell me. It's rather wonderful, isn't it, Roland?'

'Wonderful and terrible, dear. You remember everything?'

She nodded, her face grave now, her dark eyes fathomless. Below the crystal purity of them he could read her pain.

'Everything. It's got to hurt us now that I am better, hasn't it?'

'I am afraid so.'

'She knows? Your wife?'

'No, dear.'

'It isn't possible to tell her? To find a way out like that?'

'Gretel, I wonder whether I can make you understand without seeming brutal to you?'

'Try, dearest. I am an understanding person and I love you.'

'Then—Hermione cares, too. Not as we do, but in her own way. More than anything she cares for her position, her name, for absolute integrity. I wonder if you understand?'

'A little. She would care much more about possible scandal than actually losing you?'

'I think so, though I may be misjudging her. She is very difficult to know, and she must have cared a lot for me when she married me, for I had nothing to offer her save my—reputation.'

He spoke the word steadily, though it pierced him whilst her candid eyes were upon him.

'Poor Roland. It hasn't been all honey to you, has it?'

'Honey? It's been gall ever since we've been married. I don't think I realised until afterwards that she'd been making a sort of hero of me. It was May Carter she really loved – poor May who wrote my book – and your father, who wrote my music. She's quoted that book to me until I've gone nearly raving mad and have had to smirk and smile and look pleased. God!'

'My father used to be fond of quoting "the way of transgressors is hard", but I never believed it,' said Gretel. 'It always looked delightfully easy and comfortable to me.'

He bent and laid his cheek against her hand.

'Darling,' he said, 'I want you more than anything in the whole world. I love and desire you with everything in me. I've never wanted anything in my life as I want you – and it's the first time I've refrained from grasping at the thing I want. You've done that to me, Gretel. I didn't know I had it in me to be—decent until you showed me that I had. I want to be decent to you, little Gretel, and to—my wife. You've both given me more than I can ever repay, and the only thing I can do is to keep things as they are. Do you understand? You see, I could leave Hermione and take you away – but you've both made it impossible for me to snatch at that sort of happiness because you're both too good for me. I'm making an awful mess of this explanation, but you are so blessedly understanding, my dearest dear. Do you understand this?'

She lay back on her pillows, one hand still beneath his cheek, and in her eyes was pain mingled with something that was almost happiness. He was justifying her love for him, and even though it meant separation and heartache, she knew he had climbed back on his pedestal and she was glad.

'I think I do understand, dear,' she said gently after a while. 'I have refused to face it, and yet deep in my heart I have known it. What does it mean exactly? The end of everything for us? I can face it – if I must,' and her voice quivered.

He lifted his head and looked into her eyes, his own dark with unhappiness'It should mean that, for wisdom. But, darling, I can't give you up entirely – not just yet. Must I?'

'I don't want it any more than you do, dear, but we're only human, both of us, and it might come to that. Roland, I feel so tired,' with a sudden change of tone so that he jumped up, remorseful.

'Darling, I've worn you out! Will you have the draught the doctor left? You ought to get some sleep. I must be mad!'

She smiled, though she did not open her eyes.

'Not mad. Only very, very dear,' she said. 'If I have the

draught, will you stay until the morning? And then – no more nights.'

'Of course I'll stay, my dear,' he said unsteadily, and his hand shook as he measured out the draught and held it to her lips.

Just before she slept, she opened her eyes for a moment.

'You'll come sometimes?' she asked him wistfully.

'As often as I can, darling,' and he bent and kissed her gently, as one kisses a child, his life in that moment utterly selfless.

She smiled and slept, her hand in his, and in the quiet hours he passed through the bitterness of renunciation.

In the morning he stayed to see the doctor and assure himself that, with the daily woman sleeping in the house and within call, Gretel could safely be left alone at nights. The doctor had been as much intrigued as anyone at the strange position in the early days of his patient's illness. Then a photograph seen by chance in one of the magazines had revealed the identity of Roland Wade to him, and he had imagined that he understood. He kept his own counsel, but he was careful not to put anything in the way of a discontinuance of the night arrangements. He had a comfortable practice and had no desire to be mixed up in any society divorce case.

'You will not fail to get in touch with me, Dr. Grey, if Miss Baumer has a relapse or if she needs anything?' he asked anxiously. 'Of course I shall see her as often as I can, but— business—and so on . . .'

'Quite, quite,' agreed the doctor gravely. 'I do not anticipate any further trouble, and I would suggest that the less she is roused and excited now the better. She needs perfect rest and quiet.'

Wade flushed a little but met the doctor's glance steadily.

'She shall have it,' he promised quietly, and the other nodded and went his way. After all, it was no business of his, he reflected comfortably.

Meantime Fate had been busy elsewhere with the shuttle on which was wound the thread of Roland Wade's life.

Hermione, resolved to bring matters to a head without further dallying, had come down to breakfast for once and was disappointed to find her husband not there. Surprise followed when a message to his room brought forth the information that, according to Louis, Wade had already breakfasted and had gone out.

She breakfasted alone, feeling unreasonably irritated but trying not to feed the annoyance by speculating as to what made Roland get up and go out early when she knew he had been very late the night before. She herself had been out until after midnight, and he had not returned when she went to bed, for his door had been open as she passed it.

On her way out of the morning-room she overheard an altercation going on between the dignified Jarvis and an excited little man who seemed to be trying to force an entry.

'I tell you, I've been to see Mr. Wade half a dozen times,' the little man was saying in a voice that carried to the far end of the hall. Every time he puts me off by saying he's not in, and if he isn't in now I'll see her ladyship, as I said I would.'

'Her ladyship is not . . .' began Jarvis loftily, when Hermione herself came forward and stayed the words on his lips.

'What is it, Jarvis?' she asked.

'Beg pardon, my lady, but this man keeps calling to see the master, and I can't make him understand that 'e isn't 'in.'

The colossal dignity of Jarvis sometimes got beyond control of his aitches.

The angry little man darted forward.

'My name's Carter,' he said, 'and well Mr. Wade knows it. I'm not wasting my time coming here anymore to see him, and if you're Lady Wade I'll see you for a minute.'

'I am Lady Hermione Wade,' she said composedly. 'Perhaps you had better come in here,' opening the door of a little room off the hall. 'All right, Jarvis. I'll ring when I want you.'

When he was in the small office-like room and actually faced by this dignified and ice-cold woman Carter felt slightly abashed. He had called several times to see Wade, but had never found him at home. He had refused to give his name, so that when the message was given that 'a man had called, no name, would call again', Roland had thought little about it, and had certainly never connected it with Carter, whom he thought he had settled for some time, if not for ever.

'Well, Mr. Carter?' asked Hermione composedly, wondering what phase of his life this strange visitor of Roland's represented.

He cleared his throat noisily.

'Er—well—just a little matter of business, my lady,' he began nervously. 'Business with Mr. Wade, you know.'

'Yes, Mr. Carter?'

There was a supercilious note in her voice now which, had she known it, was a mistake. It roused the ire of Mr. Carter. Lording it over him, indeed! And him able to send her precious husband to quod if he liked!

'Well, it's like this, my lady. Mr. Wade owes me some money. A regular pot of money.'

Hermione flushed delicately. She had not anticipated this. Whatever Roland's faults, he had never been unduly extravagant, nor had he, to her knowledge, contracted debts. She was beginning to wonder just how much she knew about her husband.

'Indeed? You have an account there? A bill or something?' she asked coldly.

Again that supercilious note with its instant effect on the little man whose anger had not yet evaporated.

'Oh no. There aren't any bills or receipts for a deal of this sort, Lady Wade,' he said aggressively.

'Lady Hermione,' she corrected icily, but he took no notice.

'Your husband owes me money and if he doesn't pay, I can send him to prison,' he said bluntly.

'I can see no reason why you should be so truculent or insolent,' she said, and her voice had a knife-edge. 'My husband is not in the habit of owing money, and if it is due it will be paid you. What is the amount of the bill and for what was it incurred?'

'The amount of the bill, at present, is one thousand pounds,' said Carter defiantly, doubling the amount he had intended to demand. 'And here's what it's for,' thrusting into her hand the sheaf of manuscript pages which, for some reason, he brought with him on each visit.

She took the papers distastefully, but her grip tightened and she forgot her distaste of mere soiled paper as the meaning of the thing sank into her mind. She had read and re-read that book of her husband's so often that it was impossible for her not to recognise the sentences she read, and already the sinister explanation had leapt to her mind, outrageous and impossible though at first it seemed.

She laid the papers down on the table with fingers that trembled slightly, but when she spoke again there was no sign in her voice of the deadly fear and nausea that gripped her.

'What am I to understand from this?' she asked steadily.

That those words were written and composed by my daughter, madam, my daughter May who died before her book could be published. I don't know how your husband got hold of it, except that he was very friendly with her just before she died – very friendly indeed,' he added viciously, seeing that at last he had pierced that armour of hers and made her wince. 'I see you recognise it. And that's my bill, Lady Wade, and I want a thousand pounds for it.'

She recovered herself quickly and held her mind in supreme control with the training of years, facing him steadily, her eyes as cold as steel.

'You are making a most extraordinary allegation against my husband, Mr. Carter, and one which I do not for a moment think you could substantiate. I presume you are aware of the penalties of blackmail?'

'Oh yes, I know all about them. It's worth the risk, seeing that you are who you are and Mr. Roland Wade your husband.'

She felt that she was touching indescribable filth, her very soul recoiling from it, but there was no sign of her feelings in her cold, expressionless face. Even Carter had to admire her secretly. She was certainly a thoroughbred, for this must have been a knock-out blow.

'I must, of course, confer with my husband as to what steps are to be taken in this matter,' she said icily.

He snatched the papers from the table and put them back into his pocket.

'All right. I'll come again this evening, eight o'clock, for an answer, and the answer I want is a thousand pounds in notes. I wish you good day, my lady,' and he was gone, letting himself out at the front door, which banged noisily behind him.

Hermione dropped in a chair and sat as if turned to stone. Part of her refused to believe in the possibility of this horror, whilst another part of her remembered tiny details she had not known to have impressed her mind, remembered particularly that conversation she had had with Roland only the day before. What was it he had said? 'I can't compose. I can't write. I shall never be able to.' Was that what he had meant? Was that why he had spoken like that?

'Can't write. Can't *compose.*'

Her mind fastened on the new train of thought, followed it back to its logical conclusion. He could not write. He had stolen the writing of someone else. He could not compose. He had stolen . . .

Impossible! Impossible!

She rose and paced the little room, her mind in agony. What sort of man was this whom she had married, whom she had loved, of whom she had made a god to worship?

Someone came to the door and knocked. She bade them harshly to go away. For more than an hour she stayed there alone, facing this thing as she had met everything else in life, defiantly alone. Then she went to her own room, rang for Germaine and telephoned a message to Mrs. Jeffson that she would be unable to keep her luncheon engagement.

The maid looked at her ravaged face in some concern.

'You are ill, my lady?' she asked.

'No. Get me into something else, Germaine – the blue *crêpe.*

And find out if Mr. Wade is in, will you?'

A discreet conversation on the house telephone elicited the information that Mr. Wade was in, but resting.

'Have a message sent to him that I should be glad if he will come to me, in my sitting room. Tell Louis that it is very important.'

There was something in her manner which made the maid's further message to Louis definite enough to send him reluctantly to wake his master.

Hermione had always felt the influence of the clothes she wore, expressing her moods in colour and line. The need to change her dress, to change even the rings she wore, had been urgent after that wretched hour downstairs. She felt that she could never again wear the trim little morning suit. It was impregnated with horror. Now, in her gown of deep blue, soft and clinging, she felt more herself again though she hated the thought of the interview to come.

The news that Roland was 'resting' had given her a further shock. Did this odd habit he had acquired of sleeping in the daytime betoken anything else? Did it hide any other secret? Was he spending so much of the night time in unknown pursuits that he must use the day for sleep?

She tried to shake off the thought, but it persisted, and she knew that it would return to harass her.

Roland came to her, pale and strained and obviously apprehensive.

'You wanted to see me, dear? I am sorry if I kept you waiting,' he said as easily as he could.

She found it difficult to begin. It was such a horrible accusation to bring against him, and yet what else could she do? She plunged into the subject without preamble since it had to be done.

'Roland, do you know a man called Carter?' she asked, looking at him steadily.

His reaction to the totally unexpected question told her all she needed to know. She realised it with a sick certainty.

He made no attempt to hedge. He knew that it could do no good, and in some measure he could even feel relief that the thing was done, that he could start to shuffle off some of this coil which he had wound about himself.

'I do,' he said quietly.

She was rather at a loss how to go on after that admission, but he did not help her, standing there looking at her gravely, his mouth set in a grim line, his eyes deep-shadowed with fatigue.

'He has been to see me. He tells me an extraordinary story about your book *The Silken Tassel*. You know what he told me?'

'That I did not write it? It is quite true. It was written by his daughter. May Carter, whom I knew slightly.'

His voice was clear and unemotional as he made the overwhelming admission. Until that moment Hermione had not realised that she was still clinging to a hope of reprieve. He gave her none.

'He suggests that you knew her more than slightly,' she said, her colour rising a little though she faced him proudly.

His glance did not waver.

'That, at least, is not true,' he said. 'She was a cripple, hopelessly deformed. I was sorry for her and took her out in my car now and then. She couldn't walk properly and had very little pleasure. That was all. You believe me?'

She drew a deep breath.

'Yes,' she said simply. 'Then—the book? How did that happen?'

'She died – suicide. She was unhappy and, I suppose, hopeless about the future because of her deformity. A few weeks after her death a girl friend of hers brought me the manuscript of a book May had written. With it was a letter giving the book to me and suggesting that I should take it for my own. There were songs, too, which she had written for my show – and other poems, a whole heap of stuff.'

'And you took them?'

'Yes.'

She moved restlessly, burrowing the point of her slipper in the thick pile of the carpet, tracing the design with meticulous care. There seemed so little that could be said – so much that must be said.

She raised her eyes to his at last. He had not moved, nor did he attempt to avoid her glance.

'Why did you do it, Roland?'

'Ambition and greed,' he told her steadily. 'As a matter of fact, she might never have got the thing published in her own name. But I'm not going to make excuses. I did it. That's all there is to it.'

'But—your plays. Weren't they enough? Couldn't you have gone on with them? Wouldn't they have satisfied your ambition, brought you in all the money you needed?'

She felt how terribly near they were getting to a horror which had lain in the back of her mind all this time, but she closed her thoughts to it. She could not, dare not, loose it.

'I stole my plays too,' he said.

She drew a sharp breath.

'How? From whom?' she asked.

'From an old German music teacher who occupied rooms in the house in which I lived. He had never been able to get anyone to make a fair offer for his work, but he believed in it and gave it into my care when he was dying.'

'And he, too, invited you to publish his work as your own?'

He flinched under the contempt in her voice.

'No. It was for the benefit of his daughter,' he said shortly.

'And she?'

'Chose to go into a convent school, leaving me with that temptation.'

'Does she know?'

'Yes.'

'Have you made any recompense to her?'

'No. She refused when I tried to. Now I can't. The money is all gone. Carter fleeced me of my last five hundred.'

'Then she can blackmail you as well?'

253

'I suppose she could – but she won't,' he said, and Hermione was quick to catch the difference in his tone, a hint of softening. She noted it, and remembered it.

'So I married—a fraud. I, who have always prided myself on possessing nothing imperfect, nothing not absolutely genuine I I have heard the phrase "the laughter of the gods", but I have never appreciated it until now,' and her voice, low and controlled, was pregnant with bitterness and scorn.

He could find nothing to say. No excuse, no explanation, could avail him now. He stood there silently, arraigned before the tribunal at which she was both accuser and judge. He had no defence.

She spoke again, the question coming this time with something startled in it, as at some undreamt-of horror.

'And I? I was stolen, too, to satisfy your ambition and greed?'

'No, Hermione, not that!'

The denial was wrung from him almost before he realised he was going to make it. He could not bear to see this proud woman so humiliated, stripped of all that she had worn so regally, beaten into the dust. At that moment even Gretel was forgotten and only Hermione remained, his wife, who had given him her love and her faith.

'What am I to think and believe then?' she asked him, not daring to gather to her even the shred of self-respect which he offered her.

'I loved you, Hermione. You were like a being from another world to me, and the most beautiful woman I had ever seen. It wasn't for your money that I married you,' he said, and his feverish desire to save her pain made that half-truth seem almost believable.

'Yet you would not have wanted me if I had been poor?' she could not forbear to ask.

He struggled to be honest and yet not to wound her too much.

'I don't suppose I should have wanted to marry you,' he admitted bravely. 'Ambition has always been my curse. I saw everything from the view-point of personal gain. I had always had to fight for myself, and I wanted all the things people like you had – comfort and ease and pleasure, servants to wait on me, cars, important friends, the best of everything wherever I went. You were a terrible temptation to me, Hermione, but I was in love with you, too, for yourself. Can't you believe that? It ought to be easy. So many men must have loved you.'

Her mouth never relaxed its bitter line.

'I wonder! Many men have desired me, asked me to marry them. Would they have done it, any more than you, if I had been poor and not the Lady Hermione Wakelyn? Oh, Roland, why had you to do this to me?'

It was the same cry that he had heard before, Gretel's cry, the cry of a suffering and disillusioned woman, and he knew that he was draining the very dregs of his cup of bitterness.

He came to her and took her hand, held it even though she made an instinctive movement to draw away from his touch.

'I daren't say I'm sorry, Hermione. The words are too futile and inadequate. I am absolutely in the dust at your feet. But I would have loved you if you had let me. Don't you realise that? I meant to play the game with you as far as I could. I don't think I understood until after we were married that you really loved your ideal of me, the mind you believed I had, my 'genius' as people called it – and not me myself. If you had let me love you as a man, we could have been happy, Hermione. I feel sure of it. But you've always kept me at arm's length, been afraid to let yourself love me, refused my own love. That's what makes it ten thousand times worse now. Oh, I'm not making excuses for myself, my dear. There aren't any. Only—try to understand that I did love you for yourself, that I could have loved you enough to make you happy, if you had let me.'

She drew her hand away resolutely, and her eyes met his coldly, disbelievingly.

'I could have loved what I thought you were, never what you really are,' she said, and he knew that in that moment she hated him.

He turned away with a little hopeless gesture.

'What do you want me to do about it now?' he asked. Against his desire, against the struggle of his mind, the thought of Gretel rose insistently. What might this mean to her? He knew it was despicable of him to allow such a thought to invade a mind which should, in barest decency, be given entirely to Hermione at this time – and yet the thought thrust itself in and out of his mind.

'There is nothing to do,' she said in that ice-cold voice of hers.

Suddenly to her came the memory of his comings and goings, his odd programme which could surely not be accounted for by his 'work'.

'Is there anything else I ought to know, Roland?' she asked him, her voice edged with that new suspicion which had occurred to her.

He faced her steadily, not avoiding her searching eyes.

'Nothing, Hermione,' he said quietly.

'There is nothing else I shall have to face? Roland, I beg you will be utterly and entirely honest with me. You owe me that, at least.'

'You will have to face nothing else,' he said.

'There is no other woman? You have been faithful to me at least in that?' she insisted bitterly.

His eyes did not waver before hers, and he was thankful that in this one thing he could be absolutely truthful to her.

'I have been faithful, Hermione,' he said.

She drew a deep breath, held his eyes for another moment and then turned away.

'I believe that, at least,' she said, and he knew that she was catching at such empty satisfaction in her hour of humiliation, though he failed to see how that could matter to her, considering everything.

As she did not speak again, he repeated the question whose answer he must know.

'What are you going to do about it, Hermione?'

'This man Carter must be bought,' she said, and the inference killed at once that faint hope of which he had been ashamed even whilst he harboured it. 'You say he has already had five hundred pounds?'

'Yes.'

'The man is a blackmailer, of course. Well, he must be bought but only on condition that he gives up every scrap of paper he has, and that he signs a paper which I will think over and draw up. You must make arrangements to see him and settle it. He will be here tonight at eight o'clock. You must make him understand that the money will be handed over only in exchange for every scrap of evidence he has. Give him a time when you will meet him outside this house. You must arrange to hand over the money after, and not until, he has signed the paper I will let you have. You understand, don't you? There must be no scandal, no publicity. That I could not bear.'

'I understand,' he said in a low voice.

'For the rest – we go on outwardly as usual. You agree?'

'I have no choice,' he said. 'You want me to continue as your husband? In spite of everything?'

Her mouth drew into an even more bitter line.

'What else is there to do? My life, as far as contentment and happiness is concerned, is finished. I have only my little rag of pride left, and I will not lower it before the world. Do you quite understand that, Roland?'

'Yes.'

'And I can rely on you to spare me at least public scandal and disgrace?'

'You are very bitter against me, Hermione.'

'I feel bitter. You've pulled down the fabric of my life like a house of cards and trodden it into the dirt,' she said, and he realised how deep was her hurt, how utterly hopeless their outlook.

'Hermione, is it worth it to go on?' he burst out. 'Why not let us make a clean sweep of it, both of us? You hate me. You'll never trust me again. You can't possibly want to go on living with me as my wife . . .'

Her voice cut across his.

'I shall never live with you again as your wife, Roland. As for what you suggest, I thought I had made it clear that it is impossible. I will not be mixed up in any sort of unsavoury scandal, nor will I allow myself to become party to a divorce on any grounds whatever. You owe me that, at least. It is the only thing I ask of you. Is it too much?'

He knew that she had him fettered and bound. What other course was open to him? As she said, he owed her that at least. He had wrecked her happiness, and if she demanded that he leave her her pride, how could he refuse? Besides, he had nothing to offer to any other woman even if he snatched at his freedom. How could he take to Gretel the rotten husk of his life, with not even the power to marry her? Hermione would never divorce him.

'I have no choice,' he repeated.

'We can't think of mere personal happiness any more, either of us,' she said, her voice cold and utterly unfeeling. 'All that is left to us is to face the world and keep our private failure to ourselves. It would kill me to have to bear publicity, scandal, people's pity and triumph. You are prepared to stand by me in this?'

'Yes. I'm getting the benefit of it as well, aren't I?' he said bitterly.

'I am afraid I am not concerned with that. Will you please go now? And you will be at luncheon? Lady Elstow and the Graveneys are coming.'

He recognised it as a command and bowed to the new order of things. After all, since he had lost Gretel and love for ever, what did anything else matter.

'If you wish,' he said shortly.

'Then, please go now, won't you?'

For the first time he caught signs of strain about her, heard the quiver in her voice, the hint of the breaking of her iron control.

'Hermione . . .'
'Please go.'
He turned and left her with the ruins of her life about her.

17

'Hermione!'

'On the terrace, darling.'

This is an adorable place. It always goes to my head,' said Diana, coming through the French windows to find her half-sister in her favourite corner of the wide, flagged terrace with its orderly tangle of climbing roses diffusing a thousand scents into the air.

It was summer again at Heseldene, and summer there was a fragrant and lovely thing.

Hermione held out a welcoming hand and smiled the special smile reserved for this particular visitor. She had never desired motherhood, and her feeling for Diana filled the need another woman might have experienced after three years of marriage.

'Such a long time since you've been down,' she said. 'Any news?'

Diana flung off her travelling coat, pulled the jaunty little cap from her flaming hair and perched on the stone rail beside Hermione, a smile on her face that was half mischievous, half defiant.

'Hot news,' she said.

Hermione looked up quickly.

'Tell me?'

'I'm going to be married, Hermione.'

'Darling!'

There was comical dismay on Lady Hermione's face. She knew Diana so well.

'He is quite, quite impossible. I might as well tell you that at the outset,' said the girl cheerfully.

'A chimney-sweep, by any chance?' asked her sister dryly.

'In a way, yes,' chuckled Diana. 'His chimneys are immaterial, though. He's a parson.'

Hermione sighed with relief. This was better than anything for which she had dared to hope.

'Thank heaven he's a gentleman,' she said fervently.

'But he's not,' said Diana serenely, and her grey eyes twinkled.

'It's usually considered a gentleman's profession,' said Hermione in a tone of satisfaction.

'Not the way Joe takes it.'

'Joe!' murmured her sister.

'His name isn't really Joe. It's Joshua, but I couldn't possibly call him that. His mother and sisters call him Josh.'

'Hadn't you better get it all over at once, my dear? The knife is always preferable to the drill, you know.'

'His full name is the Reverend Joshua Horn. He is twenty-six, has hair like an advertisement for mops, eyes like gimlets, absolutely no ability to look after himself, a mother rather like a horse, two sisters who neigh in unison, and a small tin chapel which brings him in four hundred and fifty a year, if he's lucky.'

Hermione was horrified.

'Diana! Not even Church of England?'

'No, my sweet. Wesleyan Methodist.'

'But, Diana, you can't seriously think of marrying this man?'

'Most emphatically, darling,' said Diana, swinging her expensively clad legs and enjoying the effect.

'But why?'

'You'd never guess! I love the man!' and she rolled her eyes and hunched up her shoulders in the best approved melodramatic style.

'What are you going to live on? Four hundred and fifty a year?' asked Hermione sceptically.

'He allows the horse and the two neighers a pound a week. Lots of people live on less than eight pounds a week.'

'Exist on it, my dear, not live on it. Is there any prospect of his ever earning more, may I ask? You're the sort to have babies, Di, and clergymen are always so delightfully unworldly about the size of their families.'

'Of course I shall have babies. Why else should I get married? It's the only thing not already catered for in single life. He'll get on, especially with me to push behind.'

'But, Di, darling – you couldn't possibly be a clergyman's wife! You're most unsuitable. Look at you now, for instance.'

Diana laughed.

'I shall set a fashion in ministers' wives – not clergymen, my love. You'll have to learn to appreciate the difference. By the way, Joe's coming to fetch me this evening. All right?'

'Of course,' said Hermione helplessly. 'Have you really made up your mind, dear?'

'Unalterably.'

'But, what are his people, Di? Who are they? Do I know any of them at all?'

'His father – prepare for a shock, dear – was a butcher. Joe could not possibly handle meat, cut up cows and things, and I quite agree with him. He is practically a vegetarian because he says that even when the meat is cooked he cannot help visualising it as all raw and red and bleeding.'

'Diana, spare me the details!'

'Well, you might just as well know the worst. Fortunately for you, Horn *pére* is dead, and Mrs. Horn and Marion and Beechy live with Joe near his tin tabernacle for the moment. Of course when we are married they'll go elsewhere. They have a little income left from the meat, and I expect they'll go to the seaside and take in boarders.'

'I always knew you'd do something dreadful about your marriage,' said Hermione helplessly. 'And you've had such heaps and heaps of really good chances.'

Diana slipped from the stone rail and came to kneel at her sister's side, her strong young arms about her, her bright head resting against her.

'Hermione, dearest, don't take it too hardly. You see, I happen to love Joe and all those others left me cold. And it isn't as if I really belong here, amongst your people and your friends or your life. You can transplant a wild flower, set it in a garden and make it produce the most marvellous blooms, with all sorts of new twists and turns to its petals. But it's hardier and sweeter and happier in its own hedgerow. You transplanted me, darling, and I've been terribly happy, terribly grateful. But I belong to Joe's sort. His life is the one to which I was born. I can understand him, and he understands me much better than even you do. I think you'll see that when you meet him. I've put it in its worst light to you, but he's really quite presentable, my lamb, and you won't have to blush for his table manners.'

'But, Diana, if, as you say, I've transplanted you, haven't you been living this sort of life too long to take happily to the old sort? You've learnt the art of being comfortable. Can you unlearn it?'

The girl smiled a wise little smile, a happy and contented smile.

'I shall have a lot more difficult things than that to unlearn before I can make Joe a good wife,' she said.

'I feel sure you are making a mistake, dear. You really belong to my kind of life now, after all these years, and – people should marry into their own social class, Diana.'

The last words were in a lower voice, spoken almost as if they were dragged from her unwilling mind, and Diana kissed her almost fiercely.

'Hermione, I hate you to be unhappy!' she said suddenly.

It was the first time such a thought had been spoken between them, and Hermione drew away from it abruptly.

'I'm not unhappy, dear," she said with quiet dignity.

Diana sighed and rose to her feet. It was impossible to pierce the veil of Hermione's reserve, and she felt already that she was taking her leave of this artificial, too easy life of which she had never actually formed a part. She was essentially a worker, a struggler, a standard-bearer.

At the bottom of the rose-walk which led from the terraces to the miniature lake which had been cleared and drained for a swimming pool she caught sight of a tall figure in earnest conversation with the head gardener.

'There's Roland,' she said. 'May I tell him the news myself?'

'Of course,' said Hermione with studied indifference, and Diana sped away.

The past eighteen months had left more mark on Hermione's husband than on her own serene, unchanging beauty. He looked his full thirty years, and his grave face, his eyes which held a brooding melancholy, might often have belonged to the forties instead of to thirty. Yet face and eyes lit up as Diana came down the path, calling to him.

'Hullo, small sister!'

'Hullo yourself. Afternoon, Cummings. How's every little thing?'

'Very fine indeed, miss, thank ye,' said the broad countryman, smiling at her. Very few people had no smile for Diana.

'I've come down on weighty business, brother-in-law,' she said. 'It's just left Hermione almost prostrate.'

Diana slipped a hand through Roland's arm and led him across the rustic bridge which spanned one of the tributaries of the natural lake and led into the part of the grounds known as the Wilderness. Unconsciously they had both taken the path which would hide them from Hermione's eyes.

Once in the patch of unspoiled, tree-shaded woodland, Diana stopped and faced her companion.

'Roland, I'm going to marry Joe,' she said. 'I've just told Hermione.'

He smiled, his grave face lighting up.

'I'm glad you are, Di. He's a great chap. How did Hermione take it?'

'Rather sadly, I fear,' she said ruefully.

'I suppose you didn't start by telling her what a fine chap he is? Talked a lot of drivel about the butcher and the tin church and so on instead?'

'My dear, she's got to know the worst. It's better for her to hear it first of all and then the best, when it comes, will seem a lot better by comparison,' said Diana sagely.

'You're a wise woman in your way, small sister. What line did she take in her objections?'

'Marrying out of my class chiefly. Marrying on insufficient means as a secondary reason, though I dare say she'll give me a *dot* which I shan't hesitate to accept. If Joe's fiery chariot is to forge ahead he's going to need a little grease on the wheels, and Hermione's quite able to find it. No one has any right to have thousands and thousands in the bank nowadays. Joe and I will help to distribute as much as Hermione is inclined to part with!'

Roland chuckled. Diana was perfectly right, of course, but nine out of ten girls would have wrapped up the sentiment in pretty wrappings instead of presenting it baldly.

Then his face grew grave again.

'She's quite right about the social class, dear,' he said.

Diana made a grimace at him.

'You ought to know that Joe is my class. I belong to the workers, not to the leisured classes, as I believe the entirely useless members of the community style themselves. Joe and I belong.'

'Yes, I think perhaps you do. Anyway, you're big enough, both of you, to find a common meeting-ground and live on it.'

She slid a hand within his arm.

'Poor old Roland,' she said softly, but knew that she dare say no more. The affair of these two was too delicate, too complicated, too difficult for even her fearless handling.

They wandered on, she talking happily of the man with whom she was so soon to link her joyous existence, he listening with the memory of a pain which the years could do little to assuage.

The woodland path led around to the newly prepared swimming pool, and they stopped to watch the final touches to the small pavilion which had been designed and constructed so as not to spoil the rustic setting.

One of the men came across to speak to Roland, touching his cap respectfully to Diana and receiving her bright nod in reply.

'I am afraid we shall have to take the diving-board forward another foot, sir. A deep diver might not clear the stanchion we had to put under the platform.'

The two men walked forward to look down into the water, Roland taking a spring measure from his pocket and jotting down figures in his notebook. Diana waited, thinking her own thoughts as she watched the little scene.

She had no more idea than had any other of their friends just what was wrong with the marriage of the Wades. There had been no rumours, no breath of scandal, nothing tangible on which to base the opinion that something was wrong – and yet everybody suspected deeply hidden trouble and waited for the volcano to erupt.

Outwardly the pair were the best of friends, courteous, kind, considerate, charming. They visited together, received their own visitors either in the London house or here at Heseldene, on which Hermione had spent a fortune and which was one of the show-houses of England now that so many famous and historic places had had to be given up, or allowed to go into disrepair for want of money.

Wade had taken over the management of the place more than a year previously, and working long and hard to acquire the knowledge and experience necessary for him to do so. He had no difficulty in getting the support and co-operation of the staff for he was generally liked and was always ready to learn and to defer to the opinions of the experts whom he admitted the head men to be. It was Hermione who planned and schemed and decided on the laying-out of grounds, the purchase of another twenty acres of preserves, the addition of a new wing to the house, the diverting of the stream to widen the lake and provide the swimming pool, but it was Wade who put the plans into operation and worked indefatigably so that her slightest wish might be fulfilled. This necessitated his being at Heseldene for the greater part of the year, even when the London house was open and the season in full swing, or during the weeks when Hermione was in Paris or Deauville, where she had bought a villa.

Yet he was always available when she needed his escort, or his presence at the head of her table, or at one of the great receptions which were beginning to make history. Not the most pessimistic of their friends, or the most intimate of their enemies could find any peg on which to hang a possible future catastrophe – yet it was anticipated.

Diana, perched on a rustic stile and waiting for her brother-in-law to be free to join her again, wrinkled her brows in the thought which so often nagged at her mind. What was wrong with these two whom she loved? She had been so glad when Wade took over the management of Heseldene, justifying his marriage to Hermione at last, making himself an active and useful partner after eighteen months of loafing about whilst the world waited in vain for another 'masterpiece' from him. Now she wondered whether she had been right. Beyond shadow of doubt they had drifted very far apart. For what reason? She could attach blame to neither of them, and her worry was the greater now that she herself contemplated marriage – a love marriage, such as surely Hermione's and Roland's had been.

'Sorry, dear,' said his voice close to her, and she smiled and slid from her perch.

'You love Heseldene, don't you?' she asked as she slid a friendly hand through his arm and walked beside him.

'In a way I suppose I do,' he said. 'It's been—an outlet. Something to fill my life.'

It was rather as if he spoke to himself than to her, and she was wise enough to say nothing, though she heard the regret, the note of something unsatisfied, in his voice. Why should he have to seek something with which to fill his life? What was there to regret? Why was he so unsatisfied? Many men – most men – would have regarded Roland Wade as having fulfilled all the dreams to which a normal, everyday man might be prone.

A lovely and contented wife – almost unlimited means – houses, cars, a private yacht, even an aeroplane at his disposal, though he never elected to use it. Diana sometimes wondered whether it was the lack of children which made him so unsatisfied and Hermione so cold. Yet if so, why on earth did they go on leading the semi-detached existence of which an habitué of the house, such as she was, could not fail to be aware?

They strolled back to the house to find Martin Hale helping Hermione to dispense tea to two elderly ladies who considered themselves 'county' and were so selective that they spent in isolated splendour such parts of the years as did not bring Lady Hermione and her friends down to Heseldene.

'Hullo, Hale!' said Roland casually, when he had greeted the two ladies. 'Shan't be a minute, Hermione. I had to do some crawling about by the swimming pool,' and he went off to wash his hands, catching a comical grimace from Diana as he did so. She shared his horror at the two gossiping old women who would have loved nothing better than to tear the reputation of 'darling Lady Hermione' and 'dear Mr. Wade' to shreds, and who had been more than delighted to find Martin Hale in intimate possession of the terrace and of its owner.

In the middle of the meal a taxi brought the Rev. Joshua Horn to join them, and Roland watched with amused interest the effect of the fiery young preacher on that sedate, ultra-conservative gathering, with its inherent respect for every tradition which could boast a hoary head.

The Rev. Joshua was six feet tall and broad in proportion. He had a voice that was like a rumbling of thunder, deep and with what one felt was hidden violence, and his face was rugged as if rough-hewn by some sculptor and left so that no chiselling should fine down or mar its strength. He had eyes of deep fiery blue and the sudden, lovely smile of a child.

For the rest, as Diana had said, his manners did not disgrace Hermione's sense of fitness, and if he looked enormous and out of place, his huge feet did not tread on anything but the floor, and his enormous hands held the fragile and priceless china reverently. One could see that he regarded Diana in some such light as that delicate china, and only she knew how at times he almost crushed her in a bear-like hug which left her breathless, bruised and exultant.

Amazingly, Hermione liked him, was gracious and unusually gentle with him, and even suggested, with a smile, that the lovers should go and wander in the gardens when they had finished their tea.

When the Misses Lovegrove had departed, leaving the two men and Hermione alone, she turned to them with a smile.

'Mr. Horn is too good-looking for the term "Beauty and the Beast",' she said. 'He is rather—overpowering, though, isn't he? More tea, Martin?'

'Please. A most extraordinary choice of Diana's after all the men of our own sort who have been dangling after her for years.'

'I like him,' said Roland unexpectedly. He so seldom offered an opinion when these two were together that they both looked at him in surprise. "He is such a thorough chap, good right through.'

'Oh, you know him then?' asked Hermione, lifting her eyebrows.

'I've met him, yes,' he admitted. 'By the way, I'm going up to town and I may as well offer them a lift if they're going soon,' and he rose and strolled out. He could never feel quite at his ease with Martin Hale. He seemed always to be watching him and waiting for—what? Surely not still for Hermione, who seemed entirely and unalterably content with her life.

They watched him go.

'Hermione, how long is this going on? Not for ever surely.'

She sighed rather impatiently.

'Martin, dear, why go over all that again? We have finished that discussion surely. There is no other solution than the one I have chosen.'

'You're the most exasperating as well as the most beloved woman I have ever known, Hermione. It must be as obvious to

269

you as to me that Wade is no happier than you are. If, as I feel quite sure, he goes to some woman on these mysterious Thursday nights of his, the sensible course is plain. Have him watched, Hermione, and get your evidence. These things are so much easier now, and he won't fight once he sees you are determined.'

She rose, a frown on her face, displeasure in glance and tone.

'Please, Martin. You know quite well that I cannot possibly face the publicity and scandal of a divorce. I made a mistake, and I am perfectly willing to stand by it. Roland makes no objection to your coming here . . .'

'In the circumstances, how could he? It's yours,' put in Hale quickly.

'I am his wife,' said Hermione smoothly. 'Whilst he allows me perfect freedom with my friends, how can I reasonably object to his taking one evening a week for his own pursuits, I absolutely refuse to discuss it with you again, Martin.'

He caught her hand and held it firmly in his own. It would have been beneath her dignity to struggle for release.

'Hermione, you have admitted that you care for me,' he said.

'In a moment of weakness,' she said.

'The admission was the moment of weakness, not the caring. I have loved you for years, very faithfully and unselfishly, haven't I?'

Her face softened and for a second she returned the pressure of his hand.

'I know, Martin, dear. You have been the best and kindest of friends. Don't think I don't appreciate it because I can't accept more.'

'Friends! I'm no longer your friend, Hermione. I'm going to be your husband, somehow and some day.'

She hesitated between anger and amusement and in the end compromised with a rather wistful smile.

'I sometimes wonder if I know what love really is, Martin. I thought I loved Roland, but where is it all gone now, if I did?'

'You never loved him, dear. You were romantic. Oh yes, you

were. You were romantic, and loved an idol which you dressed up in his voice, his smile, his music and that one book he wrote.'

She turned away from him, catching her breath sharply. He had no idea, of course, how sharp was that knife, nor even that he used a knife. She had always lived in fear of the discovery of that shocking business of Roland's music and his writing, though she had bought Carter off by a payment of five thousand pounds and burnt to ashes all the manuscripts and May Carter's diary and got a signed statement from the man that his daughter had had nothing to do with the book published as *The Silken Tassel*. There still remained that girl, the daughter of the old German from whom Roland had stolen his music. Where and what was she? Always she had connected with her, for some unknown reason, those Thursday evenings which Roland took for his own, week after week, and which even Hermione had come to recognise and respect.

'We won't discuss it any more, Martin,' she said. 'I have quite made up my mind.'

'And I,' he said smiling. 'You won't mind if I don't stay tonight, dear? I've got to meet a man in town.'

'Of course. Come down again soon, Martin. I like to have you.'

He held her hand unnecessarily hard.

'I wonder if you are deliberately cruel when you speak like that, or only conventionally insincere?'

'Martin, what's changed you so?' she asked, frowning. 'You never used to be like this, bad-tempered and rather fierce.'

'You've changed me, my dear, with that "moment of weakness" of yours. Don't trust me quite as much as you used to. I'm in sight of my goal at last,' and he was gone, leaving her troubled and uneasy.

She scarcely knew herself the nature of her feeling for this old friend who was gradually ceasing to be a friend. He had been in the background of her life for so long, stable and dependable in a shifting and unsound world, that the whole picture seemed unfamiliar now that he was making a place for himself in the foreground instead. She did not know whether to be glad or sorry. It provided a fresh interest in a life grown almost unendurably flat and uneventful. Yet quite definitely she did not want matters between herself and her husband brought to a climax which would necessitate some action on her part. Everything within her revolted against the thought of divorce, of the sordidness and publicity of the whole procedure, no matter how discreetly it might be conducted. Far rather would she go on leading this austere travesty of marriage with Roland, for whom she acknowledged to herself now she had neither love nor physical desire.

She was not content, or she would not have experienced moods of restlessness, of irritability foreign to her nature and bewildering to those who knew her best. Rather was she acquiescent, seeing no release save through the divorce courts. She believed that she could find cause if she investigated these Thursday visits of his, but she did not want to investigate them. She preferred the comparative comfort of ignorance.

Diana and her lover came to say goodbye to her, and she was gracious and charming to the young minister, though slightly aloof.

'Roland's taking us up to town,' said Diana. 'Have you seen him lately? We lost him round by the cowsheds. Joe wanted to go natural and scratch the pigs' backs with a stick.'

Hermione sent a maid to find him, and he came back with the car he used, a rather weather-beaten Morris which he preferred to Hermione's enormous Bentley.

'Will you be back tonight, Roland?' she asked him smoothly.

'I expect so,' he said. 'Dannet wants me to look over those plans for the new five-acre field first thing tomorrow morning. Ready, Di? You two had better get in the back. I'll tell you when we get to Fulham.'

They laughed and packed themselves in.

Roland turned to Hermione.

'Good night, my dear, in case you've gone to bed before I get back.'

'Good night. Take care, won't you? Barter says the road from Copperton is up for two miles and not too well lighted.'

'I'll take care,' he said, exchanged a perfunctory smile with her, and climbed into the driving-seat.

Hermione sighed and went inside. Roland, his thoughts automatically concerned with the road and his eyes fixed steadily ahead, felt his spirits rising with every mile put between him and Heseldene, which meant a mile nearer his weekly glimpse of heaven. In the back of the car he could hear the Rev. Joshua's deep rumble and Diana's answering chuckle, with intervals of silence. These two, at least, were not throwing away the substance to grasp at the shadow.

He drew up before the little tin church where, some months previously, Diana had taken him to meet the popular and most unorthodox young preacher who could teach a handful of boys to box scientifically with just as much enthusiasm as he could lead a meeting or preach what Diana called a 'hell-fire' sermon.

'Coming in?' asked the Rev. Joshua of his lady rather wistfully.

She made a grimace, but stepped from the car.

'Don't pray at too great length, darling.' she said. 'It does so spoil the shape of my knees, which are really rather nice at present. When I cough, you'll know that I've reached the length of my endurance, so begin to pray for ships at sea and old ladies in lighthouses directly you hear me,' and she nodded a laughing good night to Roland and wait up the asphalt path on her fiancée's arm, her ridiculous little heels clicking gaily beside him, two steps to his one.

18

Roland released the brake with a gesture that was almost a flourish and spun down the road in the direction of Chelsea.

Thursday again!

His objective was a small flat perched at the top of a house recently converted into self-contained suites. He parked his car in a side street with the ease of familiarity, nodded in friendly fashion to the strolling police officer, and raced up the stairs two at a time.

The door of Flat No. 4 stood open, and he walked straight into the charming little sitting room from which opened bedroom, bath and diminutive kitchen. He whistled as he entered.

'In the kitchen!' called a voice, and he turned in that direction.

Gretel, a gay cretonne overall over her summer frock, stood in rapt attention over the gas cooker.

'Whafflette!' she said. 'Little cousins to the lordly whaffle. Have a bit? I've nibbled that one.'

He took a bite.

'Scrummy,' he said. 'Let me do one,' taking the iron from her hand. 'Cute little beggars, aren't they? This the gadget we saw at the Exhibition?'

'M . . . m. I sent for one. That one's done, Roland. Hook it out,' and she handed him the cooking fork.

'You wouldn't let me buy one at the time,' he complained.

'Don't be feeble,' said Gretel. 'Do you think we've done enough to start on?'

'Sure. I'm ravenous.'

'Bring the syrup in the yellow jug. Oh, and light the gas under the coffee, dear, will you?'

He followed her into the sitting room and helped her set the table, revealing an exhaustive knowledge of the whereabouts of every requirement and sighing with pure satisfaction when they were seated on opposite sides of the gate-leg table facing the piled dish, the yellow jug, and each other.

She talked rather a lot at that meal. More than usual, he thought, and with a restless gaiety that was a trifle forced. When the meal was finished and the dishes washed and put away, Roland doing his share with tea-towel and plate-basket, he put an arm firmly about her and led her back to the sitting- room.

'Come and tell Poppa all about it,' he said, pushing her down on the deep old Chesterfield which she had picked up secondhand and re-sprung with his help.

'Go and sit down over there, then,' she said, pointing to a chair opposite.

He noticed that the gaiety had fled from her face, leaving it unusually grave and a little sad. Always on these Thursday evenings they were gay and happy, as if by tacit consent leaving outside anything that might mar the perfection of their brief hours together.

'Something wrong, darling?' he asked her, lighting a cigarette and observing her closely as he did so.

'I—don't quite know,' she said. 'No, I don't think it is wrong. I think it is—entirely and unmistakably right.'

'Then it is probably unpleasant,' he observed.

She smiled, but the smile did not reach her eyes.

'Yes,' she said simply. 'It's going to make us suffer, both of us, for the time being, my dear.'

He braced himself up, knowing what this meant. He had been facing it for eighteen months.

'Does that mean—parting, Gretel?'

She rose from her seat and went across to him, dropping down at his feet, her head against his knee.

'Darling, don't look like that,' she said. 'I can't bear it. I feel so horribly—cruel.'

'Why not tell me what you propose to do? Marry someone?'

'No. Not that. I shall never marry. You know that. I'm going away, Roland.'

'Very far?' he asked evenly, controlling his voice so that not even by a quiver should it betray what he felt, the exquisite agony of that moment, no easier to bear because he had expected it so long.

'To South Africa,' she said quietly, and she pressed her head against him at the sound of his quickly drawn breath. She had known how it would hurt, but she felt convinced that she was doing the right thing.

'But, my dear, in the name of all that's marvellous – why?' he asked.

'Garners can't keep me on. Things have been getting gradually worse, and they feel quite rightly that it is better for me to go than for the men. They're all married and most of them have children as well as wives. I have only myself, and so—well, that's that.'

'But why go to South Africa to find a job?' he asked, reasonably enough.

'Mr. Garner's sister has a business in Durban, hats and frocks and so on. She wants a sort of secretary companion, to live with her and learn to look after the financial side of the business. She is in London just now, and she has seen me and offered me the job, on Mr. Garner's recommendation. I am going back with her.'

'When?' he asked dully, realising the inevitability of it. Her mind was made up. She was not seeking advice from him.

'Next Tuesday,' said Gretel, and took his hands and held them in hers, her head bent on them.

For a long moment they sat in silence. Then he spoke, and his voice was heavy and lifeless.

Then this is the end?'

Yes.'

'Gretel, do you want to go?' he asked her suddenly.

She lifted her face to his, the look of a madonna in her dark eyes. She loved him so, and she was hurting him and she had no way in which she might heal him.

'Darling, don't you see that I've got to go?' she asked. 'Come and sit over here with me and let's talk so that you will realise how right it all is.'

He went with her to the old couch, and she made no demur when he put his arm about her and held her closely. Long ago they had decided, these two lovers, that they could keep their love sacred and beautiful only if they kept it on a plane which could not be touched by physical passion. Tonight both felt that they had gone beyond the possibilities of the limits they had set. Like children in the dark, they clung to each other.

'Tell me, Gretel,' he said, though he knew all the arguments by heart already.

'Dear, you know as well as I do that we can't go on like this. We set a boundary and we've kept within it. For over a year we have not even kissed. We smile and pretend, but within ourselves we both know that it can't last. We love one another and we're normal man and woman and we can no more deny nature than can anything else created. I'm being terribly honest with you, Roland. I love you and I am afraid. That's why I must go.'

'Dear, I didn't know you felt like that about me,' he said, and he could not help the little thrill of joy in his voice.

'Well, don't you?' she asked.

'You know I do. I haven't hidden it as perfectly as you have.'

'You've been wonderful. I'm not a fool, Roland, though I am inexperienced in love. You realise that?'

His arm gathered her more closely.

'Of course I do, my darling. If you weren't, I couldn't have held out as I have done.'

'Well, we couldn't either of us hold out for ever, and to yield would be to spoil the one perfect thing in our lives. You must realise I am right, Roland.'

'Dear, why should it?' he asked her desperately. 'It isn't as if this were the passing fancy of an hour, a thing which we should either of us take lightly and fling aside lightly. I shall love you till I die, whatever you are to me or I to you.'

She shook her head.

'Tradition, experience, history, literature – all give the lie to that probability,' she said. 'The flower that once has bloomed for ever dies.'

'Rubbish. You quote the philosophy of an immoral old tippler,' he said vigorously.

She laughed at that, even in the midst of her distress. He had often quoted Omar himself with due reverence and admiration.

'But a wise old bird,' she said. 'No, darling. There are only two courses open to us. One is for me to stay on here and develop into your—mistress and make sordid all the loveliness we've known and in the end spoil every memory of each other. The other is for us to part. My dear, be honest. You know I'm right.'

'I emphatically deny the necessity for making it a sordid affair for us to—love one another completely, Gretel. There have been great lovers before us who could not marry.'

'Do you think they got any real happiness out of it? How do you think I should feel to have you go away from me, back to your wife and to her claims on you, playing second fiddle to her, content with the odd hours of your life that she could not use?'

'Dear, you know that we have been married only in name for more than two years.'

'I have guessed that. Otherwise I should not have let you come here at all. No, dear, my mind is made up. I must have all of you or none of you, and you are beginning to feel the same about me.'

Then let us take a chance on it. Come away with me, Gretel. Let's make a new start somewhere. Hermione will divorce me when she realises I am really gone.'

Gretel shook her head.

'For one thing, I don't think she would. You've told me so

often how she dreads scandal, and she'd wrap the thing up in obscurity for ever rather than drag it out to the light of day. Also – I'm not going to steal you from another woman, and one who has been good to you, kind and generous and—forgiving. She's had things to forgive, you know, my dear.'

'Oh, I know, I know I But you're wrong when you say she's been forgiving. She has never forgiven me. She never will.'

'That proves that she loves you after her fashion,' said Gretel.

'She loves herself and her pride. It was her pride I hurt by deceiving her. She thought she had secured a genuine piece, a real, dyed-in-the-wool genius to add lustre to her name and ancestry, and to the possible descendants which I imagine were in her scheme of things when we married. That's what she can't forgive – the fact that she accepted as genuine something which was only a fake.'

'The plaster cast,' said Gretel with a rueful little smile.

She had never met Roland's wife, though she had been curious enough to see her at a distance, but she had formed a fairly accurate impression of her and she could appreciate that there was probably a good deal of truth in what he said.

'Darling Gretel, won't you? I'd make you happy. I swear it.'

She shook her head.

'You wouldn't, Roland. You couldn't. In me flows the blood of the Lutherans, and I know I could never be happy if I took my happiness that way. It wouldn't be right. Oh, I know it's hopelessly old-fashioned to own a conscience nowadays, especially in such matters as love and marriage. I was born into an age which takes what it wants when it wants it – but I am an anachronism. Dear, don't you really know me very well, after all?'

He took his arm from about her and sat hunched forward on the low couch, his clasped hands hanging listlessly between his knees, his whole attitude one of dejection and despair. Until this moment he had not realised how much Gretel meant to him, how deeply he had taken her into his life, how utterly it had been sustained on the thoughts of her and on these evenings with her when he had been himself and at peace, loved, honoured, believed in, desired.

She watched him, not daring to touch him or to speak lest he find renewed hope in caress or word. She knew beyond the shadow of a doubt that she was doing the right thing. She spoke truly when she described that strong, essential uprightness of mind, that ineradicable belief in right and wrong. She could never be happy taking him from Hermione, either openly or in secret as his mistress. Far, far better that they should part.

He spoke at last.

'You'll write to me, Gretel?'

Her face was pitiful but unyielding.

'No, dear. Why lengthen out the agony? Let us be brave and make a clean cut and begin to build up what we can of the rest of our lives. We are not old. You are thirty and I twenty-four – both of us still nearer the beginning than the end. This isn't going to down either of us for good, is it?'

'You'll marry eventually?'

'I don't know. I don't think so. I don't believe in marriage without love on both sides, and I shouldn't be able to give love. Don't let's talk of the future tonight, dear. Let's enjoy the little hour we've got. Will you kiss me, Roland, and try to understand?'

He held her closely within his arms as he had done so seldom, trying to satisfy at her lips the aching passion within him, but at last he could bear it no longer.

'Darling, I've got to go,' he said. 'I'll—I'll see you again before you go?'

'Come to me here on Monday evening,' she said, and, white-faced and dry-eyed, she watched him go, stumbling a little as he went, treading carefully on each stair as though it was difficult to find it and harder to let it go.

On the Monday evening he came to her, his hands full of violets and lilies in which she smothered her white, strained, pitifully cheerful face as she felt his arms about her.

'Shall we go out, sweetheart, or stay here?' he asked her

unsteadily.

'Oh, stay here!' she cried, and he smiled as resolutely as she.

They had a farcical meal, neither eating, only Gretel even knowing what was on the table. She had cooked it and had imagined herself telling him with a smile that she had salted it with tears, but she could not tell him even that.

They talked, wildly hilarious at one moment, at the next letting the tragedy in their eyes stalk across the table between them and back again.

Gretel spoke of the journey. She would have to start very early as she had to meet Miss Garner at Tilbury at eight o'clock.

'We're going by some extraordinary route which will take another week, but which will enable her to get on friendly terms with some wealthy potential customers who are to visit Durban during the winter. It's going to be odd to me working in terms of frocks and hats and undies instead of shipping and cargo.'

'Yes, it will be – very odd – terribly odd,' said Roland, scarcely knowing what he said, and the laughter slipped from her face like a mask.

She caught his hand across the table.

'Darling,' she said brokenly.

'Don't.'

They washed up the dishes afterwards, lingering over it as they lingered over all these 'last time' things, so small in themselves, so potent in effect. That blue and orange jug they had won at a fair, shooting at absurd little rubber ducks bobbing on a make-believe lake. He had brought her the grapefruit glasses the first time he had come to see her at the new flat. She had waived her general rule for once and accepted them. They had 'christened' them by drinking cider out of them and pretending it was champagne.

They lengthened out the process, dreading that hour when they would sit with nothing to do but realise what the passing of that evening meant.

They sat in the room which held so many memories, hand in

hand, silent for the most part, talking now and then gently, as one speaks in the house of the dying, fearful of silence and yet more fearful of the thoughts which crowded for utterance.

At last, with the hands of the clock pointing to eleven, Wade rose.

'You have to be up early in the morning,' he said. 'You must go to sleep.'

He dare not utter the smallest tenderness at that moment.

'I shan't be able to sleep,' she said.

They were silent again, standing hand in hand.

'Shall I come to the boat?' he asked.

'No. I couldn't bear it.'

Her voice broke, and he gathered her into his arms with a little cry like an animal in mortal pain.

'My darling, my beautiful,' he said, and because she knew she was not beautiful it had the lovelier sound in her ears.

She clung to him, and now nothing mattered save that he should not go, should not break that bond that held them until he had knotted it so that life could never tear it entirely asunder.

'Roland, stay with me,' she said, her words coming quickly, desperately. 'I can't let you go. Give me this one night to dream about, to remember in all the lonely nights to come, all the empty nights.'

He held her closely.

'Gretel, do you mean that? You won't regret it?'

The blood was singing in his ears and every pulse in his body seemed a leaping flame.

She shook her head, and there were stars in her eyes.

'I shall regret it only if you go, my dear, only if you leave me without letting me know just once in my life what love means. I shall never know it again. One night for memory out of all the nights there are, my beloved.'

He lifted his head and laughed, an oddly exultant sound, and picked her up in his arms and carried her across the room.

In the morning she was gone.

He came up through the deep waters of the sleep that had drowned him, and found himself alone. He touched her pillow. It was wet with her tears, and as he sat up, bewildered, half afraid of he knew not what, he saw a folded slip of paper propped up against the bowl which had held his lilies and violets – the empty bowl.

My darling, [she had written, and the words were blurred with her tears], *For the splendour of the joy you brought me, for happiness and love, for memory to take down the yews which can never be quite empty of you, I thank you. Gretel.*

19

The steady clop-clop of a pony's hoofs had been carried for a mile or more through the clear, rain-washed air before the man on the creeper-hung verandah lifted his head from the catalogues he was studying and made ready to receive his visitor. He had known who it was from the sound of the hoofs. One came to recognise every sound and associate with the right individual the few sounds of a civilised world which drifted into the clearing which held the one substantially built bungalow, the collection of shacks and the curious mounds of the Masai huts, built of mud and leaves plastered over light poles.

Picking up the wide, double-brimmed felt hat with automatic care and pulling it over his grey-streaked hair, George Dawe strode out into the clearing and waited for the little cart on its solidly built springs to pull up, a smile on his rather worn, good-looking face.

Thank heaven you're visible, George,' laughed the pretty little woman who accepted his helping hand and leant rather heavily on his arm, slightly breathless from her ten-mile drive across the rough-hewn path which was dignified by the name of road. 'Anything to drink?'

'Soda,' he said with a smile.

She made a grimace.

'All right. Frightfully bad for the nerves, though.'

'If women thought less about nerves out here, Kenya would be rid of an undeserved stigma,' said Dawe, leading the way into the main room of his bungalow, a wide and many-windowed place with its walls beautifully panelled in the lovely, local woods, pencil-cedar, Podocarpus and the finely-grained olive. The floor was of parquet in the same woods, and one or two rugs of native weave broke its smooth surface. The furniture was hand-made, simple and beautiful, and the dearth of cushions and hangings betrayed the complete lack of feminine influence.

Jean Winglos smiled at its cool beauty and sniffed at its lack of what she knew as comfort.

'For the fifty-eighth time or thereabouts, you need a wife, George Dawe,' she said, sinking down on a chair of woven, coloured cane and watching him unlock a cupboard which in most bungalows in those parts contained whisky, good, bad, but for the most part indifferent.

'For the fifty-ninth or thereabouts. I have not the remotest intention of taking one even if a woman could be induced to live here in the forest ten months out of the twelve,' he said. 'I rather gather that isn't what you came to see me about, though?'

'No. When are you going to Nairobi? Frank says you are going.'

'I am. Tomorrow. Want me to buy you a new frock or something?' with a smile which made his rather weather-beaten face look attractive. So, indeed, thought Jean Winglos, the one woman of the colony to whom he ever unbent. Her husband, Frank Winglos, was the District Commissioner at Nyeri, and from him Dawe had received many gratuitous kindnesses when he had first arrived in Kenya, ten years ago, and come to work in a part of the colony where white labour was scarce and the native Kikuyu lazy and suspicious. Hard work and good luck combined had made it possible for him to acquire the forestry rights of the tract on which he had now built the bungalow where he lived alone, except for the casual and intermittent company of Billings, his head-man, who preferred as a rule his own rough and not entirely weather-proof shack a couple of miles from the main clearing.

'I don't think I'm exactly in trim for new frocks or hats just now,' said Mrs. Winglos with a grimace, and Dawe gave her a sympathetic smile.

She was expecting her third baby, but she had weathered too many years in Kenya to let a little matter like that upset her, in spite of her talk of nerves.

'Feeling fit?' he asked.

'Feeling splendid,' she assured him. 'But about Nairobi. You aren't going to stay there?'

'Only the night, and not that if I think I can get back. Why?'

'I want you to do me a favour. Bring something back with you.'

'Why not? What is it?'

'A woman.'

'Good Lord, Jean!' he protested.

'Oh, I know all about the anti-woman complex, and I'm not trying to push off a wife on you or anything like that. She's a dressmaker and I don't know her from Eve – except that she'll probably wear more clothes.'

'But why import her? Aren't there enough shops at Nyeri in the circumstances?'

'This is someone special. I've always got my things and the kiddies' from Nairobi, from one of the shops just by the European School, Delmar's. I can't go all that way over those roads just now, so Delmar's have offered to let me have the woman who makes their best things if I can send for her. She'll stay with us for a week or two and fit me and the girls out with clothes. We look like savages at present.'

He ran a protesting eye over the cool and charming vision she made in her white linen and wide, green-lined hat

'Can't you wait till someone else goes in?' he suggested.

'Now, George, don't be annoying. I've set my heart on having her before another weekend, and who on earth could I ask to fetch her but you? You're the only European about here who doesn't seize on a trip to Nairobi for a periodic drink orgy, and this woman is probably ultra-respectable and would have fifty fits if a slightly blotto man offered to escort her through a hundred-odd miles of Kenya. Be a sport, George.'

He shrugged his shoulders. Mercifully his ancient car was a saloon, for he used it for transport purposes, and he could probably find room amongst the various farm and forestry implements for one passenger. He felt that, however distasteful it might be, he could hardly refuse the service to Frank Winglos' wife.

'Very well. She mustn't expect to be entertained, however, and she'll have to sit in the back so as to leave me with all my faculties clear for driving. It's a brute of a road in parts.'

'Don't I know it? Well, seeing that you're so wildly enthusiastic over it, I'll let you bring her,' she laughed.

'What's her name?'

She made a grimace.

'Blest if I know! I never thought to ask. Anyway, she'll be at Delmar's any time you say. You can leave a message there and there can't be any trouble about finding her.'

'I dare say I shall want to start about six in the morning,' he warned her.

Jean Winglos chuckled.

'Just to be as darned aggravating as you can, you old woman-hater? Well, she's a woman who works for her living, so I dare say she'll manage to survive six o'clock starts. Drive me back, George? Frank will let you have a horse, or you can drive the cart back and send one of the boys with it in the morning.'

'I'm rather busy, Jean.'

'Oh, all right,' she said, rising in pretended offence, and flinging him a smile.

'Take Omtago. He's very steady, and he'll walk back through the swamp.'

'Thanks, no. I'll manage. In all these years, I've never got really friendly towards the Kikuyu boys.'

He drove with her to the edge of the forest, above which rose the slopes of Kenya Mountain, and stood watching her jolting along the rough road for a few minutes before he turned back to his beloved trees. He always had a curious feeling akin to home-sickness just at this particular point. Between his own land and the forest zone of the mountain was a natural clearing, the sparsely covered ground dotted with yellow cassia bushes which might almost have been gorse on a Surrey common.

He flung the sentiment aside. He had done with England for ever, and save for such moments as this, knew no regret, no desire to return. Kenya had taken him, eaten into his soul, might someday destroy him as she had destroyed thousands before him who had dared to love her and presume to seek succour and life at her fertile breast. Whatever she did to him, he belonged to her, body and soul, and he strode back through the trees, dense but never giving a tropical oppression, the undergrowth filled with the rustles and cries of a thousand insects, the higher branches alive with multi-coloured birds and chattering, daring monkeys, mostly of the Colobus type with striking black and white fur and ludicrously human faces.

He frowned as he thought of that woman in Nairobi. He always loved the journey back alone, a hundred and twenty-odd miles of virgin forest and pasture land, broken by streams and waterfalls and peopled by the wilder, shyer herds of animals driven from the neighbourhood of the fast upspringing towns to seek shelter in the still untamed tracts. Why on earth must Jean pick on him? Damn it, if a woman chose to ply her trade a hundred and twenty miles from its legitimate source, she must take the consequences of a chance and probably bibulous escort. Nevertheless, he knew in his heart that he would do as he had promised. One had a habit of doing things for Jean Winglos.

She had left a pile of papers and magazines, as was her kindly custom, on his table. Most of them were months old, but what did it matter? The world beyond the forest, except for these occasional visits to Nairobi or an evening now and then with Frank Winglos in Nyeri, the administrative centre of the province, had receded into a mist of unreality. The people who stalked through the pages of those journals, who loved and quarrelled, argued the same old questions, burnt with zeal for the same old political schemes, were dream people. Dawe read of them tolerantly, with now and then a gleam of sardonic amusement as a familiar name caught his eye, pulling at the beloved old pipe which had no flavour until the heat of the day had gone.

He glanced now at an ancient copy of *The Times*, and suddenly a name caught his eye. He read the short paragraph again, re-read it once more, and then laid the paper down, sucking at the old pipe, his face expressing nothing in particular but his grey eyes lit with an impersonal amusement like the eyes of a grown up watching children at play. How small and unnecessary it all seemed!Permission of the Court has been prayed, and granted, for the assumption by Lady Hermione Wade of the death of her husband, Mr. Roland Wade, who disappeared in mysterious circumstances more than nine years ago. Nothing has since been heard of him in spite of exhaustive enquiries.

For a long time Dawe lay back in his chair in a brown study. Then he gave a short laugh and turned to the other papers, seeking something more interesting.

The next evening, his business in Nairobi concluded, he found the shop near the European School and left a message there that Mrs. Winglos' dressmaker was to be ready for him by six o'clock the next morning.

'Tell her I will pick her up outside here, and she will please not be late. The heavy rains have flooded part of the road and I shall have to take a longer and rougher route.'

The girl who took the message gave him the required promise and he strode away to his hotel.

Soon after five the next morning he was about, packing the ancient Ford back and front with parcels of every description, leaving just enough space on the back seat for one person. He still felt resentful, but the morning was clear and cool and he was returning to his beloved forest, so he whistled as he packed, hoping that the roof of the car would not protest too strongly at the rather unwieldy implements which he had to fasten on top of it.

People were astir already. Up and down the wide, white street, with here and there a tree of brilliant tropical foliage or the curious, essential African candelabrum of the sisal – across the rather desolate-looking stretch of sparse grass in front of Government House – in and out of the squat, white, ugly buildings which had been someone's idea of architecture – a few whites went about their business, with the white-blanketed or almost unclothed Kikuyu dawdling and gossiping in the sunshine which as yet had attained no uncomfortable power.

Dawe drove rapidly down the main street, thankful to be on his way again, and he saw with some satisfaction that a woman's figure stood outlined against the white front of Delmar's, suitcase in hand, the usual wide-brimmed hat shading eyes and neck.

He drew alongside and pulled up, looked across indifferently at his passenger – and then sat perfectly still, staring out under the hood in startled unbelief.

She came slowly across to him, herself in a dream, her eyes – those wide, fathomless, dark eyes – wide with amazement.

'It's—you," she said, and her voice shook.

He had no power of movement, but just sat there, saying her name over and over again, softly, monotonously.

'Gretel – Gretel – Gretel . . .'

'It's—*you*' she said again, and this time there was a thrill on the words and a light in her eyes as if she had wakened from her dream to find it no dream but a magical reality.

He opened the door of the car and stepped out to stand beside her, looking down on her, devouring her with his eyes, worshipping her.

'Oh, my dear,' he said softly at last, and again, 'My dear!'

'Are you Mr. George Dawe?' she asked, and there was laughter in her voice, though it still trembled oddly.

'And are you Mrs. Winglos' dressmaker?'

She nodded and laughed.

'You're coming with me, Gretel,' he said, and could scarcely believe that he was speaking of something actually about to happen.

She laughed happily. 'I am,' she said. 'Where do I sit?' peering at the laden interior of the car and at the piled front seat.

'Here,' he said, and began to bundle into the back the parcels with which he had so laboriously planned to intercept any attempt on the part of his passenger to occupy the front seat with him.

She climbed in, a little breathless, her eyes starry, her cheeks flushed, and he took his seat beside her and swung along the street, his pulses hammering but his head cool and clear. He had such precious freight on board that he would not even look at her until he had cleared any chance of trouble and was out on the steady slope which led from the town to his beloved backwoods. Here the country was drier in spite of the beginning of the rains, and the huge flowers of the sisal took the place of the less conspicuous coffee.

They spoke no word until at length he ran the car off the road, stopped it, got out and took her hand.

'Come and let's talk, Gretel,' he said, and his voice lingered on her name as if he could even now scarcely believe that he spoke it to her very self. For so many years that name had been spoken only in his thoughts.

He led her a little way off the road, pushed a way for her through the dense, tropical undergrowth and brought her out beside the falls, the water thundering and tossing, flung up into a million sprays of colour to reunite into a thin, white stream in the gorge below. Where had been arid country broken by little but the sisal bushes were now palms, lianas, and all the thousand shades of green made possible by the leaping spray of water.

Gretel took a deep breath of the cool and fragrant air.

'To be here—with you, Roland,' she said, and her voice was soft with the magic of it.

Their hands went out to each other's instinctively and then

they laughed but did not release their hold.

'We should be sedate and middle-aged about it, I suppose,' he said, but knew that the wine of youth still sparkled in the cup of his life. What have the years to do with youth at such an hour?

Gretel's eyes never left his face. It was as if they could not drink their fill of him. She scarcely heard what he said even.

'You've changed, my dear,' she said, looking at the greying hair, the thin, sunburnt cheeks, the tall form which was almost gaunt within the loose clothes he wore, the washed-out khaki shirt and shorts, the inevitable double-brimmed felt hat. Yet he looked strong and virile, hard as nails, weather-beaten, broken in to this domineering country with her insatiable demands, her rewards wrested from her with blood and sweat, rewards magnificently royal once they had been torn from her reluctant hands.

'Ten years – a long stretch, Gretel. And yet you're just the same.'

To no one but a man who loved her would she have seemed the same. She was thinner, even angular, and her complexion had assumed that leathery, yellow-brown which is Africa's answer to those who come to her with that particular, pale ivory skin that had been Gretel's. Her ash-blonde hair was bleached until it was almost colourless, and about her eyes and her wide, generous mouth were fine lines and tiny wrinkles. Only her eyes remained the same, steadfast and ageless. Few men would have troubled to take a second look at her, but to Roland Wade she was beautiful.

She laughed softly.

'That's a lovely thing to hear even though I know it's not true,' she said. 'Do you realise I am . . .'

He put up a hand to stop her.

'Don't tell me how old you are. What does it matter? You're Gretel.'

Again they stood in silent wonder at the miracle which had come to them. Then she gave a little quivering laugh that was almost a sob. The very depths of her being were astir.

'Talk to me, Roland. Tell me how this miracle has happened—how you got here—what you're doing—what you're going to do . . . everything. There's nothing too small to tell me, nothing too big.'

They sat down on a fallen tree-trunk, hand in hand, and he told her of his life in the forest, the life of a man, hard, comfortless according to the standards he had once held, with more of failure than success, with little rest, with none of the things which he had accounted pleasure in the life that was dead.

'And yet you love it,' she said softly as he paused.

He smiled down into her eyes.

'You always understood.' he said. 'Yes, I love it,' and his eyes looked out over the valley, an abiding peace in their depths which she had never seen in the old days. 'I could never go back. It is my life, part of me, something on which I have grafted my very existence.'

'Tell me how it began, Roland. Everyone thought you were dead, you know.'

'You, too, Gretel?'

She shook her head.

'No. I don't think I ever believed that. I felt that I should have known. It would have been as if part of me had gone, and I never had that feeling.'

It was curious how openly and confidently they spoke now that those first few moments of incredulous wonder, of adjustment of mind, had passed. The years had rolled away as if they had been but a dream.

'I couldn't stay,' he said, groping back amongst half- forgotten memories. 'After that night, I couldn't stay. Hale had said something that day, too – Martin Hale. You remember?'

She nodded her head but did not speak to break the thread of his memory.

'I had suspected for some time that Hermione cared for him, and something he said made me sure that it was only the fear of scandal which made her keep up the farce of our marriage. Then I came to you for that last evening and – in the morning – I knew I could never go back. I was like a madman when I found you had gone. I rushed out of the house, took a succession of trains and taxis, and got to the docks just after the last tender had come back. I offered all I possessed, and a lot I had no hope of possessing, to have myself put on board your boat, but I had to stand there and see you go away from me.'

He paused, lost for a moment in the memory of that long-past anguish.

'And you never went back?' she prompted him softly.

'After those hours with you – your loveliness, Gretel – your dear love? We belonged. Even if I were never to see you again, there could never be anyone else. I couldn't have gone back to Hermione, no matter in what capacity. I meant to follow you to Durban. You'll smile when I tell you how I did it, for I found I had only a few pounds on me and I wouldn't risk trying to get more. I found a man who had been knocked out in a drunken brawl in one of those queer streets at the back of the docks. He had been signed on as a stoker on a cargo boat bound for the African coast, and I took his name and went in his place.'

'As a stoker, Roland?' she asked incredulously.

'Even so,' he laughed. 'Gosh, it was hard work! I never had much superfluous flesh on me, but that trip left me with nothing but a skinful of bones, and I finally landed in Capetown a harder and a wiser man. I don't think my hands would have done much piano-playing at the end of that jaunt! I had to do the last hundred-odd miles by land as a porter attached to some baggage lorries on trek.

'I worked my way to Durban, but I had had time to do some hard thinking and I realised that I could do you nothing but harm if I made any attempt to lay claim to you. I had nothing to offer you, and I ferreted out from the papers in Capetown the information that Hermione was making exhaustive enquiries about me. I found out where you were working, hung about without your seeing me until I knew you were all right, and then I worked my way north and finally landed in Kenya.'

'You were in Durban, and I never knew!' said Gretel.

'I was right, Gretel, wasn't I?'

'Yes, I suppose you were,' she said slowly. 'I missed you so horribly, though. It was a mistake, that last night together, my dear. It made it impossible to forget. It was like that with you?'

'Yes – but I didn't want to forget. You were all the memory I wanted to keep, and I've kept it.'

It was odd how calmly they could discuss it, and each knew the tiny prick of regret that they could be so calm. It was only in semblance that they had been caught back into the past. Actually these years stretched between what they had been and the man and woman who sat in that Kenya forest and held each other's hands and thought to bridge them.

'Hermione honestly tried to find you, Roland. I don't know how she got hold of me in connection with you, but she did. Private enquiry agents haunted me for quite a time until at last they must have decided I knew no more than they did and went away.'

'She got leave to presume me dead,' he said.

'Is that all you know?' asked Gretel.

'Should I know anything else?'

She fumbled in the pocket of her coat and brought out a crumpled newspaper, smoothing it out on her knee as she talked.

'Oddly enough, I've got this with me. I found it when I was packing, and—well, I was sentimental about it and stuck it in my pocket,' with a little laugh. 'See what it says?'

He bent over the paper with her and read where her finger pointed.

To Hermione, wife of Sir Martin Hale, on Tuesday, 21st March, twin sons, Jasper and Martin.

He stared at it, his mind caught back again into the past and finding Hermione, proud, aloof, self-possessed – and Martin

Hale, the Faithful Heart. Twin sons – Hermione's and Martin Hale's.

Gretel broke in on his reverie at last.

'Roland, you don't mind?' she laughed, an odd note in her voice.

He flung back his head and laughed, and for the first time she glimpsed the man he had been in the reckless days gone by.

'Mind? Ye gods, no! I'm glad. I'm *free*, Gretel – gloriously and fearlessly free!' and the grip on her hand tightened involuntarily.

Even that announcement he had come across in his bungalow two days previously had not given him this sense of freedom. Hermione would certainly not want to find him and lay claim to him now. The only thing she could possibly desire of him for the rest of his life was to keep away from her, never to let his existence be known. Free!

He laughed again, a different quality in this laughter.

'How like Hermione to have twin sons! She was always so thorough in what she did!'

Gretel laughed with him, aware of the intensity of her relief. For one appalling moment she had thought he was regretting Hermione.

'And all this time I've talked of myself, Gretel. What of you? How do you come to be in Nairobi at all? And a dressmaker.'

'I had bad luck. Miss Garner died and for a time I helped to keep the business together, doing three people's work and learning more than I should ever have learnt in ordinary circumstances. It went to pieces, though, and then I went to Madame Delmar's. She has a shop in Durban and she let me go into her workroom. Last year she sent me to the branch in Nairobi and – well, here I am!'

'Are you happy, Gretel?'

She let him hold her eyes and they spoke to him in a language which made him hear but vaguely the words her voice said.

'I am content, my dear. And you?'

'I thought I was content.'

'Well – aren't you?' she asked him softly.

'Gretel, I'm forty and I've had to wrestle with life to prevent it from getting me down. I'm not the man you used to know. I'm harder, rougher

'You're Roland – and a man, my dear,' she broke in softly.

He shook his head even though he smiled.

'I'm a man, but I'm not Roland Wade any longer. I'm George Dawe, and everything for which George Dawe stands. I'm a working man, Gretel – a labourer. I live in the heart of the forest, in a bungalow which I've been told has none of the refinements of life. I work early and late, month in and month out, and there's no fun there – no visiting, no parties, no dressing up – nothing but working hard so that one can live. There are native boys who work only and as long as someone is behind them to see that they work, and I have imported a Goan, a decent little chap, who does my cooking and helps me bully the Kikuyu boys. In the summer we're too hot and dry; in the wet weather we're often flooded; in any weather we have so much to do that at night we're too dog-tired for anything but bed.'

Gretel laughed softly, and her eyes never left his.

'It sounds—beautiful,' she said in a whisper.

For a long time he looked down into her eyes, those fearless, steadfast eyes in which a man might lose his soul and find it anew. Then he set his arms about her and held her.

'I've dreamed of you here, Gretel – my Gretel,' he said, and his voice was deep and quiet. 'Here in the forest I built a home for myself and thought to live there alone – but you came with me and stayed with me in my fear and my despair and in the new hope that was born there. I have found peace, Gretel – and never knew until this hour that there was one thing lacking to make it perfection.'

'Have you found it now, Roland, that one thing lacking?' she asked him.

'Oh, Gretel, have I?'

She leaned her head against him, and he drew her closely, holding her there, looking out over her bent head to the waving trees of the great forest land which had given him life and hope and courage and had left him only this one thing lacking, this one beloved woman – and which now had brought him even that.

She lifted her face at last, a face made beautiful by sorrow, by laughter, and by tears. 'I love you, my dear,' she said.

He cranked up the car with a grinding sound which sent a flurry of small birds screaming from the brushwood into the arching trees above.

'Where to, my lady?' he asked her as he climbed in beside her.

She smiled into his eyes. 'Home, George,' she said.

Give Back Yesterday

Helena Clurey has it all – a devoted husband, money and family. She is happy and secure, but her apparent contentment is about to be shattered by a voice from the past. Mistress she may have been, but that is not the way it is put to her: 'you were not my mistress - you were, and are, my wife.'

The Weir House

Philip wants to marry Eve. It is her way out - he is rich, not too old, and has been in love for years – but not a man she can accept. He has even secretly funded her lifestyle, such that it is. Eve feels trapped. Unlike her friend Marcia, who cheerfully accepts an 'ordinary' life without complaint, Eve has known better and wants better. A chance encounter then changesthings – Lewis Belamie pays her to act as his fiancée for a week. Adventure, ambition, and disappointment all follow after she journeys to Cornwall with him, where she eventually nearly dies after what appears to be a suicide attempt because of a marriage that has seemingly failed. However, the mysterious and mocking Felix really does love her. Just who is he; how does Eve end up with him; and what part does 'The Weir House' play in her life? Has Eve's restlessness and relentless search for stability ended?

Through Many Waters

Jeff has got himself into a mess. It is, on the face of it, a classic scenario. He has a settled relationship with one woman, but loves another. What is he to do? It is now necessary to face reality, rather than continually making excuses to himself, but can he face the unpalatable truth? Then something beyond his influence intervenes and once again decisions have to be made. But in the end it is not Jeff that decides.

Misadventure

Olive Heriot and Hugh Manning had been in love for years, but marriage had been out of the question because of the intervention of Olive's mother. Now, at last, she was of age and due to gain her inheritance and be free to choose. A dinner party had been arranged at the Heriot's home, 'The Hermitage' and Hugh expects to be able to announce their engagement. Things start to change after a gruesomely realistic game entitled 'murder', which relies on someone drawing the Knave of Spades after cards are dealt. Tragedy strikes and other relationships are tested and consummated – but is this all real, or imagined?

Printed in Great Britain
by Amazon